MORETA: DRAGONLADY OF PERN

MORETA: DRAGONLADY OF PERN

Anne McCaffrey

A Del Rey Book
BALLANTINE BOOKS • NEW YORK

A Del Rey Book
Published by Ballantine Books

Copyright © 1983 by Anne McCaffrey

Manufactured in the United States of America

First Edition: November 1983

Map by Bob Porter

Library of Congress Cataloging in Publication Data
McCaffrey, Anne.
    Moreta, dragonlady of Pern.

    "A Del Rey book."
    I. Title.
PS3561.A255M6   1983   813'.54   83-4630
ISBN 0-345-29874-8

10   9   8   7   6   5   4   3   2   1

This book is dedicated
to my daughter
Georgeanne Johnson
with great affection and respect
for her courage

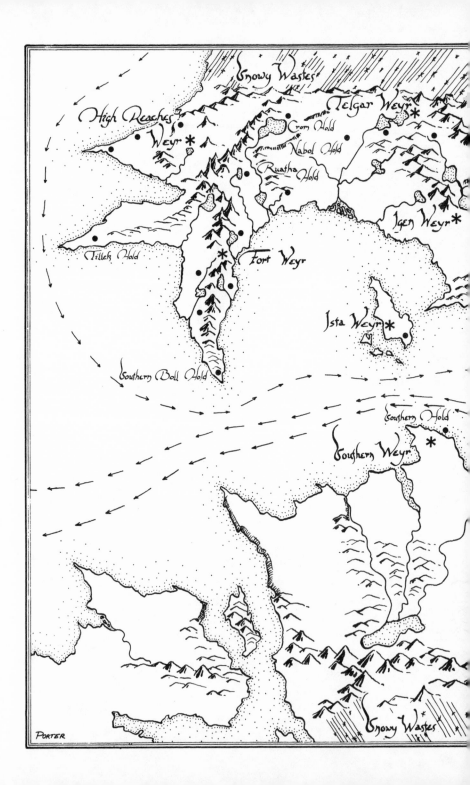

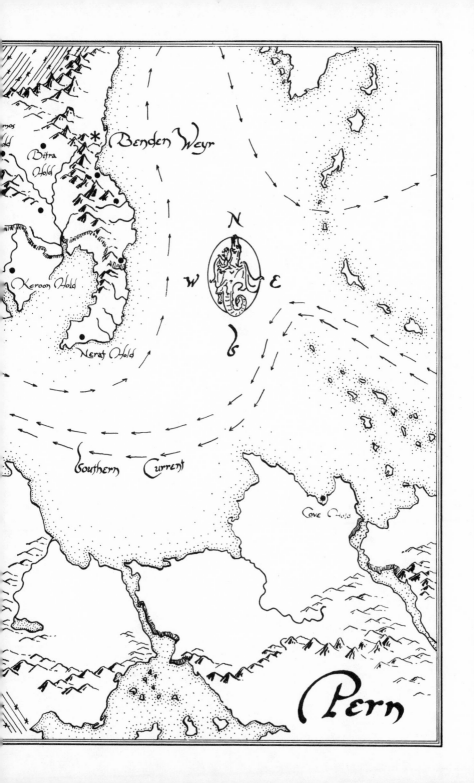

Contents

PROLOGUE

RUKBAT, in the Sagittarian Sector, was a golden G-type star. It had five planets, two asteroid belts, and a stray planet that it had attracted and held in recent millennia. When men first settled on Rukbat's third world and called it Pern, they had taken little notice of the strange planet swinging around its adopted primary in a wildly erratic orbit. For two generations, the colonists gave the bright Red Star little thought—until the path of the wanderer brought it close to its stepsister at perihelion. When such aspects were harmonious and not distorted by conjunctions with other planets in the system, the indigenous life form of the wandering planet sought to bridge the space gap between its home and the more temperate and hospitable planet. At these times, silver Threads dropped through Pern's skies, destroying anything they touched. The initial losses the colonists suffered were staggering. As a result, during the subsequent struggle to survive and combat the menace, Pern's tenuous contact with the mother planet was broken.

To control the incursions of the dreadful Threads—for the Pernese had cannibalized their transport ships early on and abandoned such technological sophistication as was irrelevant to the pastoral planet—the more resourceful men embarked on a long-term plan. The first phase involved breeding a highly specialized variety of fire-lizard, a life form indigenous to their new world. Men and women with high empathy ratings and some innate telepathic ability were trained to use and preserve the unusual animals. The dragons—named for the mythical Terran beast they resembled—had two valuable characteristics: They could instantaneously travel from one place to another and, after chewing a phosphine-bearing rock, they could emit a flaming gas. Because the dragons could fly, they could intercept and char the Thread in midair before it reached the surface.

It took generations to develop to the fullest the potential of the dragons. The second phase of the proposed defense against the deadly incursions would take even longer. For Thread, a space-traveling mycorrhizoid spore, devoured with mindless voracity all organic matter and, once grounded, burrowed and proliferated with terrifying speed. So a symbiote of the same strain was developed to counter this parasite, and the resulting grub was introduced into the soil of the Southern Continent. It was planned that the dragons would be a visible protection, charring Thread while it was still skyborne and protecting the dwellings and the livestock of the colonists. The grub-symbiote would protect vegetation by devouring what Thread managed to evade the dragons' fire.

The originators of the two-stage defense did not allow for change or for hard geological fact. The Southern Continent, though seemingly more attractive than the harsher northern land, proved unstable, and the entire colony was eventually forced to seek refuge from the Threads on the continental shield rock of the north.

On the northern continent the original Fort, Fort Hold, constructed on the eastern face of the Great West Mountain Range, was soon outgrown by the colonists, and its capacious beasthold could not contain the growing numbers of dragons. Another settlement was started slightly to the north, where a great lake had formed near a cave-filled cliff. But Ruatha Hold, too, became overcrowded within a few generations.

Since the Red Star rose in the east, the people of Pern decided to establish a holding in the eastern mountains, provided a suitable cavesite could be found. Only solid rock and metal, both of which were in distressingly short supply on Pern, were impervious to the burning score of Thread.

The winged, tailed, fire-breathing dragons had by then been bred to a size that required more spacious accommodations than the cliffside holds could provide. The cave-pocked cones of extinct volcanoes, one high above the first Fort, the other in the Benden Mountains, proved to be adequate and required only a few improvements to be made habitable. However, such projects took the last of the fuel for the great stone-cutters, which had been programmed only for regular mining operations, not for wholesale cliff excavations. Subsequent holds and Weyrs had to be hand-hewn.

The dragons and their riders in their high places and the people in their cave holds went about their separate tasks, and each developed habits that became custom, which solidified into tradition as incontrovertible as law. And when a Fall of Thread was imminent—when the Red Star was visible at dawn through the Star Stones erected on the rim of each Weyr—the dragons and their riders mobilized to protect the people of Pern.

Then came an interval of two hundred Turns of the planet Pern around its primary—when the Red Star was at the far end of its erratic orbit, a frozen, lonely captive. No Thread fell on Pern. The inhabitants erased the signs of Thread depredation and grew crops, planted orchards and thought of reforestation for the slopes denuded by Thread. They even managed to forget that they had once been in great danger of extinction. Then, when the wandering planet returned, the Threads fell again, bringing another fifty years of attack from the skies. Once again the Pernese thanked their ancestors, now many generations removed, for providing the dragons whose fiery breath seared the falling Thread midair.

Dragonkind, too, had prospered during that Interval and had settled in four other locations, following the master plan of interim defense.

Recollections of Earth receded further from Pernese memories with each generation until knowledge of Mankind's origins degenerated into a myth. The significance of the southern hemisphere—and the Instructions formulated by the colonial defenders of dragon and grub—became garbled and lost in the more immediate struggle to survive.

By the Sixth Pass of the Red Star, a complicated sociopolitical-economic structure had been developed to deal with the recurrent evil. The six Weyrs, as the old volcanic habitations of the dragonfolk were called, pledged themselves to protect Pern, each Weyr having a geographical section of the Northern Continent literally under its wing. The rest of the population agreed to tithe support to the Weyrs since the dragonmen did not have arable land in their volcanic homes, could not afford to take time away from nurturing their dragons to learn other trades during peacetime, and could not take time away from protecting the planet during Passes.

Settlements, called holds, developed wherever natural caves were found—some, of course, more extensive or strategically placed than others. It took a strong man to exercise control over terrified people during Thread attacks; it took wise administration to conserve victuals when nothing could be safely grown, and it took extraordinary measures to control population and keep it productive and healthy until such time as the menace passed.

Men with special skills in metalworking, weaving, animal husbandry, farming, fishing, and mining formed crafthalls in each large Hold and looked to one Mastercrafthall where the precepts of their craft were taught and craft skills were preserved and guarded from one generation to another. One Lord Holder could not deny the products of the crafthall

situated in his Hold to others, since the Crafts were deemed independent
of a Hold affiliation. Each Craftmaster of a hall owed allegiance to the
Master of his particular craft—an elected office based on proficiency
in the craft and on administrative ability. The Mastercraftsman was
responsible for the output of his halls and the distribution, fair and
unprejudiced, of all craft products on a planetary rather than parochial
basis.

Certain rights and privileges accrued to different leaders of Holds
and Masters of Crafts and, naturally, to the dragonriders whom all Pern
looked to for protection during the Threadfalls.

It was within the Weyrs that the greatest social revolution took place,
for the needs of the dragons took priority over all other considerations.
Of the dragons, the gold and green were female, the bronze, brown,
and blue male. Of the female dragons, only the golden were fertile; the
greens were rendered sterile by the chewing of firestone, which was as
well since the sexual proclivities of the small greens would soon have
resulted in overpopulation. They were the most agile, however, and
invaluable as fighters of Thread, fearless and aggressive. But the price
of fertility was inconvenience, and riders of queen dragons carried
flamethrowers to char Thread. The blue males were sturdier than their
smaller sisters, while the browns and bronzes had the staying power
for long, arduous battles against Thread. In theory, the great golden
fertile queens were mated with whichever dragon could catch them in
their strenuous mating flights. Generally speaking, the bronzes did the
honor. Consequently the rider of the bronze dragon who flew the senior
queen of a Weyr became its Leader and had charge of the fighting
Wings during a Pass. The rider of the senior queen dragon, however,
held the most responsibility for the Weyr during and after a Pass when
it was the Weyrwoman's job to nurture and preserve the dragons, to
sustain and improve the Weyr and all its folk. A strong Weyrwoman
was as essential to the survival of the Weyr as dragons were to the
survival of Pern.

To her fell the task of supplying the Weyr, fostering its children,
and Searching for likely candidates from hall and hold to pair with the
newly hatched candidates. As life in the Weyrs was not only prestigious
but easier for women and men alike, hold and hall were proud to have
their children taken on Search and boasted of the illustrious members
of the bloodline who had become dragon riders.

We begin our story toward the end of the Sixth Pass of the Red Star,
some fourteen hundred Turns after men first came to Pern....

MORETA: DRAGONLADY OF PERN

CHAPTER I

Fort Weyr, Present Pass, 3.10.43 – 1541, and Ruatha Hold

"SH'GALL IS OUT on other Weyr business," Moreta told Nesso for the third time, beginning to loosen her sweat-and oil-stained tunic as a hint.

"His Weyr business should be accompanying you to Ruatha Gather." Nesso's voice had a whining note to it in the best of her humors. Now the Fort Weyr Headwoman was filled with aggrieved indignation at the fancied slight to her Weyrwoman, and her voice grated like a bone saw in Moreta's ear.

"He saw Lord Alessan yesterday. A Gather is not a time to discuss serious matters." Moreta rose, seeking to end an interview she hadn't wanted to give, one that could continue as long as Nesso could dredge up complaints, real or imaginary, against Sh'gall. Their antagonism was mutual, and Moreta often found herself in the position of placating or explaining the one to the other. She could not change Sh'gall and was loathe to displace Nesso for, despite her faults, the woman was an exceedingly efficient and hard-working Headwoman. "I must bathe, Nesso, or I'll be unpardonably late at Ruatha. I know you've arranged a good meal for those who remain. K'lon's comfortable now that the fever has broken. Berchar will look in on him. Just leave him alone."

Moreta fixed Nesso with an admonitory gaze, reinforcing her injunction. Nesso had an officious habit of "taking" Moreta's place whenever the Weyrwoman was absent unless specifically ordered not to. "Away with you now, Nesso. You've enough to do, and I'm longing to be clean." Moreta accompanied her words with a smile as she gave

Nesso a gentle shove toward the exit from her sleeping room.
"Sh'gall should go with you. He should," the irrepressible woman
muttered as Moreta held aside the vivid door-curtain. Only when Nesso
neared the sleeping queen dragon did she cease her imprecations.
Heavy with egg, Orlith dozed on, oblivious to the woman's passing.
The golden dragon had arranged herself on the stony couch so as not
to mar the fine gleam of oil that Moreta had rubbed into her hide as
part of the morning's preparation for the Gather at Ruatha. Moreta was
heading for her own much-needed wash when she was asked to examine
K'lon, so she'd been late for her chat with Leri to be sure the old
Weyrwoman had what she required for the day. Leri would have no
ministrations from Nesso's hands.

The interview with Nesso had proved unavoidable. The Headwoman
had "heard" that Sh'gall and Moreta had "had words" that had caused
the Weyrleader's abrupt departure, dressed in riding gear rather than in
his Gather finery. Nesso had also to be reassured that K'lon was not
wasting from a virulent fever that would spread rapidly through the
Weyr, it being only three days to a Fall.

Moreta stripped off her clothes. She ought to have been at the Gather
long since, getting through the obligatory courtesies before the racing
started.

"Orlith?" Moreta called softly, concentrating the strength of her
gentle summons in her head. As always, the sleepy response of
her queen cheered her of Nesso's petulance. "Rouse yourself, my golden
beauty. We'll be leaving soon for Ruatha's Gatherday."

It's still sunny at Ruatha? Orlith asked hopefully.

"It should be. T'ral did the morning sweep," Moreta said, opening
her robe chest. The new gown lay in gold and soft, warm-brown folds,
colors that would accent Moreta's eyes. "You know how accurate T'ral's
weather sense is."

The dragon rumbled with satisfaction, and Moreta could hear her
stretching and turning.

"Don't roll too much now," Moreta said politely.

I know. I mustn't lose my shine. Orlith spoke with patient acknowledgment. *I will keep clean until we reach Ruatha. And then I'll sun.
When I get hot enough, I'll swim in Ruatha Lake.*

"Would that be wise so close to clutching, my dear? That lake's cold
as *between.*" Moreta shivered at her memory of those ice-fed waters.

Nothing is colder than between. Orlith spoke definitively.

Having laid out her Gather finery, Moreta strode into the bathing
room. She grabbed a handful of sweet sand, then swung her legs over
the lip of the raised pool, whose surface was faintly steaming. Standing
waist deep, she sanded her body until her skin tingled. Submerging for
a moment, she surfaced, tipping her head until her short hair fanned

out in the water. Then she pushed back to the edge of the pool, reaching for more sand, which she scrubbed into her scalp and hair.

You take a long time to get clean though there's not much of you, Orlith remarked, somewhat impatient now that she was fully awake.

"There may not be much of me, but there was a great deal of *you* to be bathed and oiled."

You always say that.

"So do you."

The countercomplaints were lodged with total affection and understanding. Queen and rider had been partnered for nearly twenty Turns, though they had only recently become the leading pair at Fort Weyr when Leri's Holth had not risen to mate the previous winter.

Moreta gave her head a final drubbing, then flicked her fingers through her hair to make the short crop settle into natural waves. Wearing a leather cap during Threadfall made her scalp sweat so much that the long blond braids in which she had taken so much pride as a holder girl had been shorn. Once this Pass was completed, she could grow her hair!

Once the Pass was completed... In the act of pulling on a clean undertunic, Moreta paused in surprise. Why, this Pass would end in another eight Turns. No, seven if one counted this Turn a quarter gone. Moreta sternly corrected an optimistic attitude. The Turn was barely seventy days old. Eight Turns then. In eight Turns, she, Moreta, would no longer *have* to fly with Orlith against Thread. The Red Star would have passed too far to rain the devastating parasitic Thread over Pern's tired continent. Dragonriders would not have to fly because no Thread would blur the sky.

Did Thread just stop, Moreta wondered as she slipped on her soft brown shoes, like a sudden summer storm? Or did it dribble off like a winter rain?

They could use some rain. Snow would be even better. Or a good hard frost. Frost was always a Weyr ally.

She slipped into the dress now, smoothing it over her rather too broad shoulders, over breasts firm rather than large, a waist that was trim, and buttocks flat from long hours of riding astride. The gown hid muscled thighs that she sometimes resented, but they, too, were the legacy of twenty Turns riding a dragon and little enough inconvenience for being a queen's rider.

She did wish that Sh'gall had chosen to come with her. She wasn't acquainted with the new Ruathan Lord Holder, Alessan. She had a vague recollection that he was the leggy young man with light-green eyes that were an odd contrast to his dark complexion and shaggy black hair. He had always stood most correctly behind the old Lord Holder, his father. Lord Leef had been a stern if just holder from whom the

Weyr could expect every traditional duty and the last tittle of tithe: just the sort of man the Weyr, and Pern, needed in command of such a prosperous Hold. But then, at Ruatha traditions had always been zealously maintained, and many of that bloodline had impressed queen as well as bronze.

None of the many sons that the old Lord Leef had bred had known which would be named his successor. Lord Leef had kept the whole tangle of them in hand, preventing discord. Despite Threadfall and the other dangers of a Pass, Lord Leef had contrived to build several new holds into the sides of Ruatha's steep valleys, to accommodate the worthiest of his sons and their families. Such expansion had been one of his many schemes to keep order in his Hold. Lord Leef had planned ahead for the end of the Pass as well as for an orderly succession. Moreta could not fault such provisions though Sh'gall, among other dragonriders, had become concerned over the creeping expansion of the hold populations. Six Weyrs, twenty-three hundred dragons, were hard-pressed to keep cultivated lands Threadfree in this Pass. There had been talk of founding another Weyr during the Interval. That would not be her problem, however.

Moreta set the gold and green jeweled band at her neck and slipped on her heavy bracelets. The light-eyed man *must* be Alessan. She had often seen him at the end of Fall with the flamethrower gangs. Always correct in his manner, nevertheless Alessan's presence was felt despite his reserve. For the life of her, Moreta couldn't remember as distinctly any of the other nine sons though they all seemed to have inherited the strong craggy features of their sire rather than those of their various mothers.

Today would be Alessan's first Gather since the Conclave of Lord Holders had confirmed his accession to Ruathan honors at the beginning of the Turn. Rest days, Threadfree days, and clear weather combined infrequently.

"Since there are the two Gathers, I shall attend Ista's," Sh'gall had told her that morning. "I told Alessan so yesterday, and it didn't displease him." Sh'gall gave a scornful snort. "He's got every rag and tag at the race meeting of his so you should enjoy yourself." Sh'gall did not approve of Moreta's uninhibited enjoyment of racing and, on those few occasions when they had attended a Gather since Orlith's mating flight with Kadith, he had put quite a damper on her pleasure in the sport. "I shall enjoy the sun and the seafood. Lord Fitatric always provides superb feasts. I can only hope you'll do as well at Ruatha."

"I've never found fault with Ruathan hospitality." Something in Sh'gall's tone required her to defend the Hold. Sh'gall had been awed by Lord Leef, but not be the new young Lord. Moreta did not always agree with Sh'gall's snap judgments so she would wait and form her own opinion of Alessan.

"Besides, I've promised to convey Lord Ratoshigan to Ista. He does not care to attend Ruatha. He does wish to see the curious new animal to be displayed at Ista."

"Oh?"

"Thought you might have heard?" Sh'gall's tone implied she should have known what he was talking about. "Seamen from Igen Sea Hold found the beast adrift in the Great Current, clinging to a floating tree. They'd never seen its like and took it to the Master Herdsman in Keroon."

Ah, Moreta thought, that was why she should have known. Why Sh'gall assumed she knew everything that transpired in her native hold she did not know. She was firmly and totally committed to Fort Weyr, and had been for ten Turns.

"It's some species of feline, I hear," Sh'gall added. "Probably something left behind on the Southern Continent. Quite a fierce beast. Wiser to leave that sort."

"With the way we're being overrun by tunnel snakes, a fierce, hungry feline might be useful. The canines aren't quick enough." Her comment annoyed Sh'gall, who gave her one of his dark, ambiguous glares and stalked out of the weyr. His unexpected reaction irritated Moreta. Not for the first time, she heartily wished that Sh'gall's Kadith had not flown Orlith a second time. Then she told herself firmly that old L'mal had considered Sh'gall one of the ablest wingleaders. Until the end of the Pass, Fort Weyr needed the ablest wingleader. Everyone had thought L'mal would last out the Pass, so his sudden illness and death had been a great loss. Moreta had always liked L'mal, and Leri spoke very highly of him as a weyrmate. Sh'gall was young, Moreta reminded herself; this was not an easy time to assume Weyrleadership, and Sh'gall suffered by comparison to the older, more experienced L'mal. Time would teach Sh'gall tolerance and understanding. Meanwhile Moreta must have those qualities in full measure to survive his learning period.

As Moreta lifted the fur cape about her shoulders, the bracelets slid up her arms. They had been the gift of old Lord Leef for her having ridden Thread down—perilously close for the safety of Orlith—to the Lord's cherished fruit trees, which were threatened by the parasite. Aided by Orlith's agile maneuvering, Moreta had seared the Thread to harmless char with her flamethrower. She had been very young then, just transferred to Fort Weyr from Ista and eager to prove to her new folk just how keen and clever Orlith was. She wouldn't take such a risk now, though it was not due to the memory of the rage in the eyes of L'mal, who had been Weyrleader then, when he had berated her for recklessness. Leef's gift had not appreciably lessened her disgrace or eased her conscience, but they looked well with her new gown.

Are we going to the Gather at all? Orlith asked wistfully.

"Yes, we are going to the Gather," Moreta replied, shaking her head clear of such reflections.

She'd have a good Gather, too, for Ruatha Hold would be gay and
bright, dominated by the young Alessan's young friends. Sh'gall had
said that they were still full of their success, that he'd had to remind
Alessan that Thread brought no joy and he must attend his duties as
Lord Holder before attending to his pleasures.

"Perhaps it's just as well Sh'gall decided to go to Ista . . . and take
Lord Ratoshigan with him," Moreta told Orlith, convincing herself in
the process.

He and Kadith are well occupied, Orlith said complacently as she
followed her rider from their weyr.

Orlith paused on the ledge, glancing around the Weyr Bowl. Most
of the sun-struck ledges usually occupied by dragons were empty.

Have they all gone? Orlith asked in surprise, craning her neck to
see the shadowed west ledges.

"With two Gathers? Of course. I hope we're not too late for the
racing."

Orlith blinked her great, many-faceted eyes. *You and your racing.*

"You enjoy it as much as I do and generally have a far better view
on the fire-heights. Don't fret. It's fun to watch, but I ride only you."

Mollified by her rider's teasing assurance, Orlith crouched, setting
her forearm so Moreta could climb to her place between the last two
neck ridges above her shoulder. Moreta settled her skirts and pulled the
cloak about her. Nothing would really keep her warm in the awesome
total cold of *between* but the transition lasted only a few breaths, which
anyone could endure.

Orlith sprang from the ledge. Though gravid, she was not a lazy
dragon, to tumble off into the air before making first use of her wings.
The old queen, Holth, trumpeted a farewell; the watchdragon spread
his wings, masking the Star Stones on the summit. The watchrider
extended his arm, completing the salute as Moreta waved acknowledgment.

Orlith caught the wind flowing down the oblong Bowl, the crater of
an extinct volcano which was home to the Weyr. In a distant Turn, an
earthslide had rampaged down the range, broken through the southwest
part of the Weyr and into the lake. Stonecraftsmen had cleared the lake
and shored up the edge in a massive wall but little could be done to
clear the lost caverns and weyrs, or restore the symmetry of the Bowl.

"Surveying your Weyr, o Queen?" Moreta asked, indulging Orlith's
leisurely glide.

At height, one sees many details in proper order. All is well.

Moreta's laugh was blown from her lips, and she had to hang on to
the riding straps. Orlith constantly surprised her with gratuitous obser-
vations. Conversely, when Moreta needed guidance, Orlith might reply
that she didn't understand any rider but Moreta. The queen could be

counted on to comment on the Weyr in general, or on the morale of the fighting wings, or to supply information about the Weyrleader's dragon, Kadith. Orlith was not so forthcoming about Sh'gall. But, after twenty Turns of their symbiotic relationship, Moreta had learned to discover as much in the queen's impartiality or evasion as from her candid remarks. Being a queen's rider was never easy. Being the Weyrwoman, Leri had more than once told Moreta, doubled both honors and horrors. One took the good with the bad and used fellis sparingly.

Now Moreta visualized the fire-heights of Ruatha Hold, with its distinctive pattern of fire-gutters and beacons and the eastern watch rampart.

Take us to Ruatha, she said to Orlith and clenched her teeth against the cold of *between*.

"Black, blacker, blackest; colder beyond frozen things,
Where is *between* when there is naught
To Life but fragile dragon wings."

Moreta often held the words of the old song as a talisman against the bitter breathless journey. Ruatha was not far from Fort Weyr by any means of travel, and Moreta had only reached "colder" when the warm sun shone on them and on Ruatha's fire-heights below. The host of dragons lounging on the rocky cliff summit, whole wings of them, voiced greetings at Orlith's appearance in the air. Orlith's thoughts echoed her pleasure in the accolade. Dragons met so rarely for pleasure, Moreta mused. Thread was the cause. Soon, in eight Turns...

As the queen glided down, Moreta recognized some of the dragons from other Weyrs by the scar patterns on their bodies and wings.

Bronzes from Telgar and High Reaches, Orlith reported, making her own identifications, *browns, blues, and greens. But Benden has been and gone. We should have come earlier.* The last held a plaintive note because Orlith had a partiality for the Benden bronze Tuzuth.

"Sorry, dear heart, but I had so much to do."

Orlith snorted. Moreta felt the jerk of chest muscles through the dragon's withers. She had begun to circle, dropping toward the fire-heights. Anticipating a landing, Moreta tightened her hold on the straps. Orlith overshot the heights, clearly headed down over the roadway crowded with the stalls of the Gather and a milling throng of folk gaily dressed for the occasion. Suddenly Moreta realized that Orlith meant to land in the empty dancing square ringed by lamp standards, trestle tables, and benches.

I do not forget that we are senior now, Orlith said primly, *and that the Hold's honors are due the Fort Weyrwoman.*

Orlith landed with neat precision in the dance square, her broad pinions vaned high to avoid excessive backwinds. The banners on the lamp standards flapped vigorously, but little dust rose from the square already swept to hard ground.

"Well done, dear heart," Moreta said, scratching her mount's back ridge affectionately.

She glanced over at the imposing precipice that housed Ruatha Hold, magnificently topped by ranks of sunbathing dragons. The Hold's un- shuttered windows displayed banners and brightly woven rugs. Tables and chairs had been set out on the open forecourt so distinguished visitors could view the gather stalls and the dancing square without obstruction. Moreta glanced quickly in the other direction, toward the flats where the racing was held. She could see the picket lines off to the right. The brightly painted starting poles were not in position so she hadn't missed any racing.

The entire Gather had ceased its activity to watch Orlith's landing. Now there was a stir among the onlookers, who parted to allow a man to step from their midst.

See! The Lord Holder approaches, Orlith said.

Moreta swung her right leg over Orlith's neck, pulling her skirts about, preparatory to dismounting. Then she glanced at the man ap- proaching them. She could just make out his features, which corre- sponded to her recollection of Lord Leef's light-eyed son. His broad shoulders were held at a confident angle and his rangy stride was as- sured, neither diffident nor hasty.

He came to an abrupt halt, bowing to Orlith, who lowered her head to acknowledge his greeting. Then he moved on quickly to assist Moreta to dismount, looking intently up at her.

His light-green eyes, unusual in one so dark-skinned, caught hers. His gaze was as formal and impersonal as his hands as he seized her by the waist and swung her down from Orlith's forearm. He bowed, and Moreta couldn't but notice that his shaggy hair had been neatly trimmed and attractively shaped.

"Weyrwoman, welcome to Ruatha Hold. I had begun to think that you and Orlith were not going to attend." His voice was unexpectedly tenor for a man so tall and lean, his words clearly spoken.

"I bring the Weyrleader's regrets."

"He gave them in advance yesterday. It would have been your regrets which I, and Ruatha, would have been sad to receive. Orlith is in splendid color," he added, his voice unexpectedly warming, "for a queen so near clutching."

The queen blinked her rainbow-hued eyes, echoing the surprise that Moreta felt in Alessan's adherence to formalities. Moreta hadn't ex- pected so polished a delivery from so young a man but, after all, Leef had drilled his heir in the proprieties. Besides, she was always ready to discuss Orlith.

"She's in great health and she's always that unusual shade."

As her reply deviated from the tradition, Alessan hesitated.

"Now, some dragons are so light as to be more pale yellow than gold while others are dark enough to vie with the bronzes. Yet she is *not*"—Moreta eyed her queen candidly—"the classic shade."

Alessan chuckled. "Does shade make any difference?"

"Certainly not to me. I would scarcely mind if Orlith were green-gold. She is my queen, and I am her rider." She glanced at Alessan, wondering if he was mocking her. But his green eyes, with their tiny flecks of brown around the pupil, registered only polite query.

Alessan smiled. "And senior at Fort Weyr."

"As you are Lord of Ruatha." She felt slightly defensive for, despite the innocuous and formal phrases, she sensed an undercurrent in his speech. Had Sh'gall discussed his Weyrwoman with a Lord Holder? *Orlith?*

The fire-height is warm in the full sun, the dragon replied evasively, swinging her head toward her rider. The many facets of her eyes were tinged with the blue of longing.

"Off you go, dear heart." Moreta gave Orlith's shoulder a loving thump and then, with Alessan at her side, she walked from the dancing square. As they reached the edge, Orlith leaped, her broad wings clearing the ground in the first downward sweep. The dragon had launched herself in a very shallow angle toward the sheer rock of Ruatha. As the queen flew a mere length above the stalls and gatherers, Moreta could hear the spate of startled cries. Beside her, Alessan stiffened.

Do you know what you're doing, my love? Moreta asked, reasonably but firm. *You're a bit egg-heavy for antics.*

I am demonstrating the abilities of their queen. It will do them good and me no harm. See?

Orlith had judged her angle finely, though from Moreta's perspective, she looked to be in danger of clipping her forearms on the cliff edge. But Orlith cleared the cliff easily and, dropping her shoulder, spun almost on wingtip. She set her hindquarters down directly over the Hold's main entrance, in the space vacated by other dragons. Then she flipped her wings to her back, sank down, and rested her triangular head on her forearms.

Exhibitionist! Moreta sent without rancor. "She's comfortable now, Lord Alessan."

"I had heard of Orlith's reputation for close flying," he replied, his eyes flicking to the jewelry Moreta wore.

So the young Lord knew of the old Lord's gift.

"An advantage in Threadfall."

"This is a Gather." With that slight emphasis on the pronoun, Alessan spoke as Lord Holder.

"And where is it more appropriate to display skill and craft and beauty?" Moreta gestured toward the gaily caparisoned stalls and the richly colored tunics and dresses of the crowd. She removed her hand from his arm, partly to show her annoyance with his criticism and partly to loosen her cloak. The chill of *between* had been replaced by the warmth of the afternoon sun. "Come now, Lord Alessan"—and she linked her arm through his again—"let us have no uncharitable words at your first Gather as Lord of Ruatha and my first outing since the winter solstice."

They had reached the roadway and the stalls where people were examining wares and bargaining. Moreta smiled up at Lord Alessan to prove her firm intention of enjoying herself. He looked down at her, blinking and creasing his dark brows slightly. His expression cleared to a smile, still reserved but considerably more genuine than his stiff formality.

"I fear I have none of my dam's virtues, Lady Moreta."

"And all of your sire's vices?"

"My good Lord Leef had no vices," Alessan said very properly, but his eyes had begun to gleam with an amusement that proved to Moreta that the man had at least a vestige of his sire's humor.

"The races haven't started yet?"

Alessan missed a stride and glanced sharply at her.

"No, not yet." His tone was wary. "We have been waiting for late arrivals."

"There seemed to be a good number at the pickets. How many races?" She gave him a quick glance. Didn't he approve of racing?

"Ten races are planned, but the entries have been lighter than I had anticipated. You enjoy racing, Lady Moreta?"

"I came from a runnerhold in Keroon, Lord Alessan, and I have never lost my interest in the breed."

"So you know where to place your wagers?"

"Lord Alessan," she said in a determinedly light tone, "I never wager. The sight of a good race well run is always a pleasure and excitement enough." His manner was still uncertain so she changed the subject. "I believe that we've missed the eastern visitors."

"The Benden Weyrwoman and Weyrleader have only just left us." Alessan's eyes sparkled at having acted the host to such prestigious guests.

"I had hoped to exchange news with them." Moreta's regret was sincere, but she was also relieved. The Benden Weyrleaders did not like Orlith's fascination with Tuzuth, the Benden bronze, any more than she herself did. Such cross-weyr interests were encouraged in young queens but not in seniors. "Did Benden's Lord Holder come, too?"

"Yes." Pleasure tinged Alessan's tone. "Lord Shadder and I had only the briefest but most congenial of talks. Most congenial. East and West don't often have much chance to meet. Have you met Lord Shadder?"

"When I was in Ista Weyr." Moreta smiled back at Alessan, for Shadder of Benden was undoubtedly the most popular Lord Holder on Pern. His warmth and concern always seemed intensely personal. She sighed. "I really wish I had been able to come sooner. Who else attends?"

The briefest of frowns crossed Alessan's face. "At the moment," he said briskly, "holders and Craftmasters from Ruatha, Fort, Crom, Nabol, Tillek and High Reaches. A long journey for some, but everyone seems well pleased that the warm weather had held for the Gather." He glanced about the crowded stalls, noting trades in the making. "Tillek's Lord Holder may arrive later with the High Reaches Weyrleader. Lord Tolocamp rode in an hour ago and is changing."

Moreta grinned in sympathy with Alessan. Lord Tolocamp was an energetic, forceful man who spoke his mind and gave his opinion on every topic as if he were the universal expert. As he did not have the least sense of humor, exchanges with him were apt to be awkward and boring. Moreta preferred to avoid his company whenever possible. But, as she was now senior Weyrwoman, she had fewer excuses to do so.

"How many of his ladies came with him?"

"Five." Alessan's voice was carefully neutral. "My mother, Lady Oma, always enjoys a visit with Lady Pendra."

Moreta had to choke back a laugh and turned her face slightly away. All Pern knew that Lady Pendra was angling to get Alessan to marry one of her numerous daughters, nieces, or cousins. Alessan's young wife, Suriana, had died the previous Turn in a fall. At the time, Lord Leef had not pressed his son to make another marriage, a fact that many had taken to mean that Alessan was not to succeed. As the Fort Hold girls were as plain as they were capable, Moreta didn't think much of Fort's chances, but Alessan would be obliged to marry soon if he wished his own bloodline to succeed.

"Would it please the Fort Weyrwoman for Lord Alessan to take a Fort Holder as wife?" His voice was cold and stiff.

"You can surely do better than that," Moreta replied crisply and then laughed. "I'm sorry. It is not really a subject for levity, but you don't know how you sound."

"And how do I sound?" Alessan's eyes glinted.

"Like a man sorely pressed in a direction he does not wish to travel. This is your first Gather. You should enjoy it, too."

"Will you help me?" Pure mischief played across his face now.

"How?"

"You're my Weyrwoman." His face assumed a proper respect. "Since Sh'gall has not accompanied you, I must be your partner."

"In conscience, I could not monopolize your time." Even as she spoke, Moreta realized that that was what she would rather like to do. There was a rebellion in him that attracted her.

"Most of it?" His voice was wistfully pleading, quite a variance with his sparkling eyes and grin. "I know what I have to do but. . . ."

"There'll be girls here from *all* over—"

"Yes, a Search has been conducted for my benefit."

"What else did you expect, Lord Alessan, when you're now such a suitable match?"

"Suriana liked *me*, not my prospects," Alessan said in a flat bleak voice. "When that match was arranged, of course, I had none, so we could suit ourselves. And we did."

So that explained why he had been allowed to grieve and defer a second marriage. Moreta hadn't thought Lord Leef had so much compassion in him. "You were more fortunate than most," she said, oddly envious. Once she had Impressed a queen, personal choice had been denied her. Once she had Impressed Orlith, their love compensated for many things; love for another human paled in comparison.

"I was acutely aware of my good luck." In that quiet phrase, Alessan implied not only his loss but his realization that he must discharge the responsibilites of his new rank. Moreta wondered why Sh'gall had developed a curious antipathy to the man.

They were moving through the Gatherers, past the stalls. Moreta sniffed deeply of the aromas of spicy stew and sweet fruit pies, the odor of well-tanned leathers, the acrid smell from the glass-blowers' booth, the mingled smells of perfumes and garment herbs, the sweat of human and animal. And above all, the pleasant excitement that permeated the atmosphere.

"Within the bounds of Gather propriety, I accept your partnering. Provided that you like racing and dancing."

"In that order?"

"Since the one comes before the other, yes."

"I appreciate your courtesy, Weyrwoman!" His tone was mock-formal.

"Have the harpers arrived yet?"

"Yesterday . . ." Alessan grimaced.

"They *do* eat, don't they?"

"They *talk*. There are enough of them, however, to keep the dancing square filled until dawn, now that your queen has graced it. And our ever jovial Masterharper has promised to dignify our Gather with his presence."

Moreta frowned at yet another undercurrent in Alessan's speech. Didn't he like Tirone? The Masterharper was a big hearty man with a robust bass voice that he allowed to dominate every group he sang in. He favored the rousing ballads and stirrings sagas that best displayed his own talents, but that was his one conceit, and Moreta had never considered it a flaw. But then, herself only lately the Weyrwoman, she had not seen as much of him in his capacity as Masterharper of Pern as had Alessan. She didn't think she would like to antagonize Tirone.

"He has a beautiful voice," she said noncommitally. "Is Master Capiam coming?"

"So I believe."

Shells, thought Moreta to herself at Alessan's terse reply. With the exception of Lord Shadder, Alessan apparently did not share any of her preferences among the leaders of Pern. She'd never heard of anyone who didn't like Masterhealer Capiam. Could Alessan fault the man for failing to mend his wife's broken back?

"Is that sort of exercise good for Orlith at this time, Moreta?" demanded Lord Tolocamp, bearing down on them suddenly. He must have been following their progress along the roadway to have intercepted them so neatly.

"She's not due to clutch for another ten days." Moreta stiffened, annoyed both by the question and the questioner.

"Orlith flew with great precision," Alessan said. "An ability well appreciated by Ruatha."

Lord Tolocamp checked, coughed, covering his mouth belatedly and plainly not understanding Alessan's reference.

"She's thoroughly shameless," Moreta said, "whenever there's a new audience for her tricks. She's never so much as bunged a claw."

"Yes, well, ah, Lady Pendra is just over here, Moreta," Tolocamp went on with his usual ponderous geniality. "Alessan, I would like you to become better acquainted with my daughters."

"At the moment, Lord Tolocamp, I am obliged to become better acquainted with the Weyrwoman, as Sh'gall is not here as her escort. Your daughters"—Alessan looked over at the young women, who were talking placidly with some of his subordinates—"seem well suited."

Tolocamp began to huff.

"A glass of wine, Moreta? This way." Alessan firmly propelled her away from Lord Tolocamp, who stood staring after them, somewhat surprised by their abrupt departure.

"I'll never hear the last of this from him, you know," Moreta said as she allowed herself to be hurried off.

"Then you can drown your sorrow in a Benden white wine I have chilling." He beckoned to a servitor, pantomiming the pouring of wine into a glass.

"Benden white? Why, that's my favorite!"

"And here I thought you were partial to Tillek's."

Moreta made a face. "I'm obliged to *assume* a partiality for Tillek wines."

"I find them sharp. Soil's acid in Tillek."

"True, but Tillek tithes its wines to Fort Weyr. And it's far easier to agree with Lord Diatis than argue with him."

Alessan laughed.

As the servitor returned with two finely engraved cups and a small wineskin, Moreta glimpsed Lord Tolocamp, Lady Pendra, and Lady Oma shepherding the daughters toward them. Just then a stentorian voice proclaimed the start of the runner races.

"We'll never elude Lady Pendra. Where can we go?" Moreta asked, but Alessan was staring toward the race course.

"I have a particular reason for wanting to watch that first race. If we hurry..." He pointed to the roadway that wound to the racing flats, but that path would not avoid the Fortian progression.

"Short of calling on Orlith's assistance, we'd never make it. And she's asleep." Then Moreta saw the scaffold surrounding the wall being built at the southern edge of the forecourt. "Why not up there?" She pointed.

"Perfect—and you've a head for heights!" Alessan took her hand and guided her deftly through the guests and away from the Fortians.

Those already standing by the unfinished courses of the wall made room for the Lord Holder and the Weyrwoman. Alessan put his goblet in her free hand and neatly jumped to the top course. Then he knelt, gesturing for her to hand up both wine cups.

For just a moment, Moreta hesitated. L'mal had often chided her about the dignity expected of Weyrwomen, especially outside the precincts of the Weyr, where holder, crafter, and harper could observe and criticise. Quite likely she had been stimulated by Orlith's outrageous exhibition. What affected dragon affected rider. It was a lovely warm Gather, just the respite she'd needed from her onerous responsibilities all Turn. There was racing and Benden wine, there'd be dancing later. Moreta, Weyrwoman of Fort Weyr, was going to enjoy herself.

You should, you know, Orlith commented sleepily.

"Hurry," Alessan said. "They're milling at the start."

Moreta turned to the nearest dragonrider at the wall.

"Give me a leg up, R'limeak, would you?"

"Moreta!"

"Oh, don't be scandalized. I want to see the race start." She arranged her skirts and bent her left knee. "A good lift, R'limeak. I'd rather not scrape my nose on the stones."

R'limeak's lift was not wholehearted. If Alessan's strong hands had not steadied her, she would have slipped.

"How shocked he looks!" Alessan laughed, his green eyes merry.

"It'll do him good. Blue riders can be so prim!" She took her wine from Alessan. "Ah, what a marvelous view!" Having observed that the race was not about to start, she turned slowly, to appreciate the sweep of the land from the foot of Ruatha's cliff hold, over the crude roofs of the decorated stalls, to the empty dancing square, the fields beyond, the walled orchards on each side, and then the slope that descended gradually to Ruatha's river, its source the Ice Lake high in the mountains above. True, the orchards were bare, the fields browned by what frost had fallen that Turn, but the sky was a vivid green-blue, not a cloud in sight, and the air was pleasantly warm. Favored with a long eye, Moreta saw that three laggard racers had yet to join the starters.

"Ruatha's looking so gay," she said. "Generally when I'm here, the shutters are all in place against Thread, not a soul or beast in sight. Today it's a different place entirely."

"We are often good company here," Alessan said. His eyes lay on the scene at the starting poles. "Ruatha is considered one of the best-placed Holds. Fort may be older but, I think, not so well laid out."

"The harpers tell us that Fort Hold was thrown together as a temporary accommodation after the Crossing."

"A mere fourteen hundred Turns *temporary*. Whereas we of Ruatha have always been planners. We even have special accommodations for visiting race enthusiasts."

Moreta grinned at him. She realized that they were both rambling on in excitement at the impending race.

"Look! They're finally lined up!"

The mild breeze cooperated by blowing the churned dust of the racing flats away from the straggling line of cavorting beasts. She saw the white flag drop, caught her breath at the incredible leap as the animals surged forward.

"This is the sprint?" she asked, trying to make out an early leader in the knot of nodding heads, bobbing bodies, and flashing legs. So close packed were the runners that neither riders' hat colors nor saddle pads could be identified.

"As is usual," Alessan replied absently, shielding his eyes with his hand to see better.

"Good field, too. Spreading out and . . . I'd swear the leader is wearing Ruathan colors!"

"I hope so!" Alessan cried in considerable excitement.

Cheers and exhortations rose from nearby and drifted up from the race course.

"Fort is challenging!" Moreta said as a second beast separated from the pack. "And fast!"

"It has only to hold!" Alessan's words were half threat, half entreaty.

"It will!" Moreta's calm assurance elicited a quick disbelieving glare from Alessan, who remained taut with suspense until the winners passed the post. "It did!"

"Are you sure?"

"Certainly. The poles are parallel to this vantage point. You've a winner! Did you breed it yourself?"

"Yes, yes, I did. And it did win!" He seemed to need her confirmation of his achievement.

"It certainly did. A very respectable two lengths the winner or I miss my mark. And I don't miss in racing. To your winner then!" She raised her goblet to his.

"My winner!" His voice was curiously fierce, and the light in his eyes became more defiant than triumphant.

"I'll come with you to the finish," she suggested, noticing that the sprinters were finally pulling up in the stubble.

"I can savor this moment just as fully in your company," he said unexpectedly. "And with no inhibitions," he added with a grin. "Dag's there. He's my herdsman, and this is as much his victory as it is mine. I won't detract from his moment. Then, too, it would be highly inappropriate for the Gathering Lord Holder to caper about like a fool over a mere sprint win."

Moreta found his admission of unlordly glee rather charming. "Surely this isn't your first winner?"

"Actually, it is." He was searching the enclosure and suddenly beckoned peremptorily at a servitor, signaling for more wine. "Breeding for special traits was the project Lord Leef assigned me eight Turns ago." Alessan went on in a more conversational tone though his voice still carried an edge. "A well-established Pernese tradition is breeding."

"Eight Turns ago?" Moreta gave Alessan a long look. "If you've been breeding since then, surely this can't be your *first* winner?"

"A race, yes. The quality Lord Leef wished me to perpetuate was stamina for long-distance carting, combined with more efficient use of fodder."

"More work out of fewer animals for less food?" Moreta didn't find that hard to believe of the old Lord, but she stared at Alessan with confused respect. "And out of that breeding, you got a sprint racer?"

"Not intentionally." Alessan gave her a rueful smile. "That winner is from a strain of rejects from the original project: tough, hardy, good doers even on poor feed, but small bodied and thin boned. They don't eat much, and everything they consume goes into short spurts of energy—fifty dragon-length sprint distances, to be truthful. Over the ninety-length mark, they're useless. Give 'em half an hour's rest and they can repeat that sort of winning performance. And they live long. It was Dag who saw the sprint potential in the scrubs."

"But, of course, you couldn't race the beasts during your father's lifetime." Moreta started to chuckle at Alessan's deception.

"Hardly." Alessan grinned.

"I imagine that your winnings today—an untried beast in its first race—will be substantial."

"I should hope so. Considering how long Dag and I have succored that wretched creature for just such an occasion as this."

"My sincerest congratulations, Lord Alessan!" Moreta raised her newly filled goblet. "For putting one over on Lord Leef and winning your first race at your first Gather. You're not only devious, you're a menace to racing men."

"Had I known you were such a race enthusiast, I'd've given you odds—"

"Spectator, not speculator. You'll race it next at Fort's Gather?"

"Considering its capability, I could race in the last sprint today and be sure of its winning, but that would not be courteous." The gleam in his eye suggested that if he weren't Lord Holder, he would not have felt any such restraint. "At that, most will assume it a lucky win. Only the one race in it, like as not." Alessan's voice imitated the pitch and inflection of the confirmed racer, querulous and skeptical. "So I shall get it to whatever Gathers we can reach. I like winning. It's a new experience."

His candor surprised her. "Are you sure your sire didn't know what you were about? Lord Leef always struck me as a man who had firm control of everything that occurred in his Hold—in the entire west."

Alessan gave her a long hard look, mulling her remark. "D'you know, I wouldn't be at all surprised if he *had* found out. We, Dag and I, took such extraordinary precautions. We thought we'd covered every possibility of discovery." Then Alessan shook his head, chuckling. "You wouldn't believe the lengths to which we went—but you could be right. The old Lord could have known."

"I expect he wouldn't have named you successor on your merits as a breeder alone. What else have you been up to?"

Alessan winked at her. "The Weyr commands my services, Lady, not my secrets."

"I've found *one* out. Shall I—" Moreta paused, suddenly aware that their laughing exchanges were being closely observed. Why shouldn't she laugh at a Gather? She gave R'limeak a stern glare, and the blue rider looked away.

Noting her change of expression, Alessan glanced about them and swore under his breath. "Not even on a half-built wall in full sight of a Gather!" he said acidly. He swore again as he saw Lord Tolocamp and the women moving purposefully toward the wall.

"Shards!" Moreta said. "I will not have the racing spoiled by chitchat and courtship. Look, we'll be able to see just as well from over there!" She pointed to a slight rise in the field below the roadway. Then she gathered her skirts and started to pick a careful path down the pile of stones waiting to be set into the wall. "And do collect that skin of white wine."

"Be careful, you'll break your neck!" Alessan urgently signaled the servitor to hand over the wineskin, then he was following her before anyone was aware of their intentions.

Rocks shifting under their feet, Moreta and Alessan reached the roadway without mishap, then hurried behind the stalls and down the open field to the rise. When Moreta felt burrs pulling at her full skirts, she bundled them higher.

"No propriety in you at all today." Alessan shook his head at her undignified lope, though he was placing his elegantly booted feet with a care for rough ground.

"This is a Gather. An informal occasion."

"You are not dressed informally." He caught her by the elbow as she tripped. "That gown was not designed for cross-country scrambles. Ah! Here we are"—he came to an abrupt halt, "an unimpeded view of the start and finish lines. Let me fill your goblet."

"Please." Moreta held it up.

"Why didn't I know that the Fort Weyrwoman liked racing enough to desert the forecourt and its pleasures?"

"I've been at all Ruatha's Gathers the past ten Turns—"

"Up *there*, though." He gestured back to the forecourt.

"Of course, as befits my rank. L'mal didn't like me to roam the picket lines."

"Which was where I generally was." Alessan grinned.

"Learning how to breed winners?"

"Of course not." Alessan feigned shocked innocence. "I was supposed to breed stamina, not speed. *My* Gather duties were to assist our race-course manager, Norman."

Moreta lifted her goblet again. "To the man who perservered and won the race!"

Alessan was quick-witted and grinned at her subtlety. Their eyes met in a candid gaze. Moreta felt a growing affinity for the new Lord Holder and not only because of their mutual interest in race runners. His mind was unpredictable, certainly not in the pattern of the usual Lord Holder, if she compared him to Tolocamp, Ratoshigan, or Diatis. He was good company, with a fine sense of humor; if he danced as well as he did everything else, she might just monopolize him this evening.

Two more dragons arrived midair as she glanced up, away from Alessan's light-green, compelling gaze. Then her eyes dropped slightly to admire Orlith, ensconced right above the main hold door, and she thought how well Orlith's golden hide complimented the window hangings on the top tier. Embarrassed, she looked away, aware that Alessan had been watching her.

"A habit, really," she said with a self-conscious shrug.

"Surely after twenty Turns as partners—"

"Are you already accustomed to being Lord of Ruatha Hold?"

"Not yet. I've only been—" Alessan broke off, his eyes on her face, noting her fond smile. "Even after twenty Turns?"

"Ah, look. The flag for the next race!" She diverted his attention. One could never explain the bond to someone who wasn't a dragonrider. Impression was a private miracle, a very private miracle.

CHAPTER II

Ruatha Hold, Present Pass, 3.10.43

THE SECOND RACE was over a greater length, the winning poles having been moved down the field and farther apart to accommodate the larger number of middle-distance runners.

"Have you an entry in this race, too?" she asked Alessan as the runners charged away from the start.

"No. I got either spindly sprinters or massive carters from my crosses. But one of my holders has a strong contestant—blue with red hatching are the colors. Not that you can distinguish them."

The field had already begun to stretch out when suddenly an animal in the middle of the pack fell, tripping two others. Moreta could never watch a bad tangle without apprehension. She was holding her breath as she silently urged each animal to its feet. Two rose, one groggily shaking its head, the second running on down the field, riderless. The third made no effort to rise.

Moreta picked up her skirts and began to run toward the fallen runner.

"It shouldn't've fallen." *Orlith!*

"Close-packed field. Tripped." Alessan kept pace with her, caught up in her concern.

"Not that close, and it wasn't a trip fall." She saved her breath for running even when she had seen that the two riders were examining the fallen beast and that handlers were running up from the starting line. *Orlith, what's wrong? Why doesn't it get up?*

As she got closer, Moreta could see the sprawled beast's sides heaving. Its nose touched the ground yet it made no effort to rise. That was unusual enough. Runners preferred to stand.

Did it break a leg, Orlith?

"It can't get its breath," one rider was saying to the other. "It's got a bloody nose."

"Probably ruptured a vein falling. Just get it to its feet. Here, I'll help." The second rider begun to tug at the bridle.

Orlith, wake up! I need you.

"It should've got to its feet. Lord Alessan! Lady Moreta!" The first rider turned anxiously to them, and Moreta recognized the man as Helly, a capable herdsman and racer.

It cannot breathe, Orlith responded sleepily. She sounded a bit grumpy at being roused. *Its lungs are full of liquid.*

Moreta knelt at the animal's head, noticing the distressed flare of the nostrils, the bloody discharge. She felt for the pulse in its throat, weak and far too erratic for an animal that had only run a few dragonlengths before falling.

Around her men were shouting that the runner should be assisted to its feet. Several positioned themselves to heave. Moreta waved them off imperiously.

"It can't breathe. No air is getting into its lungs."

"Cut into its windpipe. Who's got a sharp blade?"

"It's too late," Moreta said as she peeled back the upper lip, exposing the whitened gums.

The onlookers knew, as she did, that the animal was dying. From the finishing line the sound of cheering drifted back to those circling the faller. It gave one final sigh, almost apologetic, and the head rolled to the side.

"Ain't seen nothing like this before," the second rider said. "And I been riding since I could tighten a girth."

"You were riding it, Helly?" Alessan asked.

"Yes, doing a favor for Vander. His jock was sick. I've never ridden it before. Seemed quiet." Helly stopped, considered. "Too quiet, now I think about it. Rode in the first race, and this one was all ready for me... Broke well at the start as if it wanted to work!" Helly's tone was a mixture of despair, anger, and surprise.

"Could've been the heart," one of the onlookers suggested in a tone of broad experience. "That takes 'em sudden. No way of telling. Runner in good spirit one moment, dead the next. Takes people that way, too."

Not, Moreta thought, with a bloody nasal discharge.

"Here now," a loud voice cried. "What's the matter here? Why isn't this animal... Oh, Lord Alessan. Didn't know you were here!" The race manager had pushed his way into the circle. "It's dead? Excuse me, Lord Alessan, but we do have to clear the track for the next race."

Alessan took the shaken Helly by the arm. Moreta stepped to the man's other side, leading him through the pathway courteously made by the crowd.

"I don't understand it. No, I don't." Helly was obviously in shock. Moreta realized that she still had the wine goblet and held it up to Alessan, who quickly unslung the wineskin and poured a full cup. Moreta gave it to Helly. The racer drank the contents in one gulp.

"Helly, what happened? Did it plait its legs or something?"

The stocky man, dressed in Ruathan colors, staggered as he realized who was assisting Helly. While trying to hold a pad of wet toweling to his forehead, he also attempted to bow to Alessan and Moreta. And staggered again.

"Helly, what happened? Oh, shards!" The last was said in a low voice as a cart bearing the dead animal off the track rumbled into view.

"Vander, are you all right?" Helly demanded. He handed Moreta her goblet and went to the stunned holder. Helly supported Vander in the wake of the cart.

Moreta, Alessan by her side, watched the activity of Gather races swirl and close behind the sad procession. Men, laden with tack or blankets or buckets of water, briskly moved toward the picket lines. The sound of urgent conversations and shouts was occasionally punctuated by the squeal of excited runners.

"I *cannot* remember a respiratory illness that would result in such a remarkably swift death," Moreta said.

"I'd've said the animal was only stunned by the fall and would have gotten it to its feet," Alessan remarked. "How did you know what ailed it so fast?"

"My family has always raised runners," she explained quickly, for it was not common knowledge outside the Weyrs that she and Orlith worked together in healing.

"Your early training must have been remarkable. I thought I'd learned a thing or two about runners."

"If you bred that sprinter while looking for endurance stock, you have."

Just then two runners, long-distance racers by the look of them, were led past, and Moreta kept her eyes on them until they mixed into the crowd.

"Nothing wrong with them, is there?"

"Oh, no. They look racing fit. Not so much as a nervous sweat on them."

"Has it been crossing your mind that Vander's runner dropped dead of an illness?"

"It crossed my mind," Moreta agreed, "but it's highly unlikely. Helly said the runner *wanted* to race. A sick one wouldn't. Could have been the heart."

"Well, I'm not looking for trouble. Not today, at my first Gather." Alessan frowned and turned slowly on his right heel, casting his eyes down the rows of picketed runners. "It has to be a fluke. I know Vander. His hold's a good day's ride south. He's been saving that particular runner for this race." Alessan sighed. "We can have a look at the rest of his string. They'd be picketed over here if I recall the assignments." Alessan took Moreta's arm, guiding her to the right.

If the beast had been fit, Moreta thought, how could its lungs have filled so quickly? She considered asking Orlith but she sensed that the queen had returned to sleep. Runners did not have the same priority with the dragon as they did with the rider.

Alessan pulled Moreta to him suddenly as a rangy beast plunged past them, its eyes wild as it anticipated its race, the rider barely able to stay in the pad. Two handlers jogged along, at a distance respectful of the kicking range of an excited runner. Moreta watched its progress to the starting line.

"Well?" Alessan's tenor voice asked in her ear.

She was abruptly aware that she was still in his loose protective embrace.

"No, that one seemed far from ill." She moved away from him.

"And here's Vander's picket." Alessan counted them. "As I recall he'd entered seven. Did you say you were from Keroon? This is a runner he bought from Keroon last Turn."

Moreta laughed as she let the runner sniff her hand. She stroked its head until it accepted her touch then she felt its warm ear for the breed tattoo.

"No, it didn't come from my family's hold."

Alessan grinned at her whimsy as he examined the other animals. "They're in good shape. Vander got here two days ago to rest them well before the races. I'll have a word with him later. Shall we get back to the races—Shells!" The shouts and movements of the crowd indicated that the next race had started. Alessan looked abashed. "Now you've missed *another* race."

"I watch the racing because, in my exalted position as Weyrwoman, that is much more dignified than scrambling around the pickets. Which is what I would rather do. Now that we're here, could I see your winner? I've a suspicion that only a sense of duty to your guest has kept you from checking it."

The relief and delight in Alessan's eyes confirmed her guess. He had just indicated the proper direction when a short man with the heavy chest, well-developed arms, and thin shanks of a rider trotted toward them, his face wearing the broadest of smiles.

"Lord Alessan? Have you been looking for Squealer?"

"I have indeed, Dag. Well done! Well done!" Alessan shook Dag by the hand and thumped him across the shoulders. "A fine race. Perfect!"

Dag gave Moreta a stiffly correct bow.

"You are to be congratulated on training a winner," Moreta said. Then she couldn't resist adding, "It's a few people could contrive against Lord Leef."

Dag's expression was one of shock, betrayal, and consternation. "Lady Moreta, I wouldn't...I didn't."

Alessan laughed and gave Dag a reassuring clout on the shoulder. "Lady Moreta's runnerhold bred. She approves."

"Where is this Squealer of yours, Dag? I very much want a closer look at such a success."

"This way, Lady. And now he's not all that much to look at close on, mind you," Dag began in the deprecating way of all devoted handlers. "Over to the right, if you would. I walked him cool, Lord Alessan, and washed him down with tepid water. Race didn't take a thing out of him. He could go again..." Dag caught himself short with a startled glance at the Lord Holder and the Weyrwoman.

"It's a full male then?" Moreta asked, rescuing Dag from indiscretion.

"That he is. On account of him looking so weedy, I always managed to convince the herdmaster that he was too young yet to be gelded, or too sickly, and shouldn't we wait awhile. Then I'd sneak him off to another field."

"Turn after Turn?" Moreta was impressed by such devotion.

"Squealer doesn't have any distinguishing marks to set him in a man's mind," Alessan said. "There he is."

Suddenly Moreta faced a scrawny, thin-legged, big-kneed, mid-brown runner, standing all by itself at the end of a half-empty picket line. In a pause during which she wracked her brain to find something creditable to say about the beast, all she could see was the length of empty pickets.

"He has a kind eye," she said, blurting it out. "Well placed in the head."

As if Squealer knew he was under discussion, he turned his head and regarded her.

"Intelligence, too. Heart. Calm."

Squealer ducked his head, seemingly agreeing with her points so that all three laughed.

"There really isn't much good you can say about Squealer," Alessan said, absolving her from further comment. He swatted the runner affectionately on the neck.

"Squealer won his first race, Lord Alessan. That's all that needs to be said of him. May he win many more. But not," Moreta added slyly, "all on the same day."

Dag groaned and turned away with embarrassed mortification.

"Lord Alessan, had you expected many more entries?" Moreta asked, gesturing toward the unused pickets.

"Dag, you were assisting Norman..."

"Well, we did expect a fair turnout, what with fine weather over the past sevendays and plenty of holds to shelter strings on the road. Come to think on it, I'd expected Lord Ratoshigan to sail his sprinter up— that one he's been winning with all season. That herdsman of his was boasting at their Gather—"

"I'm not sorry that we didn't get to pit Squealer against the best in the west, but perhaps Ratoshigan's absence ensured his win."

"It did no such thing," Dag protested vehemently and then realized that he was being teased. "He's cooled off now. I'll just take him back to the beasthold above."

"Starting line or finishing?" Alessan asked Moreta.

"Let's see if we can get in a finish."

They moved at a leisurely pace for people wishing to see an imminent finish, but their path took them between pickets and that pleased Moreta as well.

"I wonder why Ratoshigan didn't come."

"His absence is a boon." Moreta did not try to mask the acid edge to her voice.

"Perhaps, but I'd've liked to pit Squealer against that sprinter of his."

"For the joy of beating Ratoshigan? Well, I'd approve of that."

"Southern Boll is beholden to Fort Weyr, isn't it?"

"That doesn't mean I have to like him."

"Yet you'd drink that sour wine Lord Diatis makes."

Moreta had opened her mouth to reply when she was suddenly drenched with water. A colorful and original string of invective in Alessan's angry voice told her that he had not escaped the slops.

Who has distressed you? Orlith's response was immediate and, as Moreta stood there, eyes closed against the water draining from her hair, she needed the moral support of her queen.

"I'm only wet!" Moreta stolidly informed her queen.

The sun is warm. You will dry fast.

"Only wet?" Alessan roared. "You're soaked."

The erring handler, belatedly discovering that he had launched a full bucket of dirty water at the Weyrwoman and the Lord Holder—who didn't ought to be strolling along picket lines when everyone else was off watching the races—proffered Moreta a towel, but the rag had been used for many purposes and merely compounded the problem. Alessan was shouting for clean water and fresh clothes and the location of a vacant tent.

The commotion was sufficient to attract everyone not engrossed in the race just starting. Assistance was offered, and people began running here and there on Alessan's orders while Moreta stood, her beautiful new brown-and-gold gown plastered to her body. She tried to reassure the mortified handler that she took no offense, all the while knowing her long-awaited afternoon of racing was doomed. She might just as well summon Orlith and go back to the Weyr. She might get her death of cold going *between* in the soggy ruins of her Gather dress, but what choice had she now?

"I know this is not what you're accustomed to, Moreta," Alessan was saying, pulling at her sleeve to get her attention. "But it's clean and it's dry and will do to watch the rest of the races. I can't be sure if my mother's ladies or my sister can get your gown and cloak dry by evening, but I am certain that suitable gowns will be displayed in the Hold for your consideration when the races are over."

Alessan was holding out a clean brown shift in one hand, sandals and a pretty belt of colored cords in the other. He was gesturing toward the race manager's striped tent when the handler rushed up with clean, steaming water in his bucket and a bundle of clean towels draped over his shoulder.

"Come, Moreta, do let us set things to rights?" The softly spoken appeal and the very real distress evident in Alessan's eyes and manner would have swayed a character far more obdurate than Moreta's.

"And yourself, Alessan?" she asked courteously as she bundled her soaking skirts for the short walk to the tent. The right side of Alessan's Gather finery was soaked.

"You, I fear, took the brunt. I'll dry out in the sun. While we watch the races?" His sly question was part entreaty.

"I'll be quick."

She took the fresh clothing and let the handler place the bucket and clothes in the tent then she entered, dropping the flap.

Her undershift was wet as well, so she was pleased that the brown shift was woven of a sturdy fabric. Her hair was gritty from the slop water, which had been used to sponge down a runner's dusty legs. She buried her head quickly in the clean water, washed her face and arms thoroughly, making lavish use of the supply of cloths. She was dressed and outside the tent just as the cheers announced the finish of the fourth race.

"Now I believe that you were once a holder lass," Alessan said with a soft chuckle. He handed her a full goblet of wine. "The Benden did not get wet."

"Well, that's luck!"

The handler bobbed an approach, apologizing and bowing and generally so abasing himself that Moreta cut him short by remarking that worse things had come flying out of a picket line, and she was grateful it was no more than dirty water. Alessan escorted her toward the finish line.

"Last one was a sprint, only five entries," he mentioned as they walked.

"And Squealer wasn't entered?" She laughed as Alessan gave her a pained look, imitating Dag.

The next races were exciting enough to make up for those she had missed and to blot out the tragedy of the second. She and Alessan, looking far less the Lord of the Hold with his fine clothes puckered and soiled, found themselves vantages near the finish and sipped wine. They made private bets about winners when Moreta refused to allow Alessan to mark her with the wagermen. She enjoyed, too, being right in the midst of the racing crowd as she had so often been as a young girl in Keroon, in the company of her childhood friend Talpan. She hadn't thought of him in Turns.

An enterprising baker passed among the finish-line crowds with a tray of hot spiced rolls. Moreta hadn't realized how hungry she was until the aroma wafted over to her.

"I'm host today," Alessan said, noticing her reaction. He took her arm and they pushed their way through to the baker.

The flaky pastry was stuffed with a savory mix, and Moreta quickly devoured three rolls.

"Don't they feed you in the Weyr on a Gather day?" Alessan asked.

"Oh, the stew pot's always simmering in the Cavern," she replied, licking her fingers appreciatively. "But stew wouldn't taste half as good as these spiced rolls do right now."

Alessan was eyeing her, a curious expression on his face.

"You're not at all what I expected in Weyrwoman Moreta," he said in a candid tone that captured her complete attention. Wearily she wondered what Sh'gall had said of her. Alessan went on, "I got to know Leri rather well. She usually stays on for a word with the ground crews . . ."

"I would if I could," Moreta said, countering his tacit criticism, "but I have to return to the Weyr immediately after Fall."

"Have to?" Alessan's right eye quirked high.

"Did you never wonder who takes care of dragon injuries?" She spoke more sharply than she intended because she had been able to forget that they would rise to Fall in two more days, and more dragons might be injured.

"I'd thought that the Weyr must have the best of the healers, of course." Alessan's reply was so formal that Moreta regretted the quick retort. She laid her hand on his arm, hoping to restore the ease of their relationship.

"I never realized it might be you." He smiled and covered her hand with his. "What about another spiced roll before someone else eats them all?"

"Lord Alessan . . ." Dag came rolling up to them. "Runel's going on about Squealer being a sport. I tol'im the breeding, but he won't take it from me."

Alessan's expression became pained, and he closed his eyes briefly.
"I was hoping to avoid Runel this Gather."

"You done pretty well with everyone else, Lord, but I can't do this for you."

Alessan inhaled the breath of one resigned.

"Who's Runel?" Moreta asked.

The two men regarded her with astonishment.

"You mean, you've escaped Runel?" Amusement chased resignation from Alessan's expression. "Well, you must meet him at least once."

Dag made a sound, half protest, half fear.

"And the race *is* due to start," Alessan reminded Dag. "Weyrwoman, that's the only thing, short of Fall, that will halt Runel's recitations."

By now, Moreta was intrigued.

"He's over there, with those cronies of his." Dag pointed.

Moreta noted first that the three men stood isolated by a clear space from any immediate neighbors. Two were holders by their badges, one from Fort and the other wearing Ruathan colors; the third was a wizened herdsman whose clothes reeked of his craft despite the fact that they looked well brushed. The tallest of the men, the Ruathan holder, drew himself up proudly as he noticed Alessan's approach. He spared Moreta only a passing glance.

"About that sprinter of mine, Runel," Alessan began briskly, addressing himself to the herdsman. "I bred the beast myself, four Turns ago, out of the sprint mare Dextra, Lord Leef's by Vander's brown stallion, Evest."

Runel's expression altered dramatically. He threw back his head and unfocused his eyes, wide-opened. "Alessan's sprinter, Squealer, won the first sprint race at the Ruathan Gather, third month, forty-third Turn of the sixth Pass, bred by Alessan out of Dextra, five times winner at sprint races in the west, Leef by Vander's Evest which was nine times winner over sprint distances. Dextra's sire, twice winner, by Dimnal out of Tran, nineteen times winner. Dimnal by Fairex out of Crick, Fairex . . ."

"There he goes," Dag said to Moreta in an undertone, shaking his head ruefully.

"He just keeps on?"

"And on and on. He'll recite the lineage of Squealer back to the Crossing," Alessan murmured, standing with hands clasped in front of him and seeming to give Runel the courtesy of his attention.

"He's only good with western racing, though," Dag added critically.

"He's eidetic? I've *heard* about them, but I've never heard one personally."

"Just give him a name of a racer and he's away. Trouble is he has to start at the beginning."

"Isn't he starting at the end with Squealer's win today?"

Runel's voice had settled into the sing-song of winners, sires, and dams.

"The latest race *is* his beginning, Lady Moreta."

"Does he go to all the Gathers?"

"Those he can get to." Dag shot Alessan a look.

I would be surprised if the Lord Holder knows half the races Runel attends, Moreta thought to herself.

"He's not much good otherwise, that's certain," Alessan said, unconcerned. "My father saw that the oldest sons were well apprenticed. Runel's memory serves a purpose—"

"Bore you to death, it would," Dag muttered unappreciatively, glancing over his shoulder at the race flats. "It's starting!" Reprieve was the overwhelming emotion. "Race!" he said in a loud voice directly at Runel.

Runel's companions began to tug at his arms. "Race, Runel! Race is starting!"

Runel came out of his recitation trance and looked about in surprise.

"Race is starting, Runel," the Fort holder said reassuringly as he began to guide the eidetic toward the finish line.

Alessan drew Moreta to one side, and Dag scurried behind the Lord Holder while the trio marched off. Moreta could not help but see that a path cleared before Runel more quickly than if Alessan and she had wished passage.

"You should hear him on the 'begats.'"

"As you have?"

"Indeed and I have, at every birthfeast." Alessan spoke with feeling and rolled his eyes upward.

"I'd've thought the man would be more valuable in the Harper Hall than in a hold."

"My father had the good sense to prevent that."

"Why? With that memory..."

"Because his granduncle was a harper here and remembered more than was prudent on too many occasions." Alessan grinned with malice. "I think my grandsire made sure to turn the trait to less...ah, shall we say...remunerative topics? I believe there have always been blood relations in the Harper Hall, undoubtedly in the Records Rooms, scanning hides and committing them to memory before the ink fades completely."

They found a place at the line and observed the hotly contested finish of the sixth race. As they passed the wait for the next race, they overheard bits and snatches of conversations. References to the new Lord Holder and the quality of the Gather were in the main complimentary, though Moreta enjoyed Alessan's discomfiture at some of the candid remarks. The weather dominated most discussions.

"Too warm, too soon. We'll melt this summer."

"Can't say as I mind mild days instead of rain and blizzard, but it ain't natural. Upsets the rhythm of the Turn."

"M'herds won't settle with insects hanging on in the warm, pestering 'em. Terrible cases of sores. Beasts don't want to eat. Don't want to move. Muddle and moan together, they do."

"A bit of frost would do us the world of good. Freeze down those tunnel snakes. Breeding fierce they are this year with no cold to lay 'em."

"Can't decide to shear now for a short crop and give 'em relief from the heat or let 'em lose condition panting under long hair."

"We needs us some snow. We needs it to kill what grubs beneath the soil, what sucks life from our good seed, and what makes a field sour. We needs frost and snow in good measure."

"You ought to be relieved, Alessan, that all they complain about *is* the weather. After all, no holder expects the Lord Holder to be able to change the weather. The Weyrs do that, you know." She pulled her mouth down in a grimace that made him grin.

The final race had a surprise ending for two runners crossed the finish line, right in front of Moreta and Alessan, without so much as a nose between them. The argument over which animal won grew so heated that Alessan came forward to mediate, dragging Moreta with him. To settle what could have been a nasty situation, Alessan loudly proclaimed that he doubled the purse so that neither contender would be disappointed for the fine excitement they had provided the Gather.

That was just the right decision to end the race meeting on a high note. Owners, riders, handlers, and spectators dispersed from the flats in the best of all spirits.

"You're a sensibly generous man, Alessan."

"I thank you, Lady Moreta. Ah, just in time," he said, and Moreta turned as a handler lead up a big-boned, long-backed runnerbeast saddled with a thick pad in Ruathan colors. "My lady, your mount."

"*This* is what your father expected you to breed?"

"This is what I *did* breed for my father," Alessan replied with a broad grin. "Squealer's type was a bonus." He gave her a leg up and waited while she hooked her leg on the broad pommel before he swung up behind her.

"I think I prefer your Squealer," she said as the beast lurched forward at Alessan's urging.

"There speaks the racing enthusiast, not the prudent holder." He turned his head left as they moved off across the stubble field, and Moreta knew that Alessan had only deferred the puzzle of the empty picket lines for the duration of the races.

"It's not like Ratoshigan to miss a chance for Ruathan marks. They could sail right up the Ruathan River," Alessan said, giving her a tight smile for his inattention. "Soover—you know him from Southern Boll—ought to have come short of Fall, fire, or fog. I hadn't realized that the weather—for all your unwillingness to change it—was of such widespread concern."

"There's no lack of people at this Gather," Moreta said. The stalls were still doing a good business despite the numbers attracted by the racing.

People had already begun to take places at the tables about the dancing square. The aromas of roasting meats wafted enticingly on the wind, the pungency of spiced wherry dominating.

Alessan had ridden straight up across the field and now turned their mount up the roadway. Moreta glanced up to the fire-heights, covered in sun-baking dragons. There seemed to be more, and she noticed Orlith flanked by another queen. Tamianth of the High Reaches, judging by her size and color.

"Some creatures like the sun and the warm," Alessan said. "Does all the sunning help them endure the cold of *between*?"

Moreta shivered involuntarily, and Alessan's arms tightened about her. She rather enjoyed the unexpected intimacy.

"When we fly Thread, I'm grateful to the cold of *between*," she replied obliquely, her thoughts on the Fall in two days.

Then Alessan reined the beast up the ramp to the forecourt, its heavy feet clumping hollowly and alerting the guests there. Moreta waved cheerfully at Falga, the High Reaches Weyrwoman.

"Wasn't your new gown ready, Moreta?" Falga asked as she walked to meet them while Alessan halted their mount.

"A new gown?" Alessan's startled question fell on Moreta's ears only.

"You'll see it next Gather, Falga," Moreta replied blithely. "This is my race-watching dress."

"Oh, you and your races!" Falga smiled tolerantly and turned back to the holders with whom she'd been talking.

Suddenly Tolocamp appeared, his genial smile not completely masking his disapproval of Moreta's dusty appearance.

"I'll just slide off, thank you, Lord Tolocamp," she said, politely ignoring his offer of assistance.

"If you'll follow me, Lady Moreta," Lady Oma said, breaking through the press of people and taking charge.

Relieved to be able to retire gracefully from Tolocamp's critical gaze, Moreta followed Alessan's mother. In the instant her eyes met Lady Oma's, Moreta knew the woman disapproved of her as much as Tolocamp did but more for upsetting her own plans for her son's afternoon entertainment than for Moreta's hoyden behavior. As they proceeded through the Hall, splendidly decorated for the Gather, and up the stairs into the Hold's private corridors, Moreta felt the weight of Lady Oma's rebuke in her silence. In Lady Oma's own apartments, however, a variety of gowns, skirts, and tunics had been hastily assembled, and from the bathroom drifted the moist scent of perfumed water and the giggles of the girls who were preparing it.

"Your gown has been cleaned, Lady Moreta," Lady Oma said, closing the door behind Moreta. "But I doubt it will be dry before the dancing." She cast a measuring glance at Moreta, ignoring the dusty brown shift. "You're thinner than I'd thought. Perhaps the rust . . ." She indicated the garment, then canceled that suggestion with an impatient gesture of her hand. It was reminiscent of Alessan. "It is in no way comparable to your own gown. This green one is more suited to your rank."

Moreta went to the rust dress, fingering the texture of the plain but soft fabric. She held it up to her waist and shoulders. The fit would be good through the body, though the skirt was short above her ankles. She glanced at the fine material of the green dress. She'd sweat in it dancing the way she intended to dance for having lost part of her racing.

"The rust will do very well, and I'm grateful for the loan of it." She smiled around at the women in the room, trying to locate the donor but no one met her glance. "This will be fine. I won't be long," she added, smiling again as she entered the bathing room and pulled the curtain across. She hoped they would all take the hint and leave.

She lolled longer in the warm scented water than she intended, easing muscles made tense by the afternoon's excitements. Only when she finally emerged and was rubbing her hair dry did she hear a noise in the outer chamber and realize that someone was waiting for her.

"Lady Oma?" she called out, dreading the answer.

"No, it's only Oklina," an apologetic young voice replied. "Did you find the shift?"

"I'm in it."

"Do you need help with your hair?"

"It's short enough to dry quickly."

"Oh!"

Moreta smiled to herself for the chagrin in the young voice. "I'm distressingly self-sufficient, Lady Oklina," Moreta said, pulling the rust dress over her head, "except that I cannot do up the back of the gown." She pulled the curtain aside as Oklina rushed forward, nearly colliding with Moreta and almost collapsing with embarrassment at her awkwardness.

Oklina bore a marked resemblance to her brother but none to Lady Oma, if indeed the woman was the girl's mother. The dark complexion, which suited Alessan, did nothing for the girl yet she had a sensitivity in her face and a grace of movement that had its own appeal. And,

Moreta noted enviously, thick long black plaits gleamed in the well-lit room.

"I'm awfully sorry it's only me, Lady Moreta, but it's time to serve the roasts and with so many guests . . ." Oklina deftly settled the bodice to Moreta's hips and began lacing the back.

"If I had been watching where I walked—"

"Oh, Marl wanted to sink into the ground with the slops, Lady Moreta. He rushed here to us with your gown and hovered in the washroom, fretting about the stains. You must have been furious to have a new gown ruined in the first wearing, before you had a chance to show it off or dance in it." Oklina's voice reflected her awe, which was quite understandable since she was obviously wearing a dress handed down from older sisters.

"I shall dance much more easily in this." Moreta twitched experimentally at the rust skirts.

"Alessan sent word that you *had* to be enticed with a gown pretty enough to make you stay for the dancing."

"Oh?"

"Oh!" Oklina's eyes widened at her indiscretion, and she blinked back sudden tears, her expression very solemn. "He hasn't been to a Gather or danced or sung or been himself since Suriana died. Not even when he became Lord Holder. Tell me, was he *pleased* when Squealer won?"

"Ecstatic!" Moreta smiled gently at the girl's obvious adoration of her brother. "Creditable win, too. Five lengths."

"And he actually smiled? And *enjoyed* himself?" At Moreta's reassurance, the girl clasped her hands under her chin, her dark eyes shining. "I did see the start"—her expressive face clouded briefly— "and *heard* the yells. I'll bet the loudest was from Alessan. Did you *see* Squealer afterward? And you met Dag. Dag is never far from that runner. He's been so devoted. He knows so much about racing because he rode for Lord Leef before he got so old. He can spot winners every time. He had faith in Alessan's breeding when everyone else thought he ought to give it up before Lord Leef—" Oklina broke off with a gasp. "I talk too much."

"I've been listening." Moreta was not unaccustomed to outpourings of repressed emotions. "I think Squealer is going to repay all the time and effort Alessan—and Dag—have put into him."

"Oh, do you really think so?" The prospect brought a fresh spasm of delight to Oklina. "Listen, the harpers have begun." At the sound of music, the girl wheeled to the window, its metal shutters open to the darkening sky.

"Well, then, let's go dance. It's time to enjoy ourselves."

For a moment, Oklina looked apprehensive, as if she wouldn't be allowed to enjoy herself. Younger members of Hold families were often saddled with the onerous duties of a Gather, but Moreta would make it a point to see that Oklina did dance. The girl smiled graciously and gestured for Moreta to precede her from the room.

The corridors and the Hall were empty, but drudges were opening the glowbaskets arranged on the forecourt as Moreta and Oklina hastened by. Moreta paused on the ramp, to look up to the fire-heights. Orlith slept, eyes closed, in the setting sun, likely to remain somnolent until the evening breeze chilled the air. Other dragons, their rainbow-colored eyes gleaming, watched the scene below.

"Oh!" Oklina's tone was a yip of delighted fear. "They are such awesome creatures." She paused, then blurted out, "Were you terribly scared?"

"When I Impressed? Very much so. The Search reached my father's hold the very day of Impression. I was scooped up and taken to Ista in a scurry, told to change, and then shoved onto the Hatching Ground before I knew exactly what was taking place. Orlith"—and Moreta could never suppress an exultant smile at the memory—"forgave me for being late!"

"*Ohhhh!*" Oklina expelled a long sigh of bliss.

Moreta smiled, recognizing the girl's yearning to be found on Search and to impress a queen dragon. Once when faced with such envious yearnings, Moreta had felt unaccountable guilt over her good fortune at Impressing Orlith, her friend, her sure consolation, her life. That reaction had gradually been replaced by the knowledge of the great gap between wish, fulfillment, and acceptance. So Moreta could smile kindly at Oklina while her mind reached out to her sleeping dragon.

"If my brother hadn't been my father's successor, he might have been a dragonrider," Oklina confided to Moreta in a sudden whisper.

"Really?" Moreta was startled. She hadn't heard that Ruatha Hold had been approached for one of its sons, not since she joined the Weyr ten Turns before.

"Dag told me." And Oklina nodded her head vigorously to support her statement. "It was twelve Turns ago. Dag said Lord Leef was in a fury because Alessan was to be the heir, and though Lord Leef told the dragonriders they could have any other member of his Hold, Dag said that no one else was acceptable to the dragons—how do dragons know?"

"*Search* dragons know," Moreta said in a mysterious voice, a rote reply after so many repetitions. "Each Weyr has dragons who sense the potential in youngsters." Moreta deepened the mystery in her voice. "There are folk, weyrborn, who've known dragons and riders all their lives who don't Impress, and complete strangers—like myself—who do. The dragons always know."

"The dragons always know..." Oklina's whisper was half prayer, half imprecation. She stole a quick look up the fire-heights as if she feared the somnolent dragons might take offense if they heard.

"Come, Oklina," Moreta said briskly. "I'm dying to dance."

CHAPTER III

Ruatha Hold, Present Pass, 3.11.43

To Moreta, of all the Gathers she'd ever attended, the Ruathan
Gather at that moment of dusk evoked best what Gathers should be—
folk from weyr, hold, and craft assembled to eat, drink, dance, and
enjoy one another's company. The glowbaskets on their standards cast
patches of golden light on the crowded tables, on the dancers, on the
clusters of people standing about talking, and on the circles of men
near the wine barrels. The darting figures of children wove in and out
of the light patches, and occasionally their laughter and shouts cut across
the music and the stamping of the dancers. The smell of roasted meats
and warm evening air, of dust and pungent glows, and wine reinforced
all prospect of entertainment.

Nine harpers graced the platform and five more sat waiting their
turns. Moreta couldn't pick out Tirone, but the Masterharper might be
circulating among the tables. Alessan might not like the Masterharper,
but Tirone would discharge his obligation to the new Lord Holder's
first Gather.

Moreta and Oklina had reached the edge of the onlookers, who parted
while respectfully murmuring greetings as the two moved closer to the
dance square. Having guided Moreta to the head table, opposite the
harpers' platform, Oklina would have left, but Moreta took the girl by
the hand. When Alessan rose to his feet, gesturing for Moreta to sit
beside him, she pulled Oklina down, too, ignoring the girl's protest.

"There's room enough, isn't there?" Moreta asked, giving Alessan a significant glare. "She was so good about waiting for me."

"Room enough, of course," Alessan replied graciously, motioning to the table's other occupants to adjust. As Moreta seated herself, Alessan peered at her, a frown beginning to pucker his brows. "Is that the best that could be supplied you?" He pinched at the sleeve with disapproval.

"This suits me very well. Much better for dancing than mine. Though I had many to choose from," she added hastily as the reason for his frown became clear to her. "I think I should make it a practice to bring two dresses to a Gather: one to see races in"—she grinned mischievously up at him—"and one to be seen in." She gave her chin an arrogant tilt and pretended hauteur.

Placated, Alessan smiled back at her and signaled for wine to be poured in her cup. "I've more of the Benden white for *you*." He raised his cup in a quick toast.

She had had not more than a sip when the harpers struck up a loud and lively dance tune.

"Will you honor me with a dance, Weyrwoman?" Alessan asked, jumping to his feet and extending his hand.

"Why else am I here?" She turned to Oklina with a smile. "Guard my place and my cup." Then she took Alessan's hand and allowed herself to be spun onto the square, finding the beat of the measure and stepping out into the pattern with a strong man's body against hers and firm hands guiding her.

She loved to dance and, though the Weyr had musicians and songs in the evening from time to time, dancing was generally reserved for Hatching festivities. Occasionally the blue and green riders indulged in wild acrobatics, usually when they were well into the wine after a bad Fall or the death of a dragon and rider, but Moreta dreaded those dances. Leri and L'mal had felt that such excesses purged the riders, but Moreta preferred to absent herself, taking flight on Orlith to be far from the maddening drum beat and the posturing dance.

But the Gather's music soon exorcised those memories and she was breathless by the time Alessan whirled her back to the table, both of them heartily applauding the harpers' music, the sweet, uncomplicated, merry, familiar tunes.

"I must dance now with Falga," Alessan said, seeing Moreta settled, "but save me another dance?"

"Did you enjoy dancing with Alessan?" Oklina asked in a shy wistful voice as she set the goblet of Benden wine before Moreta.

"Indeed I did. He's light on his feet and knows the dance well."

"Alessan taught me to dance. When there's music in the Hall, he always asks me at least once but I don't expect he'll be able to tonight with so many other girls."

"Then I shall find you another partner." Moreta turned to search out an idle dragonrider.

"Oh, I mustn't." Oklina looked scared and her eyes flitted nervously to the crowded square where a new dance was forming. "I'm expected to help with the guests."

"You are, by making sure of my comfort and guarding my Benden wine." Moreta smiled warmly at the child. "But you *must* dance tonight!"

"Moreta!" A firm hand clasped her on the shoulder, and she looked up at B'lerion, bronze Nabeth's rider from the High Reaches Weyr. "There's good music begging your step. And me!"

The bronze rider did not wait for her consent, but took her hand and pulled her into his arms, laughing down at her. "I knew you couldn't resist me." And he winked over Moreta's shoulder at the astonished Oklina as he spun the Weyrwoman off to the square.

Moreta did not miss the wistful, yearning expression on Oklina's face, but then B'lerion had that effect on many women. He was handsome and tall with a fine strong body, sparkling dark eyes, a mobile expression, a ready laugh. He always had a quick remark and a fund of light gossip. Moreta and he had enjoyed a brief association when she'd first come to Fort Weyr and she was certain that he was the father of her third child. She regretted that she had had to foster, but she had always been the healer and that duty had priority. Though B'lerion was not the same caliber wingleader as Sh'gall, Moreta had hoped that Nabeth would have flown her queen during that crucial mating flight. But then, the strongest, cleverest dragon flew the queen: That was the only way to improve the breed. Twice Sh'gall's Kadith had been strongest and fastest. Or so Moreta kept telling herself.

B'lerion was in a good mood, not yet deep in his wine for his words weren't slurred and his step was firm. He'd heard of her dousing, teased her about monopolizing the young Lord Holder, told her that her love of racing would be her undoing, and asked why Sh'gall was not there to protect his interests.

"I never understood why you let Kadith fly your queen when she could have done much better with Nabeth and I'd be Fort Weyrleader. I'm much more fun to be with than Sh'gall. Or so you used to tell me."

By the intense gleam in his eyes and the sharp hold he took of her waist for the last figure of the dance, B'lerion was half in earnest, Moreta realized. Moreta reminded herself that B'lerion was always in earnest for the duration of any given encounter. A charming opportunist who didn't limit his activities to any one Weyr or Hold.

"What? You be Fort Weyrleader? You don't like that much responsibility."

"With you as Weyrwoman, I'd've improved beyond all knowing.

And it's only eight more Turns and then we're all free to enjoy our-selves." He pulled her tighter still. "We did enjoy ourselves before, you know."

"When didn't you enjoy yourself, light wing?"

"True, and tonight is meant for enjoyment, isn't it."

She laughed and swung away from an embrace that had best be broken. B'lerion's attentions might be misconstrued by some. She owed Sh'gall her undiverted support at least until the Fall ended. As she made her way back to the table, B'lerion followed, smiling at Oklina in imperturbable good humor. Moreta wished he hadn't followed her, noting Oklina's breathless reaction as B'lerion smoothly set himself down beside the girl.

"May I have the next dance with you, Lady Oklina? Moreta will tell you I'm harmless. I'm also B'lerion, bronze Nabeth's rider from the High Reaches. May I have a sip of your wine?"

"Oh, that's Lady Moreta's wine," Oklina protested, trying to regain possession of the cup that B'lerion had seized.

"She'd never deny me a sip of wine, but I'll drink to you and your big dark eyes."

Schooling her own expression, Moreta watched Oklina's, saw her blushing confusion at B'lerion's compliments. She could see the pulse of excitement beating in the girl's slender neck, her quickened breathing. Oklina could not have been more than sixteen Turns. Hold-bred, she'd be married off very soon to some holder or craftmaster to the east or the south, far from Ruatha, strengthening Bloodlines. By the time the Pass ended, Oklina would have children and this Gather day would have been long forgotten. Or, perhaps, better remembered for B'lerion's attentions. She smiled when the harpers struck up a slow and stately dance and B'lerion lead the delighted girl onto the square.

As most people felt their talents adequate to that dance, the tables had emptied. Lady Oma remained at one end, listening gravely to a prosperously dressed holderwoman. When both smiled indulgently to-ward the dance square, Moreta caught sight of Alessan sedately guiding a young girl. The holderwoman's daughter, possible candidate for sec-ond wife? Lady Oma's faint smile was speculative. As Moreta made her own evaluation, the girl, pretty enough with dark curling hair, smiled simperingly up at Alessan. Such an innocent would never attract Ales-san, now that as Lord Holder he could have his choice from any hold or hall on the continent. Then Moreta noticed S'peren, a Fort Weyr bronzerider, watching the dance. She'd thought S'peren had been to Ista.

"Is the Ista Gather over so soon?" she asked him, surprised.

"A bit disappointing, really, once they'd taken the animal away. No racing." S'peren gave her a tolerant smile. "Nowhere near as many people as Ruatha . . ." He nodded with satisfaction at the crowded dance square. "People weren't in such a festive mood, either. There's illness in Igen, Keroon, and Telgar."

"Runners?" The memory of the beast's unexpected fall flashed across her mind.

"Runners? No. People. A fever, I heard. Master Capiam was someplace about, I heard, though I didn't see him."

"Ista's Weyrleaders are well?" F'gal and Wimmia had been good friends during her Turns at Ista Weyr.

"And sent you their good wishes, as usual. Oh, by the way, I bear greetings for you from an animal healer named Talpan. Said he knew you from your father's hold."

Strange, Moreta thought, moving on after exchanging pleasantries with the High Reaches riders chatting with S'peren. Until that day she hadn't been reminded of Talpan in Turns, and now she even had greetings from him.

The dance ended and she tried to locate Alessan for another with him. He was such a good partner. Then she saw him in the square, partnering a girl whose long black hair made Moreta think at first he was dancing with Oklina. The girl turned slightly, and Moreta realized that he was doing his duty by yet another marriageable woman. She felt great sympathy for Alessan, remembering how bronze riders had besieged her before Orlith rose to mate two Turns ago.

Moreta drained her goblet, then went in search of more wine or a partner. She very much wanted to dance again but paused by the nearest wine keg first. The barman quickly filled her cup and she thanked him. At the first sip, she realized her mistake. This wine had an acid aftertaste: Tillek, not the rich full mouth of the Benden. She nearly spat it out.

This dance was a short wild hop, as much fun to watch for the people losing balance as to dance. When the harpers finished with a swirl, they added the chords that announced an intermission. It was the time for harper songs. Moreta half expected Tirone to stride in, for he should be leading singer of a Ruathan Gather, but the young Masterharper of Ruatha Hold and an older journeyman moved to the fore in his stead.

When Moreta looked toward the head table, she saw Alessan flanked by a pair of pretty girls, one of them a redhead. Lady Oma was certainly wasting no time at this Gather. Disinclined to return to the head table, Moreta found an unoccupied stool.

She enjoyed the first song, a rousing ballad, and joined in the chorus with as much verve as those around her. Fine voices near helped her find the harmony for she didn't have a high enough voice to stay with the soprano line. Halfway through the second chorus, Moreta was conscious of Orlith's mind.

You do like the singing, too, don't you? she sent to the queen.

Singing is a pleasant occupation. It lightens the mind and all minds are together.

Moreta's voice faltered into a laugh, which she quickly suppressed for it wouldn't do, even if she were the Weyrwoman, to laugh through a serious song.

The harpers led the Gather in four traditional songs, each one sung with increasing zest as the dancers recovered their breaths. The young Ruathan harper, an excellent tenor, sang an unfamiliar song that he announced he'd found while going through old Records. The melody was haunting and the interval between the notes unexpected. A very old song, Moreta decided, but a good choice for the tenor's voice. Orlith liked it, too.

Our tastes generally coincide, Moreta said.

Not always.

What do you mean by that?

The harpers sing, Orlith replied, evading, and Moreta knew that she'd get no direct answer.

Then the harpers asked for favorites from the audience. Moreta would have liked to request one of the plains songs from her own Keroon, but it was a mournful tune unsuited to the mood of the evening. Talpan had often hummed it. Coincidence again!

After the serenading, Alessan went up on the platform, thanking the harpers and offering compliments for their music and their presence. He enjoined them to make as free of Ruatha's wine as necessary to keep them playing until the last dancer surrendered the square. Everyone applauded loudly, cheering and thumping the tables and kegs to signify their appreciation of a Lord Holder who would not stint on his first Gather. The cheering went on long past what was a courteous spate and followed Alessan back to his table.

The harpers began the next session with a circle dance that permitted Alessan to accompany both of the girls. B'lerion was on his feet with Oklina again. Lady Oma seemed not to notice, so concentrated was her attention on Alessan's partners.

Her throat dry from singing and cheering, Moreta was determined to find more of Alessan's Benden white. As she made her way to the head table, she was stopped by holders asking after Leri and Holth and expressing sincere regret that the Weyrwoman had not attended.

Pass the greetings on, Orlith. They'll like to know they were missed.

After a pause, Orlith replied that Holth was just as glad that she didn't have to sit through a long night on a cold cliff.

You're not feeling the chill, are you? Moreta asked anxiously.

The fire-heights hold the sun heat, and Nabeth and Tamianth keep me warm. You should eat. You're always telling me to eat. Now I you.

The smugness in Orlith's tone Moreta found amusing. And merited, for the rough Tillek wine was making her a trifle lightheaded. She was aware of a belly rumbling, and she'd best get to the food before the circle dance ended. She detoured to acquire a full platter of spiced roast wherry, tubers, and other tempting morsels. As she was making her way to the head table and more of the Benden wine, the circle dance ended. Alessan had no sooner bowed to his two partners when Lady Oma was introducing him to yet another girl. Then Moreta caught sight of Lord Tolocamp bearing down on her and she moved off quickly at a tangent, as if she hadn't seen him. His expression was grim and she was not going to endure one of his lectures at a Gather. She wended her way through the crowds, briefly considered stopping at the harpers' table for they would have the best wine, but she decided she was no safer from Tolocamp in the harpers' company. Besides, they'd probably had enough of him since the Harper Hall was situated so close to Fort Hold. So, instead, she ducked behind the harpers' platform, standing a moment to accustom her eyes to the welcome darkness.

As it was, she nearly fell over the pack saddles stacked behind the dais. She upended one to make an informal seat and was quite delighted with her solitude and escaping Tolocamp. Come the end of Pass, that man was going to be high-flying irritant, and she didn't think that Sh'gall was going to be able to handle him as well as he handled Fall.

This is good, you are eating! Orlith said.

Moreta neatly folded a slice of the roast wherry and took a huge bite. The meat was as tender and succulent as its roasting odor had advertised.

It's beautiful! she told her queen.

She ate eagerly, licking her fingers, not wishing to miss a drop of the juices. Someone stumbled around the corner of the platform and Moreta, balancing her plate and cursing the interruption, slipped into the deeper shadow. Could Tolocamp have followed her? Or was this someone answering natural needs?

Alessan, Orlith told her, which surprised Moreta for Orlith wasn't all that good on remembering people names.

"Moreta?" Alessan sounded uncertain. "Ah, you are here," he added as she stepped forward. "I thought I saw you slip away to elude Tolocamp. I come laden with food and drink. Am I intruding on your privacy?"

"You're not if you happened to bring any more of that Benden wine. Mind you, the Tillek you're serving is not bad—"

"—But it doesn't at all compare with the Benden, and I hope you haven't mentioned the difference to anyone."

"What? And miss out on my share? And you brought more wherry! My compliments to your cook: The roast is superior and I'm starving. Here, sit on a pack saddle." She pushed one toward him and, after emptying her cup of the inferior wine, held it out to him. "More Benden, please?"

"I've a full skin here." Alessan poured carefully.

"But surely you must share it with your partners?"

"Don't you dare—" Alessan reached for her goblet in a mock attempt to retrieve the wine from her.

"That wasn't fair of me. You were doing your duty as Lord Holder, and very nicely, if I may say so."

"Well, I've done my duty as Lord Holder and will now resume the responsibilities of being your escort. I will now enjoy the Gather."

"Hosts rarely do."

"My mother, the good and worthy—"

"—and duty conscious—"

"Has paraded every eligible girl in the west, with all of whom I have dutifully danced. They're not much on talking. By the way, speaking of talking, is that bronze rider who's been monopolizing Oklina a kind and honorable man?"

"B'lerion is kind, and very good company. Is Oklina aware of dragonriders' propensities?"

"As every proper hold girl is." Alessan's tone was dry, acknowledging dragonrider whims and foibles.

"B'lerion is kind and I have known him many Turns," Moreta went on by way of reassurance. Oklina's adoration of her brother was not misplaced if he troubled himself to speak to a Weyrwoman about a bronze rider who was paying marked attention to his sister.

They ate in companionable silence, for Alessan was as hungry as Moreta. Suddenly the harpers struck up another tune, one of the spritelier dances, more of a patterned run, requiring the lighter partner to be lifted, twirled, and caught. She recognized the challenge gleaming in Alessan's eyes; only the young and fit usually attempted the toss dance's acrobatics. She laughed low in her throat. She was no timid adolescent, uncertain of herself, and no decorous hold woman, vitality and body drained by constant childbearing; she was the fighting-fit rider of a queen dragon and she could outdance any man—holder, crafter, rider. In addition, Orlith was encouraging her.

Deserting the remains of her food and her wine, she caught Alessan by the hand and pulled him after her toward the dancing square where already one pair had come to grief and lay sprawled, the subject of goodnatured teasing.

Weyrwoman and Lord Holder were the only pair to survive the rigors of that dance without incident. Cheers and clapping rewarded their agility. Gasping for breath and trying not to weave with the dizziness generated by the final spins, Moreta reeled to the sidelines. A goblet was put in her hand and she knew before sipping that it would be the

Benden. She toasted Alessan as he stood beside her, chest heaving, face suffused with blood, but thoroughly delighted by their performance.

"By the Shell, with the right partner, you can really show your quality," Falga cried, as she walked up to them. "You're in rare form tonight, Moreta. Alessan, best Gather I've been to in Turns. You've outshone your sire who is, as of this moment, no longer lamented. He set a good spread but nothing to compare to this. S'ligar will be sorry he didn't come with me."

The other dragonriders with Falga lifted their cups to Alessan.

"See you at Crom," Falga said to Moreta in parting as the harpers began a gentle old melody.

"Can you move at all?" Alessan asked Moreta, bending to speak quietly in her ear.

"Of course!" Moreta cast a glance in the direction of Alessan's gaze and saw Lady Oma escorting a girl across the floor.

"I've had my shins kicked enough this evening!" Alessan clasped Moreta firmly, his right hand flat against her shoulder blade, the fingers of his left hand twining in hers as he guided her out in the center of the square.

As she surrendered to the swaying step and glide of the stately dance, Moreta had a brief glimpse of the smileless face of Lady Oma. She could feel Alessan's heart pounding, as hers still was, from the exertions of the previous dance but gradually the thudding eased, her face cooled, and her muscles stopped trembling. She realized that she had not danced to this melody since leaving Keroon—since the last Gather she had attended with Talpan, so many Turns ago.

"You're thinking of another man," Alessan whispered, his lips close to her ear.

"A boy I knew. In Keroon."

"And you remember him fondly?"

"We were to be apprenticed to the same Masterhealer." Could she detect a note of jealousy in Alessan's voice? "He continued in the craft. I was taken to Ista and Impressed Orlith."

"And now you heal dragons." For a moment, Alessan loosened his grip but only, it seemed, to take a fresh and firmer hold of her. "Dance, Moreta of Keroon. The moons are up. We can dance all night."

"The harpers may have other plans."

"Not as long as my supply of Benden white lasts . . ."

So Alessan remained by her side, making sure her goblet was full and insisting that she eat some of the small hot spiced rolls that were being served to the dwindling revellers. Nor did he relinquish her to other partners.

The wine got to the harpers before the new day. Even Alessan's incredible store of energy was flagging by the time Orlith landed again in the dancing square.

"It has been a memorable gather, Lord Alessan," Moreta said formally.

"Your presence has made it so, Weyrwoman Moreta," he replied, assisting her to Orlith's forearm. "Shells! Don't slip, woman. Can you reach your own weyr without falling asleep?" His voice carried an edge of anxiety despite his flippant words.

"I can always reach my own weyr."

"Can she, Orlith?"

"Lord Alessan!" The audacity of the man consulting her dragon in her presence.

Orlith turned her head, her eyes sleepily golden. *He means well.*

"You mean well, Orlith says!" Moreta knew that fatigue was making her sound silly, so she made herself laugh. She didn't wish to end the marvelous evening on a sour note.

"Yes, my lady of the golden dragon, I mean well. Safe back!"

Alessan gave her a final wave and then moved slowly through the disarray of fallen benches and messy tables, toward the deserted roadway where most of the stalls had been dismantled and packed away.

"Let's get back to Fort Weyr," Moreta said softly, reluctantly. Her eyes were heavy, her body limp with a pleasant if thorough fatigue. It took an effort to think of the pattern of Fort Weyr's Star Stones. Then Orlith sprang off the dancing square, the standards whipping about with the force of her backwing stroke. They were aloft and Ruatha receding, the darkness punctuated by the last few surviving glows.

CHAPTER IV

South Boll and Fort Weyr, Present Pass, 3.11.43

"WELL?"

Capiam raised his head from the pillow he had made of his arms on the small wooden table in the dispensary. Fatigue and the tremendous strain disoriented him and at first he couldn't identify the figure standing imperiously in front of him.

"Well, Masterhealer? You said you would return immediately to bring me your conclusions. That was several hours ago. Now I find you sleeping."

The testy voice and overbearing manner belonged to Lord Ratoshigan. Behind him, just outside the door, was the tall figure of the Weyrleader who had conveyed Capiam and Lord Ratoshigan from Ista's Gather to Southern Boll.

"I sat down only for a moment, Lord Ratoshigan"—Capiam lifted his hand in a gesture of dismay—"to organize my notes."

"Well?" The third prompting was a bark of unequivocal displeasure. "What *is* your diagnosis of these..." Ratoshigan did not say "malingerers" but the implication would have been plain enough even if the anxious infirmarian had not repeatedly told Capiam that Lord Ratoshigan regarded any man as a malingerer who took his bread and protection but did not deliver a fair day's work in return.

"They are very ill, Lord Ratoshigan."

"They seemed well enough when I left for Ista! They're not wasted or scored." Ratoshigan rocked from heel to toe, a thin man with a long thin, bony face, pinched nostrils above a thin, pinch-lipped mouth and hard small eyes in dry sockets. Capiam thought the Lord Holder looked considerably more unwell than the men dying in the infirmary beds.

"Two have died of whatever it is that afflicts them," Capiam said slowly, reluctant to utter the terrifying conclusion that he had reached before exhaustion had overcome him.

"Dead? Two? And you don't *know* what ailed them?"

Out of the corner of his eye, Capiam noticed that Sh'gall had stepped back from the doorway at the mention of death. The Weyrleader was not a man who tolerated injury or illness, having managed to avoid both.

"No, I don't know precisely what ails them. The symptoms—a fever, headache, lack of appetite, the dry hacking cough—are unusually severe and do not respond to any of the commonly effective treatments."

"But you *must* know. You are the Masterhealer!"

"Rank does not confer total knowledge of my Craft." Capiam had been keeping his voice low, out of deference to the exhausted healers sleeping in the next room, but Ratoshigan exercised no such courtesy and his voice had been rising with his sense of indignation. Capiam rose and walked around the table, Ratoshigan giving way before him, backing out into the close night. "There is much we have forgotten through disuse." Capiam sighed, filled with a weary despair. He ought not to have allowed himself to sleep. There was so much to be done. "These deaths are but the beginning, Lord Ratoshigan. An epidemic is loose on Pern."

"Is that why you and Talpan had that animal killed?" Sh'gall spoke for the first time, angry surprise in his voice.

"Epidemic?" Ratoshigan waved Sh'gall to silence. "Epidemic! What *are* you saying, man? Just a few sick—"

"Not a few, Lord Ratoshigan." Capiam pulled his shoulders back and leaned against the cool stucco wall behind him. "Two days ago I was urgently called to Igen Sea Hold. *Forty* were dead, including three of the sailors who had rescued that animal from the sea. Far better that they had left it on its tree trunk!"

"Forty dead?" Ratoshigan was incredulous, and Sh'gall stepped farther back from the infirmary.

"More are falling ill at the Sea Hold and in the nearby mountain hold whose men had come down to see the incredible seagoing feline!"

"Then why was it brought to Ista Gather?" The Lord Holder was outraged now.

"To be seen," Capiam said bitterly. "Before the illnesses started, it was taken from the Sea Hold to Keroon for the Herdmaster to identify. I was doing what I could to assist the Sea Hold healers when a drum message summoned me to Keroon. Herdmaster Sufur had people and animals sickening rapidly and curiously. The illness followed the same course as that at Igen Sea Hold. Another drum message, and I was conveyed by brown dragon to Telgar. The sickness is there, too, brought back from Keroon by two holders who were buying runnerstock. All the beasts were dead, and so were the holders and twenty others. I cannot estimate how many hundreds of people have been infected by the merest contact with those so contagious. Those of us who live to tell the Harper will thank Talpan's quick wits"—Capiam looked severely at Sh'gall—"that he linked the journey of the feline to the spread of the disease."

"But that animal was the picture of health!" Sh'gall protested.

"It was." Capiam spoke with dry humor. "It seemed immune to the disease it brought to Igen, Keroon, Telgar, and Ista!"

Sh'gall defensively crossed his arms over his chest.

"How could a caged animal spread disease?" Ratoshigan demanded, his thin nostrils flaring.

"It wasn't caged at Igen, nor on the ship when it was weak from thirst and its voyage. At Keroon, Master Sufur kept it in a run when he was trying to identify it. It had ample opportunity to infect people and plenty of time." Capiam despaired as he thought of how much time and opportunity. The healers would never be able to trace all the people who had seen the rarity, touched its tawny coat, and returned to their holds, incubating the disease.

"But...but...I just received a shipload of valuable runners from Keroon!"

Capiam sighed. "I know, Lord Ratoshigan. Master Quitrin informed me that the dead men worked in the beasthold. He's also had an urgent message of illness from the hold at which the men and the beasts halted overnight on the way from the coast."

Ratoshigan and Sh'gall at last began to appreciate the gravity of the situation.

"We're in the middle of a Pass!" Sh'gall said.

"This virus is as indifferent to us as Thread is," Capiam said.

"You have all those Records in your Crafthall. Search them! You have only to search properly!"

Sh'gall had never had an unfruitful Search, had he? thought Capiam, and suppressed his errant sense of humor. One day, though, he meant to record the various and sundry ways in which men and women reacted to disaster. If he survived it!

"An exhaustive search was initiated as soon as I saw the reports on the Igen Sea Hold death toll. Here is what you must do, Lord Ratoshigan."

"What *I* must do?" The Lord Holder drew himself up.

"Yes, Lord Ratoshigan, what you *must* do. You came to seek my diagnosis. I have diagnosed an epidemic. As Masterhealer of Pern, I have authority over Hold, Hall, and Weyr in these circumstances." He glanced at Sh'gall to be sure the Weyrleader was listening, too. "I hereby order you to announce by drum that a quarantine exists on this Hold and the one your beasthandlers used on the way from the coast. No one is to come or go from the Hold proper. There is to be no travel anywhere in your Hold, no congregating."

"But they must gather fruit and—"

"You will gather the sick, human and animal, and arrange for their care. Master Quitrin and I have discussed empiric treatments since homeopathic remedies have proved ineffectual. Inform your Warder and your ladies to prepare your Hall for the sick—"

"My Hall?" Ratoshigan was aghast at the idea.

"And you will clear the new beastholds of animals to relieve the crowding in your dormitories."

"I *knew* you'd bring that subject up!" Ratoshigan was nearly spitting with rage.

"To your sorrow, you will find that the healers' past objections have validity!" Capiam vented his pent-up anxieties and fears by shouting down Ratoshigan's objections. "You will isolate the sick and care for them, which is your duty as Lord Holder! Or come the end of the Pass, you'll find you hold nothing!"

The passion with which Capiam spoke reduced Lord Ratoshigan to silence. Then Capiam turned on Sh'gall.

"Weyrleader, convey me to Fort Hold. It is imperative that I return to my Hall as quickly as possible. You will wish to waste no time alerting your Weyr."

Sh'gall hesitated, but it was not to speak to his dragon.

"Weyrleader!"

Sh'gall swallowed. "Did you *touch* that animal?"

"No, I did not. Talpan warned me." Out of the corner of his eye, Capiam saw Ratoshigan recoil.

"You cannot leave here, Master Capiam," Ratoshigan cried, skittering fearfully to grab his hand. "I touched that animal. I might die, too."

"So you might. You went to Ista Gather to poke and prod a caged creature that has exacted an unexpected revenge for cruelty."

Sh'gall and Ratoshigan stared at the usually tactful Masterhealer.

"Come, Sh'gall, no time is to be wasted. You'll want to isolate those riders who attended Ista Gather, especially those who might have been close to the beast."

"But what shall I do, Master Capiam, what shall I do?"

"What I told you to do. You'll know in two or three days if you've caught the sickness. So I recommend that you order your Hold as quickly as possible."

Capiam gestured Sh'gall to lead the way to the courtyard where the bronze dragon was waiting. The great glowing eyes of Kadith guided the two men to his side in the predawn darkness.

"Dragons!" Sh'gall halted abruptly. "Do dragons get it?"

"Talpan said not. Believe me, Weyrleader, it was his primary concern."

"You're positive?"

"Talpan was. No whers, watchwhers, or wherries have been affected though individuals of all those species had contact with the feline at Igen Sea Hold or Keroon Beasthold. Runners are seriously affected but not herdbeasts or the indigenous whers and wherries. Since dragons are related..."

"Not to wherries!"

Capiam did not bother to disagree, though in his Craft the kinship was tacitly acknowledged.

"The dragon that took the feline from Igen to Keroon has not become ill, and he conveyed it over ten days ago."

Sh'gall looked dubious but he gestured for them to proceed to Kadith.

The bronze dragon had lowered his forequarters for his rider and the healer to mount. Riding dragonback was one of the most enjoyable perogatives of Capiam's Mastery, though he tried not to presume on that privilege. Gratefully he settled himself behind Sh'gall. He had no compunctions about drafting Sh'gall and Kadith to convey him to his Hall in this extreme emergency. The Weyrleader was strong and healthy and might survive any contagion Capiam carried.

Capiam's mind was too busy with all he must accomplish in the next few hours to enjoy the dragon's launching into air. Talpan had promised to initiate quarantine at Ista, to warn the east, and to isolate any who might have had contact with the beast. He would try to trace all runners leaving Keroon Beasthold in the past eighteen days. Capiam would alert the west and intensify the search of Records. The Fort drums would be hot tomorrow with all the messages he must send. The first priority would be Ruatha Hold. Dragonriders had attended Ista Gather and then flown in for a few more hours of dancing and wine at Ruatha. If only Capiam had not succumbed to fatigue. He had already lost valuable time in which the disease would be innocently spread.

Sh'gall's low warning gave Capiam time to take a good hold of the fighting straps. As they went *between*, he did wonder if the awful cold might kill off any trace of the disease.

They were abruptly above Fort Hold fire-heights and gliding in for a fast landing in the field before the Hall. Sh'gall was not going to stay in the company of the Masterhealer any longer than he had to. He waited until Capiam dismounted and then asked the healer to repeat his instructions.

"Tell Berchar and Moreta to treat the symptoms empirically. I'll inform you of any effective treatment immediately. The plague incubates in two to four days. There have been survivors. Try to establish where your riders and weyrfolk have been." The freedom to travel as they pleased had worked to the disadvantage of the Weyrs. "Don't congregate . . ."

"There's Fall!"

"The Weyrs do have their duty to the people . . . but try to limit contact with ground crews." Capiam gave Kadith's shoulder a grateful thump. Kadith turned his gleaming eyes toward the Masterhealer and then, walking forward a few paces, sprang into the air.

Capiam watched until the pair went *between* against the lightening eastern sky, the journey of a breath to the mountains beyond Fort Hold. Then he stumbled up the gentle slope toward the Hall and the bed he was going to welcome. But first he had to compose the drum messages that must go out to Ruatha.

The early-morning air held a bit of dampness that suggested fog was on its way. No glowbaskets were set in the forecourt of Fort Hold and only the one in the entryway of the Harper Hall. Capiam was surprised to see how much progress had been made on the annex of the Hall in the two days. Then the watchwher came snorting up to him, recognizing his smell and gurgling its greeting. Capiam slapped affectionately at Burr's ugly head, digging his fingers into its skull ridges and smiling at the happy alteration of its noise. Watchwhers had their uses, to be sure, but due to the freak of breeding that had perpetuated them, the creatures were so ugly that they revolted those who saw their debased resemblance to the graceful dragons. Yet the watchwher was as loyal and faithful as any dragon and could be trained to recognize those who were allowed to come and go with impunity. Legends said that watchwhers had been used in the earliest holds as the last-ditch defense against Thread. Though how, since watchwhers were nocturnal creatures that could not tolerate sunlight, Capiam didn't know.

Burr was quite young, only a few Turns old, and Capiam had cultivated an association with it since it had been hatched. He and Tirone had made it strictly understood that they would not tolerate apprentice abuse of the creature. When Thread fell on Fort, Capiam or Tirone, whichever of the two Masters was present, would take the watchwher into the main entrance of the Hall to remind the young men and women that the watchwher could provide an important function in that perilous period.

If Burr's ecstatic welcome nearly knocked him off his feet, at least the greeting was sincere, and Capiam was oddly touched by it. Burr

bumbled along beside him, his chain rattling on the flagstone. He gave
Burr a last drubbing across the scalp and then ran up the stairs to open
the heavy door of the Hall.

One dim glow illuminated the inner hall. Capiam closed the door
and moved quickly, so near his bed and much needed rest. He went to
the left in the main hall, through the doorway that led to the Archives.

Discordant snores surprised him, and he peered into the vaulted
library room. Two apprentices, one with head pillowed on the Records
he had been examining, the other propped more comfortably against
the wall, were vying unmusically. Annoyance warred with tolerance in
Capiam's mind. Dawn was near and would bring Master Fortine to
prod them to their labors and scold them for weakness. They'd be the
better readers for his rebuke and the rest. Suddenly Capiam was too
tired to answer the questions they would certainly tax him with if he
did wake them.

Quietly then, he took a sheet of well-scraped hide and composed a
terse message for the drummaster to broadcast to the Weyrs and the
major Holds, to be relayed to lesser holds and halls. He put the message
on Master Fortine's writing desk right on the page the Archivist was
using. Fortine would see it as soon as he finished his breakfast, which
was usually early, so the news of the epidemic would be spread before
noon.

To the sound of the discordant snores, Capiam dragged his feet
to his quarters. He'd get some sleep before the drums started. Quite
possibly he was weary enough to sleep through them for a while. He
walked up the steps into the healers' section of the Harper Hall. When
the Pass was over, he must really start the construction of a Healer
Crafthall.

He reached his room and opened the door. A mellow glow softly lit
the chamber. A bowl of fresh fruit and a small wine jar had been placed
on his bedside table, and his bed fur turned back invitingly. Desdra!
He was once more grateful for her thoughtfulness. Tossing his pack to
the corner, he sat on the bed, the effort of pulling off his boots almost
beyond his remaining physical strength. He loosened his belt, then
decided not to remove his tunic and pants—too much effort required.
He rolled onto the mattress and in the same movement jerked the fur
over his shoulder. The pillow was remarkably welcoming to his tired
aching head.

He groaned. He had left the drum messages. Fortine would know
that he had returned, but not at what hour. He had to have sleep! He
had been across Pern and up and down it. If he wasn't extra careful of
his own health, he'd be a victim of the plague before he found out what
it was.

He staggered from his bed to his table. "Disturb me not!" he printed boldly and, hanging onto the door to keep himself erect for that one last task, he pinned the note where it could not be missed.

Then when he sank into the comfort of his bed, he could relax into sleep.

CHAPTER V

Fort Weyr, Present Pass, 3.11.43

MORETA WAS CERTAIN that she had only been asleep a few minutes when Orlith woke her.

Two hours you have slept but Kadith is in a frenzy.

"Why?" Moreta found it very difficult to lift her head from the pillow. It didn't ache, but her legs did. Whether from the dancing or from the wine, Moreta didn't know and probably would not have time to discover if Sh'gall was in one of his moods.

A sickness in the land, Orlith replied, sounding puzzled. *Sh'gall went first to see K'lon and woke him.*

"Woke K'lon?" Moreta was disgusted as she pulled on the first tunic she could reach. The clothing was slightly damp and her sleeping quarters were clammy. The weather must have changed.

There is a fine mist over the Weyr, Orlith obligingly reported.

Moreta shivered as she dressed. "Why on earth should he wake K'lon? The man's been ill and needs his rest."

He is convinced that K'lon has brought the illness here. Orlith sounded truly perplexed. *K'lon was in Igen.*

"K'lon is often in Igen. His friend is a green rider there."

Moreta splashed water into her face then rubbed the mint stick over her teeth, but it did little to improve the taste in her mouth. She ran her fingers through her short hair with one hand as she fumbled for a goru pear from the dish in her room. The tart fruit might neutralise the aftereffects of all that Benden wine.

"Moreta!" Sh'gall's summons resounded from the entrance to her weyr.

Moreta had time to give Orlith's muzzle a swift caress before Sh'gall burst into the chamber. The queen blinked her eyes shut, feigning sleep. Sh'gall charged ten paces into the weyr and stopped, holding his hand up as if fending off an approach.

"A sickness is all over Pern. Men are dying and nothing can be done. Runners are dying, too. No one must leave the Weyr."

Sh'gall's eyes were wide with a genuine fear, and Moreta stared at him in surprise for a moment.

"Thread falls tomorrow, Sh'gall. The dragonriders must leave the Weyr."

"Don't come close to me. I may have been infected, too."

Moreta hadn't moved. "Suppose you give me some details," she said, speaking calmly.

"That animal they showed off at Ista—it was infected with a deadly disease. It's spread from Igen to Keroon Beasthold to Telgar. It's even in Southern Boll! Men are *dead* of it in Lord Ratoshigan's Hold. And he's been quarantined by Master Capiam. So are we!"

"Runners, you said?" Moreta's breath caught in her throat and she turned fearfully toward her dragon. "Dragons?" She'd touched that runner and if she'd contaminated Orlith...

"No, no, not dragons! Capiam said Talpan agreed they weren't affected. They had the beast killed. It hadn't looked sick to me!"

"Tell me please how men could die in Southern Boll when that feline was still in Ista?"

"Because there's an epidemic! It started when the seamen hauled that beast out of the water and brought it home. Everyone wanted to see it, so they took it to Igen Hold, then Keroon Beasthold and Ista before this Talpan fellow realized it was a carrier. Yes, that's what Capiam said: The feline was a carrier."

"And they displayed it at Ista Gather?"

"No one knew! Not until this Talpan fellow came along and talked to Capiam. He'd been to all the infected holds."

"Who? Talpan?"

"No, Capiam! Talpan's an animal healer."

"Yes, I know." Moreta held on to her patience because Sh'gall was obviously so rattled as to be incoherent. "Nothing was mentioned of this at Ruatha Gather."

Sh'gall gave her a patient glare. "Of course, the truth wasn't known. Besides, who talks of unpleasant things at a Gather! But I just conveyed Capiam to his hall. I also had to convey Ratoshigan and Capiam to Southern Boll because Ratoshigan received an urgent drum message to return. *He* had deaths. He also had new runners in from Keroon; they probably brought that sickness to the west." Sh'gall glowered and then shuddered violently. "Capiam said that if I didn't touch the feline I might not get sick. I can't get sick. I'm the Weyrleader." He shuddered again.

Moreta looked at him apprehensively. His hair was damp, pressed in a wet ridge about his forehead by his riding helmet. His lips were slightly blue and his skin very pale. "You don't look well."

"I'm fine! I'm fine. I bathed in the Ice Lake. Capiam said that the disease is like Thread. Cold kills Thread and so does water."

Moreta took up her fur cloak, which lay where it had fallen from her shoulders a scant two hours before, and approached him with it.

"Don't come near me." He stepped backward, his hands extended to fend her off.

"Sh'gall, don't be idiotic!" She flung the cloak at him. "Put that about you so you won't get sick of a chill. A chill would make you more susceptible to whatever disease is about." She turned back to the table and poured wine, splashing it in her haste. "Drink this. Wine is also antiseptic. No, I won't come near you." She was relieved to see him settled, the cloak about his shoulders, and stepped back from the table so he could reach the wine. "An utterly foolish thing to do, plunge yourself into the Ice Lake before the sun is up and then travel *between*. Now sit down and tell me again what happened at Ista Gather. And where you went with Capiam and exactly what he said."

She listened with half her attention to Sh'gall's more orderly recounting while she mentally reviewed what precautions and measures she could take to ensure the health of the Weyr.

"No good comes from the Southern Continent!" Sh'gall commented gratuitously. "There's a very sound reason why no one is permitted there."

"Permission has never been denied. I always understood that everything we need was taken over in the Crossing. Now, what are the symptoms of the disease that's spreading?" Moreta recalled the bloody discharge from the dead runner's nose, the only external sign of its mortal distress.

Sh'gall stared uncomprehendingly for a long moment, then collected his thoughts. "Fever. Yes, there's fever." He glanced at her for approval.

"There are many kinds of fevers, Sh'gall."

"Berchar will know, then. Fever, Capiam said, and headache and a dry cough. Why should that be enough to kill people and animals?"

"What remedies did Capiam specify?"

"How could he specify when he doesn't know what the plague is? They'll find out. They've only to search hard enough. Oh, he said to treat the symptoms empirically."

"Did he mention an incubation period? We can't just stay quarantined in the Weyr forever, you know."

"I know. But Capiam said we mustn't congregate. He really tore into Ratoshigan for the overcrowding in his Hold." Sh'gall grinned unpleasantly. "We have been warning the Holders, but would they listen? They'll pay for it now."

"Sh'gall, Capiam must have told you how long it takes the disease to incubate."

The Weyrleader had finished the wine. He frowned and rubbed at his face. "I'm tired. I waited half the night for the Masterhealer at Ratoshigan's. He said it incubates in two to four days. He told me to find out where everyone has been and to order them not to congregate. The Weyr has its duties, too. I've got to get some sleep. Since you're up, you make sure everyone knows about this. Tell them all just what they may have caught yesterday." He gave her a hard, warning stare. "I don't want to find out when I wake up that you've jollied people along."

"An epidemic is a far different affair from reassuring a rider with a wing-damaged dragon."

"And find Berchar. I want to know exactly what K'lon was ill of. K'lon didn't know, and Berchar wasn't in his quarters!" Sh'gall didn't approve of that. Fully male and hold-bred, Sh'gall had never developed any compassion or understanding of the green and blue riders and their associations.

"I'll speak to Berchar." She had a fairly good idea she'd find him with S'gor, a green rider.

"And warn the Weyr?" He rose, groggy with fatigue and the wine he'd taken on an empty stomach. "And no one's to leave the Weyr and no one's to come in. You be sure that the watchrider passes on that order!" He waggled an admonitory finger at her.

"It's a bit late to cry Thread when the burrow's set, isn't it?" she replied bitterly. "The Gathers should have been canceled."

"No one knew how serious this was yesterday. You transmit my orders straightaway!"

Still clutching her fur around him, Sh'gall stumbled from the weyr. Moreta watched him go, her head throbbing. Why hadn't they canceled the Gathers? All those people at Ruatha! And dragonriders from every Weyr in and out of Ista *and* Ruatha. What was it S'peren had told her— sickness in Igen, Keroon, and Telgar? But he hadn't said anything about an epidemic. Or deaths. And that runner of Vander's? Had Alessan mentioned a new runner from Keroon in Vander's hold? Thinking of the long picket lines on Ruatha's race flat, Moreta groaned. And all those people! How infectious would that runner have been at the moment of his death, when anxious riders and helpful spectators had crowded around it? She shouldn't have interfered. It was not her business!

You are distressed, Orlith said, her eyes whirling in a soothing blue. *You should not be distressed by a runnerbeast.*

Moreta leaned against her dragon's head, stroking the near eye ridge, calming her anxiety with the soft feel of Orlith's skin.

"It's not just the runnerbeast, my love. A sickness is in the land. A very dangerous sickness. Where's Berchar?"

With S'gor. Asleep. It is very early. And foggy.

"And yesterday was so beautiful!" She remembered Alessan's strong arms about her in the toss dance, the challenge in his light-green eyes.

You enjoyed yourself! Orlith said with deep satisfaction.

"Yes, indeed I did." Moreta sighed ruefully.

Nothing will change yesterday, Orlith remarked philosophically. *So now you must deal with today.* As Moreta chuckled over dragon logic, the queen added, *Leri wishes to speak with you since you are awake.*

"Yes, and Leri might have heard about an epidemic like this. She might also know how I'm going to break the news to the Weyr the day before Fall."

Since Sh'gall had gone off with her cloak, Moreta slipped into her riding jacket. Orlith had been correct, as always, about the weather. As Moreta left her weyr and started up the steps to Leri's, the fog was swirling down from the ranges. Thread would Fall tomorrow, fog or not, so she devoutly hoped the weather would clear. If the wind failed to clear the mist, the possibility of collision would be trebled. Dragons could see through fog but their riders couldn't. Sometimes riders did not heed their dragons and found themselves in one-sided arguments with bare ridges.

Orlith, please tell the watchrider that no one, dragonrider or holder, is permitted into the Weyr today. And no one is to leave it, either. The order is to be passed to each watchrider.

Who would visit the Weyr in such fog? Orlith asked. *And the day after two Gathers.*

"Orlith?"

I have relayed the message. Balgeth is too sleepy to question why. Orlith sounded suspiciously meek.

"Good day to you, Holth," Moreta said courteously as she entered the old Weyrwoman's quarters.

Holth turned her head briefly in acknowledgment before closing her eyelids and snuggling her head more firmly into her forelegs. The old queen was nearly bronze with age.

Beside her, on the edge of the stone platform that was the dragon's couch, Leri sat on a heap of pillows, her body swathed in thick woven rugs. Leri said she slept beside Holth as much for the warmth the dragon had stored up in her from so much sunning over so many Turns as to save herself the bother of moving. The last few Turns, Leri's joints rebelled against too much use. Repeatedly Moreta and Master Capiam had urged the woman to take up the standing invitation to remove to the south to Ista Weyr. Leri adamantly refused, declaring that she wasn't a tunnel snake to change her skin: She'd been born in Fort Weyr and intended to live out her Turn with those few old friends who remained, and in her own familiar quarters.

"Hear you enjoyed yourself past the first watch," Leri said. She raised her eyebrows questioningly. "Was that why Sh'gall was berating you?"

"He wasn't berating. He was bemoaning. An epidemic's loose on Pern."

Concern wiped the amusement from Leri's face. "What? We've never had an epidemic on Pern. Not that I ever heard about. Nor read either."

Her movement restricted by her joint ailment, Leri kept the Weyr's records to allow Moreta more time for her nursing. Leri often browsed through the older Records, for "the gossip," she said.

"Shards! I'd hoped you'd read something somewhere. Something encouraging! Sh'gall's in a rare taking and this time with due cause."

"Perhaps I haven't read far enough back for exciting things like epidemics." Leri tossed Moreta a pillow from her pile and pointed imperiously at the small wooden stool set aside for visitors. "We're a healthy lot, by and large. Tend to break a lot of bones, Threadscores, occasional fevers, but nothing on a continent-wide scale. What sort of disease is it?"

"Master Capiam has not yet identified it."

"Oh, I don't like the sound of that!" Leri rolled her eyes. "And, by the Egg, there were *two* Gathers yesterday, weren't there?"

"The danger was not fully appreciated. Master Capiam and Talpan—"

"The Talpan who was a friend of yours?"

"Yes, well, he's been an animal healer, you know, and *he* realized that the feline they had on display at Ista was the disease carrier."

"The feline from the Southern Continent?" Leri clacked her tongue. "And some bloody fool has been taking that creature here, there, and everywhere, showing it off, so the disease is also here, there, and everywhere! With riders, including our noble Weyrleader, all going to have a little peek!"

"Sh'gall's story was a little incoherent but he'd taken Lord Rato-shigan to Ista to see the feline; Capiam had arrived from seeing what ailed Igen Sea Hold, Keroon, and Telgar—"

"Great Faranth!"

Moreta nodded. "Ista, of course. Then Ratoshigan had an urgent drum message summoning him back because of illness, so Sh'gall conveyed him and Master Capiam."

"How did the sickness get there so fast? The beast only got as far as Ista!"

"Yes, but it was first at Keroon Beasthold to be identified by Master Sufur and no one realized that it was carrying sickness—"

"And because it's been an open winter, they've been shipping runners all over the continent!" Leri concluded, and the two women looked at each other gravely.

"Talpan told Capiam that dragons are not affected."

"We should be grateful for small mercies, I suppose," Leri said.

"And Fall's tomorrow. We'll have that over with before any of us fall sick. Incubation's two to four days."

"That's not a big mercy, is it? But you weren't at Ista." Leri frowned.

"No, Sh'gall was. However, a runner fell in the second race at Ruatha and it shouldn't have . . ."

Leri nodded, her comprehension complete. "And naturally you were close enough to go have a look. It died?"

"And shouldn't have. Its owner had just received some new stock from Keroon."

"Hooooo!" Leri rolled her eyes and sighed in resignation. "So, what medication does Capiam recommend? Surely he must have some idea if he's been flipping across the continent?"

"He recommends that we treat the symptoms empirically until he finds out just what it is and what the specific medicine is."

"And what is it we treat empirically?"

"Headache, fever, and a dry cough."

"They don't kill."

"Until now."

"I don't like this at all," Leri said, pulling her shawl across her shoulders and hunching into its warmth. "Though mind, we'd a harper here—though L'mal shooed him off for he was doleful—who used to say 'there's nothing new under the sun.' A slim hope in these circumstances, but I don't think we can ignore any avenues of exploration. You just bring me up more Records. Say the ones starting the last Pass. Fortunately I hadn't planned on going anywhere this morning."

As Leri only left her weyr to fly with the queens' wing, Moreta offered her a smile for her attempt to lighten the bad tidings.

"Sh'gall's left it to you to tell the Weyr?"

"Those who are awake. And Nesso . . ."

Leri snorted. "That's the right one to start with. Be sure she gets the facts right or we'll have hysteria as well as hangovers by noontime.

And since you're up, would you fix my wine for me, please, Moreta?" Leri shifted uneasily. "The change in the weather does get to my joints." She saw Moreta's reluctance. "Look, if you fix it, then you'll know I haven't exceeded the proper amount of fellis juice." Eyes sparkling with challenge, she cocked her head at the younger Weyrwoman. Moreta did not like Leri to use much fellis juice and contended that if Leri went south where the warmer weather would ease her condition, she wouldn't need fellis juice at all.

But Moreta did not hesitate. The clammy cold made her feel stiff so it would certainly be making Leri miserable.

"Now, tell me, did you enjoy the Gather?" Leri asked as Moreta measured the fellis juice into her tall goblet.

"Yes, I did. And I got down on the race flats and watched most of the races from a very good vantage point with Lord Alessan."

"What? You monopolized Alessan when his mother and the mother of every eligible girl able to creep or crawl to that Gather..."

Moreta grinned. "He did his duty with the girls on the dance square. And we," she added, smiling more broadly than ever, "managed to stay upright in a toss dance!"

Leri grinned back at Moreta. "Alessan could be quite a temptation. I assume he's got over the death of that wild one he married. Sad, that! Now, his grandfather, Leef's sire... Ah, no, you'll have heard all that." Moreta had not, but Leri's comment meant she was unlikely to. "I always chat Alessan up while the ground crews are reporting. Always has a flask of Benden white with him."

"He does, does he?"

Leri laughed at Moreta's alert tone.

"Don't tell me he tried it on you, too, at his own Gather?" Leri chortled and then assumed a masculine pitch to her voice, "'I just happen to have one skin of Benden white...'" And she laughed all the more as Moreta reacted to the mimicry. "He's got a full cave of 'em, I'd say. However, I'm glad Leef gave him the succession. He's got more guts than that elder brother of his—never could remember the man's name. Never mind. Alessan's worth three of him. Did you know that Alessan was Searched?"

"And that Lord Leef refused." Moreta frowned. Alessan would have made a superb bronze rider.

"Well, if the lad was to succeed, Leef was entitled to refuse. That was twelve Turns ago. Before you arrived from Ista. Alessan would have Impressed a bronze, I'm sure."

Moreta nodded, bringing Leri her fellis juice and wine.

"Your health!" she said ironically, raising the cup to Moreta before she took a careful sip. "Hmmm. Do get some rest today, Moreta," she said more briskly. "Two hours' sleep is not enough when there's Fall tomorrow and who know how many dragonriders will do stupid things thanks to two Gathers, let alone Capiam's unidentified disease."

"I'll get some rest once I've organized a few matters."

"I sometimes wonder if we did right, L'mal and I, monopolizing your healing arts for the Weyr."

"Yes!" Moreta's quick reply was echoed by Holth and Orlith.

"Well, ask a silly question!" Leri was reassured, and she patted Holth's cheek.

"Quite. Now, what Records should I send you?"

"The oldest ones you can find that are still legible."

Moreta scooped up the pillow Leri had loaned her and threw it back to the old Weyrwoman, who caught it deftly.

"And eat something!" Leri shouted as Moreta turned and left the weyr.

Wisps of fog were infiltrating the valleys, oozing toward the western rim of the Bowl, and the watchrider was standing within the forearms of his dragon, finding what protection he could from the elements. Moreta shuddered. She didn't like the northern fogs even after ten Turns, but she hadn't liked the humidity of the southern latitude at Ista any better. And it was far too late to return to the comfortable climate of the highlands of Keroon. Was the disease in the highlands, too? And Talpan diagnosing it! How strange that he had been in her mind yesterday. Would the epidemic bring them together again?

She gave herself a little shake and began the descent to the floor of the Bowl. First she would see K'lon, then find Berchar, even if it meant invading the privacy of S'gor's weyr.

K'lon was asleep when she reached the infirmary and there was not so much as a bead of fever perspiration on his brow or upper lip. His fair skin was a healthy color, wind-darkened where the eyepieces left the cheek bare. Berchar had attended K'lon during the initial days of his fever so Moreta saw no point in rousing the blue rider again.

Folk were moving about the Bowl by then, swirling fog about them as they began the preparations for the next day's Threadfall. The shouts and laughter of the weyrlings filling firestone sacks was muted by the mist. Moreta thought to check with Weyrlingmaster F'neldril to find out how many of the weyrlings had drawn convey duty the day before. A rare animal in Ista might well have attracted some of them despite their strict orders to convey and return directly.

"Put some energy into the task, lads. Here's the Weyrwoman to see the sacks are properly filled for tomorrow's Fall."

Many Fort dragonriders insisted that F'neldril was the one rider all Fort dragons obeyed, a holdover from weyrling days under his tutelage. He did have an uncanny instinct, Moreta thought, if he could see her through the rolling fog. He appeared right beside her, a craggy-faced man with a deep Thread scar from forehead to ear, and the lobe missing, but she had always liked him and he was one of her first friends at Fort Weyr.

"You're well, Weyrwoman? And Orlith thrives? She's near clutching now, isn't she?"

"More weyrlings for you to tyrannize, F'neldril?"

"Me?" He pointed his long curved thumb at his chest in mock dismay. "Me? Tyrannize?"

But the old established exchange did not lift her spirits. "There's trouble, F'neldril . . ."

"Which one?" he demanded.

"No, not your weyrlings. There's a disease of epidemic proportion spreading over the southeast and coming west. I'll want to know how many of the weyrlings were on convey duty yesterday and where they took their passengers, and how long they stayed on the ground at Ista. The entire Weyr will be answering the same questions. If we are to prevent the epidemic's spreading here, we'll need to know."

"I'll find out exactly. Never fear on that count, Moreta!"

"I don't, but we must avoid panic even though the situation is very serious. And Leri would like to have some of the oldest Records, the still legible ones, brought to her weyr."

"What's the Masterhealer doing then with his time, and all those apprentices of his, that we have to do his job for him?"

"The more to look the quicker to find; the sooner the better," Moreta replied. F'neldril could be so parochial.

"Leri'll have her Records as soon as the lads have finished sacking firestone and had a bit of a wash. Wouldn't do to have stone-dust messing up our Records—You there, M'barak, that sack's not what I'd call full. Top it off."

Another of F'neldril's quirks was to finish one job before starting the next. But Moreta moved off, secure in the knowledge that Leri would not have a long wait for her Records.

She went on to the Lower Caverns and stood for a moment in the entrance, noting how few people occupied the tables, most of those few obviously nursing wineheads. How awkward and inconvenient it all was, Moreta thought with a rush of distressed exasperation, for an epidemic to break out the day after two Gathers, when half the riders would consider the news a bad joke and the rest wouldn't be sober enough to understand what was happening. And Fall tomorrow! How could she *tell* the Weyr if they weren't available to tell?

If you eat, you'll think of something, came the calm imperturbable voice of her dragon.

"An excellent notion." Moreta went to the small breakfast hearth and poured herself a cup of klah, added a huge spoonful of sweetener, took a fresh roll from the warming oven and looked around for a place to sit and think. Then she saw Peterpar, the Weyr herdsman, sharpening his hoof knife. His hair was rumpled and his face sleep creased. He was not really attending to the job at hand, which was honing an edge against the strop.

"Don't cut yourself," she said quietly, sitting down.

Peterpar winced at the sound of her voice but he kept on stropping.

"Were you at Ista or Ruatha?"

"Both, for my folly. Beer at Ista. That foully acid Tillek wine at Ruatha."

"Did you see the feline at Ista?" Moreta thought that it would be kinder to break the news gently to a man in Peterpar's fragile state.

"Aye." Peterpar frowned. "Master Talpan was there. He told me not to get too close though it was caged and all. He sent you his regards, by the way. Afterward"—Peterpar's frown deepened as if he didn't quite trust his memory of events—"they put the animal down."

"For a good reason." Moreta told him why.

Peterpar held the knife suspended, midstrop, shocked. By the time she had finished, he had recovered his equanimity.

"If it's to come, it'll come." He went on stropping.

"That last drove of runnerbeasts we received in tithe," she asked, "from which hold did it come?" She sipped at the klah, grateful for its warmth and stimulation.

"Part of Tillek's contribution." Peterpar's expression reflected the relief he felt. "Heard tell at Ista that there's been an illness among runners at Keroon. Same thing?" The tone in Peterpar's voice begged Moreta to deny it.

She nodded.

"Now, how can a feline that came from the Southern Continent give us, man and runnerbeast, a sickness?"

"Master Talpan decided that it did. Apparently neither man nor runnerbeast has any immunity from the infection that feline brought with it."

Peterpar cocked his head to one side, contorting his face. "Then that runnerbeast that dropped dead at Ruatha races had it?"

"Quite possibly."

"Tillek doesn't get breeding stock from Keroon. Just as well. But soon's I finish my klah, I'll check the herds." He returned his hoof knife to its case, rolled up his strop and shoved it into his tunic pocket. "Dragons don't get this, do they?"

"No, Master Talpan didn't believe they could." Moreta rose to her feet. "But riders can."

"Oh, we're a hardy lot, we weyrfolk," Peterpar said pridefully, shaking his head that she would doubt it. "We'll be careful now. You wait and see. Won't be many of *us* coming down sick. Don't you worry about that now, Moreta. Not with Fall tomorrow."

One was offered reassurance from unlikely sources, Moreta thought. Yet his advice reminded her that one of the reasons weyrfolk were so hardy was because they ate well and sensibly. Many illnesses could be prevented, or diminished, by proper diet. One of her most important duties as Weyrwoman was altering that diet from season to season. Moreta looked about the Cavern, to see if Nesso was up. She had better not be laggard with the tidings to Nesso who would relish disseminating information of such caliber.

"Nesso, I'd like you to add spearleek and white bulb to your stews for a while, please."

Nesso gave one of her little offended sniffs. "I've already planned to do so and there's citron in the morning rolls. If you'd had one, you'd know. A pinch of prevention's worth a pound of cure."

"You'd already planned to? You've heard of the sickness?"

Nesso sniffed again. "Being waked up at the crack of dawn—"

"Sh'gall told you?"

"No, he didn't tell me. He was banging around the night hearth muttering to himself half-demented, without a thought or a consideration for those of us sleeping nearby."

Moreta knew very well why Nesso imposed on herself the night-hearth duty on a Gather night. The prying woman loved to catch people sneaking in or out; that knowledge gave her a feeling of power.

"Who else in the Weyr knows?"

"Whoever you've been telling before you came to me." And she cast a dark look over her shoulder at Peterpar, who was trudging out of the Cavern.

"What did you actually hear Sh'gall saying?" Moreta knew Nesso's penchant for gossip and also her fallibility in repeating it correctly.

"That there's an epidemic on Pern and everyone will die." Nesso gave Moreta a look of pure indignation. "Which is downright foolish."

"Master Capiam has declared that there is."

"Well, we haven't got one here!" Nesso pointed her ladle at the floor. "K'lon's fine and healthy, sleeping like a babe for all he was woke up and questioned sharp. *Holders* die of epidemics." Nesso was contemptuous of anyone not connected intimately with Weyrs. "What else could be expected when so many people are crammed into living space that wouldn't suit a watchwher!" All of Nesso's indignation drained out of her as she looked up and saw Moreta's expression. "You're serious?" Her eyes widened. "I thought Sh'gall just had too much wine! Oh! And everyone here was either to Ista or Ruatha!" Nesso might love to gossip but she was not stupid, and she was quite able to see the enormity of the situation. She gave herself a little shake, picked up the ladle, wiped it off with her clout, and gave the porridge such a stirring that globs fell to the burning blackstone. "What're the signs?"

"Headache, fever, chills, a dry cough."

"That's exactly what put K'lon in his bed."

"You're sure?"

"Of course I'm sure. And for that matter, K'lon's fine. Weyrfolk are healthy folk!" Nesso's assertion was as prideful as Peterpar's and a matter of some consolation to Moreta. "And, saving your look-in on him yesterday afternoon, only Berchar tended him—but he was recovered by then. Mind you, I shouldn't go telling everyone suddenlike about the symptoms, as we'll have enough sore heads this morning and it's an epidemic of wine they had last night, that'll be all." She gave the porridge a final decisive poke and turned fully toward Moreta. "How long does it take this sickness to come on people?"

"Capiam says two to four days."

"Well, at least the riders can concentrate on Fall tomorrow with a clear mind."

"There's to be no congregating. No visitors into the Weyr and none to go out. I've told the watchrider so."

"Visitors aren't likely today in any case, with Gathers yesterday and the fog so thick you can't hardly see the other side of the Bowl. You'll find Berchar in S'gor's weyr, you know."

"I thought that likely. Sh'gall's not to be disturbed."

"Oh?" Nesso's eyebrows rose to meet her hairline. "Does he fancy he's already got this disease? And Thread Falling tomorrow? What do I tell the wingleaders if they ask for him?"

"Tell them to seek me. He's not ill in any case but he was conveying Master Capiam yesterday and he's exhausted."

Moreta left Nesso on that. By sleeping, Sh'gall would recover from the first flare of panic and be as eager as ever for the stimulation of a Fall. He was always at his best leading the Weyr's fighting wings.

Fog swirled around her as Moreta stepped out of the Lower Cavern.

Orlith, would you please bespeak Malth for me and ask for a lift to her weyr?

I'll come.

I know you would, my love, but you are egg-heavy, the fog is thick, and by making such a request, I give them due notice of my coming.

Malth comes. Something in Orlith's tone made Moreta wonder if Malth had been reluctant to obey the summons. Malth should have known that the Weyrwoman would not intrude unnecessarily.

Malth does, was Orlith's quick rejoinder, implying that the rider was at fault.

No sooner had the queen spoken than the fog roiled violently and the green dragon settled herself right beside Moreta so that the Weyr-woman need only to take one step.

Express my gratitude, Orlith, and compliment her on her flying.
I did.

Moreta swung her leg over Malth's neck ridge. She always felt a trifle strange when mounted on so much smaller a dragon than her great queen. It was ridiculous to think that she might be too heavy for the green, whose rider S'gor was a tall, heavily built man, but Moreta could never dispell that notion on the infrequent occasions when she rode the lesser dragons of the Weyr.

Malth waited a respectful moment to be sure that Moreta was settled and then sprang lightly upward. Diving blind into the fog disoriented Moreta despite her absolute faith in Malth.

You would not worry on me, Orlith said plaintively. *I'm not that egg-heavy yet.*

I know, love!

Malth hovered for a moment in the gray gloom, then Moreta felt the lightest of jars through the dragon's slender frame as she landed on her weyr ledge.

"Thank you, Malth!" Moreta projected her voice loudly to give further warning to the weyr occupants then dismounted and walked toward the yellow gleam spilling from the weyr into the corridor. She couldn't see her feet or the ledge. She looked behind her, at the dragon who appeared to be suspended in the fog, but Malth's eyes whirled slowly with encouragement.

"Don't come in here," S'gor called urgently, and his figure blocked the light.

"S'gor, I really cannot stand out here in the fog. I gave you plenty of warning." This was not the time for a rider to be coy.

"It's the illness, Moreta. Berchar's got it. He's terribly unwell and he said I mustn't let anyone in the weyr." S'gor stepped back as he spoke, whereupon Moreta walked purposefully down the aisle and into the weyr. S'gor backed to the sleeping alcove, which he now guarded with outstretched arms.

"I must speak with him, S'gor." Moreta continued toward the alcove.

"No, really, Moreta. It won't do you any good. He's out of his head. And don't touch me, either. I'm probably contaminated . . ." S'gor moved to one side rather than risk contact with his Weyrwoman. The incoherent mumbles of a feverish man grew audible during the slight pause in the conversation. "You see?" S'gor felt himself vindicated.

Moreta pushed back the curtain that separated the sleeping quarters from the weyr and stood on the threshold. Even in the dim light she could see the change sickness had made in Berchar. His features were now drawn by fever and his skin was pale and moist. Moreta saw

Berchar's medicine case lay open on the table and walked over to it. "How long has he been ill?" She lifted the first bottle left on the table.

"He was feeling wretched yesterday—terrible headache, so we didn't go to either of the Gathers as we'd planned." S'gor fiddled nervously with the bottles on the table. "He was perfectly all right at breakfast. We were going to Ista, to see that animal. Then Berch says he has this splitting headache and he'd have to lie down. I didn't believe him at first—"

"He took sweatroot for headache?"

"No. He took willow salic, of course." S'gor held up the bottle of crystals.

"Then sweatroot?"

"Yes, for all the good it did him. He was burning up by midday and then insisted on having this"—S'gor read the label—"this aconite. I thought that very odd indeed since I have been of assistance to him several times and he told me off rather abruptly for questioning a healer. This morning, though, he asked me to make him an infusion of featherfern, which I did, and told me to add ten drops of fellis juice. He said he ached all over."

Moreta nodded in what she hoped was a reassuring manner. Aconite for a headache and fever? She could understand featherfern and fellis juice.

"Was his fever high?"

"He knew what he was doing, if that's what you mean." S'gor sounded defensive.

"I'm sure he did, S'gor. He is a Masterhealer, and Fort Weyr's been fortunate to have him assigned to us. What else did he tell you to do?"

"To keep everyone from visiting." He stared resentfully at Moreta. She did not blink or look away, merely waited until he had himself in control again. "Essence of featherfern undiluted every two hours until the fever abates and fellis juice every four hours, but no sooner than four hours."

"Did he think he had contracted the fever from K'lon?"

"Berchar would never discuss his patients with me!"

"I wish he had this once."

S'gor looked frightened. "Has K'lon taken a turn for the worst?"

"No, he's sleeping quite naturally." Moreta wished that she could enjoy the same privilege. "I would like a few words with Berchar when his fever drops, S'gor. Do not fail to inform me. It's very important." She looked down at the sick man with conflicting doubts. If K'lon had the same disease that Master Capiam had diagnosed as an epidemic, why had he recovered when people in southeast Pern were dying? Could it be due to the circumstances of hold life? Were overcrowding in the holds and the unseasonably warm weather promoting the spread of the disease? She realized that her pause was alarming S'gor. "Follow Berchar's instructions. I'll see that you won't be troubled further. Have Malth inform Orlith when Berchar may talk to me. And do thank Malth for conveying me. I know that she was reluctant to disobey."

S'gor's eyes assumed the unfocused gaze that indicated he was conversing with his dragon. But he smiled as he looked down at Moreta.

"Malth says you're welcome and she'll take you down now."

Dropping back to the Bowl through the thick mist was an eerie sensation.

Malth would not dare drop her Weyrwoman, Orlith said stoutly.

I sincerely trust not but I cannot see my hand in front of my nose.

Then the green dragon daintily backwinged to land Moreta in the same spot by the Lower Caverns from which she had taken off. The fog rolled in a huge spiral as Malth spurted back to her weyr.

Not sweatroot, Moreta was thinking, to bring a fever out of a body. Featherfern to reduce it. Aconite to ease the heart? *That* bad a fever. And fellis juice for aches. Sh'gall had not reported aches in Capiam's symptoms. She wished she'd had a chance to talk to Berchar. Maybe she should see if K'lon was awake.

He sleeps, Orlith said. *You should sleep awhile.*

Moreta did feel weary now that the stimulus provided by Sh'gall's startling announcement had worn off. What had begun as a mist was now an impenetrable fog. She could get lost trying to find the infirmary.

You can always find me, Orlith assured her. *Turn slightly to your left and all you'll have to do is walk straight toward me. I'll have you back in the weyr safely.*

"I'll just have a few hours' sleep," Moreta said. She needed the rest that had been interrupted by Sh'gall's precipitous entry. She'd done what she could for now, and she'd check on her medicines before she went up the stairs to her weyr. She made the slight left turn.

Now just walk straight, Orlith advised her.

That was far easier for the dragon to say than for Moreta to do. In a few steps she couldn't even distinguish the bright yellow light from the Lower Caverns; then Orlith's mental touch steadied her and she walked on confidently, the mist swirling in behind her and pushing away before each time she raised a knee.

K'lon had recovered; her mind dwelled on that thought. Even if holders died, K'lon the dragonrider had survived. Sh'gall had been very tired, hadn't slept when he burst in on her, perhaps he had not got all his facts straight. No, S'peren had said something about illness. Fall was tomorrow and she'd had such a good day, with the exception of the runnerbeast's collapse.

Don't fret so, Orlith advised. *You have done all you can with so few people awake to tell. There is sure to be something in the Records. Leri will find it.*

"It's the fog, silly. It's depressing. I feel as if I'm moving nowhere forever."

You are near me now. You are almost at the steps.

And soon enough for Moreta to be wary. She kicked the bottom step with her right foot. Behind her the mist surged. She found the wall with one hand and then the frame to the storeroom. The tumblers of the lock were so old that Moreta often wondered why they bothered to use it. When the Pass was over, she'd speak to one of the mastersmiths. Now she didn't even need light for there was a click as the tumblers fell into place. She heaved at the massive door to start it swinging on its hinges. Even the fog could not mask the compound odors released by its opening. Moreta reached up and flipped open the glowbasket, her senses pleasantly assailed and reassured by the pungent spicyness of stored herbs. As she moved farther into the room, she could identify the subtler fragrances and smells. She didn't need to uncover the central light; she knew where the febrifuges were stored. To her eyes, the well-filled shelves and the bundles of featherfern drying on the rack looked more than adequate even if everyone in the Weyr were to come down with illness. She could very faintly hear the furtive slither of tunnel snakes. The pests had their own ways in and out of solid rock. She must get Nesso to put down more poison. Aconite was to the right: a square glass container full of the powdered root. Plenty of willow salic, and four large jars of fellis juice. Sh'gall had mentioned a cough. Moreta turned to those remedies: tussilago, comfrey, hyssop, thymus, ezob, borrago. More than enough. When the Ancients had made the Crossing, they had brought with them all the medicinal herbs and trees with which they had eased illness and discomfort. Surely some would answer the problem of the new disease.

She walked back to the door, closed the glow, resting her hand a moment on the door frame, smooth from generations of hands resting just as she did. Generations! Yes, generations that had survived all kinds of bizarre happenings and unusual illnesses, and would survive this one!

The fog had not abated, and she could see the staircase as only a darker shadow. Her foot kicked the first riser.

Be careful, Orlith said.

"I will." Moreta's right hand crept along the wall as she ascended. She seemed to be walking upward into nothing until her lead foot discovered the safety of the next step and the mist churned about her. But Orlith kept murmuring encouragement until Moreta laughed, saying she was only a few steps from her weyr and her bed. For all of that, she nearly missed her step at the landing for the light from her weyr was diminished to a feeble glow.

The weyr was noticeably warmer. The golden dragon's eyes gleamed as Moreta crossed to caress her, scratching Orlith's eye ridges. She leaned gratefully against Orlith's head, thinking that Orlith exuded an odor that was a combination of all the best herbs and spices.

You are tired. You must get some sleep now.

"Ordering me about again, huh?" But Moreta was on her way to her sleeping quarters. She pulled off tunic and trousers and, sliding into the furs, arranged them around her shoulders and was very quickly asleep.

CHAPTER VI

Ruatha Hold, Present Pass, 3.11.43

ALESSAN WATCHED AS the great dragon sprang into the air with Moreta lifting her arm in farewell. The dragon glowed in the dark-gray sky, and not from the feeble light of the dying lamp standards. Did her gravid state account for that luminescence? Then the phenomenon occurred for which Alessan waited: The golden glowing queen and her lovely Weyrwoman disappeared. A *whoosh* of air made the languid banners flutter.

Smiling, Alessan took a deep breath, well satisfied by the high moments of his first Gather as Lord of Ruatha Hold. As his sire had often repeated, good planning was the essence of success. True enough that good planning had resulted in his sprinter's win, but he had never counted on Moreta's company at the races—she had been such a spontaneous companion. Nor had he anticipated her dancing with him. He'd never had such an agile partner in the toss dance. Now, if his mother could find a girl in any way comparable to Moreta...

"Lord Alessan..."

He swung around, surprised out of his pleasant reverie by the hoarse whisper. Dag scuttled out of the shadows and stopped, bolt still, half a dozen paces from him.

"Lord Alessan..." The anxiety in Dag's voice and the formal address alerted Alessan.

"What's the matter, Dag? Squealer—"

"He's fine. But all Vander's animals is down with the cough, hacking out their lungs, feverish and breaking out in cold sweats. Some of those picketed next to Vander's lot are coughing, too, and sweating. Norman don't know what to make of it, it's so sudden. I know what I make of it, Lord Alessan, and so I'm going to take *our* animals, those that have been in the beasthold and ain't been near that lot in the pickets. I'm going to take 'em away before that cough spreads."

"Dag, I'm not—"

"Now, I ain't saying, Lord Alessan"—Dag raised his hand in a placatory gesture—"but what the cough could be the warm weather and a change of grass, but I'm not risking Squealer. Not after him winning."

Alessan suppressed a smile at Dag's vehemence.

"I'll just take our bloodstock up to the high nursery meadows—till *they* clear away." He jerked his thumb at the race flats. "I've packed some provisions and there're plenty of crevice snakes for eating. And I'll take that ruffian of a grandson of mine with me."

Second only to Squealer in Dag's affections was his daughter's youngest son, Fergal, a lively rascal who was more often in the black records than any other holdling. Alessan had a sneaking admiration for the lad's ingenuity, but as Lord Holder he could no longer condone the antics that Fergal inspired. His most recent prank had so angered Lady Oma, involving as it did the smirching of guest linens, that he had been forbidden to attend the Gather, and the punishment was enforced by locking the boy in the Hold's cell.

"If I thought—"

Dag laid a finger along his snub nose. "Better safe than sorry."

"Get along then." Alessan longed for sleep and Dag was plainly in an obstinate frame of mind. "And take that . . . that . . ."

"Dirty piece of laundry?" Dag's grin was slyly infectious.

"Yes, that's an apt description."

"I'll wait for a message from you, Alessan, that all the visitors have gone and taken their cough with 'em." Dag's grin broadened and he turned smartly on one heel, setting off toward the beasthold at such a clip that his bandy figure rolled from side to side.

Alessan watched his departure thoughtfully for a moment, wondering if he gave Dag too much latitude. Perhaps the old handler was covering up some new prank Fergal had pulled. But a cough spreading through the pickets was not so easily dismissed. When he'd had some sleep, he'd have a word with Norman, see if they had discovered why Vander's runner had died. That incident bothered Alessan. But a cough hadn't killed the runner. Was it possible that Vander, keen to win at the Gather, had ignored the signs of illness to bring his middistance runner? Alessan would prefer not to think so, but he knew well how the desire to win could grip a man.

Alessan made his way back to the hold on the roadway, passing dark lumps of people rolled in sleeping furs. It had been a good Gather and the weather had held. A slight dampness in the dawn air heralded fog or mist. But the weather wouldn't be the only thing foggy that day.

The Hall, too, was crowded with sleepers, and he walked carefully so as not to disturb anyone. Even the wide corridor outside his apartment accommodated Gatherers on straw pallets. He considered himself fortunate that his mother had not insisted he share his quarters. But then, perhaps she had hoped that he would! He smiled as he closed the door behind him and began to strip off his finery. It was only then he remembered that Moreta had not retrieved her Gather gown. No matter. That gave him an excuse to talk to her at the next Fall. He stretched out on his bed, pulled the furs over him, and was asleep in moments.

In what seemed like no time he was being so vigorously shaken that, for one disoriented moment, he thought he was a boy again, being attacked by his brothers.

"Alessan!" Lady Oma's indignant exclamation brought him to complete awareness. "Holder Vander is extremely ill and Masterhealer Scand insists that it is not from overindulgence. Two of the men who accompanied Vander are also feverish. Your race-course manager informs me also that four animals are dead and more appear to be sickening."

"Whose animals?" Alessan wondered if Dag had known more than he'd admitted.

"How should I know, Alessan?" Lady Oma had no interest at all in the runnerbeasts that were Ruatha's principal industry. "Lord Tolocamp is discussing it with—"

"Lord Tolocamp presumes!" Alessan rolled out of the bed, reached for his trousers in a fluid movement, stuffed his feet into the legs and pulled them up as he rose. He dragged a tunic over his head, slammed his feet into boots, kicking aside his discarded Gather finery. He forgot about the sleepers in the hallway and nearly trod on an arm before he checked his haste. Most of those who had slept in the Hall were awake and there was a clear path to the door. Cursing Tolocamp under his breath, Alessan managed a smile for those who noticed his passing.

Tolocamp was in the forecourt, an arm across his chest, propping the elbow of the other arm as he rubbed his chin, deep in thought. Norman was with him, shifting anxiously from foot to foot, his face gaunt from a sleepless night. As Alessan strode out, Norman's face brightened, and he turned eagerly toward his own Lord Holder.

"Good day to you, Tolocamp," Alessan said with scant courtesy, controlling the anger he felt at the older man's interference, however well intentioned. "Yes, Norman?"

He tried to draw the manager to one side but Tolocamp was not so easily evaded.

"This could be a very serious matter, Alessan," Tolocamp said, his heavy features set in a frown of portentous concern.

"I'll decide that, thank you." Alessan spoke so curtly that Tolocamp regarded him with astonishment. Alessan took the opportunity to move aside with Norman.

"Four of Vander's runners are dead," Norman said in a low voice, "and the other is dying. Nineteen beasts near them have broken out in sweats and coughing something pathetic."

"Have you isolated them from the healthy?"

"I've had men working on that since first light, Lord Alessan."

"Lady Oma said that Vander's ill as are two of his men?"

"Yes, sir. I called Masterhealer Scand to attend them last night. At first I thought that Vander was upset from losing his runner, but his two men are fevered. Now Helly's complaining of a terrible headache. As Helly don't drink, it can't be from last night."

"Vander had a headache yesterday, didn't he?"

"I don't rightly remember, Lord Alessan." Norman released a heavy sigh, pulling his hand across his forehead.

"Yes, of course, you did have rather a lot to manage, and the races went off very well indeed." Alessan grinned, reminding Norman of the times when he had been his assistant.

"I'm glad you think so, but—" Norman's attention was held by something in the road and he pointed at a travel wagon, four runners led from its tailgate. "I'm worried about Kulan's leaving."

Even as the men watched, one of the led horses coughed violently.

"I told Kulan he hadn't ought to be traveling with that runner but he won't listen to me."

"How many decamped this morning?" Alessan felt the first stir of real apprehension. If a coughing illness spread through the Hold with the plowing only half completed . . .

"Some dozen left first light, mainly wagontravelers. Their stock wasn't pastured near the racers. It's just that I know Kulan's one is sick."

"I'll speak to him. You find out how many have started home. Tell some of the holders to report to me here as messengers. We'll retrieve our departed guests. No animals are to leave this Hold until we know what causes that cough."

"What about people?"

"Since the one usually takes the other, no, no people. And I'll want to have a word with Master Scand about Vander, too."

Kulan was not pleased to be halted. The animal only had a morning cough, he asserted, from the dust raised the night before and the change in grass. It'd be fine once it got moving. Kulan was anxious. He had three days' hard travel before he reached his hold. He'd left his next oldest son in charge and had doubts about the lad's capabilities. Alessan pointed out firmly that Kulan wouldn't want to bring an infected beast home to mingle with his healthy stock. Another day to find out what the ailment was would be well worth a delay.

Tolocamp followed, reaching Alessan and his holderman in time to catch the end of the argument. The older Lord's polite concern became an active anxiety but he held his peace until Kulan and his handlers had turned back to the Gather fields.

"Are such drastic measures necessary? I mean, these people must get back to their holds, as I must return to mine—"

"A slight delay, Tolocamp, until we see how the animals fare. Surely you and your good ladies would be glad of a longer visit?"

Tolocamp blinked, surprised by Alessan's smiling intransigence. "They may stay if they wish but I was about to request you to drum Fort Weyr for a conveyance."

"As you yourself said a few minutes ago, Tolocamp, this could be a serious matter. It is. Neither of us can afford to have a sickness run through our stock. Not at this time of the Turn. Of course, we may find that it only affects the racers, but I would fault myself severely if I didn't take preventive measures now, before the infection can spread from the Hold proper." Alessan watched Tolocamp's obvious reflections over the merits of a delay. "Kulan's one of mine, but I'd take it kindly if you would speak to those of your own Hold who gathered with us. I'm not spreading alarm but four racers dead and more coughing in the picket lines . . ."

"Well, now . . ."

"Thank you, Tolocamp. I knew I could count on your cooperation."

Alessan moved away swiftly before Tolocamp could muster an argument. He made for the kitchens where weary drudges were preparing large pitchers of klah and trays of fruits and sweetbreads. As he had hoped, he found Oklina supervising. From the fatigue apparent on her face, she hadn't had any sleep.

"Oklina, there's trouble," he told her quietly. "Sickness down at the flats. Tell Lady Oma that, until I'm sure what it is and how it can be cured, no one is to leave the Hold. Her powers of persuasion and hospitality are required."

Oklina's dark eyes had widened with alarm but she controlled her expression and peremptorily called one of the drudges to task for spilling klah.

"Where's our brother, Makfar?" Alessan asked. "Asleep above?"

"He's gone. They left about two hours ago."

Alessan rubbed his face. Makfar had had two runners in the racing. "When you've spoken to Mother, send a messenger after them. The way Makfar travels, they won't have gone far. Say, say . . ."

"That you have urgent need of Makfar's *advice*." Oklina grinned.

"Exactly." He gave her an affectionate pat on the shoulder. "And inform our other brothers that security is required for the Hold proper."

By the time Alessan returned to the forecourt, Norman had arrived with a number of Ruathan holders. Alessan told them to find short swords and ride in pairs along the main roads to turn back travelers on whatever pretext came to mind. The holders were ordered to use force where persuasion failed. His brothers, in varying stages of discontent, reported to him. He dispatched them to get arms and assist the messengers, if need be, but to be sure that no one else left the Hold. Just then Lord Tolocamp bustled out of the Hall. He looked full of arguments.

"Alessan, now I'm not sure that all this fuss is absolutely necessary—"

Echoing up from the south, the message drums of River Hold could be heard plainly. As Alessan counted the double-urgent salutation and heard the healer code as originator, he took a moment's pleasure in the astonishment on Tolocamp's face, but lost it as the meat of the message boomed out. Those who could not understand the code caught the fear generated by those who did. Drums were a fine method of communication but too bloody public, Alessan thought savagely.

Epidemic disease, the drums rolled, *spreading rapidly across continent from Igen, Keroon, Telgar, Ista. Highly infectious. Highly contagious. Two to four days' incubation. Headache. Fever. Cough. Prevent secondary infection. Fatalities high. Medicate symptoms. Isolate victims. Quarantine effective immediately. Runnerbeasts highly susceptible. Repeat Epidemic warning. No travel permitted. Congregating discouraged. Capiam.*

The final roll commanded the pass-on of the message.

"But there's been a Gather here!" Tolocamp exclaimed fatuously. "No one's sick but a handful of runners. And they haven't been at Igen or Keroon, or anywhere!" Tolocamp glared at Alessan as if the alarm was somehow at his instigation.

"Vander's sick and two of his handlers—"

"Too much to drink," Tolocamp asserted. "It can't be the same thing. Capiam just says the illness is spreading, not that it's here in Ruatha."

"When the Masterhealer of Pern calls a quarantine," Alessan said in a soft angry voice, "it is my duty, and yours, Lord Tolocamp, to respect his authority!" Alessan didn't realize that he sounded very much like his sire at that moment, but Tolocamp was silenced.

That was all the time they had to speak for those who had understood the drum message were now searching for the two Lords Holder.

"What's Capiam talking about?"

"We can't be quarantined! I've got to get back to my hold."

"I left stock near to birthing..."

"My wife stayed at the cot with our babies..."

Tolocamp rallied, standing stolidly by Alessan's side, confirming the dreadful message and Capiam's right to broadcast a quarantine restriction.

"Master Capiam is not an alarmist!" "We'll have further details once that message has passed." "This is just a precaution." "Yes, a runner-beast did die yesterday." "Master Scand will tell us more." "No, no one may be permitted to leave. Might endanger your own hold and spread illness further." "A few days is not too much for health's sake."

Alessan answered almost by rote, letting the first panic roll over his head. He had already taken the first steps toward recalling people and to avert a mass exodus. He and Tolocamp did their best to quiet apprehension. Alessan rapidly calculated how much food he had in convenient storage. The Gatherers would soon exhaust their travel rations. Assuming some people might catch Vander's illness—if it was Capiam's epidemic, would it be better to house them in the Hall? Or clear one of the beastholds? The Hold's infirmary could accommodate no more than twenty and that with crowding. Four dead animals, another dying, and Norman said nineteen more were coughing? Twenty-four animals out of a hundred twenty-two in twenty-four hours? The emergency had nothing to do with what he had been trained to meet. Nothing to do with the immemorial evil that ravaged Pern. As impartially as Thread, this new and equally insidious menace would blight the inhabitants as Thread could devastate the land. "Fatalities high," the message had said. Were there no dragons to combat disease? Was this sort of disaster provided for in the Hold Records his father had always referred to?

"Here comes your healer, Alessan," said Tolocamp.

The two Lords Holder moved to intercept Master Scand before he reached the forecourt. The man's usually placid round face was nearly purple with his exertions, his mouth thinned by annoyance. He was sweating copiously and blotting his face and neck with a none-too-clean cloth. Alessan had always thought Scand merely an adequate healer, suitable to attend the Hold's large number of pregnancies and treat occasional accidents, but not up to a major emergency.

"Lord Alessan, Lord Tolocamp," Scand panted, his chest heaving, "I came as soon as I received your summons. Did I not hear drums? Did I not recognize the healer code? Is something the matter?"

"What ails Vander?"

The sharpness of Alessan's question put Scand on his guard. He cleared his throat and mopped his face, reluctant to commit himself. "Well, now, as to that I am perplexed for he has not responded to the draught of sweatroot which I prepared for him last night. A dose, I might add, that would have made a dragon perspire. It was ineffectual." Scand blotted his face again. "The man complains of terrible heart palpitations and of a headache that has nothing to do with wine because I was assured that he didn't indulge—he felt unwell yesterday even before the races."

"And the other two men? His handlers?"

"They, too, are legitimately ill." Scand's pompous speech had always irritated Alessan. Today he brandished his sweaty cloth in his affected pauses. "Legitimately ill, I fear, with severe headaches that render them unable to rise from their pallets, as well as the palpitations of which Holder Vander complains. Indeed, I am inclined to treat them for those two symptoms, rather than sweat them, although that is the specific treatment for unidentified sudden fevers. Now, may I inquire if that message from the Healer Hall in any way concerns me?" Scand cocked his head inquisitively.

"Master Capiam has called a quarantine."

"Quarantine? For three men?"

"Lord Alessan," said a tall lean man, wearing harper blue. He had grizzled hair and a nose that had suffered from many an unexpected adjustment to its direction. His glance was direct and his manner quietly capable. "I'm Tuero, journeyman harper. I can give Master Scand the full text so that you can get on." Tuero jerked his head to the people milling excitedly in the forecourt.

Just then Ruatha's drummer began to relay the news onward to the large northerly and western holds, the instruments' deep reverberations adding to the general atmosphere of apprehension. Lady Oma emerged from the Hall with Lady Pendra and her daughters. Lady Oma listened intently to the drum then gave Alessan one long steady look. She and the Fort Hold women converged on Harper Tuero and the healer, who was now dithering, his face cloth hanging from his limp hand.

For the first time in his life, Alessan had cause to be grateful for the unquestioning support of his bloodkin and even for the officiousness of Lord Tolocamp. A rider galloped back to request aid in bringing in one of the more aggressive holders with whom Alessan had already had trouble. Then Makfar's family wagon thundered in, scattering folk in the roadway. Alessan put him in charge of improvising shelters from Gather stalls and travel wagons. It was one thing to doss down in a corridor for a night or grab a few hours' sleep in the Hall, but quite another matter to be so cramped for four nights. Tolocamp was not the only one who failed to see the irony of that as he countered Makfar's suggestions with some of his own. Alessan left the two to solve the housing problem so that he could accompany Norman to the race flats and survey the sick runners. People were already making small camps in the first of the fields.

Despite his errand, it was a relief to Alessan to get away from the turmoil about the forecourt.

"Never saw anything bring down so many so fast, Lord Alessan."
Norman had almost to run to keep up with Alessan's long-legged stride.
"And I can't think what to do for 'em. If there is anything. Healer's
message didn't say much about animals, did it?" His voice was bleak.
"A runner can't tell you if it ails."

"It goes off feed and water."

"Not wagon beasts. They go till they drop."

Both men looked across the fields where the Hold's sturdy cart and
wagon runnerbeasts grazed—the ones Alessan had bred to his sire's
specifications.

"Set up a buffer area. Keep racers and wagoners well separated."

"I will, Lord Alessan, but the racers have been drinking upriver of
them!"

"It's a wide river, Norman. Hope for the best."

The first thing Alessan noticed at the flats was that the manager had
utilized the entire spread of picket lines. The healthy beasts were on
the outside, well away from the cleared circle surrounding the sick ones.
The coughing of the infected beasts was audible on the still, slightly
chill air. They coughed, necks extended, mouths gaping, in hard painful-
sounding barks. Their legs were swollen, their hides dull and starring.

"Add featherfern and thymus to their water. If they'll drink, Norman.
Use a syringe to get fluid into them before they dehydrate completely.
We might offer nettleweed, too. Some runners are smart enough to
know what's good for them. Nettles, at least, are in plentiful supply."
Alessan gazed out over the meadows where the annual battle to reduce
the perennial had not yet started. "Any coughs among the herdbeasts?"
He swung in the other direction.

"Truth to tell, I've had little time to think about them." Norman had
the dedicated racer's almost contemptuous disdain for the placid herd
creatures. "Harper told me the drums only mentioned runners."

"Well, we'll have to slaughter herdbeasts to feed our unexpected
guests. I don't have enough fresh meat left after the Gather."

"Lord Alessan, did Dag . . ." Norman began tentatively, with a half-
gesture toward the cliff, to the great apertures where the Hold's animals
were normally sheltered during Threadfall.

Alessan gave Norman a shrewd glance.

"So, you were in on that?"

"Sir, I was," Norman replied staunchly. "Dag and I got worried
when the cough started to spread. Didn't want to interrupt your dancing,
but as the bloodstock had no contact with these—Look at that!"

"Shards!"

They watched as the leader in a team of four hitched to a big wagon
collapsed in the traces, pulling its harness mate to its knees.

"Right, Norman. Get some men up to take charge of that team. Use
them as long as they last to haul carcasses. Burn the dead animals down

there." Alessan pointed to a dip in the far fields, out of sight from the forecourt and downwind. "Keep track of the dead beasts. Reparation should be made."

"I've no recorder."

"I'll send down one of the fosterlings. I'll also want to know how many people stayed the night down here."

"Most of the handlers stayed, and some keen ones like old Runel and his two cronies. Some of the breeders were in and out, not caring much for the dancing after you were thoughtful enough to send a few kegs down here."

"I wish we knew more about this illness. 'Medicate the symptoms,' the drums said." Alessan looked back at the lines of coughing animals.

"Then we give 'em thymus and featherfern, and nettles. Maybe we'll get a message from the Masterherdsman. Could be on its way from the east right now." Norman looked confidently in that direction.

Help didn't usually come from the east, Alessan thought, but he clapped Norman reassuringly on the shoulder. "Just do the best you can!"

"You can count on me, Lord Alessan."

Norman's quietly issued assurance heartened Alessan as he took the shorter way across the stubble field to the hold. Was it only the day before that he and Moreta had paused on the rise to watch the racing? She had touched Vander's dying runner! Alessan's stride faltered. The Weyr would have received the drum message before Ruatha did. She would know by now the consequences of her act. She would also probably know better how to prevent falling ill herself.

As did everyone of Ruatha Hold, he knew the Fort Weyrwoman by sight, but Alessan had always been on the fringes of such Hold gatherings as she had attended since achieving her senior position in the Weyr. So he had thought her a distant, self-contained person, totally immersed in Weyr culture. The discovery that her fascination with racing was as keen as his own had been an unexpected delight. Lady Oma had rebuked him firmly at one point in the early evening for taking so much of Moreta's time. Alessan knew perfectly well that she meant that he was not making the most of the chance to meet eligible girls. He knew, too, that he must soon secure his bloodline and so he had tried to be properly receptive until he saw Moreta slip behind the harpers' dais. By then he had had enough of stammering insipidity and timorousness. He had acquitted his duty as Lord Holder but he was also going to enjoy himself at his first Gather. In Moreta's company. And he had. Alessan had been raised to anticipate both just reward and just punishment. Momentarily the thought that today's trials balanced yesterday's pleasures sprang to his mind but was quickly rejected as juvenile.

The situation at the racing flats observed, Alessan decided the next priority would be to send messages to those expecting the return of the Gatherers to those holds outside the message-drum system. Otherwise he would have anxious people coming to the Hold. Next he'd have to discover who else had brought in new stock from Keroon as Vander had done, whether the beasts were in holds or fields, and destroy them. He would also have to figure out how to deal with dissidents. The Hold's one small cell might secure a small boy like Fergal but not an aggressive holder.

Tolocamp, who had been directing those spreading a tent over the half-walled southern addition, intercepted Alessan.

"Lord Alessan," the older man said, stiffly formal, his face expressionless, jaw clenched, "while I realize that the quarantine affects me as well, I must return to Fort Hold. I will keep to myself in my apartment, making contact with no one. If this"—Tolocamp gestured toward the confusion in the roadway and Gather fields—"is occurring here, think of the turmoil caused by my absence from Fort Hold."

"My Lord Tolocamp, I have always been under the impression that your sons were superbly trained to take over any Hold duties and perform them flawlessly."

"So they are." Tolocamp stood even more stiffly erect. "So they are. I put Campen in charge when I left for your Gather. To give him experience in assuming leadership—"

"Good. This quarantine should afford him an unparalleled opportunity."

"My dear Alessan, this emergency is outside his experience, too."

Alessan gritted his teeth, wondering if he had underestimated Tolocamp's perception.

"Lord Tolocamp, you are more familiar than I with a double-urgent code sent by a Mastercraftsman. Would you permit anyone to disobey it?"

"No, no, of course not. But this is an unusual circumstance—"

"Quite. Your son has no Gather guests to deal with." Both men could see a group being shepherded back by two of Alessan's brothers and six men with drawn swords. "Campen has the Healer Hall as well as the Masterharper to instruct him in the emergency." Alessan moderated his harsh tone. He must not alienate Tolocamp. He'd need Tolocamp's support with some of the older men in his Hold who were not yet accustomed to taking orders from someone as young and untried in Holding. "As the drum message said, two to four days' incubation. You've been here a day already," he added persuasively, glancing up at the noon-high sun. "In another day, if you show no signs of discomfort yourself, you could discreetly return to Fort Hold. Meanwhile, you should set an example."

"Yes, well. Hold one, hold all." Tolocamp's expression mellowed.

"It is true that it would be very poor discipline for me to break a quarantine." He became noticeably more amenable. "This outbreak is probably confined to the racing flats. I never have followed the sport." A disdainful wave of his hand dismissed one of the major pastimes of Pern.

Alessan did not take umbrage because a party of men now bore purposefully down on the two Lords Holder, their expressions determined and anxious.

"Lord Alessan . . ."

"Yes, Turvine," Alessan replied to the man, a crop holder in the southeastern corner of Ruatha. His companions were herdsmen.

"We've no drums near us and we're expected back. I'm not one to go against Healer's advice but there are other considerations. We can't bide here . . ."

Makfar had noticed the deputation and, although Alessan gave Turvine his complete attention, he was aware that his brother had signaled several armed holders to converge.

"You'll bide here! That's my order!" Alessan spoke forcefully and the men backed off, looking uncertainly for support from Tolocamp. The Fort Holder stiffened, ignoring their tacit plea. Alessan raised his voice, projecting it beyond the group to those watching and listening from the roadway and the forecourt. "The drums have decreed the quarantine! I am your Lord Holder. As surely as if Thread were Falling, you are under my orders. No one, no animal leaves here until that drum"—Alessan jabbed his arm at the tower—"tells us that the quarantine is lifted!"

In the silence that ensued, Alessan strode rapidly toward the hall door, Tolocamp in step beside him.

"You will have to get messages out to prevent people coming in," Tolocamp said in a low voice when they were inside the Hall.

"I know that. I just have to figure out how. Without exposing animals or people." Alessan swung to the left, into the Hold's office where the bloody Records he did not have time to peruse were stacked in accusing ranks. Although the office had been put to use as sleeping space during the Gather, it was vacant but sleeping furs were scattered about, their owners apparently having left them in haste. Alessan kicked several aside to reach his maps. He finally located the small-scale chart of the Holding on which the roads were marked in different colors for trail, track, or path, and the holds similarly differentiated.

Tolocamp exclaimed in surprise at the fine quality of the map. "I'd no idea you were so well equipped," he said with a want of tact.

"As the harpers are fond of telling us," Alessan said, with a slight smile to sweeten his words, "Fort Hold happened, but Ruatha was planned." He traced a forefinger up the northern trail, to the dividing tracks that went northwest, west, and northeast, reaching twenty holds, large and small, and three mineholds. The main western trail through the mountains wandered with occasional hazards into the plateau.

"Lord Alessan . . ."

He turned and saw Tuero at the door, the other harpers behind him in the corridor.

"I thought we might volunteer as messengers." Tuero grinned, which made his long, crooked nose slant even more dramatically to the left. "That's the subject of rather heated discussions outside. The harpers of Pern are at your disposal."

"I thank you, but you've been as exposed as anyone else here, It's the disease I wish to contain, not the people."

"Lord Alessan"—Tuero was smilingly insistent—"a message can be *relayed*." Tuero mimed putting something down quickly with one hand and taking it up in the other with a sharp pull. He walked quickly to the map. "Someone in this hold"—he stabbed at the first one of the northern track—"could take a message to the next one, and so on, relaying instructions as well as the drum call."

Alessan stared at the map, mentally reviewing the inhabitants of the holds and cots. Even the farthest settlement, the iron minehold, was no more than three days' hard riding. Dag would have taken the fastest runners, Squealer's ilk, with him, but there would be beasts to make the first leg of the relay, and no risk to other stock if the runner returned to Ruatha. If the runner returned . . .

"And as none of us has any reason to stay away from your bountiful hospitality, you can depend on us to return. Besides, this sort of thing is *our* duty."

"A very good point," Tolocamp murmured.

"I concur. So, may I leave it to you, Tuero, to organize the contents of the messages and instructions to be forwarded by this relay system of yours? Drum messages went here, here, here, and here." Alessan tapped the cardinal holds. "I doubt if they would have thought of communicating the bad news to the smaller places. Seven holds are capable of supplying runners for the relay, each covering outlying cotholds."

"How fortunate that we are seven!"

Alessan grinned. "Indeed, Tuero. Let the harpers spread the news that heralds are available. Our drummer is still in the drum tower, I take it—well, then, his supplies are in those cupboards: ink and hide and pen. Let me know when you're available. I've travel maps. I'll arrange mounts. You'll want to be quick about this business or risk sleeping out."

"That's no novelty for harpers, I assure you."

"And you might discover, if you can, who else brought in animals from Keroon over the past few weeks."

"Oh?" Both Tuero's eyebrows lifted expressing surprise.

"Vander picked up new runners from a ship out of Keroon—"

"The drum mentioned Keroon, didn't it? We'll find out. This winter's lack of ice is not the blessing it seemed, eh?"

"Not at all!"

"Ah, well, it's not ended yet!" With a quick courteous bow of his head, Tuero led his craftfellows off to the main hall.

"Alessan, there is so much to be done, too, at Fort—" Tolocamp pleaded.

"Tolocamp, Farelly is in the drum tower and at your disposal." Alessan waved him courteously toward the tower steps and then left the office. Lord Leef had once confided that the way to avoid arguments was to keep them from starting. Tactful withdrawal, he had called it.

Alessan paused briefly in the shadow of the Hall doors, observing the activity in the forecourt, along the roadway, and beyond. Tents had been raised, small fires had tripods, kettles hung above the flames, a new fire had been started in the roasting pit and the spit reset. From the east a party of mounted riders and a string of runners were slowly walking up the road, the leader flanked by Alessan's next oldest brother, Dangel, and two Ruathan cotholders, all three men with drawn swords. He'd asked Dangel where to put Baid, the reluctant cropholder. Above the dip where he'd told Norman to burn the dead beasts, a thin gout of black smoke hovered. Yes, anyone apprehended leaving the hold proper could serve on the burial detail.

A rider, running his mount hard, galloped up the stubble field, clattering over the roadway, dodging tent and fire. The rider jumped down, looking anxiously about him. When Alessan stepped out of the shadow, the rider dropped his reins and ran to him.

"Lord Alessan, Vander's dead!"

CHAPTER VII

Healer Hall and Fort Weyr, Present Pass, 3.11.43

THE BOOMING REVERBERATED through Capiam's head until he woke, clutching at his skull defensively. The drumming had even haunted his nightmares before he woke. He could hardly call the vivid scenes that had tortured him dreams, and his awakening was as much a protest against them as against the intrusive rhythms. He lay in his bed, spent with the effort of renewed consciousness. Another drum roll caused him to haul the pillows feebly over his head.

Would they never stop? He'd no idea that the drums were so infernally loud. Why had he never noticed them before? The Healers really deserved their own quiet precinct. He was forced to add his hands to his ears to obtain some relief from the throbbing. Then he remembered the messages that he had left to be relayed to all the major Halls and Holds. Had they taken so long to send them? It must be midday! Didn't the drum master realize how important a quarantine was? Or had some snide little apprentice mislaid the messages to allow time for his own sleep?

The ache in his skull was like nothing Capiam could remember. Intolerable. And his heartbeat had speeded up to the drum tempo. Highly unusual! Capiam lay in the bed, his head painfully resounding and his heart doing its own peculiar unsyncopated palpitation.

Mercifully the drums ceased presently, but neither his head nor his heart took any notice. Rolling to his side, Capiam attempted to sit up. He must have relief from this headache. Swinging his feet to the floor, he levered his body up. A groan of agony was forced from him as he managed to sit upright. The pain in his head intensified as he staggered to his cupboard.

Fellis juice. A few drops. That would do the trick. It never failed him. He measured the dose, blinking to clear his blurred vision, then splashed water into the cup and swallowed the mixture. He wove back to his bed, unable to remain perpendicular. He was panting from the slight effort and realized that not only had the frantic beat of his heart increased, but he was sweating profusely from a simple few steps across his own room.

He had had too much experience with sleepless nights and tight schedules to chalk up his condition to such things. He groaned again. He didn't have *time* to be sick. He ought not to have contracted the damnable disease. Healers didn't *get* sick. Besides, he'd been so careful to wash thoroughly in redwort solution after examining each patient.

Why didn't the fellis juice work? He couldn't think with the headache. But he had to think. There was so much to be done. His notes to organize, to analyze the course of the disease and the probability of dangerous secondary infections, like pneumonia and other respiratory infections. But how could he work when he couldn't hold his eyes open? Groaning again at the injustice of his situation, he pressed his hands to his temples and then to his hot, moist forehead. Shards! He was burning up with fever.

He was aware that someone else was in the room before he heard the slight sound of entry. "Don't come near me," he said urgently, holding up one hand abruptly and uttering another cry of pain when his injudicious movement increased the ache in his head.

"I won't."

"Desdra!" An exaggerated breath escape his lips.

"I had an apprentice posted at your door to listen for sounds, but I wouldn't let anyone disturb you until you'd slept yourself out." Her calm unexcitable voice reassured him. "You've caught this fever of yours?"

"There's an ironic justice in that, you know." Capiam's sense of humor seldom left him.

"There would be if you weren't the most sought-after man on Pern."

"The quarantine isn't popular?"

"You might say so. Drum tower's been besieged. Fortine's been coping."

"My notes are in my pack. Give them to Fortine. He's much better at organizing than diagnosing. He'll have all I've discovered about this epidemic."

Desdra glided across the floor and took the Healer's note case from the pack. She flipped it open. "Which isn't much."

"No, but I'll soon understand it all much better."

"Nothing like personal experience. What do you need?"

"Nothing! No, not nothing. I'll want water, any fresh juice—"

"You cut off our supplies with that quarantine—"

"Then water will suffice. No one is to enter this room, and *you* are not to come farther than the door. Anything I ask for must be left on the table."

"I am quite prepared to stay in here with you."

He shook his head and regretted the motion. "No. I'd rather be by myself."

"Suffer in silence."

"Don't mock, woman. This disease is highly contagious. Has anyone else in Hall or Hold contracted it?"

"As of a half-hour ago, no."

"It's now?" Capiam was simply unable to see the timepiece.

"Late afternoon. Four."

"Anyone who was at either Gather and returns here—"

"Which is forbidden by your drum message—"

"Some wise-ass will think he knows better...Anyone who comes is to be isolated for four days. Two seem to be the usual incubation period, judging by the best reports—"

"And your good self—"

"Experience teaches. I don't know yet how long someone *stays* infectious so we must be doubly wary. I shall keep notes on my symptoms and progress. They will be here...in case..."

"My, we are being dramatic."

"You've always maintained that I'd die of something I couldn't cure."

"Don't talk like that, Capiam!" Desdra sounded more angry than fearful. "Master Fortine has apprentices and journeymen at the Records round the clock."

"I know. I heard their snores last night."

"So Master Fortine surmised when no one could tell him your time of return. Unfortunately Master Fortine must have only just retired himself for he didn't get back to his desk until noon. He will want to see you."

"He's not to come in here."

"He'll doubtless prefer not to."

Why wasn't the fellis juice taking effect? The palpitations of his heart were dramatic!

"Tell Fortine, will you, Desdra, that sweatroot has no effect and provides no relief. In fact, I think it is counterproductive. That's what they were using in Igen and Keroon for the first stage of the illness. Tell Fortine to try featherfern to reduce fever. Tell him to try other febrifuges."

"What? All on the same poor patient?"

"He will have patients enough for the different remedies." Capiam spoke from wretched certainty. "Go, Desdra. My head is a drum tower."

Desdra was cruel enough to chuckle softly. Or maybe she thought she was being sympathetic? One never knew what reaction to expect from Desdra. That was part of her charm, but she'd never make Master on the strength of it. She spoke her mind and sometimes a healer *had* to be diplomatic and soothing. She certainly didn't soothe Capiam. But he was relieved that she was in charge of him.

He lay supine, trying to rest his head as lightly as possible on a pillow that had apparently turned into stone. He willed the pain to subside, willed the fellis juice to dispense its numbing magic. His heart thudded. Erratic heartbeat had been mentioned by many of the patients. He'd had no idea that the symptom would be so severe. He hoped it would subside when the fellis juice took effect.

He lay for what seemed a very long time and, although the ache in his skull appreciably lessened, the palpitations did not. If he could just regain a normal heartbeat, he might be able to sleep. He was very conscious of his bone-deep weariness and that he had not benefited from that nightmare-filled sleep. He reviewed the appropriate herbs to relieve palpitations: whitethorn, adonis, glovecap, tansy, aconite, and decided on the latter, the old reliable root.

His rising from the bed was accompanied by much effort and suppressed moans—suppressed because Capiam did not want apprentice ears to witness masterly weakness. It was enough that the Masterhealer had basely succumbed; the grim details of his travail need not be advertised.

Two drops should suffice. It was a strong drug and must always be administered carefully. He remembered to secure a writing hide from his supply, gathered up ink and pen, and took all back to his bed, where he arranged his stool as his writing desk. Heart still pounding. Capiam composed his first entries, carefully noting the day and the exact time.

He was grateful to lie down again. He concentrated on his breathing, slowing it and willing his heart to slow. At some point in the exercise, sleep overcame him.

Holth is upset. He is angry and so is Leri. Orlith's concerned but apologetic tone roused Moreta from a profound slumber.

"Why didn't he stay asleep and leave the ordering of the Weyr to me?"

He says Leri is too old to fly, and the plague kills the elderly first.

"Scorch him! This epidemic business has addled his wits!" She dressed quickly, grimacing as she stuffed her feet into clammy boots.

Leri says that she must speak with the ground crews, especially at a time like this, to find out who gets ill and to spread the word. She says she can do so without unnecessary physical contact.

"Of course she can." Leri had never been in the habit of dismounting to accept ground-crew reports. She was not tall and remaining on her queen gave her many advantages.

Moreta raced up the stairs through the thick fog. She could hear Holth's agitated rumblings by the time she reached the weyr entrance. Sh'gall's angry voice made her quicken so that she entered the weyr in a burst of speed.

"How dare you interfere with the queens' wing?" she demanded, allowing her momentum to carry her right up to him.

He spun around and, holding both hands up to keep her at a distance, backed off. Blinking with distress, Holth was swinging her head anxiously from side to side over Leri. A Weyrleader was an unlikely source of danger for her rider.

"How dare you upset Holth and Leri?" Moreta shouted.

"I'm not yet so decrepit I can't handle an hysterical bronze rider!" Leri retorted, her eyes snapping with anger.

"You queens stick together, don't you," Sh'gall shouted back, "against all logic and reason!"

Holth roared, and from the weyr below, Orlith trumpeted; then the fog resounded with dragon queries.

"Calm down, Sh'gall! We don't need the Weyr in an uproar!" Leri spoke in a tense but controlled voice, her eyes catching and holding Sh'gall's. She might have retired as senior Weyrwoman but just then she exuded the unmistakable authority of her many Turns in that position. When Sh'gall looked away, Leri glanced sternly at Moreta. The younger Weyrwoman spoke soothingly to Orlith and the furor outside the weyr subsided. Holth stopped her agitated head-swinging.

"Now!" Leri folded her hands over the cumbersome Record she was trying to keep in her short lap. "A fine time to be quarreling over small points. The Weyr needs undivided leadership now more than ever— we've a double threat to overcome. So let me tell you a few things, Sh'gall, that you seem to have overlooked in your very laudable concern for protecting the Weyr from this plague of Capiam's. As of yesterday's Gathers there can't be many of our dragonriders who haven't been exposed to it. In fact, you're the most likely carrier since you were actually in the infirmary at Southern Boll as well as at Ista, viewing that poor beast."

"I never went into the infirmary and I never touched the feline. I washed thoroughly in the Ice Lake before I returned to the Weyr."

"So that's why your wits are slow—too bad your tongue thawed first! Hold it, Weyrleader!" Leri's forceful tone and her stern face quelled the retort on the bronze rider's lips. "Now, while you slept, Moreta was busy. So was I." She hefted the heavy Record in her lap.

"The watchriders all know to deny the Weyr, not that anyone's likely to be flying in this fog after two Gathers. The drum towers of Fort Hold have been booming all day. Peterpar's checked the herds for sign of illness, which isn't likely since the last drove came from Tillek. Nesso has been busy talking to those sober enough to absorb information. K'lon continues to improve. Moreta, exactly what do you think is wrong with Berchar?"

Moreta had never doubted that Leri kept an ear on everything that occurred outside her weyr, but the former Weyrwoman was too discreet to display her knowledge.

"Berchar?" Sh'gall exclaimed. "What's wrong with him?"

"Quite likely what ailed K'lon. At Berchar's instructions, S'gor isolated him and will himself remain weyrbound."

Sh'gall began to sputter with the questions he wanted to ask.

"If K'lon has recovered, Berchar should as well," Moreta continued reasonably.

"Two sick!" Sh'gall's hand went to his throat, then his forehead.

"If Capiam says two to four days before the onset of illness, you shouldn't be feeling ill yet," Leri said bluntly but not unkindly. "You'll lead in tomorrow's Fall. Holth and I will fly with the queens' wing and, as is my custom, I will receive ground-crew reports—that is, if any ground crew are about. It's unlikely that Nabol and Crom will panic. A disease would have to be desperate indeed to seek victims in those forsaken holds. As is my custom, I shall remain on Holth, thus keeping to a minimum any possible contagion. It is essential to the main duty of the Weyrs to keep in contact with every holder. Without ground crews to assist us, we'd have twice the work. Do you not agree, Weyrleader?"

Judging by the consternation on Sh'gall's face, he had not yet considered the possibility of inadequate ground-crew support.

"Not that it would matter if I did contract this plague of Capiam's. As well as being elderly"—Leri cast a malicious glance at Sh'gall—"I'm certainly the most expendable rider."

Holth and Orlith trumpeted in alarm. Even Kadith spoke as Moreta rushed to embrace Leri, her throat suddenly thick at the casual remark.

"You are not expendable! You are not! You're the most valiant of all the queen riders on Pern."

Leri gently disentangled herself from Moreta's fierce grasp then dismissed Sh'gall imperiously. "Go. All that can be done has been done."

"I'll get Kadith settled," he said, leaving as if pursued.

"And you settle yourself," Leri said to Moreta. "I'm worth no one's tears. Besides, it is true. I am expendable. I think Holth would like to rest and she can't until I do, you know."

"Leri! Don't say such things! What would I do without you?"

Leri gave her a long searching look, her eyes very bright. "Why, my girl, you'd do what you have to. You always will. But *I'd* miss *you*. Now, you'd best get down to the Cavern. Everyone will have heard the queens sounding off and Kadith's tizzy. They'll need to be reassured."

Moreta stepped back from Holth's couch and Leri, abashed by the intensity of her feeling.

"You're not worried because you touched that runner at Ruatha, are you?"

"Not particularly." Moreta shrugged diffidently. "But I did and it's done. My rash impulses always worried L'mal—"

"Not half as much as your ability to deal with injured dragons pleased him. Now go, before they have too much time to fret themselves. Oh, and would you take this piece of harness to T'ral to be mended?" She chucked a roll of leatherstrap to Moreta. "Would never do for me to tumble off, would it? Such an ignominious end! Go on now, girl. And check your own harness—routine is reassuring in times like these. I wish to continue my fascinating reading!" Leri made a comical grimace as she tugged the Record volume into a more comfortable position.

Moreta left Leri's weyr, her fingers finding the stretched length in the strap. She re-coiled it. In a subdued mood, Moreta dutifully inspected her own harness, which she had oiled after the last Fall and hung neatly on its pegs.

I did not like to wake you but when Holth asked, I did.

"And you did exactly as you should."

Holth is a great queen. Orlith's eyes whirled brightly.

"And Leri is marvelous." Moreta went to her queen, who lowered her head to accept her rider's caresses. "This will be the last Fall you fly for a while!" she added, assessing the bulge in Orlith's belly.

I will fly tomorrow. I can fly in need as well.

"Don't you fret about my riding Malth that short hop!"

I don't. I do wish you to know that I can always fly you.

"There could be no need so great to take you from your eggs, my love." Moreta stroked the bulges appreciatively. "A good clutch, I think."

I know. A degree of smug satisfaction tinged her tone.

"I'd best get down to the Lower Cavern." Moreta pulled her shoulders back, bracing against the stresses. Then she reminded herself that weyrfolk were hardy, not only in body but in mind. Each Fall they faced the knowledge that some among them would suffer injury, possibly death. They endured the certainty with fortitude and courage. Why should an additional transient hazard dismay them? Why should something unseen appear more dangerous than the visible Thread that scored?

Sh'gall's apprehension was insidiously affecting her. There was even no surety that contact would result in illness. K'lon and Berchar? Well, that could be dismissed as misfortune—K'lon so often visited A'murry at Igen. At that, she was more likely to take ill than Sh'gall, after succoring that runnerbeast.

Moreta took Leri's strap then, with a backward look at Orlith, who was composing herself as comfortably as she could, she left the weyr. The fog appeared to be thinning. It eddied about her more freely, and she could make out the full flight of stairs although the Lower Caverns remained invisible until she was more than halfway across the Bowl.

When Moreta arrived, the Lower Cavern was already well populated. Most of the Weyr was about, in fact. Judging by the clutter of dishes and cups on the tables, a hearty meal had been consumed. Women and weyrlings moved among the diners with klah pitchers, but not many wineskins were in evidence. The other queen riders—Lidora, Haura, and Kamiana—were at the raised table to one side of the dining area, their weyrmates seated with them.

Moreta's presence was noted, and conversations subsided briefly. She located T'ral, who was busy at his leather-mending, then made her way across the cavern, nodding and smiling to riders and weyrfolk, feeling more at ease as she began to appreciate the receptive mood of the assembled.

"Leri's neck strap needs a mend, T'ral."

"We can't be losing her!" the brown rider said, taking the strap and putting it on top of other work.

"Did we mishear the drums, Moreta?" one of the younger brown riders asked in a voice suddenly too loud and brash.

"Depends on the strength of your morning headache," she said with a laugh, which drew a scatter of echoes.

"Klah or wine?" Haura asked Moreta as she stepped up on the dais.

"Wine," Moreta said firmly, a choice that was greeted appreciatively by those nearby.

"It's her legs that wobble," someone suggested.

"The dancing was good at Ruatha, wasn't it?" She took a sip of the wine and then looked out over the faces turned toward her. "Who doesn't know what the drums have been relaying?"

"Whoever slept through them heard the news from Nesso at the breakfast hearth," someone remarked from the center of the diners. Nesso brandished her ladle in that direction.

"Then you all know as much as I do. An epidemic's loose on Pern, caused by that unusual beast the seamen rescued in the Current between Igen and Ista island. Runnerbeasts are affected but Master Talpan says that watchwhers, wherries, and dragons don't contract the disease. Master Capiam hasn't a name for it yet but if the disease originated from the Southern Continent, the odds are it'll be mentioned in the Records—"

"Like everything else," a wit called out.

"Consequently it's only a matter of time before we know how to treat it. However"—Moreta altered her voice to a serious tone—"Master Capiam warns against any congregating—"

"He should have told us *that* yesterday—"

"Agreed. We may have Fall tomorrow but I want no heroes. Headache and fever are the symptoms."

"Then K'lon had the plague?"

"It's possible, but he's hale again."

A worried voice came from the eastern side of the cavern. "What about Berchar?"

"Caught it from K'lon, more than likely, but he and S'gor have isolated themselves, as you are probably aware.

"Sh'gall?"

An uneasy stir rippled around the Cavern.

"He was fine ten minutes ago," Moreta said dryly. "He'll fly Thread tomorrow. As we all will."

"Moreta?" T'nure, green Tapeth's rider, rose from his table to speak. "How long does this quarantine condition last?"

"Until Master Capiam rescinds it." She saw the rebellious look on T'nure's face. "Fort Weyr will obey!" Before she finished that injunction, the unmistakable trumpeting of the queens was heard. No lesser dragon would disobey the queens. Moreta thanked Orlith for the timely comment. "Now, in view of Berchar's indisposition, Declan, you and Maylone share responsibility for the injured. Nesso, you and your team must be prepared to assist. S'peren, can I rely on your help?"

"Anytime, Weyrwoman."

"Haura?" The queen rider nodded, none too keen. "Now, are there any other matters to be discussed?"

"Does Holth fly?" Haura asked quietly.

"She does!" Moreta spoke in a flat voice. She would not have that right challenged by anyone. "Leri, as is her custom, will speak to the ground crews, keeping her distance up on Holth."

"Moreta?" T'ral spoke up. "What about ground crews? I know Nabol and Crom will turn out tomorrow, but what happens next Fall—over Tillek and, after that, at Ruatha—if this plague spreads and we've no ground crews?"

"Time enough to worry about that in the next Fall," Moreta said quickly, with an unconcerned smile. Ruatha! With all the Gatherers there, crowded in! "The Holds will do their duty as the Weyrs discharge theirs."

An approving applause capped her restatement as she sat down, signaling that the discussion was at an end. Nesso stepped up on the dais with a plate of food.

"I think you should know," she said in a low voice, "that all the drum messages sign Fortine as sender now."

"Not Capiam?"

Nesso shook her head slowly from side to side. "Not since the first one this noon."

"Has anyone else noticed that?"

Nesso sniffed in offended dignity. "I know my duty, too, Weyr-woman."

The headache didn't know when to quit, Capiam decided, trying for another position in which to ease his aching skull and his feverish body. His clock was slow: He had another hour before he could take a fourth draught of fellis juice. His heartbeat was more regular thanks to the aconite. Carefully the Healer rolled onto his right side. He forced himself to relax his neck muscles, let his head sink into the fiber-filled pillow. He was certain he could count every strand within the case from its pressure on the sensitized skin of his cranium.

To compound his misery, the drum tower began to transmit an urgent message. At this hour? Were they manning the drums on a twenty-four-hour basis? Could no one sleep? Capiam recognized that the message was being relayed to Telgar Weyr but that was as far as he could force himself to concentrate.

An hour before he could take more fellis juice? It was his duty to Pern not to be insensible as the disease followed its course with his resisting body. Sometimes duty was a very difficult task.

Capiam sighed again, willing his execrable headache to abate. He ought to have listened to that message to Telgar. How was he to know what was happening on Pern? How the disease was progressing? How could he think?

CHAPTER VIII

Fort Weyr, Present Pass, 3.12.43

THE NEXT MORNING when Orlith roused Moreta early, the fog had cleared from Fort Weyr's mountain slopes.

"And to the northwest? Toward Nabol and Crom?" Moreta asked as she donned riding gear.

Sweeprider's gone out. He'll know, Orlith replied.

"Sh'gall?"

Awake and dressing. Kadith says he's well and rested.

"What does Malth say about Berchar?"

The conversation paused while Orlith inquired. *Malth says the man feels worse today than he did yesterday.*

Moreta didn't like the sound of that. If Berchar had been taking sweatroot, the fever should have been sweated from his body.

Neither you nor the Weyrleader are ill, Orlith remarked by way of encouragement.

Emerging from her sleeping quarters, Moreta laughed and went to throw her arms around her queen's neck, scratching the eye ridges affectionately. She couldn't help but notice the protuberances marring the curve of Orlith's belly.

"Are you sure you should fly Fall today?"

Of course I can. Orlith craned her neck around to look at the bulges. *They will settle once I am airborne.*

"Holth and Leri?"

They still sleep.

"Staying awake until the small hours, poring over Records!"

Orlith blinked.

When Moreta had returned the mended strap to Leri after the Weyr meeting, she found the old Weyrwoman deep in her studies.

"Weyrfolk don't *get* sick," she had said with considerable disgust. "Bellyache from overeating or drinking raw wines, Threadscore, stupid collision, knife fights, abscesses, kidney and liver infections by the hundreds, but sick? I've looked through twenty Turns after the last Fall"—Leri paused to give a great yawn—"bloody boring. I'll read on, but only because duty requires. Dragonriders are a healthy lot!"

Moreta had been quite willing to take that reassurance with her to bed. Though Nesso might have found it curious that Fortine was sending drum messages, Moreta logically concluded that Capiam was sleeping off the exhaustion of his round of the afflicted Holds. Sh'gall said that the man had been traveling for days. Sh'gall's excessive alarm over the epidemic was likely compounded by his innate antipathy for injury or minor ailments. The Weyrleader had been overreacting. She felt more sanguine about her contact with the diseased runner: It had been so brief that she failed to see how she could be affected.

Consequently, after a good night's sleep, Moreta was able to face Fall in good heart as she stepped out in the brightness of a crisp wintry day. Moreta preferred an early start on a Fall day: that day especially for, with Berchar sick, she must check that the supplies for treating scored dragons had been set out properly.

Declan, Maylone, and six of the weyrfolk were already setting up supplies in the infirmary. Declan and Maylone were runnerhold bred like herself. Searched the previous Turn for Pelianth's clutch, they had not Impressed. Because Declan had proved himself useful to Berchar and Maylone was young enough to Impress again, the two had been allowed to stay on in the Weyr. Even if Declan made a dragonrider, his skill would give Moreta much needed assistance. A Weyr never had enough healers for men and dragons.

Declan, a thin-faced man of nearly twenty Turns, brought Moreta a mug of klah while she checked his efforts. Moreta had briefly considered sending a weyrling to the Healer Hall for a more experienced healer to replace Berchar, but because of the quarantine and the efficiency shown by Declan and Maylone, she decided the Weyr would be well enough tended. Most riders knew how to treat minor scores on themselves and their dragons.

She was serving herself from the porridge kettle when Sh'gall entered the cavern. He went straight to the dais and pulled all the chairs but one from the table. He sat down, beckoned to a sleepy weyrling, and, when the boy would have mounted the dais, Sh'gall warded him off with a peremptory command. While those in the cavern watched with amused surprise, the boy brought the cup of klah and the cereal bowl, placing them carefully at the far end of the table. Sh'gall waited till the boy had gone before he collected his breakfast.

Moreta felt impatience for such elaborate precautions. The Weyr had enough on its mind with Fall at midday. Out of deference to the Weyr-leader's authority, she kept her expression bland. Nesso had added something flavorful to the cereal, and Moreta concentrated on identifying the addition.

Wingleaders and wingseconds began to arrive, to report the readiness of their wings to Sh'gall. They prudently observed his isolation.

The three queen riders arrived together and sought Moreta. She signaled a weyrling to serve the women and replenish her klah. Kamiana, a few Turns younger than Moreta, was her usual imperturbable self, her short dark hair spiky from the bath, her tanned face smooth. Lidora, who had flown enough Thread not to be unduly anxious, was clearly upset about something, but she had recently changed her weyr-mate and her moods were often changeable. Haura, the youngest, was never at her best before Threadfall, but she always settled down once the queens' wing went into action.

"He's taking no risks, is he?" Kamiana said after noting Sh'gall's segregation.

"He did convey Capiam from Ista to Southern and Fort Hold."

"How's Berchar?"

"Still feverish." Moreta's gesture intimated that this was only to be expected.

"Hope there's no serious injuries." Kamiana aimed that remark at Haura, who was a capable if unenthusiastic nurse.

"Holth will fly lead," Moreta said, reproving Kamiana with a glance. "She's valiant in that position and we can all keep an eye on her. Haura and you fly as wing backs. Lidora and I will do the upper level. Nabol and Crom may not be cursed with fog—"

"Has a sweeprider gone out?"

"Sh'gall's less likely to fly blind than any other Weyrleader I've known," Moreta told Lidora dryly.

The weyrling returned with the porridge and klah, and served the Weyrwoman. Dragonriders began to arrive in groups, making their way to the breakfast hearth and then drifting to tables. The wingseconds moved about, checking their riders, giving instructions. All in a normal, perfectly routine fashion, despite Sh'gall, until the sweeprider came in.

"The High Reaches rider says it's all clear to the coast," A'dan announced in a cheerfully loud voice, peeling back his headgear as he strode to the hearth.

"The High Reaches rider says!" Sh'gall demanded. "You spoke to him?"

"Of course." A'dan turned round to the Weyrleader in surprise. "How else could I know? We met at—"

"Were you not told yesterday—" Sh'gall, appearing to enlarge with anger, rose. He glared at Moreta with piercingly accusative eyes. "Were you not told yesterday that contact with anyone was forbidden?"

"Riders aren't anyone—"

"Other riders! *Anyone!* We must keep this disease from reaching Fort Weyr and that means staying away from everyone. Today, during Fall, no rider of this Weyr is to approach any holder, any rider from High Reaches. Give any necessary orders adragonback, preferably on the wing. Touch no one and nothing belonging to anyone outside this Weyr. Have I made my orders perfectly clear this time?" He ended his outburst with another searing look at Moreta.

"What does Sh'gall think he can do to offenders?" Kamiana asked in an undertone meant for Moreta's ears alone.

Moreta gestured peremptorily for Kamiana's silence. Sh'gall had not finished speaking.

"Now," he went on in a stentorian but less forbidding tone that no one in the Lower Cavern could ignore. "We've Thread Falling today! Only dragons and their riders can keep Pern Threadfree. That is why we live apart, in Weyrs, why we must keep apart, preserving our health. Remember! Only dragonriders can keep Pern Threadfree. We must all be equal to that task!"

"He really is rousing us for Fall, isn't he?" Lidora said, leaning toward Moreta. "How long does he mean to keep us cooped up here?" Irritation colored her voice and sent a flush to her cheeks.

Moreta gave the dark woman a long measuring look, and Lidora caught at her lower lip.

"Aggravating to be sure, Lidora, but few Gather loves are ever caught for long." She had accurately guessed the source of Lidora's discontent and wondered who had caught the weyrwoman's fancy at Ruatha Gather. Moreta looked away, with apparent unconcern, but she thought again of Alessan and how much she'd enjoyed his company. She'd been showing off a bit, rushing to the runnerbeast's aid, trying to catch his attention.

The scuffling of bootheels and bench legs on stone roused her from her momentary lapse. She rose hastily. Custom dictated that she receive last-minute instructions concerning the queens' wing from Sh'gall. She stopped a few feet from the dais before he looked toward her, his expression warning her to keep her distance.

"Leri insists on flying?"

"There's no reason to stop her."

"You'll remind her, of course, to stay mounted."

"She always does."

Sh'gall shrugged, absolving himself of responsibility for Leri. "Tend your dragons, then. Threadfall is slated for midday." He turned to beckon the wingleaders forward.

"Is he complaining about Leri again?" Kamiana asked, perversely forgetting her own objections.

"Not really," Moreta replied then made her way out of the cavern, the queen riders following her.

Around the Bowl, on the ledges or on the ground, riders were harnessing dragons, arranging firestone sacks on dragon necks. Others daubed oil on recent scars and examined rough patches on hide or wing membranes. Wingleaders and wingseconds were busy overseeing the preparations. Weyrlings ducked around riders and dragons on errands. The atmosphere was busy but not frantic. The bustle had the right tone to it, Moreta decided as she made her way to the far side of the Bowl. The activity was routine, familiar, almost comforting when she considered the probability that, elsewhere on Pern, men and beasts might be dying of the plague.

That is not a good thought, Orlith said sternly.

"True. And not one to take into Fall. Forgive me."

There is no fault. The day is clear! We will meet Thread well.

Orlith's sturdy confidence imbued Moreta with optimism. The sun streamed in from the east, and the crisp air was invigorating after the clammy weather that had prevailed. A good deep frost now would be most beneficial, she thought as she climbed the stairs. Not too long a cold spell, just enough to freeze the pernicious insects and reduce the snake population.

"I'll do Holth's harness first."

Leri has help.

Moreta grinned at Orlith's impatience. That was a good spirit in a dragon. As she entered the weyr, Orlith was off her couch, her eyes sparkling, their whirl speeding up with anticipation. Orlith lowered her head. In a burst of affection and love for her partner and friend, Moreta flung her arms about the triangular muzzle, squeezing as tightly as she could, knowing that her strongest embrace would be as nothing to the husky beast. Orlith rumbled and Moreta could feel the loving vibration. Reluctantly she released Orlith. Briskly then, she turned to the harness hanging on its wall pegs.

As she arranged the straps, she ran the leather through knowing hands. The cold of *between* ate into equipment, and most riders changed harnesses three or four times a Turn. Finding all was well with the leather, Moreta then examined Orlith's wings despite the queen's growing impatience to be up on the Star Stone height, overseeing the final preparations. Next Moreta checked the gauge on the agenothree tank, made sure the nozzle head was clean, and strapped on the tank. Then queen and rider moved out to the ledge. On the one above, Holth and Leri were already waiting.

Moreta waved to Leri and received a jaunty salute. Settling her eyepieces, Moreta fastened her helmet, hitched back the cumbersome flamethrower, and mounted Orlith. With a mighty heave, Orlith launched herself toward the Rim.

"That's quite an effort, dear heart," Moreta said.

Once I am airborne, there is no effort.

To allay Moreta's anxiety, Orlith executed a very deft turn and landed with precision near Kadith. The dragon was a good-size beast, a deep rich shade of bronze with green undertones. He was not the largest bronze in Fort Weyr but, in his mating flights with Orlith, he had proved the most agile, daring, and energetic. Kadith looked up at Orlith and affectionately stroked his head on her neck. Orlith accepted the caress demurely, turning her head to touch muzzles.

Then Sh'gall signaled the blue, green, brown, and bronze riders to feed their dragons firestone. Considering it was an essential step in the destruction of Thread, Moreta could never take it as seriously as she ought. She kept her face composed and eyes straight ahead but she knew exactly the expression on the dragons' faces—pensive, eyes half closed as the dragon maneuvered firestone to the grinding surfaces of sturdy teeth, taking the greatest care to set the rock just *so* before applying pressure. The force that would pulverize firestone could also wreak considerable damage to a dragon's tongue. Dragons chewed firestone cautiously.

Once they'd stopped chewing firestone, the twelve wings of dragons—green, blue, brown, and bronze hides glistening with health in the sunlight, the many-faceted eyes taking on the reddish-yellow battle hue, wings restlessly flicking and tails slapping on the rock of the Rim—were a sight that never failed to inspire Moreta.

Orlith shifted her feet, sat back on her haunches. Moreta thumped her shoulder affectionately and told her to settle.

They are ready. Their bellies are full of firestone. Why are we not flying? Kadith?

Moreta was not one of those rare queen riders who could understand any dragon. Kadith turned his molten eyes on Orlith, and she steadied. Orlith was queen of the Weyr, as senior queen, the most powerful dragon in the Weyr, and since Fort was the first and biggest Weyr on the planet, she and her rider were the preeminent partners. But when Thread Fell, the Weyrleader was in command and Orlith had to obey Kadith and Sh'gall. So did Moreta.

Suddenly the farthest wing launched into the sky, high and straight. They would fly the high first westerly stack of the initial three wings. The second level wing moved out, then the third. Once all had achieved their assigned heights, the three wings went *between*. The north–south wings launched next for a cross-flight of the probable line of Fall. They went *between*. The diagonal wings, who would start in the northwest, went aloft and disappeared. Sh'gall lifted his arm yet again, and this time Kadith bugled, as impatient to be gone as Orlith. The Weyrleader would take his three wings east, to the line along Crom's plateau where the leading edge of Thread was due. The queens' wing took the final position, sweeping as close to the ground as they safely could. Their slower glide, their more powerful wings gave them more flight stability in erratic wind currents.

Now Kadith leaped from the Rim, Orlith following so quickly that Moreta was jerked back against the fighting straps. Then they were gliding into position. Leri on Holth had joined them, by what feat of acrobatics Moreta had not seen. Haura and Kamiana took their positions, and Lidora joined Moreta on the upper level.

Kadith says we go between.
You have the visual from him?
Very clear.
Take us between, *Orlith!*

> "Black, blacker, blackest, coldest beyond living things,
> Where is life when there is . . ."

The rugged mountains of Nabol were in the far distance, the sun warm on their backs in its cold-season arc. Below lay the bony plains of eastern Crom, glistening in patches and streaks that suggested there had been frost or a heavy dew.

Moreta's second glance was for Leri and Holth, who were perfectly fine. Haura and Kamiana were aligned behind them to form the V. Above were the fighting wings, the highest stack mere motes on a slow western glide. At the other assigned points of the defense, nine more wings were gliding toward the as-yet-unseen enemy. Now Moreta looked back over her shoulder. *Much wind?*

Not enough to matter. Orlith veered slightly to the right and left, testing.

Then Thread would make its entry on a slight slant, Moreta thought. There'd be more problems as they neared the mountains of Nabol where drafts would complicate Fall by sudden upward surges or drops. Thread fell at a faster rate during the cold season and, although the temperature was colder than it had been for recent Falls that Turn, the air wasn't frigid.

It comes!

Moreta looked back again. She saw that silvery smudging of a sky, a blurring that crept inexorably groundward. The Fall of Thread!

Leading edge! And Orlith began to pump her great wings, propelling them forward to meet the devastating rain.

Moreta caught her breath, as always exhilarated and apprehensive.

She remembered to exhale as she settled against the fighting straps. Moments would pass before the high wings would close with Thread. It would be minutes before she and the other queens might be needed. She spared another glance for Holth.

She flies well! Orlith confirmed. *The sun is warm on their backs, too.*

Leading edge was visible and the sky ahead on either side was starred with quick bursts of flame. Moreta could see the stacks of dragons at their various altitudes covering the edge well. Then, from the pattern of dragon flame, she saw that the Fall was uneven. There were gaps where no dragon breathed Thread to char.

Kadith says the Fall is ragged. Widen the formations. Second stack is closing. Southern wings have contact. Orlith would keep up her commentary until the queens' wing was called to use its flamethrowers. Then her attention would be totally involved in keeping herself and her rider unscathed. *High level is dropping down now. No injuries.*

There rarely are, Moreta thought, not in the first few exciting moments of Fall, no matter how badly it drops. The riders are all fresh, their dragons eager. Once they assessed the Fall, thick or thin, racing or languid, then mistakes would occur. The second hour of a Fall was the most dangerous. Riders and dragons lost their initial keenness, they overshot Thread, or they misjudged. Falls don't always follow the pattern of the leading edge, particularly at the end of a Pass.

Kadith is checking. Kadith is flaming. Char! Excitement tinged Orlith's previously calm tone. *He's between. Back again. Flaming. All wings are now engaged. First flight returns for second sweep.*

The wind yanked at Moreta's body and she tugged briefly to settle the flamethrower strap on her shoulder. Now the wind carried with it tiny flecks of black charred Thread. On a stormy day, sometimes her eyepieces would be covered by a muddy film. They were under the first edge of Fall now.

Nothing passed the wings, Orlith said.

Sometimes great gouts of Thread would descend on the leading edge and riders would be hard put to acquit their duty. Some older riders preferred the first drop to be heavy, swearing that the heavier the leading edge, the lighter the die-off. So many Falls, so many leading edges, so many, many variations possible and so many comparisons. No two accounts, even by riders in the same wing, ever seemed to tally.

Old L'mal had told Moreta that the efficiency of the dragon was only hampered by his rider's ability to brag. However a rider flew, so long as no Thread reached the ground, the flight was well done!

The plains of Crom flowed beneath them. Moreta kept her eyes ranging ahead as did Orlith, in a synchrony of alertness long perfected. Moreta now caught the overvision from Orlith as the dragon saw hers.

Moreta often experienced the desire to dive on Thread as the fighting dragons did, swooping down on the target, instead of having to wait passively for stray Thread to appear. Sometimes she envied the greens, who could chew firestone. That effectively sterilized them, which was all to the good or green dragons would overpopulate the planet. The danger was in the fight, but so was the excitement, and the golden queens could not indulge.

Thread!

"Haura!"

Werth sees. Werth follows!

Moreta watched as the younger queen veered, swung, and came up under the tangle of the deadly parasite. The flamethrower spat. The ash dispersed in the air as Werth accomplished the brief mission.

They are all alert now, Orlith told Moreta.

Tell them to broaden the interval since we're past leading edge. Kamiana is to stay with Leri and Holth. We'll go south. Haura, north!

Obligingly Orlith turned, gradually picked up air speed and altitude.

That was the hard part of Fall, coursing back and forth. The rich dark soil of the plateau held sufficient mineral nourishment to sustain Thread long enough to waste fields that had been brought to fertility over hundreds of Turns of careful husbandry.

They were nearing the initial rank of hills and the first of Crom's holds. The symmetry of the windows with their metal shutters tightly closed was visible against the protecting hillside. As Moreta and Orlith passed over the burning fire-heights, she wondered if all within the hold were healthy.

"Ask the watchwher, Orlith."

It knows nothing. Orlith's tone was a shade contemptuous. The queen did not enjoy interchanges with the simpleminded beasts.

"They have their uses," Moreta said. "We can check with all of them today. Sh'gall may not wish us to contact people but we can still learn something."

Orlith gained more altitude as the second fold of hills loomed. Rider and queen kept the silvery shower in sight, angling from one edge of their appointed line to the other. Over the next plateau they saw Lidora and Ilith swinging along their route.

Kadith says to converge on Crom Hold, Orlith told her after several long sweeps.

"Let's join them."

Moreta thought hard of Crom's fire-heights, chanted her talisman against *between*, and on "blackest" arrived in the air above Crom's principal Hold. It was situated near a river, the first cascade of which could be viewed from the Hold windows when unshuttered. The live-stock that usually grazed the fields had been gathered in. Moreta remembered the gay and brave decorations on Ruatha's windows and asked Orlith to speak to Crom's watchwher.

It is only worried about Thread. Knows nothing of illness. Orlith sounded disgusted. *Kadith says the Fall is heavy now and we should be careful. There have been three minor scorings. All dragons are flaming well and the wings are in order. Cross over!*

Moreta glanced at the spectacular display as all the fighting wings overlapped one another above Crom Hold. Too bad the holders couldn't see it. Cross-over was a magnificent sight but the concentration of the wings in one aerial position left many openings for Thread.

Suddenly Orlith veered. Moreta saw the Thread patch. Saw the blue dragon heading for it.

"We're in a better position," she cried, knowing that Orlith would warn off the diving blue. She flicked open the nozzle of the flame-thrower, leaning well left in her fighting straps as Orlith came up under the tangle. She pressed the button. The gout of fire found its mark but Moreta also had a blurred vision of blue wings and belly.

"Too close, you fool. Who was that?"

N'men, rider of Jelth, Orlith said. *One of the young blues. You didn't singe him.*

"A singe would teach him discipline." Moreta fumed, but was relieved that the young rider was unscathed. "Reckless stupidity to fly so low. Didn't he see us? I'll have his eyes for polishing."

More Thread! Orlith was off at another tangent. Lidora had also seen the Thread and she was nearer. Orlith desisted. *Kadith is diverting from cross-over. The others are coming.*

The queens' wing reformed, flying north, fanning out as gobbets of loose Thread Fell in a curious order caused by the dragon's distortions of the air currents. That was work indeed for the queens!

Moreta and Orlith were flying hard after this tangle, that patch, aware that Sh'gall had quickly redeployed sections of several wings to cover the upper levels. Cross-overs were hard to avoid, with the different stacks of dragons flying at varying speeds, especially when the prime requirement was that wings maintain the proper altitude and interval. Then Sh'gall sent sweep riders north to make sure there had been no burrowing.

The Fall continued as the wings reestablished their far-ranging patterns. Riders called for more firestone and set meetings with the weyrlings riding supply. Moreta checked her flamethrower and found half a tank. And Fall continued.

More casualties were reported by Orlith, none serious—wing tips and tails. Orlith and Moreta flew a watching level over the first of the snow-tipped mountains along the irregular border between Crom and Nabol. Thread would freeze and shrivel on those slopes but the queens ranged while Sh'gall and Kadith ordered the wings *between* to the far side and Nabol.

Haura said that she and Leri needed new fuel cylinders for their flamethrowers and were dropping down at the mine hold.

"Leri, please check with the watchwher!"

Holth says that the watchwhers are all stupid and know nothing of any use to us. I'll keep on asking.

Any landing was a strain for Holth, who was no longer agile. Moreta watched anxiously, but Leri had allowed for Holth's incapacity and directed the old queen to a wide ledge close to the mine hold. A green weyrling arrived from *between*, cylinders hanging on both sides of her neck. She landed daintily. Her rider detached one tank and dismounted. He ran toward Holth, up her forearm, clinging to the cylinder straps with one hand and the fighting leather with the other. The exchange of tanks was made as Moreta and Orlith glided over. Holth took several steps forward, leaning into the free air and got in her first downward sweep.

They pace themselves. All is well, Orlith said.

"Take us to Kadith!"

They went *between* and emerged above a rough valley just as a mass of Thread split across the nearest ridge.

Tapeth follows!

The green dragon, her wings flat against her dorsal ridge, fell toward the point of impact, her flaming breath searing the crest. Just when it looked as if the dragon would collide with the ridge, she unfolded her wings and swerved off.

Take us there! Moreta glanced down at the tank gauge. She'd need more to flood the ridge. No ground crew could get into the blind valley.

Then they were above the sooted stone. Obedient to her rider's mental directions, Orlith hovered so that Moreta could flame the far side of the ridge. Tendrils of Thread hissed and writhed into black ash. Methodically she pumped flame into the area, widening the arc to be sure that not a finger-length of the parasite escaped.

"We'll land a bit away, Orlith. I'll need another tank now."

It comes! Orlith landed easily.

"I want to check that ridge. I couldn't see if it was shelf, sheet, or shale."

Moreta released her fighting straps and slid down. Her feet, sore from the long ride and slightly numb despite the thick lining of her boots, were jarred by the impact of her jump. She slowly clambered on insensitive soles toward the blackened area, her finger ready on the flamethrower's ignition button. She began to sense the residual heat of the two flame attacks on the rock and moved forward more slowly as much to revive her cold feet as to be cautious. She never liked to rush in on a Thread site, not on foot. However, it had to be done and the sooner the better. Thread burrowed into any crevice or cranny.

The eastern side of the ridge was sheer rock, unmarred by a split or crack to harbor Thread. The western face was also a solid mass. Tapeth's flame must have caught the stuff on landing.

Her feet were beginning to warm up as she made her way back to Orlith. Just then a blue weyrling emerged. His claws were no more than a finger-length from the top of the protruding rock thrust. The next instant the blue backfanned his wings to land. Orlith rumbled and the blue shuddered at the queen's reprimand. The rider's expression altered abruptly from delight to apprehension.

"Don't be clever T'ragel! Be safe!" Moreta shouted at him. "You could have come out *in* the ridge, not on it! You've never been here before. Hasn't F'neldril drilled it in your skull to have air space landing as well as taking off?"

The young rider fumbled with the straps holding the tank to his blue dragon's side as Moreta stormed over to him, still seething with the fright he had given her. "Caution pleases me much more than agility."

She almost wrenched the tank from his hand.

"Get down. To make up for your error in judgment, stay until the ridge cools. Check for infestation. There's moss just below. You know how to use a flamethrower? Good. What's left in my tank should suffice. But have your dragon call if you see *anything* moving on that ridge. Anything!"

An hour or so's cold watch with fear as his companion would cool the young rider's ardor for fancy landings. No matter how often they were cautioned by the Weyrlingmaster and Weyrleader, weyrlings inexplicably disappeared and the older dragons grieved. The casualties were such a waste of the Weyr's resources.

She remounted Orlith, aware that the boy had taken a sentry's stance, but as close to the comfort of his blue dragon as possible. They looked shaken and forlorn.

Kadith calls!

"We must be nearing the end of Fall!" Moreta clipped back her fighting straps, remembering to tug them secure. Her harangue would lose its force if she came adrift on take-off.

B'lerion rides!

Moreta smiled as she told Orlith to get them airbound, to take them *between* to join the wings. She wondered, in the blackest of cold, just how B'lerion had fared with Oklina.

Then they were on the western side of the Nabol Range with Thread falling thick and fast. Moreta had no time to express gratitude for the presence of the fresh dragons and their riders. Moreta and Orlith had just dispatched a low snarl of Thread when Orlith announced abruptly, *The Fall is over!*

As the queen slowed her forward motion into a leisurely glide, Moreta leaned wearily into the fighting straps, the nozzle heavy in her tired hand. She felt the dull ache in her head from having to see too much at once, from having to concentrate on drift, and glide, and angle of the flame.

"Casualties?"

Thirty-three, mostly minor scorings. Two badly damaged wings. Four riders with cracked ribs and three with dislocated shoulders.

"Ribs and shoulders! That's bad flying!" Yet Moreta was relieved at the total. But two wings! She hated having to mend wings, but she'd had lots of practice.

B'lerion hails us. Bronze Nabeth flew well. Orlith was admiringly craning her neck as the High Reaches bronze matched their speed and level. B'lerion waved his arm in greeting.

"Ask him if he had a good Gather." Any diversion not to think of the Thread-laced wings to be mended.

He did. Orlith sounded amused. *Kadith says we should get back to the injured wings at the Weyr.*

"First ask B'lerion what he's heard of the epidemic."

Only that is exists. Then she added, *Kadith says Dilenth is very badly injured.*

Moreta waved farewell to B'lerion, wishing that Sh'gall or Kadith, or both, did not consider B'lerion and Nabeth rivals. Perhaps they were. Orlith liked B'lerion's bronze, and Moreta thought it would be far more pleasant spending the Interval with someone as merry as B'lerion.

"Take us back to the Weyr."

The utter still coldness of *between* acted as a bracer to Moreta. Then they were low over the Bowl, Orlith having judged her reentry as fine as that blue weyrling had earlier. The ground was studded with wounded dragons, each surrounded by a cluster of attendants. The piercing cry of wounded and distressed dragons filled the air and imbued Moreta with the most earnest desire to reduce their keening to a bearable level.

"Show me Dilenth," Moreta asked Orlith as the queen swung in over the Bowl.

His main wingsail is scored. I will soothe him! Pity deepened the queen's tone as she circled as close as was prudent above the thrashing blue. Riders and weyrfolk were trying to apply numbweed to the injured wing, but Dilenth was writhing with pain, making that impossible. As Orlith obligingly hovered, Moreta had a clear view of the crippled wing, its forestay tip flopping awkwardly in the dust.

It was a serious injury. From elbow to finger joint, the leading edge of Dilenth's wing had taken the brunt of the havoc wrought by Thread. The batten cartileges had wilted and were crumpled into the mass of the main wingsail; Moreta thought there was also some damage to the fingersail between the joint and batten ribs, where Thread had glanced off as Dilenth had tried to take belated evasive action. More damage marred the lub side of the wing than the leech. The spar sail appeared relatively whole. Nor could she discern if the finger rib was broken. She devoutly hoped it wasn't for without ichor to the head of the mainsail, the dragon might never regain full use and fold of his wing.

Dilenth's injury was one of the worst a dragon could sustain since both the leading and trailing edges of the mainsail were involved. Healed wing membrane might form cheloid tissue and the aileron would become less sensitive, imbalancing the dragon's glide. First Moreta would have to sort the puzzle pieces of the remaining tissue and support it, hoping that there was enough membrane left to structure repair. Dilenth was young, able to regenerate tissue, but he would be on the injured list for a long time.

Moreta saw Nesso bustling about in the group attending Dilenth. His rider, F'duril, was doing his best to comfort the dragon but Dilenth continually broke loose from his rider's grip, flailing his head about in anguish.

Orlith landed just in front of the blue dragon. As soon as her hind feet met the ground, Moreta released the fighting straps and slid to the ground. Weyrlings appeared to take the agenothree tank, her outer gear.

"Where's redwort to wash in?" she demanded loudly, more to mask the sound of the keening that beat between her ears. *Orlith, control him!*

The intensity of Dilenth's cries dwindled abruptly as the queen locked eyes with the blue. His head steadied and he submitted to his rider's ministration. The relieved F'duril alternately entreated Dilenth to be brave and thanked Orlith and Moreta.

"Half the noise is shock," Moreta said to F'duril as she scrubbed her hands in the basin of redwort. The solutions stung her cold fingers.

"The lacerations are major. The wingsail is nothing but rags and shreds," said Nesso at her elbow. "How will it ever mend?"

"We'll just see," Moreta replied, resenting Nesso for airing the doubts she herself entertained. "You can get me that bolt of fine wide cloth and the thinnest basket reeds you've got. Where're Declan and Maylone?"

"Declan's with L'rayl. Sorth took a mass of Thread on his withers. Maylone is somewhere or other with a dragon." Nesso was distracted by so many urgent requirements. "I've had to leave the injured riders with only their weyrmates and the women to tend them. Oh, why did Berchar have to be sick?"

"Can't be helped. Haura will be back shortly to help you with the riders." Moreta took a firm hold on her frustration and banished impatience as a useless luxury. "Just get me the cloth and the basket reeds. I'll want my table here, in front of the wing. Send me someone with

steady hands, oil, and thin numbweed, then get back to the riders. And
my needle case and that spool of treated thread."

As Nesso rushed off, shouting for helpers, Moreta continued her
survey of the injured wing. The main wingbones were unscathed, which
was a boon, but so much numbweed had been applied that she couldn't
see if ichor was forming. Fragments of the leading sail dangled from
elbow and finger joint. There might just be enough for reconstruction.
Any shred would help. She flexed her fingers which were still stiff from
the cold flying of Fall.

Dilenth's keening was muted but now another sound, a human one,
penetrated her concentration.

"You know I had my feeling! You know we've both been uneasy.
I *thought* we weren't flying true!" F'duril's litany of self-reproach reached
Moreta. "I should have held us *between* a breath longer. You couldn't
help yourself. It isn't your fault, Dilenth. It's mine! You'd no air space
to dodge that Thread. And I let you back in too soon. It's all my fault."

Moreta rounded on the man to shock him out of his hysterics. "F'duril,
get a grip on yourself. You're upsetting Dilenth far more than—" Moreta
broke off, suddenly noting the Threadscores on F'duril's body. "Has
no one tended you yet, F'duril?"

"I made him drink wine, Moreta." A rider in soot-smeared leathers
appeared from Dilenth's left side. "I've got numbweed dressings for
him."

"Then apply them!" Moreta looked around in exasperation. "Where
is Nesso now? Can't she organize anything today?"

"How bad is Dilenth?" the rider asked while capably slitting away
the remains of F'duril's riding jacket. Moreta now identified the slender
young man as A'dan, F'duril's weyrmate. He spoke in a low worried
voice.

"Bad enough!" She took a longer look at A'dan, who was coping
deftly with the dressings he wrapped about F'duril. "You're his weyrmate? Have you a steady hand?"

A solicitous weyrmate was preferable to no help, and certainly more
acceptable to Moreta than Nesso's moaning and pessimistic outlook.
Beads of ichor were beginning to seep through the numbweed on Dilenth's wingbone.

"Where *are* my things, Nesso?"

Moreta had taken but one pace toward the cavern to collect her
requirements when the stout Headwoman floundered into view, laden
with reeds, a pot of thin numbweed liquid, the jug of oil, and Moreta's
needle box. Behind her marched three weyrlings, one of them carrying
a hide-wrapped bolt of cloth as tall as himself and a washing bowl while
the other two wrestled the table close to the blue dragon's wing.

"Oh, a long time healing if it heals whole," Nesso moaned in a dismal undertone while shaking her head. She took one look at the expression on Moreta's face and scurried off.

Moreta took a long, settling, breath then exhaled and reached for the oil. As she began coating her hands against contact with numbweed, she issued instructions to A'dan and the weyrlings.

"You, D'ltan." She pointed to the weyrling with the strongest-looking hands. "Cut me lengths of that cloth as long as Dilenth's leading edge. A'dan, wash your hands with this oil and dry them, then repeat the process twice, just patting your hands dry after the third. We'll have to oil our hands frequently or get benumbed by the weed as we work. You, M'barak." Moreta indicated the tall weyrling. "Thread me needles with this much thread"—she held her oily hands apart to the required length—"and keep doing 'em until I tell you to stop. You, B'greal"— she looked toward the third boy—"will hand me the reeds when I ask for them. All of you wash your hands in redwort first.

"We're going to support the wing underneath with cloth stitched to the wingbone and stretched from the dorsal to the finger joint," she told A'dan, watching his face to see if he understood. "Then we must—if you have to get sick, A'dan, do it now and get it over with. Dilenth and F'duril both will find it reassuring to have you helping me. F'duril knows you'll be the most loving and gentle nurse that Dilenth could have. A'dan!" She spoke urgently because she needed his help. "Don't think of it as a dragon wing. Think of it as a fine summer tunic that needs mending. Because that's all we'll be doing. Mending!"

Her hands oiled, she took the fine-pointed needle from the weyrling's hand, willing A'dan to fortitude. *Orlith?*

I can only speak to his green, T'grath, Orlith said a bit tartly. *Dilenth needs all my concentration and none of the other queens has returned to help.*

In the next second, however, A'dan shook himself, finished washing his hands, and turned resolutely to Moreta. His complexion was better and his eyes steady though he swallowed convulsively.

"Good! Let's begin. Remember! We're mending!"

Moreta jumped up on the sturdy table, beckoned him to follow, and then reached for the first length of cloth. As Moreta made her first neat tacks along the dorsal, Dilenth and A'dan twitched almost in unison. With Orlith's control and all the numbweed on the bone, Dilenth could not be experiencing any pain. A'dan had to be anticipating the dragon's reaction. So Moreta talked to him as she stitched, occasionally asking him to stretch or relax the fine cloth.

"Now I'll just fasten this to the underside. Pull to your left. The leading edge of the wing will be thick—no help for it—but if we can just save enough of the mainsail... There! Now, A'dan, take the numbweed paddle and smear the cloth. We'll lay on it what wingsail fragments remain. This is a very fragile summer tunic. Gently does it. M'barak, cut me another length. That tendon's been badly stretched but luckily it's still attached to the elbow. *Orlith, do stop him flicking his tail. Any movement makes this operation more difficult.*

Moreta was grateful when Dilenth's exertions abruptly ceased. Probably another queen had arrived to support Orlith. She thought she saw Sh'gall but he didn't stop. He wasn't attracted to this aspect of Threadfall.

"Retaining that tendon is a boon," she said, realizing that her verbal encouragement to A'dan had faltered. "I'll have those reeds now, B'greal. The longest one. You see, A'dan, we can brace the trailing edge this way, using gauze as support. And I think there're enough fragments of membrane. Yes. Ah, yes, he'll fly again, Dilenth will! Slowly now, very gently, let's lay the tatters on the gauze. M'barak, can I have the thinner salve? We'll just float the pieces . . . so . . . ."

As she and A'dan patiently restored the main wingsail, she could see exactly how the clump of Thread had struck Dilenth. Had F'duril and the blue dragon emerged from *between* a breath earlier, F'duril would have been bowled off Dilenth by the searing mass. She must remember to point out to F'duril that good fortune had attended their reentry.

They retrieved more sail fragments than she'd initially dared believe. Moreta began to feel more confident as she stitched a reed to the tendon. In time the whole would mend although the new growth, overlapping the old, would be thicker and unsightly for seasons to come, until windblown sand had abraded the heavier tissue. Dilenth would learn to compensate for the alteration on the sail surface. Most dragons readily adapted to such inequalities once they were airborne again.

Dilenth will fly again, Orlith said placidly as Moreta stepped back from the repaired wing. *You've done as much as you can here.*

"Orlith says we've done a good job, A'dan," she told the greenrider with a weary smile. "You were marvelous assistants, M'barak, D'ltan, B'greal!" She nodded gratefully to the three weyrlings. "Now, we'll just get Dilenth over to the ground weyrs—and you can all collapse."

She jumped down from the table and would have sprawled had A'dan's hand not steadied her. His wry grin heartened her. She propped herself against the table edge for a moment. Nesso appeared, dispensing wine to Moreta first and then the others.

Dilenth, released from Orlith's rigid control, began to sag on his legs, tilting dangerously to his right. Orlith reasserted her domination while Moreta looked around for F'duril.

"He'll be no help to anyone," Nesso observed sourly as they all watched the blue rider sinking slowly to the ground in a faint.

"It was the strain and his wound," A'dan said as he rushed to his weyrmate.

Dilenth moaned and lowered his muzzle toward his rider.

"He's all right, Dilenth," A'dan said, gently turning F'duril over. "A little sandy—"

"And a lot drunk!" M'barak murmured as he signaled the other two lads to aid A'dan with F'duril.

"The worst is over now!" A'dan said with brisk cheer.

"He doesn't know what worst is," Nesso muttered gloomily at Moreta's side as the blue dragon lurched away, supported on one side by A'dan's Tigrath and K'lon and blue Rogeth on the other.

It took Moreta a few moments to realize that K'lon and Rogeth should not be about. "K'lon?...."

"He volunteered." Nesso sounded peeved. "He *said* that he was fine and he couldn't stand being idle when he was so badly needed. And he the only one!"

"The only one?"

Nesso averted her face from the Weyrwoman. "It *was* a command the Weyr could not ignore. An emergency, after all. He and F'neldril decided that he must respond to the drum message."

"What drum message are you talking about, Nesso?" Abruptly Moreta understood Nesso's averted gaze, She'd been overstepping her authority as Headwoman again.

"Fort Hold required a dragonrider to convey Lord Tolocamp from Ruatha to Fort Hold. Urgently. There is illness at Ruatha and more at Fort Hold, which cannot be deprived of its Lord Holder during such a disaster." Nesso blurted out the explanation in spurts, peering anxiously up at Moreta to gauge her reaction. "Master Capiam is sick—he must be, for it is Fortine who replies to messages, not the Masterhealer." Nesso grimaced and began to wring her hands, bringing them by degrees to her mouth as if to mask her words. "And there are sick *riders* at Igen, Ista, and many at Telgar. There's Fall in two days in the south . . . I ask you, who will fly against Thread if three Weyrs have no riders to send?"

Moreta forced herself to breathe slowly and deeply, absorbing the sense of Nesso's babbling. The woman began to weep now, whether from the relief of confession or from remorse Moreta couldn't ascertain.

"When did this drum message come?"

"There were two. The first one, calling for a conveyance for Lord Tolocamp, just after the wings left for Fall!" Nesso mopped at her eyes, appealing mutely to Moreta for forgiveness. "Curmir said we had to respond!"

"So you did!" Nesso's blubbering irritated Moreta. "I see that you could not delay until we had returned from Fall. Surely Curmir responded that the Weyr was at Fall?"

"Well, they knew that. But F'neldril and K'lon were here—no, there"—Nesso had to find the exact spot near the Cavern—"so we all heard the drum message. K'lon said immediately that he could go. He said, and we had to agree with him, that since he had been ill of the fever, he was unlikely to contract it. He wouldn't let F'neldril or one of the weyrlings or the disabled take the risk." Nesso's eyes pleaded for reassurance. "We tried to ask Berchar about the danger of infection, but S'gor would not let anyone see him and could not answer for him. And we *had* to respond to Lord Tolocamp's request! It is only right that a Lord Holder be in his Hold during such a crisis. Curmir reasoned that, in such an unusual instance, we were constrained by duty to assist the Lord Holder even if it meant disobeying the Weyrleader!"

"Not to mention the Masterhealer and a general quarantine."

"But Master Capiam is *at* Fort Hold," Nesso protested as if that sanctioned all. "And what will be happening at Fort Hold in Lord Tolocamp's absence I cannot imagine!"

It was the happenings at Ruatha Hold that concerned Moreta more vitally, and the second drum message.

"What is this of sick riders? Did it come in on open code?"

"No, indeed! Curmir had to look it up in his Record. We did nothing about that. Not even forward it for it didn't have the pass-on cadence. F'neldril and K'lon said you should know. There are forty-five riders ill at Telgar alone!" Nesso placed one hand on her chest in a dramatic gesture. "Nine are very ill! Twenty-two are ill at Igen and fourteen at Ista." Nesso seemed obscurely pleased by the numbers.

Eighty-one riders ill of this epidemic? Despair and fear welled through Moreta. *Riders* ill? Her mind reeled. It was Fall! All the dragonriders were needed. Fort Weyr was down thirty in strength from the last Fall, and thirty-three from this one. It would be a full Turn before Dilenth flew. Why this? Only eight Turns remained in this Pass and then the riders would be free of the devastation that Thread wrought on dragons, themselves, and Pern. Moreta shook her head in an effort to clear her thinking. She ought to have paid more heed to Sh'gall's agitated report of illness instead of discounting the truth because it was unpalatable. She knew that Master Capiam was not in the habit of issuing arbitrary orders. But riders were healthy, fit, less susceptible to minor ailments. Why should they, in their splendid isolation, pursuing their historic occupation, be vulnerable to an infection rampant in crowded holds, halls, and among beasts?

Yet, her rational self said, the damage was already spreading by the time Sh'gall brought her the news. Even she had already innocently compounded her involvement by showing off her sensitivity to impress Alessan. *How* could anyone at Ruatha Gather have realized the danger in approaching that dying runnerbeast? Why, when Talpan had correlated illness to the journeyings of that caged beast, she and Alessan had probably been watching the races.

You are not at fault, the tender, loving voice of Orlith said. *You did no harm to that runnerbeast. You had the right to enjoy the Gather.*

"Is there anything we should *do* about the other Weyrs, Moreta?" Nesso asked. She had stopped weeping but she still twisted and washed her hands in an indecisive way that annoyed Moreta almost as much.

"Has Sh'gall returned?"

"He was here and went off, looking for Leri. He was angry."

Orlith?

They are busy but unharmed.

"Nesso, did you tell him about the drum messages?"

Nesso cast a desperate look at Moreta and shook her head. "He wasn't on the ground long enough—really, Moreta."

"I see." And Moreta did. Nesso could never have brought herself to inform the Weyrleader of such fateful tidings had there been worlds of time. Moreta would have to present the matters to Sh'gall soon enough, a conversation that would cause more acrimony on a day when both had more problems than hours. "How is Sorth?"

"Well, now, he's going to be fine," Nesso said with considerably more enthusiasm for that topic. "He's just over here. I thought you might like to check over my work."

The westering sun glinted off the Tooth Crag above Fort Weyr and the glare hurt Moreta's tired eyes as she looked in the direction Nesso pointed. The repair of Dilenth's wing had taken far longer than she had realized.

There is still sun on your ledge, Orlith. You should enjoy it. Get the cold of between *and Fall out of your hide.*

You are as tired. When do you rest?

When I have finished what must be done, Moreta said, but her dragon's concern was comforting. Moreta scrubbed at her fingertips, which had become insensitive where numbweed had seeped through the oil. She rinsed her hands in redwort and dried them well in the cloth Nesso offered.

A blue dragon wailed plaintively from his ledge, and Moreta looked up, worried.

"His rider only has a broken shoulder," Nesso said with a sniff. "Torn harness."

Moreta remembered another blue rider. *Orlith, that blue weyrling— has he returned from the ridge?*

Yes, there was no Thread. He reported to the Weyrlingmaster. He wants to have a word with you about putting a very young rider at risk.

The lad would have been in more risk continuing his antics, and I'll have words with the Weyrlingmaster on another score. "Let's see Sorth," she said aloud to Nesso.

"He's an old dragon. I don't think he'll heal well." Nesso babbled out of a nervous desire to regain favor in Moreta's eyes, for she didn't know that much about dragon injuries and far too much about how she thought the Weyr should be managed.

Moreta had also come to the conclusion at some point in the last few moments that she would have ordered someone to convey Lord Tolocamp had she been in the Weyr when the message arrived, despite any protest Sh'gall might have raised about breaking quarantine. Fort Hold would need Tolocamp more than Ruatha needed an unwilling guest. She wondered fleetingly if any were sick at Ruatha. If so, how had Alessan permitted Tolocamp to break quarantine?

Sorth had taken a gout of tangled Thread right on the forward wing-finger, severing the bone just past the knuckle. L'rayl was full of praise for Declan's assistance, belatedly including Nesso in his recital while she glared at him. They had done a good job of splinting the bone, Moreta noted professionally, tying reeds into position on well-numbed flesh.

"Nasty enough," Moreta commented as Sorth gingerly lowered the injured wing for her scrutiny.

"A fraction closer to the knuckle and Sorth might have lost tip mobility," L'rayl said with laudable detachment. The man had a habit of clenching his teeth after he spoke, as if chopping off his words before they could offend anyone.

"A soak in the lake tomorrow will reduce the swelling once ichor has coated the wound," Moreta said, stroking the old brown's shoulder.

"Sorth says," L'rayl answered after a pause, "that floating would feel very good. The wing would be supported by the water and not ache so much." L'rayl was then caught between a grin and a grimace for his dragon's courage and, to cover his embarrassment, he turned and roughly scratched Sorth's greening muzzle.

"How many riders were injured?" she asked Nesso as they turned toward the infirmary. With eighty-one sick of the plague, they might have to send substitutes.

"More than there should be," Nesso replied, having recovered her critical tongue.

Nesso hovered while Moreta made her expected brief appearance in the infirmary. Most of the injured riders were groggy with fellis juice or asleep, so she didn't have to linger. She also seemed unable to extricate herself from Nesso's company.

"Moreta, what you need right now is a good serving of my fine stew."

Moreta was not hungry. She knew she ought to eat but she wanted to await the return of Sh'gall and Leri. In a brief flurry of malice, Moreta struck across the Bowl to the Lower Cavern in a long stride that forced Nesso to jog to keep up. Annoyed with herself, Moreta silently put up with Nesso's fussing to make sure that the cook served Moreta a huge plate. Nesso obsequiously cut bread and heaped slices on Moreta's plate before making a show of seating the Weyrwoman. Fortunately, before the last of Moreta's waning penitence was exhausted, one of the fosterlings came running up to say that Tellani needed Nesso "*right* now."

"Giving birth, no doubt. She started labor at the beginning of Fall." Nesso raised her eyes and hands ceilingward in resignation. "We'll probably never know who the father was for Tellani doesn't know."

"Babe or child, we'll have some trace to go by. Wish Tellani well for me."

Privately Moreta blessed Tellani for her timing; she would have respite from the Headwoman, and a birth after Fall was regarded as propitious. The Weyr needed a good dollop of luck. A boy, even of uncertain parentage, would please the dragonriders. She'd have a stern talk with Tellani about keeping track of her lovers—surely a simple enough task even for so loving a woman as Tellani. The Weyr had to be cautious about consanguinity. It might just be the wiser course to foster Tellani's children to other Weyrs.

It was easier to think of an imminent birth than tax her tired mind with imponderables such as sick riders in three Weyrs, a Masterhealer who was not signing outgoing messages, the disciplining of a rider and a harper who disobeyed their Weyrleader, a wing-torn dragon who would be weyrbound for months, and a sick healer who might be dying.

Malth says Berchar is very weak and S'gor is very worried, Orlith told her in a gentle, drowsy voice. *We have decided that the woman has carried a male,* Orlith continued. Moreta was astonished. Since Orlith very rarely used the plural pronoun, she must be referring to other dragons.

How kind you are, my golden love! Moreta shielded her face with her hands so that no one in the cavern would see the tears in her eyes for her dragon's unexpected kindly distraction, and her everlasting joy that, of all the girls standing on Ista's Hatching Ground that day Turns ago, Orlith had chosen the late arrival for her rider.

"Moreta?"

Startled, Moreta looked up to see Curmir, K'lon, and F'neldril standing politely before her table.

"It was I who *insisted* on conveying Lord Tolocamp," K'lon said firmly, chin up, eyes shining. "You could say that I hadn't actually *heard* the Weyrleader's order of quarantine since Rogeth and I were asleep in a lower weyr." Outrageously K'lon winked at Moreta. An older, weyr-bred rider, he had not been best pleased when Sh'gall's Kadith had flown Orlith, making the much younger bronze rider Weyrleader in L'mal's stead. K'lon's discontent with the change in leadership had been aggravated by Sh'gall's overt disapproval of K'lon's association with the Igen green rider A'murry.

Moreta tried to assume a neutral expression but knew from Curmir's expression that she failed.

"You did as custom dictates!" Moreta would allow that much latitude. "The Fort Holder must be conveyed by this Weyr. You brought his family back?"

"Indeed not, though I did offer. Rogeth would not have objected but Lady Pendra decided that she and her daughters could not break the quarantine."

Moreta caught Curmir's gaze again and knew that the harper was as aware as everyone else in the west as to why Lady Pendra would not break the quarantine. Moreta had great sympathy for Alessan's predicament. Not only was he still saddled with the Fort girls, but all the other hopefuls of the Gather were still at Ruatha.

"Lady Pendra said that she would wait out the four days."

"Four days, four Turns," F'neldril said with a snort, "and it wouldn't change their faces or improve their chances with Alessan."

"Did you see Master Capiam, K'lon?"

K'lon's expression changed, reflecting annoyance and remembered offense. "No, Moreta. Lord Tolocamp required me to set him down in the Hold forecourt, so I did. But immediately Lord Campen and Master Fortine and some other men whose names I can't recall bore him off to a meeting. I wasn't admitted to the Hall—to protect *me*, they said, from contagion, and they wouldn't listen when I explained that I'd had the plague and recovered."

Before she could speak, the watchrider's dragon bugled loudly. Sh'gall and his wing had returned at last. As Moreta rose hastily from the table, she could see the dust roiled up by the dragons' landing.

All are well, Orlith reassured her. *Kadith says the Fall ended well but he is furious that there were few ground crews.*

"No ground crews," she told the three men by way of warning.

Sh'gall came striding through the second dust cloud created as the dragons jumped to their weyrs. The riders of Sh'gall's wing followed a discreet distance behind their Weyrleader. Sh'gall made directly for Moreta, his manner so threatening that K'lon, Curmir, and F'neldril tactfully stepped to one side.

"Crom sent out no ground crews," Sh'gall shouted, slamming gloves, helmet, and goggles down on the table with a force that sent the gear skidding across the surface and onto the floor. "Nabol mustered *two* after Leri threatened them! There was no illness at Crom or Nabol. Lazy, ignorant, stupid mountaineers! They've used this plague of Capiam's as an excuse to avoid their obligations to me! If this Weyr can fly, they can bloody well do their part! And I'll have a word with Master

Capiam about those drum messages of his, panicking the holders."

"There's been another drum message," Moreta began, unable to soften her news. "Ista, Igen, and Telgar have sick riders. The Weyrs may find it hard to discharge their obligation."

"This Weyr will always discharge its duty while I'm Leader!" Sh'gall glared at her as if she had disputed him. Then he whirled and faced those lingering at the dining tables of the cavern. "Have I made myself plain to you all? Fort Weyr will do its duty!"

His declaration was punctuated by the sound that every rider dreaded, the nerve-abrading shrill high shriek of dragons announcing the death of one of their kind.

Ch'mon, bronze rider of Igen, died of fever, and his dragon, Helith, promptly went *between*. He was the first of two from that Weyr. During the evening five more died at Telgar. Fort Weyr was in shock.

Sh'gall was livid as he hauled Curmir with him to send a double-urgent message to the Healer Hall, demanding to know the state of the continent, what was being done to curb the spread, and what remedies effected a cure. He was even more upset when Fortine replied that the disease was now considered pandemic. The response repeated that there had been recoveries: Isolation was imperative. Suggested treatment was febrifuge rather than a diaporetic, judicious use of aconite for palpitations, willowsalic or fellis juice for headache, comfrey, tussilago, or preferred local cough remedy. Sh'gall made Curmir inquire double-urgent for a reply from Master Capiam. The Healer Hall acknowledged the inquiry but sent no explanation.

"Does anyone know," he demanded at the top of his voice as he rampaged back into the Lower Caverns, "if this is what K'lon had?" He glared at the stunned blue rider, his eyes brilliant with an intensity that was beyond mere fury. "What has Berchar been dosing himself with? Do you know?" Now he almost pounced on Moreta where she sat.

"S'gor tells me he has been using what Master Fortine suggests. K'lon *has* recovered."

"But Ch'mon has died!"

His statement became an accusation, and she was at fault.

"The illness is among us, Sh'gall," Moreta said, gathering strength from an inner source whose name was Orlith. "Nothing we can do or say *now* alters that. No one forced us to attend the Gathers, you know." Her wayward humor brought grim smiles to several of the faces about her. "And most of us enjoyed ourselves."

"And look what happened!" Sh'gall's body vibrated with his fury.

"We can't reverse the happening, Sh'gall. K'lon survived the plague as we have survived Thread today and every Fall the past forty-three Turns, as we have survived all the other natural disasters that have visited us since the Crossing." She smiled wearily. "We must be good at surviving to have lived so long on this planet."

The weyrfolk and the riders began to take heart at Moreta's words, but Sh'gall gave her another long stare of outraged disgust and stalked out of the Lower Caverns.

The confrontation had shaken Moreta. She was drained of all energy, even Orlith's, and it had become an effort to keep upright. She gripped the edge of her chair, trembling. It wasn't just Sh'gall's rage but the unpalatable, unavoidable knowledge that she was very likely the next victim of the plague in the Weyr. Her head was beginning to ache and it was not the kind that succeeded tension or the stress and concentration of repairing dragon injuries.

You are not well, Orlith said, confirming her self-diagnosis.

I have probably not been well since I went to that runner's rescue, Moreta replied. *L'mal always said that runners would be my downfall.*

You have not fallen down. You have fallen ill, Orlith corrected her, dryly humorous in turn. *Come now to the weyr and rest.*

"Curmir." Moreta beckoned the harper forward. "In view of Berchar's illness, I think we must demand another healer from the Hall. A Masterhealer and at least another journeyman."

Curmir nodded slowly but gave her a long, searching look.

"S'peren is to contrive a support sling for Dilenth. We cannot expect T'grath to stand under his wing until it heals. Such sacrifices sour weyrmates!" Moreta managed to rise, carefully planting her feet under her so as not to jar her aching skull. Never had a headache arrived with such speed and intensity. She was nearly blinded by it. "I think that's all for now. It's been a difficult day and I'm tired."

Curmir offered her assistance but she discouraged him with a hand gesture and walked slowly from the Lower Cavern.

Without Orlith's constant encouragement, Moreta would not have been able to cross the Bowl, which, in the sudden chill of the night air, seemed to have perversely grown wider. At the stairs, she had to brace herself several times against the inner wall.

"So, it's got to you," Leri said unexpectedly. The older Weyrwoman was sitting on the steps to her weyr, both hands resting on her walking stick.

"Don't come near me."

"You don't see me rising from my perch, do you? You're probably contagious. However, Orlith appealed to me. I can see why now. Get into your bed." Leri brandished her cane. "I've already measured out the medicine you should take, according to that drum roll of Fortine's. Willowsalic, aconite, featherfern. Oh, and the wine has a dose of fellis juice from my own stock. The sacrifices I make for you. Shoo! I can't carry you, you know. You'll have to make it on your own. You will.

You always do. And I've done more than enough for one day for this Weyr!"

Leri's chivvying gave Moreta the impetus to stagger up the last few steps and into the corridor of her weyr. At its end she could see Orlith's eyes gleaming with the pale yellow of concern. She paused for a moment, winded, her head pounding unbearably.

"I assume that no one in the Lower Caverns suspected you've been taken ill?"

"Curmir. Won't talk, though."

"Sensible of you in view of the Igen death. She'll make it, Orlith." Then Leri waved her cane angrily. "No, you will not help. You'd jam the corridor with your egg-heavy belly. Go on with you, Moreta. I'm *not* going to stand on these chilly steps all night. I need my rest. Tomorrow's going to be very busy for me."

"I hoped you'd volunteer."

"I'm not so lacking in sense that I'd let Nesso get out of hand. Go! Get yourself well," she added in a kinder tone, heaving herself to her feet.

Orlith did meet Moreta at the end of the corridor, extending her head so that Moreta could hang onto something to cross the chamber. Orlith crooned encouragement, love and devotion and comfort in almost palpable waves. Then Moreta was in her own quarters, her eyes fastening on the medicine set out on the table. She blessed Leri, knowing what an effort it had been for the old Weyrwoman to navigate the steps. Moreta took the fellis wine down in one swallow, grimacing against the bitterness not even the wine could disguise. How could Leri sip it all day? Without undressing, Moreta slid under the furs and carefully laid her head down on the pillow.

CHAPTER IX

Healer Hall, Present Pass, 3.13.43; Butte Meeting and Fort Weyr, 3.14.43; Healer Hall, 3.15.43

CAPIAM COULD NOT remain asleep, though he tried to burrow back into the crazy fever-dreams as a more acceptable alternative to the miseries total awareness brought. Something impinged on his semiconsciousness and forced him awake. Something he had to do? Yes, something he had to do. He blinked bleary, crusted eyes until he could focus on the timepiece. Nine of the clock. "Oh, it's me. Time for my medicine."

A healer couldn't even be sick without responding to his professional habits. He hauled himself up on one elbow to reach for the skin on which he was recording his progress through the disease but a coughing spasm interrupted him. The cough seemed to throw tiny knives at his throat. Such spasms were exceedingly painful, and Capiam disliked them even more than the headache, the fever, and the boneache.

Cautiously, lest he provoke another coughing fit, he dragged the note case onto his bed and fumbled for the writing tool.

"Only the third day?" His illness seemed to have made each twenty-four hours an eternity of minor miseries. That day was mercifully three quarters done.

He could take little comfort in noticing that his fever had abated, that the headache was a dullness that could be endured. He placed the fingers of his right hand lightly on the arterial pulse in the left wrist. Still faster than normal, but slowing. He made an appropriate notation and added a description of the hardy, dry, unproductive cough. As if

122

the note was the cue, he was wracked with another fit that tore at his throat and upper chest like a tunnel snake. He was forced to lie in a fetal position, knees up to his chin to relieve the muscle spasms that accompanied the cough. When it had passed, he lay back, sweating and exhausted. He roused enough to take his dose of willow salic.

He must prescribe a cough remedy for himself. What would be the most effective suppressant? He touched his painful throat. What must the lining of his throat resemble?

"This is most humiliating," he told himself, his voice hoarse. He vowed to be far more sympathetic to the afflicted in the future.

The drum tower began to throb and the message stunned him for condolences were being transmitted from Lord Tolocamp—what was *he* doing in Fort Hold when he should have remained at Ruatha?—to the Weyrleaders of Telgar and Igen for the deaths of . . . Capiam writhed on the bed, convulsed by coughing that left him weak and panting. He missed the names of the dead riders. Dead riders! Pern could ill afford to lose any of its dragonriders.

Why, oh why hadn't he been called in earlier? Surely nine people in the same Sea Hold falling sick was an unusual enough occurrence to have warrented even a courtesy report to the main Healer Hall? Would he have appreciated the significance?

"Capiam?" Desdra's query was low enough not to have aroused him had he been asleep.

"I'm awake, Desdra." His voice was a hoarse caw.

"You heard the drums?"

"Part of the message—"

"The wrong part from the sound of you."

"Don't come any closer! How many riders died?"

"The toll is now fifteen at Igen, two at Ista, and eight at Telgar."

Capiam could think of nothing to say.

"How many are ill, then?" His voice faltered.

"They report recoveries," Desdra said in a crisper voice. "Nineteen at Telgar, fourteen at Igen, five at Ista, two at Fort are all convalescing."

"And at Hall and Hold?" He dreaded her answer, clenching his fists to bear the staggering totals.

"Fortine has taken charge, Boranda and Tirone are assisting." The finality in her tone told Capiam he would not elicit any further information.

"Why are you in my room?" he demanded testily. "You know—"

"I know that you have reached the coughing stage and I have prepared a soothing syrup."

"How do you know what I would prescribe for my condition?"

"The fool who treats himself has only a fool for a patient."

Capiam wanted to laugh at her impudence, but the attempt turned into one of the hideously painful, long coughs and, by the time it had passed, tears rolled down his cheeks.

"A nice blend of comfrey, sweetener, and a touch of numbweed to deaden the throat tissues. It ought to inhibit the cough." She deposited the steaming mug on his table and was swiftly across the room by the door.

"You're a brave and compassionate woman, Desdra," he said, ignoring her sarcastic snort.

"I am also cautious. If at all possible, I would prefer to avoid the agonies which I have observed you enduring."

"Am I such a difficult patient?" Capiam asked plaintively, seeking more consolation than he could find in a mug of an odd-tasting syrup.

"What cannot be cured must be endured," Desdra replied.

"By which unkind words I assume that the Records have not given up either an account or a remedy."

"Master Tirone joined the search with all his apprentices, journeymen, and masters. They proceed backward by the decade for two hundred Turns and forward from the previous Pass."

Capiam's groan quickly degenerated into a spasm that again left him gasping for breath. Each of the two hundred bones in his body conspired to ache at once. He heard Desdra rummaging among his bottles and vials.

"I saw an aromatic salve in here. Rubbed on your chest it might relieve you, since you spilled most of that potion."

"I'll rub it on myself, woman!"

"Indeed you will. Here it is! Phew! That'll clear your sinuses."

"They don't need it." Capiam could smell the aromatic from his bed. Odd how the olfactory senses became acute in this disease. Exhausted by the last cough spasm, he lay still.

"Are you experiencing the severe lassitude as well as the dry cough?"

"Lassitude?" Capiam dared not laugh but the word was totally inadequate to describe the total inertia that gripped his usually vigorous body. "Extreme lassitude! Total inertia! Complete incapacity! I can't even drink from a mug without spilling half of it. I have never been so tired in my life—"

"Oh, then, you're proceeding well on the course of the disease."

"How consoling!" He had just enough energy for sarcasm.

"If"—and her emphasis teased him—"your notes are correct, you should be improving by tomorrow. That is, if we can keep you in your bed and prevent secondary infections."

"How comforting."

"It should be."

His head was beginning to buzz again from the willow salic. He was about to commend Desdra on the efficacy of her cough mixture when a totally unprovoked tickle bent him double to cough.

"I'll leave you to get on with it then," Desdra said cheerily.

He waved urgently for her to leave the room, then put both hands on his throat as if he could find some grip to ease the pain.

He hoped that Desdra was being careful. He didn't want her to catch the illness. Why hadn't those wretched seamen left that animal to drown? Look to what depths curiosity brought a man!

Butte Meeting, 3.14.43

Deep in the plains of Keroon and far from any hold, a granite butte had been forced to the surface during some primeval earthquake. The landmark had often been used as an objective in weyrling training flights. Just then it was the site of an unprecendented meeting of the Weyrleaders.

The great bronze dragons arrived almost simultaneously at the site, coming out of *between* full lengths clear of each other's wing tip, utilizing their uncanny perceptions of proximity. They settled to the ground in an immense circle at the southern face of the butte. The bronze riders dismounted, closing to a slightly smaller circle, each rider keeping a wary distance from those on either side until K'dren of Benden, who had an active sense of humor under any conditions, chuckled.

"None of us would be here if we were sickening," he said, nodding to S'peren who had come in Sh'gall's place.

"Too many of *us* have," L'bol of Igen replied. His eyes were red with weeping.

M'tani of Telgar scowled and clenched his fists.

"We have shared each loss," S'ligar of the High Reaches said with grave courtesy, inclining his head first to L'bol, M'tani, and F'gal of Ista. The other two bronze riders murmured their condolences. "We have gathered here to take emergency measures which discretion keeps from the drum and which our queens are unable to relay," S'ligar went on. As the oldest of the Weyrleaders, he took command of the meeting. He was also the biggest, topping the other bronze riders by a full head, and the breadth of him through chest and shoulders would have made two of most ordinary men. He was oddly gentle, never taking advantage of his size. "As our Weyrwomen have pointed out, we cannot admit the losses and numbers of the ill that the Weyrs have sustained. There is too much anxiety in the Holds as it is. They are suffering far more than we are."

"That's no consolation!" F'gal snapped. "I don't know how many times I warned Lord Fitatric that overcrowding hold and cot would have dire consequences."

"None of us had *this* in mind," K'dren said. "However, none of *us* had to run see the curious new beastie from the sea. Or attend two Gathers in one day—"

"Enough, K'dren," S'ligar said. "Cause and effect are now irrelevant. Our purpose here is to discuss how best to insure that the dragonriders of Pern fulfill their purpose."

"That *purpose* is dying out, S'ligar," L'bol cried. "What's the purpose of flying Thread to protect empty holds? Why preserve *nothing* at the risk of our skins and our dragons? We can't even defend ourselves from this plague!" L'bol's dragon crooned and extended his head toward his distressed rider. The other bronzes rumbled comfortingly and moved restlessly on the warm sand. L'bol scrubbed at his face, leaving white runnels where tears had wet his cheeks.

"We will fly Thread because that is the one service we can provide the sick in the Holds. They must not fear the incursions of Thread from without!" S'ligar said in his deep gentle unhurried voice. "We have labored too long as a Craft to surrender Pern now to the ravages of Thread because of a menace we can't see. Nor do I believe that this disease, however fiercely it spreads, however ruthless it appears, can overcome *us* who have for hundreds of Turns defended ourselves from Thread. A disease can be cured by medicines, defeated. And one day we will fly Thread to *its* source and defeat it."

"K'lon, Rogeth's rider, has recovered from the plague," S'peren announced in the silence following S'ligar's statement. "K'lon says that Master Capiam is on the mend—"

"Two?" L'bol flung the number derisively back at S'peren. "I've fifteen dead, one hundred and forty sick at Igen. Some holds in the mideast no longer respond to their drum codes. And what of the holds which have no drums to make known their needs and the toll of their dead?"

"Capiam on the mend?" S'ligar said, seizing at that hope. "I have every faith in that man's ability to lick this. And more than those two must have recovered. Keroon Beasthold still drums, and they were the hardest hit by the plague. High Reaches and Fort Weyrs have sickness, it is true, but the holds of Tillek, High Reaches, Nabol, and Crom have none." S'ligar tried to catch L'bol's despairing gaze. "We have only seven Turns to go before this Pass is over. I have lived under the scourge of Thread all my life." Suddenly he straightened his shoulders, his face severe. "I haven't fought Thread as a dragonrider for nearly fifty Turns to quit now over some fever and aches!"

"Nor I," K'dren added quickly, taking a step toward the High Reacher. "I made a vow, you know"—he gave a short laugh—"to Kuzuth, that we would see this Pass through." K'dren's tone turned brisk. "There's Fall tomorrow at Keroon, and it has become the responsibility of all the Weyrs of Pern. Benden has twelve full wings to fly."

"Igen has eight!" Anger brought L'bol out of his despondency to glare fiercely at K'dren. Timenth, his dragon, bugled defiance, rearing back onto his haunches and spreading his wings. The other bronzes reacted in surprise, sounding off. Two extended their wings and gazed skyward in alarm. "Igen will rise to Fall!"

"Of course your Weyr will rise," S'ligar said reassuringly, raising his arm in an incomplete gesture of comfort. "But our queens know how many Igen riders are ill. Fall has become the problem of all the Weyrs, as K'dren said. And we all supply the muster from our healthy riders. Until this epidemic is over, the Weyrs must consolidate. Full wings are essential since in many places, we shall be deprived of ground crews for close encounters with Thread."

S'ligar took a thick roll of hide from his pouch. With a deft flick of his wrist, the roll fell into five separate sections on the sand. Mindful to make no physical contact with the other Leaders, S'ligar slid a section to each of the other bronze riders.

"Here are the names of my wingleaders and seconds, since naming people seems to be a deficiency in our queens. I've listed my riders in order of their competence for assuming command of either wing or Weyr. B'lerion is my choice of a personal successor." Then a rare and brilliant smile crossed the High Reacher's face. "With Falga's complete accord."

K'dren roared with laughter. "Didn't she suggest him?"

S'ligar regarded K'dren with mild reproof. "It is the wise Leader who anticipates his Weyrwoman's mind."

"Enough!" M'tani called irritably. His dark eyes were angry under heavy black brows. He threw his lists down to join S'ligar's. "T'grel has always fancied himself a Leader. He reminded me that he hadn't been to either of the Gathers so I'll reward his virtue."

"You're fortunate," K'dren said with no humor in his voice. He added his lists to the others. "L'vin, W'ter, and H'grave attended both Gathers. I've recommended M'gent. He may be young but he's got a natural flair for leadership that one doesn't often see. He wasn't at the Gathers."

F'gal seemed unwilling to lose the sheets he unwound. "It's all on these," he said wearily, letting them flutter to the sand.

"Leri suggested me," S'peren said with a self-deprecating shrug, "though it's likely Sh'gall will make a change when he recovers. He was too fevered to be told of this meeting so Leri drew up the lists."

"Leri would know." K'dren nodded. He went down on his haunches to pick up the five slips of hide, aligning them at the top before rolling. "I shall be pleased if these can gather dust in my weyr." He stuffed the roll in his pouch. "It is, however, a comfort to have made plans, to have considered contingencies."

"Saves a lot of unnecessary worry," S'ligar agreed, bending to scoop up the scraps into his long-fingered hand. "I also recommend that we use entire wings as replacements, rather than send individuals as substitutes. Riders get used to their wingleaders and seconds."

The recommendation found favor with the others.

"Full wings or substitutes is not the real worry." L'bol glowered at the lists as he assembled them in his hand. "It's the lack of ground crews."

K'dren snorted. "No worry. Not when the queens have already decided among themselves to do that job. We've all been informed, no doubt, that every queen who can fly will attend every Fall."

M'tani's scowl was sour and neither L'bol or F'gal appeared happy, but S'ligar shrugged diffidently. "They will arrange matters to suit themselves no matter what but queens keep promises."

"Who suggested using weyrlings for ground crews?" M'tani asked.

"We may have to resort to them," S'ligar said.

"Weyrlings don't have enough sense—" M'tani began.

"Depends on their Weyrlingmaster, doesn't it?" K'dren asked.

"The queens intend"—S'ligar put in before M'tani could take offense at K'dren's remark—"to keep the weyrlings under control. What other choice have we in the absence of ground crews?"

"Well, I've never known a weyrling yet who would disobey a queen," F'gal admitted.

"S'peren, with Moreta ill, does Kamiana lead?"

"No. Leri." S'peren looked apprehensive. "After all, she's done it before."

The Weyrleaders murmured in surprised protest.

"Well, if any of your Weyrwoman can talk her out of it, we'd be very relieved." S'peren did not hide his distress. "She's more than done her duty by the Weyrs and Pern. On the other hand, she *knows* how to lead. With both Sh'gall and Moreta sick, the Weyr at least trusts her."

"How is Moreta?" S'ligar asked.

"Leri says Orlith doesn't seem worried. She carries her eggs well and she is very near clutching. It's as well Moreta is sick or they'd be out and about Pern. You know how keen Moreta is on runners."

M'tani snorted with disgust. "This is not the time to lose an egg-heavy queen," he said. "This sickness hits so fast and kills so quickly, the dragons don't realize what's happening. And then *they're* gone *between*." He caught his breath, clenching his teeth and swallowing against tears. The other riders pretended not to see his evident distress.

"Once Orlith has clutched she won't go until they've hatched," S'ligar said gently to no one in particular. "S'peren, have you candidates safely at Fort Weyr?"

S'peren shook his head. "We'd that yet to do and thought there was worlds of time for Search."

"Pick carefully before you bring anyone new into your Weyr!" L'bol advised sourly.

"If the need arises, High Reaches has a few promising youngsters who are healthy. I'm sure an adequate number can be made up from the other Weyrs?" S'ligar waited for the murmur of assent to go round the circle. "You'll inform Leri?"

"Fort Weyr is grateful."

"Is that all?" L'bol demanded as he turned toward his dragon.

"Not quite. One more point while we are convened." S'ligar hitched up his belt. "I know that some of us have thought of exploring the Southern Continent once this Pass is over—"

"After this?" L'bol stared at S'ligar in total disbelief.

"My point. In spite of the Instructions left to us, we cannot risk further contagions. Southern must be left alone!" S'ligar made a cutting gesture with the flat of his huge hand. He looked to the Benden Weyr-leader for comment.

"An eminently sensible prohibition," K'dren said.

M'tani flourished his hand curtly to show agreement and turned to S'peren.

"Of course, I cannot speak for Sh'gall but I cannot conceive why Fort would disagree."

"The continent will be interdicted by my Weyr, I assure you," F'gal said in a loud, strained voice.

"Then we shall leave it to the queens to communicate how many wings each Weyr supplies for Fall until this emergency is over. We've all the details we need to go on." S'ligar brandished his roll before he shoved it in his tunic. "Very well then, my friends. Good flying! May your Weyrs—" He caught himself, a flicker of uncertainty for his glib use of a courteous salutation not entirely appropriate.

"The Weyrs will prosper, S'ligar," K'dren said as he smiled confidently at the big man. "They always have!"

The bronze riders turned to their dragons, mounting with the ease and grace of long practice. Almost as one, the six dragons wheeled to the left and right of the red butte, to spring agilely into the air. Again, as if the unique maneuver had been many times rehearsed, on the third downstroke of six pairs of great wings, the dragons went *between*.

Fort Weyr, 3.14.43

At about the time the bronze dragonriders were meeting at the Butte, Capiam had discovered that if he timed a fit of coughing, he could miss some of the incoming, more painful messages. Even after the thrumming of the great drums in the tower had ceased, the cadences played ring-a-round in his head and inhibited the sleep he yearned for. Not that sleep brought any rest. He would feel more tired when he roused from such brief naps as the drums permitted. And the nightmares! He was forever being harried by that tawny, speckle-coated, tuft-eared monster that had carried its peculiar germs to a vulnerable continent. The irony was that the Ancients had probably created the agency that threatened to exterminate their descendants.

If only those seamen had let the animal die on its tree trunk in the Eastern Current. If only it had died on the ship, succumbing to thirst and exhaustion—as Capiam felt he was likely to do at any moment—before it had contaminated more than the seamen. If only the nearby holders hadn't been so bloody curious to relieve the winter's tedium. If! If! If? If wishes were dragons, all Pern would fly!

And *if* Capiam had any energy, he would apply it to finding a concoction that would relieve and, preferably, inhibit the disease. Surely the Ancients had had to cope with epidemics. There were, indeed, grand paragraphs in the oldest Records, boasting that the ailments that had plagued mankind before the Crossing had been totally elminated on Pern—which statement, Capiam maintained, meant that there had been two Crossings, not one, as many people—including Tirone—believed. The Ancients had brought many animals with them in that first Crossing, the equine from which runners originated; the bovine for the herdbeasts; the ovine, smaller, herdbeasts; the canine; and a smaller variety of the dratted feline plague carrier. The creatures had been brought, in ova (or so the Record put it) from the Ancients' planet or origin which was not the planet Pern, or why had that one point been made so specifically and repeated so often? Pern, not simply the Southern Continent. And the second Crossing had been from south to north. Probably, Capiam contemplated bitterly, to escape feline plague carriers that secreted themselves in dark lairs to nourish their fell disease until unwary humans took them off tree trunks, days from land. Couldn't the Ancients have stopped bragging about their achievements long enough to state *how* they had eradicated plague and pandemic? Their success was meaningless without the process.

Capiam plucked feebly at the sleeping furs. They smelled. They needed to be aired. He smelled. He didn't dare leave his room. "What can't be cured must be endured." Desdra's taunt returned to him often.

He was a healer: He would heal himself first and thus prove to others that one could recover from this miserable disease. He need only apply his trained mind and considerable willpower to the problem. On cue, a coughing spell wracked him. When he had recovered sufficiently, he reached for the syrup Desdra left on the beside table. He wished she would look in on him.

Fortine had, conferring three times from the doorway, seeking authority on matters Capiam could not now recall. He hoped that his responses had been sensible. Tirone had appeared, very briefly, more to assure himself and to report to the world that Capiam was still part of it than to comfort or cheer the sick man.

Fort Hold proper had not been sullied by the plague, even though healers—master, journeyman, and apprentice—had journeyed to the stricken areas. Four of Fort's seaside holds and two coastal cropholds had succumbed.

The syrup eased Capiam's raw throat. He could even taste it. Thymus was the principal ingredient, and he approved of its use on his person. If the disease ran the same course in him as it had in the cases he had studied, the cough ought soon to pass. If, by virtue of the strict quarantine in which he lay, he did not contract a secondary infection—pulmonary, penumonic, or bronchial seemed the readiest to pounce on the weakened patient—then he ought to improve rapidly.

K'lon, the blue rider from Fort Weyr, had recovered totally. Capiam hoped that the man had actually *had* the plague, not some deep cold, and his hope was substantiated by the facts that K'lon had a close friend in plague-stricken Igen, and that the Weyr healer, Berchar, and his green rider weyrmate were grievously ill at Fort Weyr. Capiam tried to censor his own painful thoughts of dragonriders dying as easily as holders. Dragonriders could *not* die. The Pass had eight Turns to go. There were hundreds of powders, roots, and barks and herbs to combat disease on Pern, but the numbers of dragons and their riders were limited.

Desdra really ought to be appearing soon with some of the restorative soup she took such pleasure in making him consume! It was her presence he wished for, not the soup, for he found the long hours of solitude without occupation tedious and fraught with unpleasant speculations. He knew he ought to be grateful to have a room to himself for the chances of further infection were thus reduced to the minimum, but he would have liked some company. Then he thought of the crowded holds and he had no doubt that some poor sod there would dearly love to exchange with him for solitude.

Capiam took no pleasure in the knowledge that his frequent haragues to the Lords Holder about indiscriminate breeding should prove so devastatingly accurate. But dragonriders ought not to be dying of this plague. They had private quarters, were hardy, inured to many of the ailments that afflicted those in poorer conditions, were supplied with the top of the tithe. Igen, Keroon, Ista: Those Weyrs had had direct contact with the feline. And Fort, High Reaches, and Benden riders had attended the Gathers. Almost every rider had had time and opportunity to catch the infection.

Capiam had had severe qualms about demanding a conveyance of Sh'gall from Southern Boll to Fort Hold. But, on the other hand, Sh'gall had conveyed Lord Ratoshigan to Ista Gather for the purpose of seeing the rare creature on display quite a few hours before Capiam and the young animal healer, Talpan, had their startling conference. It was only after Capiam had reached Southern Boll and seen Lord Ratoshigan's sick handlers that he had realized how quickly the disease incubated and how insidiously it spread. Expediency had required Capiam to use the quickest means to return to his Hall, and that had been adragonback with the Fort Weyrleader. Sh'gall had taken ill but he was young and healthy, Capiam told himself. So had Ratoshigan, but Capiam found a rather curious justice in that. Given the infinite variety of human personalities, it was impossible to like everyone. Capiam didn't like Ratoshigan but he shouldn't be glad the man was suffering along with his lowliest beasthandler.

Capiam vowed, yet again, that he would have far more tolerance for the ill when he recovered. *When! When!* Not *if. If* was defeatist. How had the many thousands of patients he tended over his Turns as a healer endured those hours of unrelieved thought and self-examination? Capiam sighed, tears forming at the corners of his eyes: a further manifestation of his terrible inertia. When—yes, *when*—would he have the strength to resume constructive thought and research?

There *had* to be an answer, a solution, a cure, a therapy, a restorative, a remedy! Something existed somewhere. If the Ancients had been able to cross unimaginable distances to breed animals from a frozen stew, to create dragons from the template of the legendary fire-lizards, they surely would have been able to overcome bacterium or virus that threatened themselves and those beasts. It could only be a matter of time, Capiam assured his weary self, before those references were discovered. Fortine had been searching the Records piled in the Library Caves. When he had had to dispatch journeymen and apprentice healers to reinforce their overworked craftsmen in the worst plague areas, Tirone had magnanimously placed his craftspeople at Fortine's disposal. But if one of those untutored readers passed over the relevant paragraphs in ignorance of the significance . . . Surely, though, something as critical as an epidemic would merit more than a single reference.

When would Desdra come with her soup to break the monotony of his anxious self-castigation? "Stop fretting," he told himself, his voice a hoarse croak that startled him. "You're peevish. You're also alive. What must be endured cannot be cured. No. What cannot be cured must be inured—endured."

Tears for his debilitation dripped down his cheekbones, falling in time to the latest urgent drum code. Capiam wanted to stop his ears against the news. It was sure to be bad. How could it possibly be anything else until they had some sort of specific treatment and some means of arresting the swift spread of this plague?

Keroon Runnerhold sent the message. They needed medicines. Healer Gorby reported dwindling stocks of borrago and aconite, and needed tussilago in quantity for pulmonary and bronchial cases, ilex for pneumonia.

A new fear enveloped Capiam. With such unprecedented demands on stillroom supplies, would there be enough of even the simple medicaments? Keroon Runnerhold, dealing as it did with many animal health problems, ought to be able to supply all its needs. Capiam despaired afresh as he thought of smaller holds. They would have on hand only a limited amount of general remedies. Most holds traded the plants and barks indigenous in their area for those they lacked. What lady holder, no matter how diligent and capable, would have laid in sufficient to deal with an epidemic?

To compound demand, the disease had struck during the cold season. Most medicinal plants were picked in flower, when their curative properties were strongest; roots and bulbs gathered in the fall. Spring and flowering, autumn and earthy harvest were too distant, the need was now!

Capiam writhed in his furs. Where was Desdra? How much longer did he have to endure before the wretched lethargy abated?

"Capiam?" Desdra's quiet voice broke into his self-pitying ruminations. "More soup?"

"Desdra? That message from Keroon Runnerhold—"

"As if we had only one febrifuge in our pharmacopia! Fortine has compiled a list of alternatives." Desdra was impatient with Gorby. "There's ash bark, box, ezob, and thymus as well as borrago and featherfern. Who's to say one of them might not prove to be specific for this? In fact, Semment of Great Reach Hold believes that thymus is more effective for the pulmonary infections he's been treating. Master Fortine holds out for featherfern, being one of the few indigenous plants. How are you feeling?"

"Like nothing! I cannot even raise my hands." He tried to demonstrate this inability.

"The lassitude is part of the illness. You wrote that symptom often enough. What can't be cured—"

Summoning strength from a sudden spurt of irrational anger, Capiam flung a pillow at her. It had neither the mass nor the impetus to reach its target, and she laughed as she collected the missile and lofted it easily back to his bed.

"I believe that you are somewhat improved in spirit. Now drink the soup." She set it down on the table.

"Are all healthy here?"

"All here, yes. Even the officious Tolocamp, immured in his quarters. He's more likely to catch pneumonia while standing at unshuttered windows to check up on the guards." Desdra chuckled maliciously. "He's got messengers stationed on the forecourt. He sails notes down to them to take to offenders. Not even a tunnel snake could slip past his notice!" A tiny smirk curved Desdra's lips. "Master Tirone had to talk long and hard to get him to set up that internment camp in the hollow. Tolocamp was certain that offering shelter would be an invitation to undesirables to lodge and feed at his expense. Tirone is furious with Tolocamp because he wants to send his harpers out with the assurance that they can return, but Tolocamp refuses to believe that harpers can avoid infection. Tolocamp sees the disease as a visible mist or fog that oozes out of meadows and streams and mountain crevices."

Desdra was trying to amuse him, Capiam thought, for she wasn't normally garrulous.

"I did order a quarantine."

Desdra snorted. "True! Tolocamp ought not to have left Ruatha. He overruled the brother when Alessan fell ill. And with every other breath, Tolocamp is said to moan for abandoning his dear wife, Lady Pendra, and those precious daughters of his to the mercies of the plague rampaging at Ruatha." Desdra's chuckle was dry. "He left them there on purpose. Or Lady Pendra insisted they all stay. They'll have insisted on nursing Alessan!"

"How *are* matters at Fort Weyr and Ruatha?"

"K'lon tells us that Moreta is doing as well as can be expected. Berchar probably has pneumonia, and nineteen riders—including Sh'gall—are weyred. Ruatha is badly hit. Fortine has dispatched volunteers. Now drink that soup before it cools. There's much to be done below. I can't stay to chat with you any longer."

Capiam found that his hand shook violently as he picked up the mug.

"Shouldn't't've wasted all that energy tossing that pillow," she said.

He used both hands to bring the mug to his lips without spilling. "What *have* you put in it?" he demanded after a careful swallow.

"A little of this, a little of that. Trying a few restoratives out on you. If they work, I'll make kettlesful."

"It's vile!"

"It's also nutritional. Drink it!"

"I'll choke."

"Drink it or I'll let Nerilka, that laundry pole daughter of Tolocamp's, come nurse you in my stead. She offers hourly."

Capiam cursed Desdra but he drained the cup.

"Well, you do sound improved!" She chuckled as she closed the door quietly behind her.

*   *   *

"I didn't say I liked it either," Leri told S'peren. "But old dragons can glide. That's why Holth and I can still fly Thread in the queens' wing." Leri gave Holth an affectionate clout on the shoulder, beaming up at her life-long friend. "It's the tip, the finger, and elbow joints that harden so the finer points of maneuverability go. Gliding's from the shoulder. Doesn't take much effort, either, with the sort of wind we're likely to get now. Why did it have to get so bloody cold on top of everything else? Rain'd be more bearable as well as more seasonable." Leri adjusted the furs across her shoulders. "I wouldn't trust the weyrlings to such dull work. They'd do something fancy, like the stunt young T'ragel tried on the ridge with Moreta.

"Now, you said L'bol is grieving badly?"

"Indeed he is. He's lost both sons." S'peren shook his head sadly before he took another sip of the wine Leri had served him "to wet your throat after the dust at Red Butte." S'peren took comfort in the familiar act of reporting to Leri. It was like the old times, only a few Turns past at that, when L'mal had been Weyrleader and S'peren had been much in this weyr. He almost expected to see L'mal's chunky figure swing into the chamber and hear the hearty voice greeting him. Now *there* was a Leader to encourage and comfort in this disastrous Turn. Still, S'peren thought with a blink, Leri was as brisk and quick as ever. "Could Igen put eight full wings up to Fall?"

"What?" Leri snapped out in surprise at the question, then snorted. "Not likely. Torenth told Holth that half the Weyr is sick and the other half looks sick. Their damned curiosity and all that sun on their heads all the time. Slows 'em down. Nothing to do with their spare time but bake their brains. Of course, they all went to gawk at a raree! And we'll never hear the last of their moans for the unexpected tariff!" She made a business of scanning the lists S'peren had handed her. "Can't say as I can put a face or pair a dragon name with some of these. Must all be new. When L'mal was Leader, I kept up with all the new riders in every Weyr."

"S'ligar asked about Moreta."

"Worried about Orlith and her eggs?" Leri peered wisely over the lists at the bronze rider.

S'peren nodded. "S'ligar volunteered candidates in case—"

"Only what I'd expect." Leri's answer was tart but, seeing the expression on S'peren's face, she relented. "It was good of him to offer. Especially since Orlith is the only queen currently bearing eggs." Leri's round face produced a slightly malicious smile.

S'peren continued to nod for he hadn't realized that. It put another light on S'ligar's concern for Moreta and Orlith.

"Don't worry, S'peren. Moreta's doing well. Orlith's with her constantly and that queen's a marvel of comfort, as everyone in this Weyr should know by now."

"I thought it was just with injured dragons."

"And no comfort for her own weyrmate and rider? Of course Orlith helps Moreta. The other Weyrs could learn a thing or two from our senior queen dragon. Wouldn't surprise me if there were some pretty crucial changes made when Moreta's well. And when Orlith rises to mate again!" Leri winked broadly at S'peren. "That girl has got to show her true preference to her queen."

S'peren managed to hide his surprise at Leri's outspokenness. Of course, they were old friends and she probably felt able to be candid in his company. Then he took a quick sip of the wine. What could Leri possibly be suggesting? He liked Moreta very much. She and Orlith had done a fine job of healing a long Threadscore on his Clioth's flank last Turn. And Clioth had risen to fly in Orlith's last mating flight. He had been perversely relieved when Clioth had failed, despite his admiration and respect for Moreta, and despite a natural desire to prove his bronze dragon superior to the other bronzes of Fort. On the other hand, he had never questioned Sh'gall's ability as a flight leader. The man had an uncanny instinct for which dragon might be failing in strength or losing his flame, or which rider might not be as courageous as he ought in following Thread out of path, but S'peren did not covet the Leadership half as much as his Clioth yearned to mate with Orlith.

"K'lon?" Leri said, breaking into his thoughts. She and her dragon looked toward the weyr entrance.

Clioth confirmed the arrival of Rogeth to S'peren, telling his rider that he was moving over to permit the blue to land on Holth's ledge.

"About bloody time that young man came back to his own Weyr," Leri said, frowning. "There *has* to be another dragonrider able to do what K'lon's doing or he'll kill himself. Misplaced guilt. Or more likely the chance to get in and out of Igen to see that lover of his."

There was no question that the blue rider was exhausted as he entered the weyr. His shoulders sagged and his step had no spring. His face was travel-stained except for the lighter patches of skin around his eyes, protected from flight dirt by his goggles. His clothes were stiff with moisture frozen into the hide by constant journeys *between*.

"Five drops from the blue vial," Leri said quickly in an undertone, leaning toward S'peren. Then she straightened, speaking in a normal tone. "S'peren, fix a mug of klah laced with that fortified wine of mine for K'lon. And sit down there, young man, before you fall." Leri pointed imperiously to a chair. She had replaced her one stool with several comfortable seats positioned, as she phrased it, in noncontagious spacing in front of Holth's couch.

K'lon barely avoided falling into the appointed chair; his legs slid out in front of him as he slouched into the seat. Dangling helmet and goggles from one limp hand, he accepted the mug from S'peren.

"Take a long swallow now, K'lon," Leri said kindly. "It'll restore your blood to normal temperature after all that *betweening*. You're nearly as blue as Rogeth. There! That tastes good, doesn't it? A brew of my own to hearten the weary." Though her voice was kind, she watched K'lon intently. "Now, what news from the halls?"

K'lon's weary face brightened. "There is *good* news. Master Capiam really is recovering. I spoke to Desdra. He's weak but he's swearing out loud. She said they'd probably have to tether him to his bed to keep him there long enough to regain his strength. He's yelling for Records. Best of all"—K'lon seemed to shrug off his fatigue in his cheerful recital—"he insists that the disease itself doesn't cause the deaths. People are actually dying from other things, like pneumonia and bronchitis and other respiratory ailments. Avoid those and"—K'lon made a wide sweep of his hand, his helmet and goggles clacking together—"all's well." Then his expression altered dolefully. "Only that's just not possible in the Holds, you know. So many people crammed into inadequate space...and not enough facilities...especially now, when it's got so cold. The Lords Holder would put people into hide tents that are well enough for a Gather but not for the sick. I've been everywhere. Even holds that don't know what's been happening elsewhere and think it's only them that're in deep trouble. I've been so many places..." His face turned bleak and his body slumped deeper into the chair.

"A'murry?" Leri spoke the green rider's name gently.

K'lon's misery broke through the tight hold he must be keeping on his private anxiety. "He's got a chest infection—one of the weyrfolk nursing him had a bad cold." His condemnation was plain. "Fortine gave me a special mixture and a comfrey salve for his chest. I made A'murry take the first dose and it really did stop him midcough. And I rubbed the salve thick on his chest and back." Some instinct made K'lon look at the other two riders and he saw their unvoiced apprehension. "I've got to go to A'murry. Whenever I can. I can't *give* him what I've got over! And don't tell me it's enough that Rogeth and Granth stay in touch. I've very much aware that they do, but *I* have a need to be with A'murry, too, you know." K'lon's face contorted. He looked about to break into tears, a display he averted by drinking deeply of the wine-laced *klah*. "That's quite tasty, really," he said courteously to Leri. Then he finished the drink. "Now, what else can I tell you from my..."

He paused, blinked, swallowed, and then his head began to loll to one side. Leri, who had been waiting for that, signaled urgently to S'peren.

"Perfectly timed, I think," she said as S'peren caught K'lon before he slid from the chair. "Here." She tossed a pillow and pulled the fur from her shoulders. "Roll him into this, pillow his head, and he'll sleep a good twelve hours. Holth, be a pet and tell Rogeth to go curl up in his own weyr and get some rest. You"—she prodded the resisting flesh of her queen with her forefinger—"will keep your ears open for Granth."

"What if he's needed?" S'peren asked, arranging K'lon comfortably. "By the Halls or the Hold or A'murry?"

"A'murry is, of course, a priority," Leri replied thoughtfully. "I can't really condone his breaking of quarantine. I'll think of some discipline later, for K'lon *has* disobeyed a direct order. I have just decided that we can use other messengers in K'lon's place. Especially if most of what he does is convey supplies or healers. Weyrlings can do that! They'll feel brave and daring, and be scared enough to be careful. Packages can certainly be deposited without making contact and messages collected at a discreet distance from cots. Let them practice setting down by a pennant instead of a ridge. Good practice." Leri peered down critically at the sleeping K'lon. "However, you'd better circulate the news he brought us from the Hall—that the plague doesn't kill. We must be more wary than ever for our convalescents. No one with the slightest sign of a head cold or even a pimple is to attend the riders."

"It's hard enough to get weyrfolk to tend them," S'peren remarked.

"Hmm! Ask the laggards who will tend *them* in their hour of need?" Leri rolled up the rider lists and stowed them carefully on the shelf beside her. "So, old friend, you'll bring the good news from the Healer Hall to the Lower Caverns and *then* tell off the wings which are rising to Fall tomorrow!"

Healer Hall, 3.15.43

The light of the many glows that Capiam had ordered to illuminate the tight and fading script of the old ledgers shone harshly on the handsome countenance of Tirone, Masterharper of Pern, who had drawn a chair up to Capiam's wide writing desk. Tirone was scowling at the healer, a totally uncharacteristic expression on a man renowned for his geniality and expansive good humor. The epidemic—no, one had to state its true proportions, *pan*demic—had marked everyone, including those lucky enough not to have contracted it.

Many believed that Tirone bore a charmed life in the pursuit of his duties across the continent. The Harper had been detained on the border between Tillek and the High Reaches on a disputation over mines, which had prevented him from attending the Ruathan Gather. Once the drums had sounded the quarantine, Tirone made his way back to the Hall by runner relays, past holds where the plague had not penetrated and some where the news had not spread. He had a fine old row with Tolocamp to be permitted within the Hold proper, but Tirone's logic and the fact that he had not entered any infected areas had prevailed. Or had one of the guards told the Masterharper how it was that Lord Tolocamp had returned from Ruatha?

Tirone had also prevailed on Desdra to permit him to visit the Master Healer.

"If I don't get details from you, Capiam, I shall be forced to rely on hearsay and that is not a proper source for a Masterharper."

"Tirone, I am not about to die. While I laud your zealous desire for a true and accurate account, I have a more pressing duty!" Capiam raised the ledger. "I may have recovered but I have to find out how to cure or stop this wretched disease before it kills further thousands."

"I'm under strict orders not to tire you or Desdra will have my gizzard to grill," Tirone replied with a jocular smile. "But the facts are that I was woefully out of touch with the Hall at this most critical time. I can't even get a decent account from the drummaster though I quite appreciate that neither he nor his journeymen had the time to log the messages which came in and out of the tower at such a rate. Tolocamp won't talk to me though it's five days since Ruatha Gather . . . and he shows no signs of the illness. So I must have something to go on besides incoherent and confused versions. The perceptions of a trained observer such as yourself are invaluable to the chronicler. I am given to understand that you talked with Talpan at Ista?" Tirone poised his pen above the clean squared sheet of hide.

"Talpan . . . now there's the man you should talk to when this is over."

"That won't be possible. Shards! Weren't you told?" The Harper half-rose from his chair, hand outstretched in sympathy.

"I'm all right. No, I didn't know." Capiam closed his eyes for a moment to absorb that shock. "I suspect they thought it would depress me. It does. He was a fine man, with a quick, clever mind. Herdmaster potential." Capiam heard another swift intake of breath from Tirone and opened his eyes. "Master Herdsman Trume as well?" And when Tirone nodded confirmation, Capiam steeled himself. So that was why Tirone had been allowed to see him: to break the news. "I think you'd better tell me the rest of the bad news that neither Desdra nor Fortine voiced. It won't hurt half as much now. I'm numb."

"There have been terrible losses, you realize—"

"Any figures?"

"At Keroon, nine out of every ten who fell ill have died! At Igen Sea Hold, fifteen were weak but alive when the relief ship from Nerat reached them. We have no totals from surrounding holds in Igen, nor do we know the extent of the epidemic's spread in Igen, Keroon, or Ruatha. You can be very proud of your Craftsmen and women, Capiam.

They did all that was humanly possible to succor the ill . . ."

"And they died, too?" Capiam asked when Tirone's voice trailed off.

"They brought honor to your hall."

Capiam's heart thumped slowly in his anguish. All dead? Mibbut, gentle Kylos, the earthy Loreana, earnest Rapal, the bone-setter Sneel, Galnish? All of them? Could it really be only *seven* days ago that he had first had word of the dreadful sickness? And those he had attended at Keroon and Igen already sick to their deaths with it? Though he was now positive that the plague itself didn't kill, the living had to face another sort of death, the death of hopes and friendships and what might have been in the futures of those whose lives were abruptly ended. And so near to the promise and freedom of an Interval! Capiam felt tears sliding down his cheeks but they eased the tight constriction in his chest. He let them flow, breathing slowly in and out until his emotions were in hand again. He couldn't think emotionally; he must think professionally. "Igen Sea Hold held nearly a thousand people; only fifty were ill when I attended them at Burdion's summons."

"Burdion is one of the survivors."

"I trust he kept notes for you." Capiam could not prevent his tone from being savage.

"I believe he did," Tirone went on, impervious to the invalid's bad temper. "The log of the *Windtoss* is also available."

"The captain was dead when I reached the Sea Hold."

"Did you *see* the animal?" Tirone leaned forward slightly, his eyes glinting with the avid curiosity he did not voice.

"Yes, I saw it!" That image was now seared in Capiam's memory. The feline had paced restlessly and vividly through his fever dreams and his restless nightmares. Capiam would never forget its snarling face, the white and black whiskers that sprang from its thick muzzle, the brown stains on its tusks, the nicks in its laid-back tufted ears, the dark-brown medallions of its markings that were so fancifully ringed with black and set off in the tawny, shining coat. He could remember its fierce defiance and had even then, when he'd first seen it, conceived the notion that the creature knew perfectly well that it would take revenge on the beings who had restricted it to a cage, who had stared at it in every hold and hall. "Yes, Tirone, I actually saw it. Like hundreds of other people attending Ista Gather. Only I've lived to tell the tale. Talpan and I spent twenty minutes observing it while he told me why he thought it had to die. In twenty minutes it probably infected many people even though Talpan was making the gawkers stand well back from the cage. In fact, I probably contracted my dose of the plague there. From the source. Instead of secondhand." That conclusion afforded Capiam some relief. Made more vulnerable by fatigue, he'd come down with the plague a bare twenty-four hours later. That was better than believing that he had been negligent of hygiene at Igen and Keroon. "Talpan deduced that the animal had to be the cause of the disease already affecting runners from Igen to Keroon. I'd been called to Keroon, too, you see, because so many of their folk were falling ill. I was tracing human contagion, Talpan was tracing runner. We both reached the same conclusion at Ista Gather. The creature was terrified of dragons, you know."

"Really?"

"So I was informed. But K'dall is among the dead at Telgar Weyr and so is his blue dragon."

Tirone murmured, all the while writing furiously. "How, then, did the disease get to Southern Boll if the creature was killed at Ista Gather?"

"You've forgotten the weather."

"Weather?"

"Yes, the weather was so mild Keroon Runnerhold started shipping early this winter, the tides and winds being favorable. So Lord Rato-shigan got his breeding stock early and an unexpected bounty. As did several other notable breeders, some of whom attended Ruatha Gather."

"Well, that is interesting. Such a devastating concatenation of so many small events."

"We should be grateful that Tillek breeds its own and supplies the High Reaches, Crom, and Nabol. That the Keroon-bred runners destined for Benden, Lemos, Bitra, and Nerat either died of the plague or were not herded overland."

"The Weyrleaders have issued an interdiction against any travel to the Southern Continent!" Tirone said. "The Ancients had excellent reason for abandoning that place. Too many threats to life."

"Get your facts straight, Tirone," Capiam said, irritated. "Most life *here* was created and nutured *there*!"

"Now, I have never seen that proved to—"

"Life and its maintenance are *my* province, Masterharper." Capiam held up the ancient ledger and waggled it at Tirone. "As the creation and development of life was once the province of our ancestors. The Ancients brought with them from the Southern Continent all the animals we have here with us today, including the dragons which they genetically engineered for their unique purpose."

Tirone's lower jaw jutted slightly, about to dispute.

"We have lost the skills that the Ancients possessed even though we can refine runners and the herdbeasts for specific qualities. And..." Capiam paused, struck by an awful consideration. "And I'm suddenly aware that we are in a double peril right now." He thought of Talpan and all his bright promise lost, of Master Herdsman Trume, of the captain of the *Windtoss*, his own dead craftsmen, each with his or her special qualities lost to a swift, mortal illness. "We may have lost a lot more than a coherent account of the progress of a plague, Tirone. And that should worry you far more. It is knowledge as well as life that is being lost all over Pern. What you should be jotting down as fast as you can push your fist is the knowledge, the techniques that are dying in men's minds and cannot be recovered." Capiam waved the Record about, Tirone eyeing it with alarm. "As we can't recover from all the ledgers and Records of the Ancients exactly how they performed the miracles they did. And it's not the miracles so much as the working, the day-to-day routine which the Ancients didn't bother to record because it was *common knowledge*. A common knowledge that is no longer common. That's what we're missing. And we may have lost a lot more of that common knowlege over the past seven days! More than we can ever replace!"

Capiam lay back, exhausted by his outburst, the Records a heavy weight on his guts. That sense of loss, the pressure of that anxiety, had been growing inside him. That morning, when the lethargy had passed, he had been disquietingly aware of the many facts, practices, and intuitions he had never written down, had never thought to elaborate in his private notes. Ordinarily he would have passed them on to his journeymen as they grasped the complexities of their craft. Some matters he had been told by his masters, which they had gleaned from their tutors or from their working experiences, but the transfer of information and its interpretation had been verbal in all too many instances, passed on to those who would need to know.

Capiam became aware that Tirone was staring at him. He had not meant to harangue; that was generally Tirone's function.

"I could not agree with you more, Capiam," Tirone began tentatively, pausing to clear his throat. "But people of all ranks and Crafts tend to keep some secrets which—"

"Shells! Not the drum again!" Capiam buried his head in his hands, pressing his thumbs tightly into his earholes, trying to block the sound.

Tirone's expression brightened and he half-rose from the chair, gesturing for Capiam to unplug his ears. "It's good news. From Igen. Threadfall has been met and all is clear. Twelve wings flew!"

"Twelve?" Capiam pulled himself up, calculating Igen's crushing losses and the numbers of its sick riders. "Igen couldn't have put twelve wings in the air today."

"'Dragonmen must fly, when Thread is in the sky!'" Tirone's resonant voice rang with pride and exultation.

Capiam stared at him, aware only of profound dismay. How had he failed to catch the significance of Tirone's mention of the Weyrleaders' joint interdiction of the Southern Continent? They'd had to consolidate Weyrs to meet Fall.

"'To fight Thread is in their blood! Despite their cruel losses, they rise, as always, to defend the continent...'"

Tirone was off in what Capiam had derisively termed his lyric trance. It was not the time to be composing sagas and ballads! Yet the ringing phrases plucked at a long forgotten memory.

"Do be quiet, Tirone. I must think! Or there won't be *any* dragonriders left to fight Thread. Get out!"

Blood! That's what Tirone had said. It's in their blood! Blood! Capiam hit his temples with the heels of his hands as if he could jolt the vagrant memory into recall. He could almost hear the creaky old voice of old Master Gallardy. Yes, he'd been preparing for his journeyman's examinations and old Gallardy had been droning on and on about unusual and obsolescent techniques. Something to do with blood. Gallardy had been talking about the curative properties of blood—blood what? Blood serum! That was it!

Blood serum as an extreme remedy for contagious or virulent disease.

"Capiam?" It was Desdra, her voice hesitant. "Are you all right? Tirone said—"

"I'm fine! I'm fine! What was that you kept telling me? What can't be cured must be endured. Well, there's another way. *Inuring* to cure. Immunizing. And it's in the blood! It's not a bark, a powder, a leaf, it's blood. And the deterrant is in my blood right now! Because I've survived the plague."

"Master Capiam!" Desdra stepped forward, hesitant, mindful of the precautions of the last five days.

"I do not think I am contagious any longer, my brave Desdra. I'm the cure! At least I believe I am." In his excitement, Capiam had crawled out of bed, flinging sleeping rugs away from him in an effort to reach the case that held his apprentice and journeyman's texts.

"Capiam! You'll fall!"

Capiam was tottering and he grasped at the chair Tirone had vacated to prevent the collapse. He couldn't summon the strength to reach to the shelves.

"Get me my notes. The oldest ones, there on the left-hand side of the top shelf." He sat down abruptly in the chair, shaking with weakness. "I must be right. I have to be right. 'The blood of a recovered patient prevents others from contracting the disease.'"

"Your blood, my fine feeble friend," Desdra said tartly, dusting off the records before she handed them to him, "is very thin and very weak, and you're going back to your bed."

"Yes, yes, in a minute." Capiam was riffling through the thin hide pages, trying in his haste not to crack the brittle fabric, forcing himself to recall exactly when Master Gallardy had delivered those lectures on "unusual techniques." Spring. It was spring. He turned to the last third of his notes. Spring, because he had allowed his mind to dwell more on normal springtime urges than ancient procedures. He felt Desdra tugging at his shoulder.

"You have me spend two hours fixing glowbaskets just to illuminate you in bed and now you read in the darkest corner of your room. Get back into bed! I haven't nursed you this far out of that plague to have you die on me from a chill caught prancing about in the dark like a broody dragon."

"And hand me my kit...please." He kept reading as he allowed himself to be escorted back to bed. Desdra tugged the furs so tightly in at the foot that he couldn't bend his knees to prop up the notes. With a tug and a kick, he undid her handiwork.

"Capiam!" Returning with his kit, she was furious at his renewed disarray. She grabbed his shoulder and laid her hand across his forehead. He pushed it away, trying not to show the irritation he felt at her interruptions.

"I'm all right. I'm all right."

"Tirone thought you'd had a relapse the way you're acting. It's not like you, you know, to cry 'blood, blood, it's in their blood.' Or in yours, for that matter."

He only half heard her for he had found the series of lectures that he had copied that spring, thirty Turns gone, when he was far more interested in urgent problems like Threadscore, infection, preventive doses, and nutrition.

"It is in my blood. That's what it says here," Capiam cried in triumph. "'The clear serum which rises to the top of the vessel after the blood has clotted produces the essential globulins which will inhibit the disease. Injected intravenously, the blood serum gives protection for at least fourteen days, which is ordinarily sufficient time for an epidemic disease to run its course.'" Capiam read on avidly. He could separate the blood components by centrifugal force. Master Gallardy had said that the Ancients had special apparatus to achieve separation, but he could suggest a homely expedient. "'The serum introduces the disease into the body in such a weakened state as to awaken the body's own defenses and thus prevent such a disease in its more virulent form.'"

Capiam lay back on his pillows, closing his eyes against a momentary weakness that was compounded of relief as well as triumph. He even recalled how he had rebelled against the tedious jotting down of a technique that might now save thousands of people. And the dragonriders!

Desdra regarded him with a curious expression on her face. "But that's homeopathic! Except for injecting directly into the vein."

"Quickly absorbed by the body, thus more effective. And we need an *effective* treatment. Desdra, how *many* dragonriders are sick?"

"We don't know, Capiam. They stopped reporting numbers. The drums did say that twelve wings flew Thread at Igen, but the last report I had, from K'lon actually, was that one hundred and seventy-five riders were ill, including one of the queen riders. L'bol lost two sons in the first deaths."

"A hundred and seventy-five ill? Any secondary infections?"

"They haven't said. But then we haven't asked...."

"At Telgar? Fort Weyr?"

"We have been thinking more of the thousands dying than the dragonriders," Desdra admitted in a bleak voice, her hands locked so tightly the knuckles were white.

"Yes, well, we *depend* on those two-thousand-odd dragonriders. So nag me no more and get what I need to make the serum. And when K'lon comes, I'll want to see him immediately. Is there anyone else here in the Halls or the Hold who has recovered from this disease?"

"Not recovered."

"Never mind. K'lon will be here soon?"

"We expect him. He's been conveying medicines and healers."

"Good. Now, I'll need a lot of sterile, two liter glass containers with screw tops, stout cord, fresh reeds span-length—I've got needlethorns—redwort and oh, boil me that syringe the cooks use to baste meats. I do have some glass ones Master Clargesh had blown for me, but I can't *think* where I stored them. Now, away with you. Oh, and Desdra, I'll want some double-destilled spirits and more of that restorative soup of yours."

"I can understand the need for spirits," she said at the door, her expression sardonic, "but more of the soup you dislike so?"

He flourished a pillow and she laughed as she closed the door behind her.

Capiam turned the pages to the beginning of Master Gallardy's lecture.

In the event of an outbreak of a communicable disease, the use of a serum prepared from the blood of a recovered victim of the same disease has proved efficacious. Where the populace is healthy, an injection of the blood serum prevents the disease. Administered to a sufferer, the blood serum mitigates the virulence. Long before the Crossings, such plagues as varicella, diphtheria, influenza, rubella, epidemic roseola, morbilli, scarlatina, variola, typhoid, typhus, poliomyelitis, tuberculosis, hepatitis, cytomegalovirus herpes, and gonococcal were eliminated by vaccination...

Typhus and typhoid were familiar to Capiam, for there had been outbreaks of each as the result of ineffective hygiene. He and the other healers had feared they would result from the current overcrowding. Diphtheria and scarlatina had flared up occasionally over the past several hundred Turns, at least often enough so that the symptoms and the treatment were part of his training. The other diseases he didn't know except from the root words, which were very very old. He would have to look them up in the Harper Hall's etymological dictionary.

He read on farther in Master Gallardy's advice. A liter and a half of blood could be taken from each recovered victim of the disease and that, separated, would give fifty mils of serum for immunization. The injectable amount varied from one mil to ten, according to Gallardy, but he wasn't very specific as to which amount for which disease. Capiam thought ruefully of the impassioned words he had poured at Tirone concerning the loss of techniques. Was he himself at fault for not attending more closely to Master Gallardy's full lecture?

No great calculation was needed for Capiam to see the enormity of the task of producing the desirable immunity even for the vital few thousand dragonriders, the Lords Holder, and Mastercraftsmen, let alone the healers who must care for the ill and prepare and administer the vaccine.

The door swung before Desdra, who looked flustered for the first time that Capiam could remember. She carried a rush basket and closed the door with a deft hook of her foot.

"I have your requirements and I have found the glass syringes that Master Genjon blew for you. Three were broken, but I have boiled the remainder."

Desdra carefully deposited the wicker basket by his bed. She pulled his bedside table to its customary place and, on it, she put the jar of redwort in its strongest solution, a parcel of reeds, the leaf-bound needlethorns, a steaming steel tray that had covered the kettle in which he could see a small glass jar, a stopper, and the Genjon syringes. From her pocket, Desdra drew a length of stout, well-twisted cord. "There!"

"That is not a two-liter jar."

"No, but you are not strong enough to be reduced by two liters of blood. Half a liter is all you can lose. K'lon will be here soon enough."

Desdra briskly scrubbed his arm with the redwort then tied the cord about his upper arm while he clenched his fist to raise the artery. It was ropy and blue beneath flesh that seemed too white to him. With tongs, she took the glass container from the boiled water. She opened the packet of reeds, then the needlethorns, took one of each and fitted the needlethorn to one end of the reed. "I know the technique but I haven't done this often."

"You'll have to! My hand shakes!"

Desdra pressed her lips in a firm line, dipped her fingers in redwort, put the glass container on the floor by his bed, tilted the reed end into it, and picked up the needlethorn. The tip of a needlethorn is so fine that the tiny opening in the point is almost invisible. Desdra punctured his skin and, with only a little force, entered the engorged vein then flipped loose the tourniquet. Capiam closed his eyes against the slight dizziness he felt when his blood pressure lowered as the blood began to flow through the needlethorn and down the reed into the container. When the spell had passed, he opened his eyes and was objectively fascinated by his blood dripping into the glass. He pumped his fist and the drip increased to a thin flow. In a curious, detached way, he seemed to feel the fluid leaving his body, being gathered from his other limbs, even from his torso, that the draining was a totally corporeal affair, not just from the fluid in one artery. He really could feel his heart beating more strongly, accommodating the flow. But that was absurd. He was beginning to feel a trifle nauseated when Desdra's fingers pressed a redwort-stained swab over the needlethorn, then removed it with a deft tweak.

"That is quite enough, Master Capiam. Almost three quarters of a liter. You've gone white. Here. Press hard and hold. Drink the spirits."

She placed the drink in his left hand and he automatically held the compress with his right. The powerful spirit seemed to take up the space left by the release of his blood. But that was a highly fanciful notion for a healer who knew very well the route taken by anything ingested.

"Now what do we do?" she asked, holding up the closed glass jar of his blood.

"That top firmly screwed on?" And when she demonstrated that it was: "Then wrap the cord tightly around the neck and knot it firmly. Good. Hand it here."

"What do you think you're going to do now?" Her face was stern and her gaze stubborn. For a woman who had often preached detachment, she was suddenly very intense.

"Gallardy says that centrifugal force, that is, whirling the jar around, will separate the components of the blood and produce the useful serum."

"Very well." Desdra stood back from the bed, made sure she had sufficient clear space to accomplish the operation, and began to swing the jar around her head.

Capiam, observing her exertions, was glad she had volunteered. He doubted that he could have managed it. "We could rig something similar with the spit canines, couldn't we? Have to prod the beasts to maintain speed. One needs a constant speed. Or perhaps a smaller arrangement, with a handle so one could control the rotational velocity?"

"Why? Do we...need...to do this...often?"

"If my theory is correct, we'll need rather a lot of serum. You did leave word that K'lon is to be shown here as soon as he arrives?"

"I did. How...much...longer?"

Capiam could not have her desist too soon, yet Master Gallardy had said "in a very short time" or—and Capiam looked more closely at his own handwriting—had *he* erred in transcribing? A concerned healer with thirty Turns of Craft life behind him, he silently cursed the diffidence of the spring-struck young apprentice he had been. "That ought to suffice, Desdra. Thank you!"

Breathless, Desdra slowed the swing of the jar and caught it, placing it on the table. Capiam hunched forward on the bed while Desdra examined the various layers with astonishment.

"That"—Desdra pointed dubiously to the straw-colored fluid in the top level—"is your cure?"

"Not a cure, exactly. An immunization." Capiam enunciated the word carefully.

"One has to drink it?" Desdra's voice was neutral with distaste.

"No, though I daresay it wouldn't taste any worse than some of the concoctions you've insisted I swallow. No, this must be injected into the vein."

She gave him a long thoughtful look. "So that's why you needed the syringes." She gave her head a little shake. "We don't have enough of them. And I think you better see Master Fortine."

"Don't you trust me?" Capiam was hurt by her response.

"Completely. That's why I suggest you go to Master Fortine. With your serum. He has been too frequent a visitor at our cautious Lord Holder's internment camp. He's coming down with the plague."

CHAPTER X

Fort Weyr and Ruatha Hold, Present Pass, 3.16.43

WHEN MORETA WOKE, she felt Orlith's joyful presence in her mind. *You are better. The worst is over!*

"I'm better?" Moreta was annoyed by the quaver in her voice, too much a remnant of the terrible lassitude that had enervated her the day before.

You are much better. Today you will get stronger every minute.

"How much of that is wishful thinking, my love?"

Even as Moreta spoke in her usual affectionate way, she realized that Orlith would know. During Moreta's illness, the queen had been as close in her mind as if the dragon had changed mental residence. Orlith had shared every moment of Moreta's discomfort, as if, by sharing, the dragon could diminish the effects of the plague on her rider. They, who had been partners in so much, had achieved a new peak of awareness, the one in the other. Orlith had dampened the pain of the fierce headache, she had eased the stress of fever and depressed the hard, racking cough. All she could do was comfort Moreta during the fourth day of physical and mental exhaustion. But by then the dragon queen had every right to rejoice.

Holth says there is other good news! Master Capiam has a serum which prevents the plague.

"Prevents it? Can he cure it?" Moreta had not been so detached in the course of her illness that she had not known that others in Fort had sickened—or that dragons and riders had died in other Weyrs. She was aware as well that two Fort Weyr wings had risen the day before to meet the Fall on Igen's behalf. That Berchar and Tellani's new babe had died. She knew as well that the epidemic had extended its insidious grip on the continent. It was time and enough for the healers to have found some specific means to control it.

The plague has a name. It is an ancient disease.

"What name do they give it then?"

I can't remember, Orlith said apologetically.

Moreta sighed. Naming was a dragon failing. Yet Orlith remembered quite a few, Moreta thought fondly.

Holth asks are you hungry yet?

"My greetings to our good Holth and our gracious Leri, and I think I am hungry." Moreta said with some surprise. For four days any thought of food had caused nausea. Thirst she had suffered, as well as the hard throat-searing cough, and a weakness so deep she feared at moments that she would never shake it. That was when Orlith had been closest to her mind. Had there been space enough, the queen would have forced her swollen body into Moreta's quarters to be physically near.

"How's Sh'gall?" Moreta inquired. She had been feverishly ill by morning when Kadith had mournfully roused Orlith and Holth with the news of his rider's collapse.

He is weak. He doesn't feel at all well.

Moreta grinned. Orlith's tone was tinged with scorn as if the queen felt her own rider had been more valiant.

"Do remember, Orlith, that Sh'gall has never been ill. This must come as a terrible shock to his self-esteem."

Orlith said nothing.

"What news from Ruatha Hold? You'd better tell me," Moreta added when she felt Orlith's resistance.

Leri comes. Relief marked Orlith's manner. *She knows.*

"Leri comes here?" Moreta tried to sit up, but gasped at the dizziness the sudden movement occasioned. She lay where she had flopped as she listened to the approach of shuffling steps and the tap of Leri's cane. "Leri, you shouldn't—"

"Why not?" Leri projected her voice from the larger weyr. "Good morning, Orlith. I'm one of the brave. I've lived my life so I'm not afraid of this 'viral influence,' as the Healers have styled it." Leri pushed back the bright door curtain, peering brightly at the younger woman. "Ah, there—you have color in your face today." A covered pot and the thong of a flask swung from her left hand. Two more containers had been stuck in her belt to allow her to use her right hand for her stick. As Leri entered the room, Moreta noticed that the old woman's gait seemed more fluid. She deposited her oddments on the chest that was now drawn to Moreta's bedside and then allowed herself to drop onto the space by Moreta's feet. "There now!" she said with great satisfaction, tucking her gnarled stick beside her. "Yes, you should do very well."

"Something smells good," Moreta said, inhaling the aroma from the pot.

"A special porridge I concocted. Made them bring me supplies and a brazier so I could nurse you myself. Nesso's finally down with it and out of my hair for a bit. Gorta's taken charge—rather well, I might add, in case you're interested." Leri looked slyly at Moreta as she spooned porridge in two bowls. "I'll join you since it's my breakfast time as well, and this stuff is as good for me as it is for you. By the way, I made Orlith eat this morning before she wasted away to nothing but the eggshells. She had four fat bucks and a wherry. She was very hungry! Now, don't look dismayed. You've scarcely been able to do for yourself, let alone her. She didn't feel neglected. She minds me very well, Orlith does, since she knows me so well. After all, Holth laid her! So she did as we told her and *she's* feeling better. She *had* to eat, Moreta. Her next stop is the Hatching Ground, and we had to wait till you recovered for that. Won't be long now."

Moreta did some swift adding. "She's early. She shouldn't clutch for another five or six days."

"There has been some stress. Don't fuss. Eat. The sooner you've got your strength back, the better all round."

"I'm much stronger today. Yesterday..." Moreta smiled ruefully. "*How* have you managed?"

"Very easily." Leri was serenely smug. "As I said, I had them bring me a brazier and supplies. I made your potions myself, I'll have you know! With Orlith listening to every breath you made and relaying the information to Holth, I'll wager you couldn't have been better cared for if Master Capiam had been at your bedside."

"Orlith says he's discovered a cure?"

"A vaccine, he calls it. But I'll not have him after your blood."

"Why should he be?" Moreta was startled and Orlith gave a bellow at Leri's protectiveness.

"He takes the blood of people who have recovered and makes a *serum* to prevent it in others. Says it's an ancient remedy. Can't say I like the notion at all!" Leri's short upright figure shuddered. "He practically attacked K'lon when he reported for conveying." Leri gave a chuckle and smiled with bland satisfaction. "K'lon was doing too much flitting *between* on Healer Hall errands. I've appointed weyrlings to the duty. Didn't like to but...they've followed orders well. Oh, there's been so much happening I hardly know where to begin!"

Beneath Leri's glib manner, Moreta could discern worry and fatigue, but the older Weyrwoman seemed to be thriving on the crisis.

"Have there been more...Weyr deaths?" Moreta asked, bracing herself for the answer.

"No!" Leri gave a defiant nod of her head and another pleased smile. "There shouldn't have been any! People weren't using the wits they were born with. You know how greens and blues panic? Well, they did just that when their riders got so sick and weak, *instead* of supporting them. In fact, there might be something to Jallora's theory that the one caused the other...." Leri stared off for a moment in deep thought. "Jallora's the journeywoman healer sent with two apprentices from the Healer Hall. So we keep in touch with the sick riders. You were very ill, you know. Exhausted, I think, after the Gather—no sleep, all the excitement, then Fall and that repair on Dilenth. He's fine, but Orlith is so strong and her need of you so great that *you* hadn't a chance of dying! You and Orlith as a healing team were the inspiration"—Leri fixed Moreta with a mock stern gaze—"so we just told the other Weyr-women to have their queen dragons keep watch on the sick and not *let* the riders die. It isn't as if the Weyrs had the crowding that's causing so much concern in the Holds and Halls. It's ridiculous for dragonriders to die of this vicious viral influence."

"How many *are* ill, if the Weyrs must consolidate to fly Fall?"

Leri grimaced. "Steel yourself! Nearly two thirds of every Weyr except High Reaches is out of action. Between the plague and injuries, we can only just manage to send our two wings to cover Fall."

"But you said Master Capiam had a cure?"

"A preventive. And not enough of this vaccine yet." Leri spoke with an angry regret. "So the Weyrwomen decided that the High Reaches' riders must be vaccinated"—she stumbled over the unfamiliar term— "since we must all look to S'ligar and Falga. As more of the serum is prepared, other Weyrs will be vaccinated. Right now Capiam has the drums burning to find more people who have recovered from this viral influence. First dragonriders"—Leri ticked off each name on a finger— "then Healers, *then* Lord Holders and other Craftsmasters, except for Tirone, which, I think no matter how Tolocamp objects, is sensible."

"Tolocamp hasn't been ill?"

"Tolocamp won't leave his apartment."

"You know a great deal about what's happening for a woman who stays in her own weyr most of the time!"

Leri chuckled. "K'lon reports to *me*! Whenever, that is, Capiam hasn't his exclusive services. Fortunately blues have good appetites and, although Capiam maintains that dragons, wherries, and watchwhers can't contract the plague, dragons had best eat from stock isolated in their own weyrs. So K'lon brings Rogeth home to eat. Daily."

"Dragons don't eat daily."

"Blue dragons who must flit *between* twice hourly do." Leri gave Moreta a stern glance. "I had a note from Capiam, could barely read his script, lauding K'lon's dedication—"

"A'murry?"

"Recovering. Very close thing but Holth was in constant touch with

Granth once I realized how vital dragon support could be. L'bol lost both his sons and he grieves constantly. M'tani's impossible, but then he has fought Thread longer than most and sees this incident as a personal affront. If it weren't for K'dren and S'ligar, I think we'd have had trouble with F'gal: He's lost heart, too."

"Leri, there's something you're not telling me."

"Yes, dear girl." Leri patted Moreta's arm gently before she filled a glass from one of her flasks. "Take a sip of this," she said peremptorily, handing it to her.

Obediently Moreta did, and she was about to ask what on earth Leri had concocted, when she felt Orlith's presence in her mind, like a buffer.

"Your family's hold..." Leri's voice thickened and she avoided Moreta's gaze, staring instead at the bright central design of the door curtain. "...was very hard hit."

Leri's voice habitually broke but that time it was pronounced, and Moreta peered at the older woman's averted face. Tears were running unheeded down the round cheek nearest her.

"There'd been no drum message in two days. The harper at Keroon heights made the trip downriver..." Leri's fingers tightened on Moreta's arm. "There was no one alive."

"No one?" Moreta was stunned. Her father's hold had supported nearly three hundred people, and another ten families had cots nearby on the river bluffs.

"Drink that down!"

Numbly Moreta complied. "No one alive? Not even someone out with the bloodstock?"

Leri shook her head slowly. "Not even the bloodstock!" Her admission was almost a whisper. Moreta could barely grasp the staggering tragedy. Obscurely, it was the deaths of the bloodstock that she regretted the most. Twenty Turns ago she had acquiesced to her family's wish that she respond to Search. She regretted their deaths, certainly, for she had been fond of her mother, and several of her brothers and sisters, and one paternal uncle; she had enormous respect for her father. The runnerbeasts—all the bloodstock that had been so carefully bred for the eight generations her family had the runnerhold—that loss cut more deeply.

Orlith crooned gently, and her dragon's compassion was subtly reinforced by a second pressure. Moreta felt the terrible weight of her grief being eased by an anodyne of love and affection, of total understanding for the complexities of her sorrow, of a commitment to share and ease the multiple pressures of bereavement.

Tears streamed down Moreta's cheeks until she felt drained but curiously detached from her body and mind, floating in an unusual sensation of remoteness. Leri had put something very powerful in that wine of hers, she thought with an odd clarity. Then she noticed that Leri was watching her intently, her eyes incredibly sad and tired, every line of her many Turns etched in her round small face.

"No stock at all?" Moreta asked finally.

"Would young runners have been wintering on the plains? The harper couldn't check. Didn't know where and there hasn't been time to send a sweeprider."

"No, no. Of course there wouldn't be time. . . ." Moreta could quite see that impossibility with the present demands on available riders but she accepted the hopeful suggestion. "Yearlings and gravid runners would be in the winter pasture. Somebody of the Hold will have been tending them and survive."

The comforting presences in her mind wrapped her with love and reassurances. *We are here!*

Is Holth with you, Orlith? Moreta asked.

Of course, was the reply from two, now distinct to her, sources.

Oh! How kind! Moreta's mind drifted, oddly divorced from her body, until she became aware of Leri's anxious expression. "I'm all right. As Holth will tell you. Did you know she speaks to me?"

"Yes, she's got rather used to checking in on you," Leri said with a kind and serene smile.

"What did you put in that wine? I feel . . . disembodied."

"That *was* rather the effect I hoped to achieve. Fellis juice, numbweed, and one of the euphorics. Just to cushion the shock."

"Are there more?" From the wavering of Leri's smile, Moreta knew that there were. "You might as well give me the whole round tale now while I'm so remote. My family's hold . . . cannot have been unique." Leri shook her head. "Ruatha Hold?" That would follow the line of catastrophe, Moreta thought.

"They have been badly hit. . . ."

"Alessan?" She asked about him first because his would be the worst loss there, before he'd even had time to enjoy being a Lord Holder.

"No, he's recovering, but the decimation among the Gather guests— his brothers, almost all the racers—"

"Dag?"

"I don't have many names. Igen Weyr and Hold have been shockingly depleted. Lord Fitatric, his Lady, half their children . . ."

"By the Egg, isn't there *any* place spared?"

"Yes, in fact, Bitra, Lemos, Nerat, Benden, and Tillek have had relatively few cases, and those were isolated promptly to avoid contagion. Those Holds have been magnificent in sending people to the stricken."

"Why?" Moreta clenched her fists, hunching herself together in a sudden convulsion that was more mental than physical. "*Why?* When we're so near the end of the Pass? It's not fair so close to an Interval. Did you know"—Moreta's voice was hard and intense—"that my family started out after the end of the last Pass? My bloodline started then? And now—just before the next Interval—it's wiped out!"

"That isn't known for certain, if what you say of wintering stock applies. *Do* consider that possibility. That probability." The dragons reinforced Leri's optimism.

Moreta's outburst passed almost as swiftly as it had consumed her. She lay back, limp, her eyelids suddenly heavy, her body flaccid. Leri seemed to be retreating from her though she was conscious that the Weyrwoman still sat on the bed.

"That's right. You sleep now," Leri said in a gentle croon echoed by two dragon voices.

"I can't stay awake!" Moreta mumbled and, sighing, relaxed into a potion-induced sleep.

Ruatha Hold, Present Pass, 3.16.43

K'lon was intensly relieved when Journeyman Healer Follen, his lips pulled down in a sorrowful line, emerged from Lord Alessan's apartment. The death-stench of the cold corridor bothered K'lon, inured though he was to plague-ridden holds.

"I've vaccinated the sister and the harper and did that other poor fellow as well. Lord Alessan says that more patients may be found along this corridor, but they did manage to clear the upper levels. I don't know how the man had managed. I'd no idea it would be so bad or I'd've insisted that Master Capiam give us more serum."

"There isn't that much to distribute, you know."

"Don't I just!"

Follen gave K'lon a thin smile. The previous evening the bluerider had conveyed the journeyman to South Boll Hold when the drums had reported survivors of the plague. As Capiam's timely visit to South Boll and his recommendations to its healers had in fact prevented the plague from spreading as insidiously as it had in midcontinent, it was only just that all the survivors donate blood for serum. Lord Ratoshigan had been a donor though the ever-irascible Lord Holder had been under the distinct impression—adroitly fostered by blue rider and journeyman—that the blood-taking was part of the prescribed treatment.

"Donations can be taken here," Follen went on, combing his hair with his fingers. "I'll give them some of Desdra's brew first, but judging from Lord Alessan's tally, the Hold will be able"—Follen gave a dour snort—"to supply those left here. Do ask Lord Shadder if he can find a few more volunteers. I'm sure we can save many of those with

secondary infections if we just have enough nurses. We've got to try. This Hold has been devastated."

K'lon acknowledged that with a slow nod of his head. The desolation and ruin of Ruatha Hall had appalled the relief party. K'lon and three Benden green dragons had conveyed Follen, an apprentice healer, and six volunteers from Benden Hold. The spectacle that greeted the party emerging from *between* over the Hold was the worst K'lon had seen. The monstrous burial mounds in the river field, the wide circle of charnel fires near the race flats, the abandoned tents built on Gather-stall frames had indicated the magnitude of Ruatha's attempt to survive. The sad tatters of the gaudy Gather flags, hanging from the upper tiers of the closely shuttered windows, had struck K'lon as grotesque, a mockery of the gaiety that was Gathering in the midst of the tragedy that had befallen the Hold. Bits and pieces of trash skittered across the forlorn dancing square and the roadway while a kettle swung noisily on its tripod over a long-dead fire, its ladle banging in time to gusts of the bitter-cold wind.

"Lady Pendra?" K'lon began.

A quick shake of Follen's head made it unnecessary for K'lon to continue. "No, nor any of the daughters he brought to Ruatha Gather. At that, Lord Tolocamp comes out better than Lord Alessan. *He's* got but the one sister left."

"Of all Leef's get?"

"Lord Alessan frets about her. And his runners. More of them survived than guests, I think. You speak to him," Follen suggested, clapping the blue rider on the shoulder before making off up the dark corridor to the next room.

K'lon squared his shoulders. In the last few days, he had learned how to keep his face from showing his emotions, how to sound not exactly cheerful, which would have been offensive, but certainly positive and encouraging. After all, with the vaccine, there was the hope of mitigating the plague and preventing the disease in those not yet infected. He knocked politely at the heavy door but entered without waiting for an acknowledgment.

Lord Alessan was kneeling by a toss-mattress, bathing the face of the occupant. There was another makeshift bed along the wall leading into the sleeping quarters. K'lon suppressed an inadvertent exclamation at the change in the young Lord Holder. Alessan might regain lost weight and his skin its healthy color, but his face would always bear the prematurely deep lines and the resigned expression that he turned toward the blue rider.

"You are many times welcome, K'lon, rider of Rogeth." Alessan inclined his head in gratitude and then folded the dampened cloth before placing it on the forehead of the man he was tending. "You may tell

Master Tirone that, without the invaluable assistance and ingenuity of his harpers, we would be worse off at Ruatha than we are. Tuero here was magnificent. The journeyman healer—what was his name?" Alessan drew a shaky hand across his forehead as if to coax the identity back.

"Follen."

"Strange, I can remember so many names . . ." Alessan broke off and stared out the window. K'lon knew the Lord Holder could see the burial mounds and wondered if the distraught man meant the names of those who lay beneath the tumbled soil of the mass graves. "It takes you that way, lying in bed, waiting to . . ." Alessan gave himself a shake and, gripping the top of the table, pulled himself slowly to his feet. "You have brought relief. Follen says that Tuero here, Deefer"—he gestured wearily toward the other bed—"and my sister will recover. He even apologized that he hadn't more . . . vaccine? Is that what it's called? Yes, well—"

"Sit down, Lord Alessan—"

"Before I fall down?" Alessan gave a slight smile with his bloodless lips, but he eased himself into the chair, sighing heavily from a weariness that went beyond any physical fatigue.

"They've stirred up the fires, and soon there'll be some restorative soup. Desdra concocted it. She tended Master Capiam, and *he* says the soup worked miracles for him."

"We shall hope it does for us as well." As they both heard the sound of coughing, Alessan turned his head sharply toward the door of his bedroom, inhaling apprehensively.

"Your sister? Well, you'll see," K'lon said with conviction. "The vaccine will effect a great improvement in her condition."

"I sincerely hope so. She's all the family I have left."

Though Alessan spoke in a light, almost diffident voice, K'lon felt his throat close tightly with compassion.

"Oh, that serum will moderate the effects of the virus for her, I assure you. I've seen amazing recoveries after its administration. In fact, the serum Follen gave her is probably derived from the blood I donated." K'lon rattled on mendaciously. Others had taken consolation from that fact so he held it out as comfort to this sadly bereaved man.

Alessan regarded him with a slightly surprised expression and his lips twitched in wry humor. "Ruatha has always been proud of its dragonrider bloodties though they've never been so direct."

K'lon responded to Alessan's retort with a thin laugh. "You haven't lost your wits."

"They're about all I have left."

"Indeed, Lord Alessan, you have much more," K'lon said stoutly. "And you shall have all the help Weyr, Hold, and Hall can supply."

"As long as what you have already brought is effective." Once more Alessan's head turned toward the room where his sister lay. "It is more than we had hoped for."

"I shall have a look at your stores and see what is most needful," K'lon began, vowing to himself that one of his first tasks would be to remove the Gather banners. If their presence had affronted him as a hideous reminder of that unfortunate occurrence, how cruelly would they affect Lord Alessan.

The Lord Holder stood far more quickly than he ought to have for he had to steady himself against the chair. "I know exactly what we need. . . ." He walked shakily to the desk at the window, absently stacking dirty dishes as he looked. He found the sheet of hide he wanted with a minimum of search. "Medicines, first of all. We have no aconite, not a gram of febrifuge left, only an ineffective syrup for that wretched cough, no thymus, hyssop, ezob, no flour, no salt. Blackstone is almost depleted, and there have been no vegetables or meat for three days." He handed the sheet to K'lon, a wry smile on his lips. "See how timely your arrival is? Tuero sent the last drum message this morning before he collapsed. I doubt I should have had the strength to climb to the drum tower."

K'lon took the sheet with a hand that shook only slightly less than the hand that offered it. He bowed to hide his face, but when he looked up, he saw that Alessan was gazing out the window, his expression unreadable.

"Follen told me that scenes like this are repeated throughout the continent."

"Not like this," K'lon said, his voice cracking.

"Follen didn't go into detail—how badly are the Weyrs affected?"

"Well, we have had our casualties, it's true, but dragonriders have met every Fall."

Alessan gave him a long puzzled look, then he turned away again to gaze out the window. "Yes, I suppose they would, if they could. You're from Fort Weyr?"

As K'lon knew that Alessan was aware of his affiliation, he sensed that the man was trying to discover something else. Then he remembered what Nesso had said, about Moreta dancing in a scandalous monopoly of the young Lord.

"Lady Moreta is recovering and so is the Weyrleader. We have had only one death at Fort, an elderly brown rider and his dragon, Koth. The toll was fifteen at Igen, eight at Telgar, and two at Ista but, because of the vaccine, we are hopeful."

"Yes, there is hope."

Why Alessan should glance from the fields to the mountains, K'lon did not know, but the action seemed to hearten the man.

"Did you know that we had over a hundred and twenty of the best western racers here a few short days ago, and seven hundred Gatherers to enjoy the dancing, the wine, the feast, the plague . . ."

"Lord Alessan, do not distress yourself so needlessly! If you had *not* held the Gather festivities here, the *entire* Hold could have been destroyed. You were able to prevent the plague's spread. All Ruathan drumholds have reported in. There are a few deaths reported and some cases of the plague, but you did what had to be done, and did it well!"

Alessan turned abruptly from the window. "You must bear to Lord Tolocamp my most profound condolences for the loss of Lady Pendra and her daughters. They nursed the sick until they were themselves overcome. They were valiant." Alessan's message was no less sincere for the abruptness of its tone.

K'lon acknowledged the message with a sharp inclination of his head. He was not the only one who would forever fault Lord Tolocamp for running from Ruatha. There were those who held the opinion that Tolocamp had been eminently correct to put the welfare of his Hold above that of his Lady and his daughters. Lord Tolocamp had remained secure in his apartment at Fort Hold while Ruatha suffered and died. Tolocamp would be spared the disease since he had vehemently insisted on being vaccinated despite the priorities set by the Weyrwomen and Master Capiam.

"I will convey your condolences. All the supplies we brought," K'lon found himself explaining, "came from Benden or Nerat Holds."

Alessan's eyes sparkled briefly, and he looked at K'lon as if he were seeing the blue rider for the first time.

"Good of you to tell me that. My profound gratitude for the generosity of Lord Shadder and Lord Gram." The view from his window again drew Alessan's glance. His obsession was beginning to perturb K'lon.

"I must go," the blue rider said. "There is so much to be done."

"There is! Thank you for answering the drums . . . and for your reassurances, K'lon. My duty to Rogeth who brought you." Alessan held out his hand.

K'lon crossed the room to take it in both of his. He was almost afraid to return the pressure on the strengthless fingers but he smiled as warmly as he could, thinking that if Ruatha was proud of dragonrider bloodties, he was as proud to be part of it. Perhaps some of his blood *had* been in that serum batch. K'lon fervently hoped so.

He quit the apartment as fast as was polite, for he did not wish to give way to the emotions that possessed him. K'lon hurried down the dark corridor—they must put up glowbaskets—into the Main Hall, where two Benden volunteers were cleaning up. Their homey noises were a welcome relief from the preternatural stillness that had shrouded the Hall on their arrival. He told them about the need for glowbaskets and asked them to remove the Gather banners as soon as possible. He could hear Rogeth bellowing outside.

This place is most distressing, the blue dragon said piteously. *It is the most distressing place we have been. How much longer must we stay?*

K'lon gave the Bendenites warm thanks and then rushed out to the forecourt. Rogeth half ran, half flew up the ramp to meet K'lon, his eyes wheeling in distress.

This place distresses you, too. Can we not see Granth and A'murry now? The "now" was accompanied by an unhappy snort.

"We can leave now." K'lon swung up to Rogeth's back, his gaze inadvertently falling on the dreadful field with its ruined shelters, the race flats, and the burial mounds. *Were* they what drew Lord Alessan's eyes? Or the handful of runnerbeasts grazing in the far field? The rumble of the dead cart, a recalcitrant pair of herdbeasts between the shafts, startled K'lon.

"Get us out of here," he told Rogeth, sick to the soul of plague and death and desolation. "I *must* spend some time with A'murry. Then I'll be able to face this sort of thing."

K'lon was overwhelmed with longing for his gentle friend, for the respite of companionship. He should go right back to the Healer Hall. There was so much to be done. Instead he projected for Rogeth the sun-dappled heights of Igen Weyr, the bright sparkle of the Weyr lake. Rogeth leaped gladly from the ramp into the air and took him *between*.

CHAPTER XI

Fort Weyr, Present Pass, 3.17.43

"Shards!" Jallora cried. "He's fainted!"

Kadith, in the outer chamber of the weyr, bellowed, and Moreta jumped up from the chair to reassure the startled dragon as the journeywoman healer examined her reluctant donor.

What has happened? Orlith asked in concern from her weyr.

"Sh'gall had a bad reaction," Moreta replied, knowing perfectly well that Leri would be instantly informed by Holth and know what had really happened. "Calm Kadith down!"

"It's generally the big strong ones who faint," Jallora was saying as Moreta resumed her place. "He's in no danger. Badly as we need the blood for serum, I wouldn't risk him."

"I didn't think for a moment that you would, Jallora," Moreta replied with a slight laugh.

The journeywoman had interrupted an interview between Moreta and Sh'gall in which he had been determined to find fault with every provision made in the Weyr since the onset of his illness. He utterly discounted the fact that Moreta had not made any of the decisions or that she herself had only just recovered.

"His sort don't generally make good patients, either," Jallora went on conversationally, though her attention was on the blood dripping into a glass container.

"Will his go to Ruatha?"

"Most of it, once the rest of your riders are vaccinated." When Moreta gestured warningly at Sh'gall, she added diplomatically, "I perfectly

161

understand, I assure you. He's still out of it. There! That's all I'll take but he could donate more and never miss it." Deftly she pressed a small pad over the needlethorn, extracted it, and motioned for Moreta to continue the pressure as she dealt with the apparatus. "He'll regain consciousness in just a few minutes." Jallora began packing her tray, carefully covering the container. "F'duril told me that you did the reconstruction on Dilenth's wing. Fine work."

"The wing is healing well, isn't it?" Recognition of her achievement by another healer was gratifying to Moreta.

"Fortunately, so is F'duril and that nice young A'dan. I've never visited a Weyr before. And—you know something else? It never occurred to me that dragons suffered so from Thread. They're so impressive—"

"Unfortunately not invulnerable."

"We can thank our lucky stars they didn't catch this viral influence!"

Just then Sh'gall moaned. Jallora hurried to gather up the rest of her paraphernalia.

"There now! Back again, Weyrleader?" She took the glass of orange liquid from the table and, deftly propping Sh'gall's pillows behind him with her free hand, put the glass to his lips. "Drink this and you'll be just fine."

"I don't really think it was wise of you to take—" Sh'gall sounded petulant and took the glass from her with a bad grace.

"The riders of Fort need it, Weyrleader. They must all be vaccinated, you know, to insure that no more have to endure what you've just been through."

The journeywoman took exactly the right tone with Sh'gall. Moreta could wish herself so fortunate as Sh'gall permitted Jallora to make a discreet departure.

"I don't think she should have!" Sh'gall repeated when he was certain Jallora was out of earshot.

"She got mine." Moreta pushed up her sleeve to exhibit the tiny bruise at the bend of her elbow. Sh'gall looked away. "We've a hundred and eighty-two riders out of action, sick or disabled."

"Why didn't Capiam attend us instead of that—woman?"

"Jallora is an experienced journeywoman healer. She was sitting her mastery exams when this plague occurred. Capiam is only just out of bed himself and he has the whole continent to worry about."

"I cannot believe that Leri did not know of my preference for P'nine as Leader." Sh'gall picked up his complaints as if Jallora had not interrupted the acrimonious interview.

"Leri made appropriate decisions based on her experience as a Weyrwoman. Kindly remember that she was one before you or I had Impressed."

"Then why does Kadith tell me that T'ral is taking *two* wings to Tillek today?" Sh'gall demanded angrily. "T'ral's a *wingsecond*."

"With the exception of the High Reaches, the Weyrs are still being led by wingseconds at this point. The sooner you can take over, the best pleased all the Weyrs will be."

That comment startled Sh'gall, but he didn't look pleased. "I've been ill. I've been very ill."

"I sympathize." Moreta tried not to sound facetious. "Believe me, you'll be feeling much better by evening."

"I don't know about that..." Sh'gall's voice faded.

"I do! I've been through it, too, don't forget."

Sh'gall gave her a look of pure loathing, but Moreta could not relent. Some of the burden of continuous Falls had to be removed from S'ligar's shoulders. Sh'gall was a damn good Leader and his abilities were desperately needed.

"Nerat's after Tillek," she went on. "You'll be in luck: *They* can supply ground crews."

"I didn't believe Kadith when he said that there hadn't been any ground crews. Don't holders realize—"

"The holders realize what this viral epidemic is like a lot more acutely than we do, Sh'gall. Talk to K'lon for a few minutes. He'll tell you a few hard unpleasant truths." She stood up. "I've a lot to do. Jallora said you must rest today. Tomorrow you can rise. Kadith may, of course, call me if you need anything today."

"I need nothing from you." Sh'gall turned away from her and jerked the sleeping furs around his ears.

Moreta was quite willing to leave him to surly convalescence. She sincerely hoped that he would want to lead his Weyr in three days more than he wanted to indulge his fancied grievances. Leading the consolidated Weyrs was a mighty temptation for a man with Sh'gall's love of power. She tried to consider him more charitably: He was shocked by the devastation caused by the pandemic and seeking refuge from the staggering losses by dwelling on the petty details he could cope with and understand. Like who rose to Fall from where, and how.

She walked down the steps to Leri's weyr at a fairly rapid pace, an exercise that did not leave her as breathless as it had the day before. She would harness Holth since she could not dissuade Leri from fighting in the queens' wing though the old woman was very tired. Then Moreta would distill and mix medicines from the Weyr's dangerously depleted stores. She knew K'lon had been raiding them but hadn't the heart to object.

"He fainted, did he?" Leri crowed in malicious jubilation. "And he wasn't satisfied with my decisions during his illness, was he?"

"Was Holth eavesdropping again?"

"She doesn't need to. I don't know another reason why you'd have anger spots on your cheeks. Ha!"

"I've as much trouble making you listen to reason." Moreta spoke more tartly than she meant and she could feel her cheeks flush again. "You *know* you're overreaching your strength—"

Leri flapped her hand. "I will *not* forgo the pleasure of flying the queens' wing. Not while I'm able. And I'm a lot abler today than I have been for Turns!" She sipped from her wineglass.

"Oh?" Moreta eyed the goblet significantly.

"I won't *have* any more fellis juice until you've brewed it, my dear Moreta," Leri reminded her with a saccharine smile.

"K'lon said he knew where he could get some dried fruit."

"Hmmm." Both women knew that many of K'lon's supplies probably came from a hold that didn't need such medicines any more. "Ah well." Leri lifted her glass in silent homage.

Moreta turned to the harness rack, tears stinging her eyes again. She must stop thinking of her family's empty hold. The memories of that place, shimmering in summer sunshine, children playing in the big meadow in front of the Hold, old aunties and uncles basking along the stone walls, seesawed with the present empty lifeless dwelling. Snakes and wild wherries must have . . .

"Moreta?" Leri's voice was soft and kind. "Moreta, Holth says K'lon has arrived," she added in a brisker tone exactly as Orlith told her rider the same news.

"I sometimes think I have more than two ears and one head."

I don't have ears, Orlith remarked.

Then K'lon was striding into the weyr, exuding an enormous amount of energy and good spirits. Moreta was suddenly struck by the warm brown tan of his face. Then, as he pulled off his flying helmet, she noticed that his hair was bleached.

"Nerat has fellis juice to spare, Moreta," he announced cheerfully, swinging the bulging pack from his back. "And Lemos says they've aconite and willow salic."

"And how was A'murry when you stopped at Igen?" She gave him a warm smile to show that she didn't object to a short detour.

"He's much, much improved." K'lon radiated relief. "Of course he's still weak, but he sits in the sun all day, which is good for his chest, and he's beginning to get an appetite."

"Done a lot of sunning with A'murry, haven't you, K'lon?" Leri asked.

Moreta shot her a quick look for her voice was suspiciously coy.

"When I've had the time." K'lon stammered slightly, fussing nervously with the pack.

"You mean"—Moreta had at last reached Leri's conclusion—"you've *taken* time to be with A'murry!"

"When I think of how hard I've worked—" Rogeth bugled outside the weyr.

"No one is faulting you, K'lon," Leri said quickly. Holth crooned reassurance, her eyes whirling bluely. "But, my dear boy, you've been taking a dreadful risking timing it. You could meet yourself coming and going—"

"But I haven't. I've been very careful!" K'lon's tone was defiant and fearful.

"Just how many hours have you been putting into your days?" Leri spoke with great understanding and compassion, even a hint of amusement.

"I don't know. I never counted hours!" K'lon jerked his chin up, rebellious. "I had to, you know. To get everything done and still make time to be with A'murry. I had *promised* him that I'd be in Igen every afternoon no matter how busy I was. I had to keep that promise. And I felt *compelled* to render Master Capiam the assistance *he* had to have—"

"Believe us, K'lon," Moreta said when he turned to her in appeal, "we are profoundly grateful to you for your courage and dedication over the past week. But timing is a very tricky business."

"And something our Weyrlingmaster certainly never mentioned," K'lon replied with an edge to his voice.

"The information is restricted to bronze and queen dragons, K'lon. I presume you discovered it by chance."

"Yes, rather." K'lon's expression mirrored the surprise he must have had. "I was late. I knew A'murry would be worried. I thought of him, waiting for me, anxious, when I didn't appear on time, and the next thing I knew, I had!"

"Bit of a shock, isn't it?" Leri had a grin on her round wise face.

K'lon grinned back. "I wasn't all that certain how I'd managed it."

"So you practiced again the next afternoon?"

K'lon nodded, relaxing imperceptibly since the Weyrwomen had apparently accepted his feat with good humor. "I report to Master Capiam in the morning and he tells me the schedule. I'm at Igen in the afternoons and everywhere else on Pern in the mornings and evenings. I'm very careful." His smile was broad delight.

"You'll be more careful from now on," Leri said, her voice austere and her manner forbidding. "A'murry has improved—so you've informed us. But *you* cannot keep on being in debt to yourself for double time. Therefore, instead of flying Fall this afternoon, you will spend it—and only this afternoon— with your friend. From now on, you will keep to the normal number of hours in a day. Holth will supervise. And we will see that Master Capiam schedules you to drop in at Igen frequently."

"But—but . . ."

"Only one mistake, K'lon," Leri pointed her forefinger, oddly twisted now by the joint disease, shaking it at him in dire emphasis, "and you're too tired timing it to realize the risks you've been taking. Only one mistake, and you will deprive A'murry of yourself forever. Not just for an afternoon." Leri paused, judging the effect of her warning on K'lon, who lowered his eyes. Holth crooned on an admonitory note and Rogeth answered, startled, from outside. K'lon looked up at Leri, his eyes wide with astonishment. "Oh yes, we can, you know, when the matter is disciplinary. I think you'd prefer Holth to Sh'gall and Kadith in the matter of this infraction?"

K'lon cast a look of entreaty at Moreta, who shook her head in slow denial. K'lon looked bereft, quite different from the energetic assured man who had entered the weyr, but he had to be restricted.

"I'll be needed at Fall this afternoon," he said finally in a low uncertain voice. "How can I explain to A'murry? We can barely make up two wings as it is, and Ista can only supply one wing and ten replacements."

"You may tell A'murry that we have been considerably worried about the pace at which you've been working. That we felt it more advisable for you to *rest* this afternoon, because you've been working so hard that your judgment in Fall might be impaired, and we can't afford to lose you!"

"K'lon, *we* need you, too," Moreta added.

"In fact, the Healer Hall and the Weyr are deeply indebted to you," Leri said, her voice and manner kindly again. "Go on with you now, and send that scamp, M'barak, on any other duties Capiam scheduled for you. And you will never, K'lon—*never*—mention to anyone, especially A'murry, that dragons can slip between one time and another."

Holth's eyes gleamed with a red tinge as she extended her neck toward K'lon. He pulled himself up straight, awed by the dragon's fierce appearance.

"Yes, Leri."

"And?" Leri indicated Moreta.

"Yes, Moreta!"

"We shall never refer to this again. Give our regards to A'murry." Leri was all affability. "If it weren't so damn cold here right now, I'd suggest that you bring him and his Granth to Fort, but I suppose he *is* better off in the sun at Igen!"

The chastened rider left the weyr with a heavy tread. The two Weyrwomen could hear Rogeth chirping.

"He's going to act the martyr for a while," Leri said with a sigh.

"Better that than a real one."

Then Leri began to chuckle. "I had the worst time keeping a proper face, Moreta. He was very clever about timing it, I must say. If he hadn't acquired that suspicious tan and bleached hair, we might never have guessed."

"He had too much energy! Positively obscene if you knew how dragged out I feel! Can Holth keep track of him?"

"As long as he thinks she is, it doesn't matter. You will check in on Rogeth now and again, won't you, my clever love?" Leri thumped her queen with affection. "Now, if you'll just harness her up, Moreta, we'll be off to Fall."

Moreta regarded her friend a long time until Leri gave an impatient shrug.

"Oh, go boil the fellis!" And she wriggled herself off the stone couch.

As Moreta harnessed the old queen, she wondered, in a very private way, if there was any restriction Orlith could put on Holth to prevent their martyrdom.

No.

Moreta blinked with surprise because she had put such a careful cap on her worry. And she didn't know which dragon had spoken, Orlith or Holth. Then she concentrated hard on the correct placement of the leather fighting straps. When Leri was ready, Moreta saw rider and queen to the ledge and watched them lumber off into the air with the two wings, Fort's contribution to Pern's protection against Fall. The bugling farewell from the Weyrbound dragons as the wings went *between* was a curious, prayerful compound of yearning, defiance, and encouragement. Moreta found that seeing so few dragons on the Rim reminded her that the Weyr was vulnerable, all the Weyrs—and Pern. It was hard enough to think of her family's hold, deserted, emptied by the pandemic in a matter of days. She knew but could not assimilate the fact that her personal loss was duplicated all over Igen, Ista, Telgar, and Keroon as well as at Ruatha. That wonderful Gather! To be so closely followed by such a disaster!

Resolutely Moreta turned from the chill blue skies and busied herself peeling and preparing the *fellis* fruit for juice. Her hands were not as shaky as they had been the day before and for that she was grateful, as the knife was sharp and the tough skins difficult. As the thick pulp was coming to the boil, she ran an inventory of the remaining stocks, amazed that what she had considered ample only six days before could have been reduced to a few bags of this or that. With all the riders vaccinated, the Weyr should not require massive amounts of febrifuges, stimulants, and chest remedies. Which was a good thing, for at that season of the year it would be impossible to restock.

"Where is K'lon?" she asked Orlith.

He is at Igen.

"How is Sh'gall?" Moreta asked out of a sense of duty.

He sleeps deeply and Kadith says that he ate well. He recovers.

Moreta was amused at the indifference in Orlith's voice—she didn't care, either, and that suited Moreta perfectly. When Orlith rose to mate again—

HOLTH COMES! Falga and Tamianth are severely wounded!

Moreta paused long enough to take the simmering *fellis* juice from the brazier before she hurried out. Holth emerged above the Star Stones and dove straight for her ledge. Moreta hurried up the stairs. With an agility that Moreta could not believe, Leri swung off her dragon, shedding the cumbersome agenothree tank so that it clanged hollowly on the stone, rolling to the wall.

"Tamianth has taken a terrible scoring, Moreta," Leri said, her face gray with shock and anxiety. "The healers can manage Falga's leg, but Tamianth's wing..." Tears runneled the flight dirt on Leri's face. "Here. Use my jacket! My helmet will fit and the goggles. Oh, go!"

"Orlith can't!" Moreta felt anguish, sensing Leri's distress through Holth.

"Orlith can't, but Holth will!" Leri was shoving her jacket sleeve on Moreta's outstretched arm. "You're more use to Falga and Tamianth than anyone else could be. You've got to go! Holth won't mind and neither will Orlith. This is an emergency!"

Both queen dragons were agitated, Orlith coming out to her ledge to croon and bellow, extending her neck up toward her rider, Leri, and Holth. Moreta pulled the jacket on. As Moreta was so much taller than Leri, it didn't quite come to her waist, and Leri's flying belt had to be cinched in to the last notch. Moreta crammed on the helmet and eyepieces and swung up on the fighting straps before she could reconsider.

Forgive me, Orlith! she cried, waving at her queen.

What is to forgive?

"Get going!" Leri bellowed.

Holth sprang, moving almost as heavily as egg-bloated Orlith. Moreta experienced confusion, linked for so many Turns to one dragon mind. How on earth was she going to understand Holth, when suddenly she did. Holth was there, with her, and Moreta could sense Orlith hovering protective. Jealously? No, she sensed nothing negative in her own dragon's mind other than a concern that Moreta could not deal with her friend Holth. Holth was by then airborne, and the first intimate connection Moreta had with the old queen was of her weariness and her compulsion to help Tamianth.

Slow and easy does it, Moreta said to Holth with all the encouragement and understanding she could muster.

The watchdragon saluted them, wishing Holth and Leri well. As the watchdragon was a green weyrling, mistaking Holth's rider could be forgiven but it stuck in Moreta's mind as Holth gallantly plowed upward in the blustery wind.

Moreta envisioned the distinctive ridge of the High Reaches Weyr, a jagged comb with seven unequal spires.

I know where we must go. Trust in me, the old dragon said.

I do, Holth, Moreta replied, aware that Holth's experience was far greater than Orlith's for all the younger queen's vigor. *Take us to the High Reaches.*

In place of her usual *between* litany, Moreta tried to analyze the difference between the two queen dragons. Holth's mind-voice was old and tired, but it was firm, rich, and deep, many layers denser than Orlith's. Perhaps, when Orlith had reached the fine age Holth enjoyed, she, too, would have the depth of Holth's responsiveness.

Then they were in the warmer air over the High reaches, and Holth was skimming the jagged spindles and swooping in a deep left-hand bank so that Moreta had an unobstructed view of the ground and the injured dragons there. Moreta blinked at the small clusters attending the wounded. Tamianth rated the most assistance. As Holth descended, Moreta could see that Tamianth had lost the trailing edge of all three wingsails. And she was badly scored down her left side.

How did that happen? Moreta was appalled.

Cross-over and too much to do. She wanted to help the wings, Holth said, and an echoing sadness welled in Moreta as Holth implanted the incident in her mind. Tamianth had risen at an angle so that Falga could bring the flamethrower into action but they had blundered into an updraft before they could correct. A great gout of Thread had fallen across her wing and into her shoulder. And across Falga's leg.

Holth could not turn on a wingtip as Orlith could, but the old queen gauged her descent to a finger and glided to a halt a wing-length from the injured Tamianth.

Can you help me ease her pain, Holth? Moreta asked as she slid in frantic haste from the dragon's back. Tamianth's howls had to be muted.

Orlith is with us, Holth said with great dignity, her eyes churning a brilliant sparkling yellow.

Falga lay to one side on a stretcher, her face turned toward her queen, but she was barely conscious. Two healers were swathing her leg in bandages soaked in numbweed.

Tamianth, Moreta said, hurrying to the dragon's injured side, hoping the dragon might hear her and would listen. *I am Moreta to heal you!*

Tamianth was thrashing her head and forearms from side to side, movement that hampered the efforts of the weyrfolk trying to apply numbweed to the wingbones. Moreta noticed in a quick glance that they had managed to salve the deep body score from which ichor flowed; the wing was causing Tamianth's agony.

"*Hold her!*" Moreta roared at the top of her voice and her mind.

The other injured dragons and the watchdragon bugled in response.

Holth reared onto her hindquarters, trumpeting, her wings extended. From the weyrs emerged High Reaches dragons whose riders were too sick to fly Fall. And suddenly Tamianth was locked by the combined wills of the dragons around her.

"Come *on!*" Moreta exhorted the weyrfolk who were gawking in astonishment. "Get the numbweed on. Now!"

She grabbed a paddle and a pot from the ground and, as she worked rapidly, she assessed the extent of the injury. It was somewhat similar to Dilenth's. Though he had lost leading edge and sustained damage to bone and finger joints, Tamianth had lost more sail. She would be a long time out of the air.

"Is there anything we can do to help the dragon?" A bright-eyed little man with a broad jaw and a broad nose appeared at her elbow. Another man, not much bigger, frowning anxiously in what seemed a permanent grimace, stood just beyond him. Both wore Healer purple and the shoulder knots of journeymen. Moreta glanced quickly at Falga's stretcher. "She is unconscious and her wound dressed. That's all we can do for her right now. I will need oil, reeds, thin gauze, needle, treated thread—"

"I'm not of this Weyr," the bright-eyed man said and turned to the bigger one who nodded acknowledgment to Moreta and ran off to the low stone building that was High Reaches' main living quarters. "My name is Pressen, Weyrwoman."

"Keep applying numbweed, Pressen. All down the bones. I want them thickly coated, especially the joints. Just as you'd do any Thread-score on a human. And keep it thick on the body wound, too. I don't want her losing so much ichor."

An old woman stumbled up with a bucket of redwort, shouting at three children behind her to bring the oil and not dawdle. Two riders, each with bandaged scores, approached Moreta; their dragons, a blue and a brown—both scored—settled to the rocky ground, their eyes, spinning with distress, on Tamianth.

Moreta suddenly had more help than she could use effectively so she sent the riders to help the other healer find her requirements and the children to get a table for her to stand on. The old woman informed her that the Weyr's healers had died and the two new ones knew absolutely nothing about dragons but were willing. She used to help but her hands had "a trembling."

Moreta sent her off to find the gauze—that was her most urgent need. In the time it took Moreta to complete her preparations to repair the wing, Tamianth's crushing pain had been reduced to a throbbing ache, according to Holth–Orlith. Tamianth's wing was considerably larger than Dilenth's and the sail fragments fewer. The two riders were of great assistance in sorting the pieces onto the gauze. "I never would have thought of gauze," Pressen had murmured, fascinated at the reconstruction. He was able to assist her in the finer stitching, for his small hands were extremely deft. Nattal, the ancient High Reaches headwoman, forced Moreta to take time for a cup of soup, claiming that she knew the Fort Weyrwoman was only just recovered from the plague and it would give the High Reaches a bad name if Moreta collapsed on them, and then what would happen to Tamianth? It was soon obvious to Moreta that the soup contained a stimulating ingredient, for when she resumed her delicate repair it was with improved concentration and precision.

Nonetheless, Moreta was trembling with fatigue by the time she finished.

We must return, Holth said in an inarguable tone.

Moreta was more than willing, but oddly disturbed by some nonspecific anxiety. She looked toward Falga, who was either unconscious or sleeping under the furs of the stretcher. Troubled, Moreta looked over the rocky Bowl, at the other injured dragons.

"You look very pale, Moreta," Pressen said, lightly touching her arm with his red-stained hand. "I'm sure we can handle any other injuries. It was just that—the whole wing! Your work was an inspiration."

"Thank you. Just keep the bones saturated with numbweed. Once the joints have started to produce ichor, that will coat the wounds and the healing process will begin."

"I had never really considered that dragons get injured by Thread," Pressen said, his expression respectful as he flicked his eyes to the dragons on the ledges and the seven pinnacles.

Come! Mount! Holth's tone was more urgent, and there was nothing of Orlith in her voice.

"I must leave." Moreta swung up onto Holth's back, noting in the back of her mind that Holth was leaner than Orlith and no longer as tall in the shoulder. Or maybe it was the way Holth had of assuming a half-crouch.

As the old queen gathered herself, Moreta suppressed a concern that the dragon was too tired for a standing start. Her hindquarters—Moreta's head snapped back as Holth sprang powerfully upward, and she devoutly hoped that the queen had been unable to track her secret doubts. To cover her embarrassment, Moreta visualized the Star Stones of Fort Weyr, the largest of those monuments, and the mountain peak that soared behind the Stones.

Please take us to Fort, Holth!

Holth complied without clearing the High Reaches Weyr rim. During the searing moment of cold *between*, Moreta's hands stung in the gloves. She ought to have oiled them again. She was always acquiring little nicks and needle scratches during a repair. The green weyrling greeted them on their return, bugling on an unexpectedly joyful note.

Holth glided to her ledge, coming in a shade too fast, Moreta thought, bracing herself for the landing.

You are needed, Holth said as Moreta loosened the straps and slid down.

"I'll just remove your harness—"

I need you now! Orlith's voice was petulant. *I've been waiting for you!*

"Of course you have, love, and very goodnatured you were to let me go—"

Leri says you shouldn't waste any time, Holth added, the facets of her eyes beginning to whirl faster.

"Something's happened to Orlith?" Moreta skipped down the stone steps as fast as she could, her heart pounding. She raced around the corner into her weyr, knocking her shoulder as she bounced into the turn.

Orlith had her head angled to catch the first possible glimpse of her rider. As Moreta barreled into the weyr, Orlith bugled repeatedly.

As she threw her arms around her dragon's head, Moreta noticed Leri standing to one side, wrapped up in sleeping furs, looking excessively pleased.

"We managed just fine," she explained between Orlith's effusions, "but the sooner you get her to the Hatching Ground the better. I don't think she could have held out *much* longer, but you *were* needed badly at High Reaches, weren't you?"

Between apologies and encouragements to her dragon, Moreta agreed.

"No one even knew you were gone," Leri said, "but I doubt I could have sustained the deception getting Orlith to the Hatching Ground."

I really need to go, Orlith said plaintively.

CHAPTER XII

Fort Hold, Fort and High Reaches Weyrs, Present Pass, 3.18.43

"I, FOR ONE, am heartily glad to hear a piece of good news," Capiam said when the echoes of the drum message had faded.

They had all heard the sound of the drums but, closeted in the thick stone walls of Lord Tolocamp's apartment in Fort Hold, they had not been able to distinguish the cadences until the Harper Hall began to relay the tidings onward.

"Twenty-five eggs is not a generous clutch," Lord Tolocamp said in exaggeratedly mournful voice.

Capiam wondered if the Lord Holder's dose of vaccine had held some curious contaminant. The man's whole personality had altered. The charitable would say that he grieved for his wife and four daughters, but Capiam knew that Tolocamp had consoled himself rather quickly by taking a new wife, so his sorrow was suspect. Tolocamp had also made his losses the excuse for a variety of shortcomings, short temper, and dithering.

"Twenty-five with a queen egg is a superb clutch this late in a Pass," Capiam replied firmly.

Lord Tolocamp pulled at his lower lip, then he sighed heavily.

"Moreta really must not permit Kadith to fly Orlith again. Sh'gall was so ill."

"That is not *our* business," Tirone remarked, entering the discussion for the first time. "Not that the illness of the rider has any effect on the performance of the dragon. Anyway, Sh'gall is flying Fall at Nerat so he's evidently fully recovered."

"I wish they would inform us of the status of each Weyr," Lord

Tolocamp said with another heavy sigh. "I worry so."

"The *Weyrs*"—Tirone spoke with a firm emphasis and a sideways look of irritation at the Lord Holder—"have been discharging their traditional duties to their Holds!"

"Did *I* bring the illness to the Weyrs? Or the Holds? If the dragon-riders were not too quick to fly here and there—"

"And Lords Holder not so eager to fill every nook and cranny of their—"

"This is *not* the time for recriminations!" Tirone shot a warning glance at Capiam. "You know as well, if not better than most people, Tolocamp, that seamen introduced that abomination onto the continent!" The deep rumbling voice of the Masterharper was acid. "Let us resume the discussion interrupted by such good news." Tirone's expression told Capiam that he must control his antipathy for Tolocamp. "I have men seriously ill in that camp of yours." Tirone caught the Lord Holder's gaze, stabbing his finger toward the windows. "There is not enough vaccine to mitigate the disease, but they could at least have the benefit of decent quarters and practical nursing."

"Healers are among them," Tolocamp countered sullenly. "Or so you tell me!"

"Healers are not immune to the viral influence and they cannot work without medicines." Capiam leaned urgently across the table to Tolo-camp, who drew back, another habit that irritated the healer. "You have a great storeroom of medicinal supplies—"

"Garnered and prepared by my lost Lady—"

Capiam ruthlessly suppressed his irritation. "Lord Tolocamp, we *need* those supplies—"

A mean look narrowed Tolocamp's eyes. "For Ruatha, eh?"

"Other holds besides Ruatha have needs!" Capiam spoke quickly to allay Tolocamp's suspicions.

"Supplies are the responsibility of the individual holder. Not mine. I cannot further deplete resources that might be needed by my own people."

"If the Weyrs, stricken as they are, can extend *their* responsibilities in the magnificent way they have, beyond the areas beholden to them, then how can you refuse?" Tirone's deep voice rang with feeling.

"Very easily." Tolocamp pushed his lips out. "By saying no. No one may pass the perimeter into the Hold from any outlying area. If they don't have the plague, they have other, equally infectious, diseases. I shall not risk more of my people. I shall make no further contributions from my stores."

"Then I withdraw my healers from your Hold," Capiam said. He rose quickly.

"But—but—you can't *do* that!"

"Indeed he can! *We* can," Tirone replied. He got to his feet and came round the table to stand by Capiam. "Craftsmen are under the jurisdiction of their Hall. You'd forgotten that, hadn't you?"

Capiam swung out of the room, so angry at Tolocamp's pettiness that bile rose sourly in his throat. Tirone was only a step behind him.

"I'll call them out! Then I'll join you in the camp."

"I didn't think it would come to this!" Capiam seized Tirone by the shoulder in an effort to express his appreciation at the Harper's swift reinforcement.

"Tolocamp has presumed once too often on the generosity of the Halls!" Tirone's usually smooth, persuasive voice had a hard edge. "I hope this example reminds others of our prerogatives."

"Call our Craftspeople out, but don't come to the camp with me, Tirone. You must stay in the hall with your people, and guide mine."

"My people"—Tirone gave a forced laugh—"with very few exceptions, are languishing in that blighted camp of his. You are the one who must bide at the halls."

"Master Capiam—"

The men whirled toward the woman's voice. The speaker emerged from the shadow of a doorway. She was one of the three remaining Fort daughters, a big-boned girl with large brown eyes well-spaced in an intelligent but plain face. Her thick black hair was pulled severely back from her face.

"I have the storeroom keys." She held them up.

"How did you?..." Tirone was uncharacteristically at a loss for words.

"Lord Tolocamp made plain his position when he received the request for medicines. I helped harvest and preserve them."

"Lady?..." Capiam could not recall her name.

"Nerilka." She supplied it quickly with the faint smile of a someone who does not expect to be remembered. "I have the right to offer you the products of my own labor." She gave Tirone an intense, challenging stare. Then she returned her direct gaze to Capiam. "There is just one condition."

"If it is within my giving." Capiam would give a lot for medicines.

"That I may leave this Hold in your company and work with the sick in that horrid camp. I've been vaccinated." A wry smile lifted one side of her mouth. "*Lord* Tolocamp was expansive that day. Be that as it may, I will not stay in a Hold to be abused by a girl younger than myself. Tolocamp permitted her and her family to enter this hallowed Hold from the fire-heights yet he leaves healers and harpers to die out there!"

And he left my mother and sisters to die at Ruatha. Her unspoken words were palpable in the brief silence.

"This way, quickly," she said, taking the initiative and pulling at Capiam's sleeve.

"I'll remove our Craftspeople from this Hold on my way out," Tirone said. He walked quickly toward the hall.

"Young woman, you do realize that once you leave the Hold without your father's knowledge, particularly in his present frame of mind—"

"Master Capiam, I doubt he'll notice I'm gone." She spoke with a light disregard for the matter, obviously more bitter about her sire's new wife. "These steps are very steep," she added and flicked open a handglow.

Steep, circular, and narrow, Capiam realized as his foot slipped on the first short step. He disliked blind stairways, of which Fort had more than its fair share. The Ancients had been fond of them in the construction of the first holds as auxiliary access between the levels of what were, essentially, natural caves. He was grateful for Nerilka's guidance and the soft glowlight but the descent seemed to take ages. Then the darkness lightened and they emerged on to a landing, with narrow high halls branching in three directions. Beside the circular stair they had just left was a second one that he hoped they would not need to use.

Nerilka led him to the right, then down a short broad flight and to the left. He was completely disoriented. Nerilka made a second left turn. Three drudges who had been lounging on long benches by a heavy wooden door got to their feet, their faces impassive.

"You are prompt, I see," Nerilka said, nodding approval to them. "Father appreciates promptness," she said to Capiam as she was separating the keys. Unlocking the door took three of the larger ones. Opening required the effort of one of the drudges and then Capiam could smell the mingled stillroom aromas, astringent, bitter, fragrant, and oddly musty.

Nerilka pulled open the glowbasket inside the door to illuminate sinks, braziers, tables, high stools, measuring apparatus and implements, gleaming basins and glass bottles. Capiam had been in the room often and when he had, he'd approached it from the other direction in the company of Lady Pendra. Now Nerilka was unlocking the storeroom and beckoning him to follow her. She smiled when she heard his surprised gasp.

Capiam had known that Fort Hold's storage rooms were ample, but he had not been beyond the dispensary. They were standing on a wide tier, balustraded from the vast, dark interior, with steps leading down to the main floor. He could hear the slither and rustle of tunnel snakes fleeing the sudden light. Capiam saw shelves, reaching, it seemed, to the high vaulted ceiling. Barrels and crates and drying racks, were ranged in rows and dusty ranks. He had the impression of staggering resources and doubly condemned Tolocamp's parsimony.

"Behold, Master Capiam, the produce of my labors since I was old enough to snip leaf and blossom or dig root and bulb." Nerilka's sarcastic voice was intended for his ears only. "I won't say I have filled every shelf, but my sisters who have predeceased me would not deny me their portions. Would that all of these hoarded supplies were usable, but even herbs and roots lose their potency in time. Waste, that's the bulk of what you see, fattening tunnel snakes. Carry-yokes are in the corner there, Sim. You and the others, take up the bales." She spoke in a pleasant authoritative tone, gesturing to the drudges. "Master Capiam, if you do not mind—that's the fellis juice." She pointed to a withy-covered demijohn. "I'll take this." She lifted the bulky container by its girth strap. In her other hand, she swung a pack over one shoulder. "I mixed fresh tussilago last night, Master Capiam. That's right, Sim. On your way now. We'll use the kitchen exit. Lord Tolocamp has been complaining again about the wear on the main hall carpets. It's as well to comply with his instructions even if it does mean extra lengths for the rest of us." She covered the glowbaskets.

She set down the demijohn to lock the storeroom, ignoring Capiam's expression, for it was apparent to him that she had gone to some pains to organize the unauthorized distribution. Her eyes met his once as she swept the chamber with one last long glance. The drudges were already halfway down the corridor with their burdens.

"I would like to take more, but four drudges added to the noon parade to the perimeter are not going to be noticed by the guard."

Only then did Capiam realize that Nerilka was dressed in the coarse fabric allotted the general worker, a plainly belted tunic over dark-gray trousers and felted winter boots.

"No one will care in the least if one of the drudges continues on to the camp." She shrugged. "Nor will anyone at the kitchen exit think it odd for the Masterhealer to leave with supplies. Indeed, they would wonder if you left empty-handed."

She had locked the outer door and now looked speculatively at the bunch of keys. "One never knows, does one?" she said to herself in the habit of one used to solitary tasks. She stuffed the keys in her belt pouch and then, noticing Capiam's look, gave him that little half smile. "My stepmother has another set. She thinks it is the only one. But *my* mother thought the stillroom a very good occupation for me. This way, Master Capiam."

Capiam followed. The docility of the Fort daughters had been the source of ribaldry at the Halls whenever Lady Pendra had invited unmarried men of rank to the Hold. Nerilka, Capiam was chagrined to remember, was one of the oldest of the eleven daughters, though she had two full elder brothers, Campen and Mostar, and four younger. Lady Pendra had been constantly pregnant, another source of indelicate comment among the apprentice healers. It had never occurred to Capiam—and certainly not to his shameless juniors—that the Fort Horde had any wits or opinions of their own. In Nerilka, rebellion was full blown.

"Lady Nerilka, if you leave now—"

"I *am* leaving," she said in a firm low voice as they entered the kitchen's back corridor.

"—and in this fashion, Lord Tolocamp—"

She halted and faced Capiam at the archway into the busy, noisy kitchen. "—will miss neither me nor my dower." She lifted the demijohn. She sighed with exasperation, glancing at the door through which the drudges had exited. "I can be of real use in the internment camp for I know about mixing medicines and decocting and infusing herbs. I shall be doing something constructive that is needed rather than sitting comfortably in a corner somewhere. I know your craftsmen are overworked. Every hand is needed.

"Besides,"—she gave him a sideways glance that was almost coquettish—"I can slip back in whenever it's necessary." She patted the keys in her pouch. "Don't look surprised. The drudges do it all the time. Why shouldn't I?"

Then she moved on and he followed her quickly, unable to think of any counterargument. The moment she passed the arch from the kitchen, her posture changed, her stride altered, and she was no longer the proud daughter of the Hold but a gawky woman, head down, shuffling, awkwardly overburdened and resentful.

Once out in the great roadway, Capiam looked, trying not to appear furtive, to his left, to the main forecourt and stairs. Tirone and the dozens of harpers and healers regularly in attendance at Fort Hold were moving down the ramp.

"He'll be watching them! Not us," Nerilka said. She chuckled. "Try to walk less proudly, Master Capiam. You are, for the moment, merely a drudge, burdened and reluctantly heading for the perimeter, terrified of coming down sick to die like everyone in the camp."

"Everyone in the camp is not dying."

"Of course not, but Lord Tolocamp thinks so. He has so informed us constantly. Ah, a belated attempt on his part to prevent the exodus! Don't pause!" she added, again in that authoritative voice.

Capiam would have halted in consternation but for her warning. He saw four guards hurrying after Tirone's group.

"You can walk as slowly as you want, that's in character, but don't stop," she advised.

She watched, too, and if her eyes sparkled and she grinned at the discomfiture of her father's guards, there was no one but Capiam to observe her unfilial delight. At that distance, Capiam couldn't tell whether the guards were halfhearted in their efforts or not. There was a brief mêlée from which Tirone and his companions continued unhurriedly down the roadway to the Harper Hall. Nerilka and Capiam continued toward the perimeter.

The internment camp had been established to the left of the massive Fort Hold cliff, in a small valley out of the direct view of the Hold. The guard lines had been set above it, in full view of Lord Tolocamp's windows. A rough timbered shack had been erected as a guard shelter from which temporary fencing had been built in both directions. Guards constantly patrolled the fence.

Nerilka's three drudges deposited their burdens at the guardhouse where others were leaving baskets of food. Then the men had begun to retrace their steps to the Hold, empty yokes balanced on their shoulders.

"If you go past the perimeter, Master Capiam, you will not be permitted back," Nerilka reminded him.

"If there is more than one way into the Hold, is there only one past the perimeter?" Capiam asked flippantly. "I'll see you later, Lady Nerilka."

As they approached the shack, guards were being assigned to carry certain of the baskets and bales into the prohibited area where a group of men and women waited patiently for the exchange to be made.

"Here now, Master Capiam." The guardleader came striding up, his expression alarmed. "You can't go in there without staying—"

"I don't want this medicine heaved about, Theng. Make sure they understand it's fragile."

"I can do that much for you," Theng replied, and he strode diffidently to add the demijohn to one side of the bales. "This is to be handled carefully and preferably by a healer. Master Capiam says it's medicine."

The internees moved forward to collect the supplies, and Theng backed up. Nerilka was right behind him and as he turned to come back to the guardhouse, she slipped past him and joined those picking up the baskets as if she were one of them.

Capiam waited for an outcry, for surely the other guards had noticed her. Nerilka was already trudging down the slope toward the tents of the internment camp when Theng took him by the arm to escort him back.

"Nah, then, Master Capiam, you know I can't allow you close contact with any of your craftsmen," Theng said as Capiam cast one more glance after Nerilka's retreating figure.

"I know, Leader Theng. The medicine was my concern. So little of its ingredients remain."

Theng made a conciliatory noise between his teeth and then his attention was taken by the spacing of his guards. Slowly Capiam turned in the direction of the halls.

As he walked, he realized that he could not walk out of his Hall as

Nerilka could leave her Hold. Withdrawing his healers from the Hold was quite within his right as Masterhealer, but he must remain in his Hall, available to those who need him throughout Pern. However, he felt the better for his brief flirtation with the idea. And the camp had gained not only supplies but a valuable assistant. He must ask for volunteers to take the remainder of Nerilka's purloined supplies to Ruatha with all possible haste.

"The ichor can be extracted from one queen and applied to the joints of another," Moreta told Leri. "And you shouldn't be coming all this way for a message someone else could have brought."

They were standing at the entrance to the Hatching Ground and talking in quiet tones, although it was doubtful that the sleeping Orlith would have paid them any attention had they bellowed. She was still exhausted from the laying of twenty-five eggs. Orlith had curled herself about the leathery eggs, the queen egg within the circle of her forearms, her head laid at an awkward angle. Her belly skin was beginning to shrink and her color was good, so Moreta had no more anxieties about her queen and time to worry about Falga's Tamianth.

"No one there is capable of doing that," Leri said with a fine scorn, "or so Holth was informed by Kilanath. Holth says she sounds very worried."

"She has reason to be if Tamianth is not producing any ichor on that damaged wing." Moreta paced up and down. "Is Falga conscious?"

"Delirious."

"Not the plague?"

"No, wound fever. Under control."

"Shards! Falga knows how to draw ichor. It would have to be Kilanath and Diona . . ." Moreta looked back at the slumbering Orlith.

"She'll be out a long while," Leri murmured, stepping inside the Hatching Ground and gripping Moreta's hands tightly in hers. "It doesn't take long to draw ichor and spread it—"

"That's abusing Orlith's trust in me!"

"She trusts me as well. Every moment you delay . . ."

"I know! I know!" Moreta thought wretchedly of Falga and Tamianth, of all that Weyr had done the last few days.

"If Orlith should rouse, Holth will know and, considering the emergency, Orlith will understand. The clutching's over!" Leri pressed urgently on Moreta's hands.

Unusual circumstances, of which there were far too many recently in Moreta's opinion, warranted unusual actions.

"Holth's willing. I asked her first, as soon as she told me about Tamianth."

Obviously Leri felt that no one at Fort realized that Moreta had been absent two days before to treat the injured High Reaches' queen. Moreta cast a distraught look toward her sleeping queen, returned Leri's clasp with an answering pressure, and walked hurriedly from the sheltering arch of the Hatching Ground, quickly leaving Leri behind.

"Don't stride so! I can't," Leri whispered after her.

Moreta adjusted her pace. Anyone really observant would have noticed the difference in height between the woman who had entered the Ground and the one who left, but it was the gray hour before dawn and no one was about. Thread would Fall later that day at Nerat and the dragonriders rested whenever possible with so difficult a schedule.

Moreta delayed long enough on her way to Holth to change into her own riding gear. Leri's had left a broad exposed band across her back and she couldn't risk kidney chill. Holth greeted her at the entrance to her weyr and Moreta stepped aside for the queen to reach the edge. Then she mounted, conscious once again of the difference between dragons. She wished fervently that she did not feel that she was somehow betraying Orlith.

"Take us to the High Reaches, please, Holth," she asked in a subdued voice.

The watchrider sleeps and the blue will not note our departure. Holth said impassively and, despite her dark reflections, Moreta smiled. So Leri and Holth had considered that detail.

Then Holth propelled herself from her ledge and was barely airborne before she went *between*. Moreta gasped at the audacity and hadn't time to think of her verse before the darkness around them was relieved by the glows surrounding the High Reaches Bowl.

Tamianth is below but it is easier for me to take off from a ledge, said Holth, neatly landing on one. *Tamianth will not object to my tenancy*. Then she added gently, *Orlith sleeps. And so does Leri*.

"The pair of you!" Moreta's exasperation was goodnatured.

Holth turned gleaming eyes toward her and huffed softly.

"Is that you? Moreta?" a quavering voice asked.

"It's Moreta."

"Oh, bless you, bless you. I'm so sorry to drag you here but I simply can't do it. I'm so afraid of hurting Kilanath. Hitting a nerve or something. They tried to explain to me how simple it all is but I can't believe them. Oh, do wake up, Kilanath. Moreta's come."

A pair of dragon eyes lit the darkness below the ledge. Moreta put her hand on the wall, her left foot seeking for the top step. Light spilled from the weyrling quarters now occupied by Tamianth but the stairs were still in confusing shadow.

"Oh, do hurry, please, Moreta!" Diona's plea was more wail.

"I would if I could see where I'm going." Moreta spoke sharply, irritated by Diona's ineffectuality.

"Oh, yes, of course. I didn't think. You don't know where anything is in this Weyr." Dutifully Diona opened a glowbasket but, before she held it up, she turned its illumination away from Moreta. "Yes, Pressen, she's here. Oh, do hurry, Moreta. Oh, yes, sorry." Then she remembered to hold the basket high enough to show Moreta the steps.

Moreta skipped down them as fast as she could before something else could distract Diona. Kilanath dipped her head close to Moreta and sniffed, as if testing the quality of the visitor.

"Now, don't fret, Kilanath," Diona crooned in a saccharine voice that Moreta thought ought to irritate a queen. "You know she came here just to help." Diona turned apologetically to Moreta. "She really will behave because she's terribly worried about Tamianth."

As Moreta entered the weyrling quarters, she could see why. Tamianth looked more green than gold except for the gray wing and gray-spread score on her side. The wing had been propped at the shoulder and put in a sling so that the queen could relax, but her hide twitched constantly from stress. Tamianth opened one lid of her eyes, which were gray with pain.

"Water! Water, please, water!" Falga's voice rose in feverish complaint.

"That's all she says." Diona was wringing her hands.

Pressen, the bright-eyed healer, ran to Falga's side and offered her water, but she pushed it away before falling back into her restless tossing.

Muttering an oath, Moreta strode to the queen, picked up a fold of hide on the neck, and cursed. The dragon was dehydrated, her skin parched.

"Water. Of course, it's *Tamianth* who needs the water! Has no one offered the queen water?" Moreta looked about for a water tank, for anything resembling a container.

"Oh, I never thought of that!" Diona snatched her hands to her mouth, her eyes wide with dismay. "Kilanath kept telling me about water but we all thought Falga..." She waved feebly at the fevered woman.

"Then, by the Egg of Faranth, get some!"

"Please, water. Water!" Falga moaned, restlessly trying to rise.

"Don't stand there, Diona. Are there weyrlings in the next building? Well, rout them out! Use a cauldron from the kitchen but get water for this poor beast. It's a wonder she's not dead! Of all the irresponsible, ineffectual, dithering idiots I have ever encountered—" Moreta saw the startled expression on Pressen's face as he rose from Falga's side. She pulled herself together, breathing deeply to dispel the impotent anger and dismay that boiled within her. "I *can't* keep coming here for oversights!"

"No, no, of course not!" Pressen's reply was conciliatory, anxious.

The poor beast was too weak to reach farther than her rider who had, even in her pain-wracked daze, tried to communicate! Fuming at Diona's ineptitude, Moreta snatched down the nearest glowbasket to examine Tamianth's wing. Two days without any lubrication and the wing fragments might not reconstruct. The glowlight glistened ominously on a stain on the floor, under Tamianth's injured side. With a muffled cry of despair, Moreta dropped to one knee, dipped her fingers in the moisture, sniffing it.

"Pressen! Bring me your kit—redwort and oil! This dragon's bleeding to death!"

"What?"

Pressen stumbled toward her and she held the basket high, at Tamianth's side. Grimly she recalled the instructions she had given Pressen, unused to dragon injuries: Keep the side wound covered with numbweed. Why hadn't she checked it? How could she have assumed, given the chaotic conditions at High Reaches, the inexperienced healers, and the tired riders, that the wound had been properly attended? Instead she had blithely flitted off, smugly pleased with her wing repair.

"The fault is mine, Pressen. I ought to have seen to the side as well. What has happened is that Threadscore ruptured veins along the side and shoulders. Numbweed covered the ooze. Ichor isn't reaching the wing. We'll need to repair the veins. The surgery is much the same sort you'd do on a human. Color is the main difference."

"Surgery is not my speciality, Lady, but," he added, seeing her desperate expression, "I have assisted and can do so now."

"I'll need surgical clamps, oil, redwort, threaded needle..."

Pressen was pouring oil and redwort into bowls. "I have all the instruments we'd need. Barly's effects were handed over to me when I arrived."

Dreading what she might find, Moreta examined the injured wing. Some ichor beaded the joints but far less than was required. Tamianth would have to be very lucky; stupidity had already worked against the poor beast. Possibly, with application of Kilanath's ichor at crucial points, the damage could still be reversed. Liberal and frequent dressings of numbweed had, at least, kept the fragments moist. Once Tamianth's veins had been mended and water brought the poor thirsty beast...

Moreta scrubbed her hands in the redwort, hissing at the sting in half-healed scratches. Then she oiled her hands thoroughly while Pressen made the same preparation.

"First we must clean the numbweed away from the wound. I'd say the stoppage is here...and here, and perhaps, even down here near the hearts." She lightly indicated the areas, then with oil-soaked pads, she and Pressen cleaned away the numbweed. Tamianth shuddered. "With all this numbweed, she can't *feel* any pain. Here! See where the ichor is oozing..." Her father had always talked as he worked on injured runners. Much of what she had heard from her earliest years she had been able to apply to dragons. She oughtn't to think of her father at a time like this, but his habit would help her teach Pressen. Someone in the Weyr had to know. "Ah, here's the first one. Just below your left hand, Pressen, should be another. Yes, and a third, a major vein leading to the hearts, and the belly vein." Moreta reached for the fine needle and the treated thread Pressen had made ready.

"Yes, the colors are different!" Pressen saw the greenish flesh and the darker green ichor that was dragon blood, the curious shining fiber that was dragon muscle. He was absorbed. "Has she had any supply to the wing at all?" His nimble fingers were suturing the first severed vein.

"Not really enough."

"Thirsty! Thirsty. Water, please, water!" Falga raved.

"Can't that idiotic woman do anything? There's a lake full of water out there!"

There was suddenly a great amount of noise, the hollow sound of metal banging against another object, the sleepy complaints of young voices. The smell of desperately desired water roused the dragon from her stupor.

Hidden from sight behind the droop of the wing, Moreta could not see what was happening but she heard the bong of the kettle being dropped and the *plash* of buckets of water being poured. She heard the greedy slurping of Tamianth as the dragon sucked water down a parched throat.

"By the Egg, she'd drink barrels!" said the bemused voice of an older man. "She mustn't have too much at once, boys, so take your time with the refills. Anything else I can do—" The Weyrlingmaster ducked carefully under the wing and stared in surprise at Moreta. "I thought your queen had clutched, Moreta."

"She has, but this one would have died..."

When Moreta pointed to the ichor-stained puddle on the floor, the disapproval in the Weyrlingmaster's face turned to shock.

"S'ligar's down with a touch of the plague, despite the vaccine," Cr'not said. "But"—he gestured impotently toward Pressen, at the sound of Diona's voice thanking the weyrlings—"I could hear Falga calling for water..."

"It's no one's fault, Cr'not. Everyone's tired, pushed beyond their strength or trying to take on unfamiliar tasks. *I* should have examined this wound two days ago!"

"Sometimes I think it's only the momentum of routine that keeps any of us going," Cr'not said, rubbing at his face and eyes.

"You could be right. There. That's the last! Thank you, Pressen. You've the makings of a good Weyr healer!"

"Once I get accustomed to such large patients!" Pressen smiled back at Moreta.

"And you're about to learn another invaluable technique for healing dragons," Moreta said, beckoning to Pressen to follow her. She took the largest syringe from Barly's kit, fitted a needlethorn to its opening, soaked a pad quickly in redwort and then ducked under Tamianth's wing. *"Diona!"*

"Oh, no," Diona moaned timorously, spreading her arms to protect her queen. "Tamianth's looking ever so much better. Her color's improved enormously."

"I should hope so, but, if we don't get some ichor on her joints, she may never fly again. Holth, tell Kilanath!"

Cr'not moved toward the weyrwoman, his expression ferocious, and Diona moaned again.

"It doesn't take long, and it won't hurt Kilanath."

The queen was a good deal more cooperative than her rider, dipping her wing as she knelt for Moreta's ministration.

"Pressen, see? Here, where the vein crosses the bone?" As Pressen nodded, Moreta rubbed on some redwort, turning the golden skin brown. The fine sharp needlethorn entered hide and vein so smoothly that the dragon never felt the prick. Moreta deftly drew ichor into the tube: It glistened green and healthy in the glowlight.

"Most interesting," Pressen said, his expression intent. Neither of them paid any attention to Diona's moaning or Cr'not's exclamation of disgust.

"Now we will apply this"—Moreta returned to Tamianth, Pressen right beside her—"to the joints and the cartilage. See how dry the cartilage is? Soaks the ichor right up. Well, ah, here, nearest the shoulder, see how the beads are forming? Tamianth's beginning to function again. We'll save that wing yet!" She grinned at the little man whose face beamed back at her. "And color's returning to Tamianth's eyes, too."

"Why, so there is! Is she winking at me?"

Moreta chuckled. The gray had certainly receded from Tamianth's huge eyes and the 'winking' was just the sparkle returning to the facets as the dragon improved. "I believe so. She knows who's helped her."

"And Falga is sleeping." Pressen hurried to the cot, feeling the pulse along Falga's neck. He sighed with relief. "She's much quieter now."

Holth? Moreta asked, aware of other obligations.

They sleep! Holth was unperturbed.

"I must get back to Fort. Cr'not, will you keep checking on the wing for me? Pressen knows how to draw ichor and where to put it but not when. You would."

"I will!" Cr'not nodded solemnly. "Now, you ought not to leave your queen," he added, shaking his head worriedly.

"There is a point at which *ought* has little to do with actions, Cr'not. I was sent for! I came! Now I'm going!" She gave him a curt nod. Weyrlingmasters were a breed of their own and felt they could criticize with impunity anyone in a Weyr. As she collected her riding gear, she gave Pressen a saucy wink and then strode out of the building.

She ran to the stairs and took the steps two at a time.

They sleep, Holth repeated, her eyes whirling serenely.

"And so shall we once we're back home," Moreta said, swinging up onto Holth's lean back. "Take us to Fort Weyr, please, Holth."

Obligingly, Holth sprang from the ledge and, once again, went *between* as soon as there was free air about her. As the chill of nothingness wrapped them, Moreta wondered if she should mention Holth's curious trick to Leri. Was it just that the queen was old and could not jump as forcefully? Did it not seem an impertinence on Moreta's part to criticize?

Then they were back in the dawn, skimming low above the lake in Fort Weyr. That was the explanation: Holth was practicing stealth. The watchrider was unlikely to notice a dragon leaving so low in darkness.

Holth glided to her own ledge and accepted Moreta's effusive thanks before lurching wearily into her weyr. Moreta ran down the stairs and into the Hatching Ground. To the Weyrwoman's relief, Orlith hadn't so much as changed the angle of her head during her rider's absence. And Leri slept soundly on Moreta's cot.

CHAPTER XIII

Ruatha Hold and Fort Weyr, Present Pass, 3.19.43

ALESSAN HAD TO stop. Sweat was beaded on his forehead, ran down his cheeks and chin. His hands were sweaty on the plowhandles and the team panting as hard as he from their labors in the rain-heavy field. Ignoring the sting of the blisters he had acquired in the last two days, he dried his hands finger by finger on the grimy rag attached to his belt. Then Ruatha Hold's Lord Holder rubbed the sweat from his face and neck, took a swallow from the flask of water, picked up the reins, slapped the rumps of his reluctant team, and managed to grab the handles of the unwieldy plow before the runners had pulled it out of the furrow.

Another day and he was sure they'd forget they'd ever been trained to race. Of course, he told himself that every day. One day it would have to be true. He had mastered feistier beasts to the saddle, and he must—if he wished to Hold—prove equally capable at retraining. With bitter humor, Alessan wondered if his predicament could be a retribution for his defiance of his father's wishes. Yet none of *that* breeding had survived. The heavier runners, the draft and plow animals, the sturdy long-distance beasts, had been especially susceptible to the lung infections that had swept the racers' camp after the first days of the plague. The light wiry runners of his breeding had survived to graze contentedly on the lush river pastures. Until he had had to harness them, and himself, to the plows.

The land had to be tilled, crops sown, the tithe offered, the Hold fed no matter how the Lord Holder managed to accomplish those responsibilities. He came to the edge of the field and wrestled the team into the wide arc, turning back on the furrows. They were uneven but the earth had been turned. He looked briefly out at the other fields of the Hold proper, to check on the other teams. He also had a view of the northern road and the mounted man approaching along it. He shaded his eyes, cursing as the off-sider took advantage of his momentary distraction. As he lined it up again with its teammate and the plow righted, he was certain that he saw a flash of harper blue. Tuero must be back from his swing of the northern holds. Who else would be brave enough to venture to Ruatha? Alessan had drummed for heavy plow-beasts and been told that no one had any to offer. Neither threats of witholding nor doubling the marks brought better results.

"It's the plague, Alessan," Tuero had said, for once unsmiling. "It was at its worst here in Ruatha. Until Master Capiam has sent the vaccine round to everyone, they won't come here. And even then they won't bring animals, I think, because so many died here."

Alessan had cursed futilely. "If they won't come, I'll have to go! I'll bring teams in myself! They can't deny their Lord Holder to his face!" While Alessan railed at his people, he understood their view-point—especially since he himself had not yet had the courage to send for Dag, Fergal, and the bloodstock. Follen had given him the most strict assurance that the plague was passed by coughing or sneezing— personal contact—and could not be in the soil of the race flats or the pickets where so many beasts had died, but Alessan would not risk the few priceless breeders that Dag had whisked away the morning after the accursed Gather.

After considerable discussion with Tuero, Deefer, and Oklina—his inner council—it had been decided that he couldn't leave the Hold proper, for there was no one else of sufficient rank to enforce his orders. He hadn't wanted Tuero to make the journey as the harper was only just out of bed. But Tuero had been a wily talker, which was why, Tuero had said at the conclusion of the council, he was a harper and why he was the best emissary to send. A few days or so in the fresh spring air on an untaxing mission would complete his recovery. After all, while a harper was generally able to turn his hand to most tasks, Tuero couldn't plow. Alessan hadn't believed a word of Tuero's cheery bluff but he had no one else to send.

Despite the awkward height of its rider, Tuero's lean mount moved easily, with a quick high step, head held high and eager once it knew itself to be home. Tuero's feet were level with the wiry beast's knees, and the harper's gaunt frame towered above its ears. Certainly not the mount that Alessan would have assigned Tuero by choice, but they seemed to have gotten along. They were riding at a right angle to Alessan's field, but he could not remove his hands from the plow to hail Tuero. He'd reached the downslope of the field and the team was fractious with the pole hitting against their hocks. The field was nearly done; he'd finish it! Once he had he could give all his attention to Tuero's news.

He would have wished to see Tuero returning with a sturdy team, but there did seem to be something in his pack. Two more furrows and the day's stint was done.

As he drove the weary team back to the beasthold, the sowers were still busy setting seed. They'd have some sort of a crop in spite of the bloody plague. That is, if the weather held, and some other disaster— like a Thread burrowing—did not overtake wretched Ruatha.

To Alessan's surprise, Tuero was waiting for him in the beasthold, sitting on an upturned pail, his saddlebags at his feet and a look of satisfaction on his long face. His mount was munching sweetgrass in its stall, all saddle marks rubbed from its back.

"I saw you at your labors, Lord Alessan," Tuero began, a sparkle of amusement in his eyes as he rose to take the bridles of the team. "Your furrows improve."

"They could stand to." Alessan began to unhook the harness.

"Your example inspires many. In fact, your industry and occupation are already legend in the Hold. Your participation does you no dis-service."

"But brought me no team. Or is there more bad news?" Alessan paused before he removed the heavy collar from the off-sider.

"No more than you've probably figured out for yourself." Tuero nodded to the saddlebags and took the collar from the other runner. "I've some bits and stashes but I saw myself how bare the cupboards are of what is needed most. At least in the north."

"And?" Alessan liked all his bad news at once so he could absorb the different shocks according to their merits.

"Others have started working the land but in some of those holds"— Tuero gestured north with the twist of straw he made to rub the mount's sweat marks—"they had severe losses. Some Gatherers left before the quarantine and made it to their homes, bringing the virus with them. I've made a list of the deaths, a sad total it is, too, and no way I can ease the telling of it. They say misery loves company, and I suppose if you're of a dismal temperament, you get joy of it." Tuero quirked his eyebrows. "I've a list of needs and musts and worries. But I'd a thought on my way back which may sweeten all.

"I was right about people's being afraid to come here, to Ruatha Hold proper. I was right about their not wanting to send good stock to their deaths for all the marks you'd be willing to give. I had a time of it to get them to let Skinny there in their holds. They were afraid."

"Afraid?"

"Afraid it carries the plague."

"That runner *survived* it!"

"Precisely. It survived, you and I survived. I got over my bout faster because I had the serum. Wouldn't serum from recovered runners protect others the way it protects people?" He grinned at Alessan's reaction. "If that notion's valid, you got a field full of cures. And a good trade item."

Alessan stared at Tuero, condemning himself for not having thought of vaccinating runners. So many of his smallholders depended on their runner breeding that he could not, in conscience, have demanded his right to a portion of their labor in this emergency, recognizing their fear of bringing plague back to their holds.

"I'm disgusted I didn't think of it myself!" he said to the grinning harper. "Come on. Let's put these two away. I need a little chat with Healer Follen." He gave his beast an exultant swat on the rear to impel it into its stall. "How could I have been so dense?"

"You have had a few other problems on your mind, you know!"

"Man! You've revived me!" Alessan gave the lean harper a clout on the shoulder, grinning in the first respite from grim reality that he had enjoyed since Oklina had recovered. "And to think I hesitated about sending you."

"*You* may have, I didn't." Tuero said impudently, scooping up his saddlebags and following Alessan's quick lead to the Hold Hall.

They found Follen quickly enough, in the main Hall tending the sick. Alessan felt his nostrils pinch against the odors that the incense could not mask. He avoided the Hall whenever possible—the coughing, the rasping breaths, and the moans of the patients were a constant reminder of the sad hospitality he had offered. Follen's anxious expression cleared when Tuero raised the saddlebags. When the men had converged into the Hold office Follen now occupied, his hopefulness waned as he examined the bags and twists of herbs. Alessan had to repeat his question about vaccinating runners.

"The premise is sound enough, Lord Alessan, but I'm not conversant with animal medicines. The Masterherdsman . . . oh, yes, well, I forgot. But there must be someone at Keroon Beasthold who could give you a considered opinion."

Tuero sighed with disappointment. "It's too late now to drum across to Keroon. They wouldn't thank us for rousing them from their beds."

"There is someone else, much closer, who would know," Alessan said in a thoughtful voice. "And Follen, is there any human vaccine left? Enough for two people?"

"I can, of course, prepare some."

"Please do while Tuero and I drum up Fort Weyr. Moreta will know if we can vaccinate runners." Then he added to himself, I can bring Dag back and see what he managed to save.

* * *

Moreta was startled when the request came in to the Weyr drummer. The quarantine no longer applied. Alessan had specifically mentioned that he had been vaccinated and was healthy. She had no reason to deny a meeting and more than a few to grant it, curiosity about why the Lord Holder of Ruatha would urgently require a meeting being the least of them. Orlith was not a broody queen and quite happy to have people admire her clutch, particularly the queen egg, though she kept it always within reach of a forearm. Once she indulged in her postclutch feeding, she had piled the other eggs in a protective circle about the unique one.

"As if anyone would rob your clutch," Moreta teased her affectionately. She had told Orlith all about her early-morning visit to High Reaches and received a serene absolution for her errand of mercy.

Leri was here. Holth was with you. Fair exchange in those conditions. I slept.

Moreta slept for a while after her return from the High Reaches, waking nervously almost as if she had expected another summons. She would have preferred to stay at Tamianth's side until she was certain that the ichor was flowing to the wing, but Pressen had learned of the dangers and was able to perform necessary countermeasures. Further, as Tamianth strengthened and Falga recovered from wound fever, another crisis was less likely to develop.

So Moreta ascribed her nagging sense of apprehension to the tensions of a long day and and sent M'barak, Leri's favorite weyrling rider, to Ruatha Hold. K'lon told Leri and Moreta how appalled he had been by Ruatha. Moreta did not like to dwell on the scenes of a derelict Ruatha that her active imagination could conjure. What could she say in condolence to a man who had suffered so many losses?

Suddenly Alessan, dressed in rough leathers but a clean shirt showing at the neck, stood to one side of the entrance to the Hatching Ground. Beside his was a lanky man in a faded, patched tunic of harper blue. M'barak was grinning at their hesitation and waved them toward the portion of the tiers that Moreta had converted to a temporary living space. Orlith was awake and watched them enter, but displayed no agitation.

Moreta rose, one hand raised in unconscious protest against the change in Alessan. Too vividly she recalled the assured, handsome, buoyant young man who had greeted her at Ruatha's Gather eight days before. He had lost weight and his tunic was belted tightly to take up the slack. His hair no longer looked trimmed or brushed. She wondered why that detail should matter so much to her. The stains on his hands, witness of his efforts to plow and plant, were honorable ones, as was the redwort on hers. She grieved, too, for the lines of worry and tension in his face, the cynical slant to his mouth, and the wary expression in his light green eyes.

"This is Tuero, Moreta, who has been invaluable to me over the... since the Gather." After the slight pause, Alessan's voice deepened as if to ward off comment. "He has a theory against which I can raise no objections, but, as we cannot reach an authority at this hour in Keroon Beasthold, I thought you might give us an opinion."

"What is it?" Moreta asked, put off by his diffidence. The change in him went far deeper than appearance.

"Tuero"—Alessan gave the harper a slight bow of acknowledgment—"wondered if a vaccine could be made from the blood of runnerbeasts to protect them from the plague."

"Of course it can! You mean it hasn't been done?" Moreta was consumed by such a surge of fury and frustration that Orlith rose to all four legs from her semirecumbent position, her eyes whirling pinkly, and a worried question rumbled from her throat.

"No." In the one word, Alessan mirrored her own intense reaction.

"No one *thought* of doing it, or there hasn't been the time?" she demanded, sick at the thought of more loss, animal or human. The grim set of Alessan's mouth and the harper's sigh gave the answer. "I would have thought that—" She broke off the angry sentence, closing her eyes and clenching her fists. She recalled the heavy losses at Keroon Beasthold—the emptiness of her family's runnerhold.

"There have been other priorities," Alessan said. He spoke without bitterness but from a resignation to harsh fact.

"Yes, of course." She pulled her wits back from useless conjecture. "Have you any healers?"

"Several."

"Runnerblood would produce the same serum by the same method, centrifugal separation. More blood can be drawn from runners, of course, and the vaccine should be administered in proportion to body weight. The heavier—"

Alessan cocked his left eyebrow just enough for her to realize that there were no more of the heavier beasts at Ruatha.

"Would you have any spare needlethorns?" Alessan asked, breaking the silence.

"Yes." At that moment Moreta would have given Alessan anything he needed to alleviate his problems. "And whatever else is needed by Ruatha."

"We've been promised a supply train from Fort," Tuero said, "but until we can assure the wagoners that man and animal in Ruatha are plague-free, no one will venture near the Hold."

Moreta assimilated that information with a slow nod of her head, her eyes on Alessan. They might be discussing something completely foreign to him to judge by his detachment. How else could he have survived his losses?

"M'barak, please take Lord Alessan and Journeyman Tuero to the storeroom. They may have anything they need from our supplies."

M'barak's eyes widened.

"I'll be right with you," Alessan told Tuero and M'barak, who left him. Alessan swung down the pack he carried. "I did not come," he said with a wry smile, "in expectation of bounty. I can, however, return your gown." He took out the carefully folded gold and brown dress and presented it to her with a courteous bow.

She managed to take it from him but her hands trembled. She thought of the racing, the dancing, her joy in a Gather as one should be, her delight in the perfection of that Gather evening as she and Oklina had made their way to the dancing square for an evening she would never forget. The pent-up frustrations, angers, suppressed griefs, the man-datory absences from Orlith that she thought of as betrayals of Impres-sion, the whole accumulation burst the barrier of self-control and she buried her face in the dress, weeping uncontrollably.

As Orlith crooned supportively, Moreta was taken into Alessan's embrace. The touch of his arms, fierce in their hold, the mixed odors of human and animal sweat, of damp earth, combined to free her tears. Abruptly she felt the heave and swell of his body as his grief found expression at last. Together they comforted and were comforted by each other's release.

You needed this, Orlith said to Moreta but she knew that the dragon included Alessan in her compassion.

It was Moreta who recovered from the catharsis first. She continued to hold Alessan tightly, to ease his shuddering body, as she murmured reassurances and encouragements, repeating all the praise for his in-domitable spirit and fortitude that had come to her through K'lon: trying to make her voice and hands convey her own respect, admiration, and empathy. She felt the shuddering subside and then, with one final deep sigh, Alessan was purged of the aggregation of sorrow, remorse, and frustration. She relaxed her grip and his arms because less fierce and clinging. Slowly they leaned apart so that they could look into each other's eyes. The lines of pain and worry had not diminished but the strain had eased about his mouth and brow.

Alessan raised his hand and with gentle fingers smoothed the tears from her cheeks. His hands tightened and he pulled her toward him again, bending his head to one side so that she could evade him if she chose. Moreta tilted her head and accepted his kiss, thinking to put the seal of comfort to their shared sorrow with that age-old benison. Neither expected their emotions to flare to passion—Moreta because she had stopped thinking of relationships outside the Weyr, Alessan because he had thought himself spent from his losses at Ruatha.

Orlith crooned serenely, almost unheard by Moreta, who was caught up by the surge of emotion, the flow of sensuality so remarkably aroused by Alessan's touch, the hard strength of his thighs against hers, the sensation of being *vital* again. Not even her girlhood love for Talpan had waked such an uninhibited response, and she clung to Alessan, willing the moment to endure.

Slowly, reluctantly, Alessan raised his mouth from hers, looking down at her with incredulous intensity. Then he, too, became aware of the dragon's crooning and looked, startled, in the queen's direction.

"She doesn't object!" That amazed him further, and he was sensible of the risk he had taken.

"If she did, you'd know about it." Moreta laughed. His expression of dismay swiftly altering to delight was marvelous. Joy welled up from a long-untapped source in her body.

Orlith's croon changed to as near a trill as the dragon larynx could manage. With great reluctance, Moreta stepped back from Alessan, her smile expressing that regret.

"They'll hear it?" he asked, smiling back at her ruefully, his hands clinging as he released her.

"It may be chalked up to the joys of clutching."

"Your gown!" He grasped at the excuse of retrieving the crumpled folds where the dress had fallen unremarked to the stone at their feet. He was passing it to her when M'barak and Tuero entered the Hatching Ground, Tuero with a keen sparkle in his expressive eyes.

"With so much on your mind, Alessan," Moreta said, amazed at her self-possession, "it is very good of you to have remembered."

"If the simple courtesy of returning what had been misplaced is always rewarded with such generosity, leave more with me!" Alessan's eyes burned with amusement at his turn of phrase but it was Tuero's full pack that he indicated.

Moreta could not but laugh. M'barak was looking from her to Orlith, Tuero was aware that something had occurred but he couldn't identify it.

"I didn't take *all* we needed," the harper said as he looked from Weyrwoman to Lord Holder with a bemused smile. "That would have stripped your stores completely."

"I shall be able to get replacements more easily than you, I think. As I was telling Alessan"—Moreta felt the need to dissemble—"I think there are old Records about this sort of animal vaccination, though I cannot remember the details. I would try the serum on a worthless beast—"

"Just now there are *no* worthless beasts at Ruatha," Alessan said quickly, a slight edge to his voice. "I have no choice but to proceed and hope the animal vaccine is as efficacious as the human."

"Did you inquire of Master Capiam?" Moreta asked, wishing that Alessan had not distanced himself from her quite so soon though she could appreciate the necessity.

"*You* know runners, not Master Capiam. Why rouse them if the notion was not feasible?"

"I think it is feasible." Moreta put her hand urgently on Alessan's arm, yearning to recapture some trace of their encounter. "I think you should inform the Healer Hall immediately. And keep me informed."

Alessan smiled with polite acknowledgment and, under the pretense of a courteous pressure on her hand, his fingers caressed hers.

"You may be sure of that."

"I know Oklina lives." The words came in a rush from her lips as Alessan turned to leave. "Did Dag . . . and Squealer?"

"Why do you think I want so desperately to vaccinate the runners? Squealer may be the only full male I have left." Alessan left, pausing briefly at the entrance to bow toward Orlith.

With a startled expression, Tuero hastened after him, and M'barak hurried after his two passengers.

Orlith crooned again, her many-faceted eyes whirling with flashes of red amid the predominant blue. Feeling rather limp after the spate of emotions and resurgent desire, Moreta sank to the stone seat, clasping her trembling hands together. She wondered if there was any chance that Holth and Leri had missed that tumultuous interview.

CHAPTER XIV

Healer Hall, Ruatha Hold, Fort Weyr, Ista Hold, Present Pass, 3.20.43

"LOOK AT THE situation as a challenge!" Capiam suggested to Master Tirone.

The harper slammed the door behind him, an uncharacteristic action that startled Desdra and sent Master Fortine into a spasm of nervous coughing.

"A challenge? Haven't we had enough of those in the past ten days?" Tirone demanded indignantly. "Half the continent sick, the other half *scared* sick, everyone suspicious of a cough or a sneeze, the dragonriders barely able to meet Thread. We've lost irreplaceable Masters and promising journeymen in every Craft. And you advise me to look on this news as a challenge?" Tirone jammed his fists against his belt and glared at the Masterhealer. He had fallen into the pose that Capiam irreverently called the "harper attitude." Capiam dared not glance at Desdra to whom he had confided the observation for it was not a moment for levity. Or perhaps that was all that was keeping his mind from buckling under the new "challenge."

"Did you not tell me yourself earlier this morning," Tirone continued, his bass voice resonant with vexation—"harper enunciator," Capiam's graceless mind decided, "that there had been no new cases of the plague reported anywhere on the continent?"

"I did. I'll be happier when the lapse is four days long. But that only means that this wave of the viral influence is passing. The 'flu'— as the Ancients nicknamed it—can recur. It's the *next* wave that worries me dreadfully."

"Next one?" Tirone stared blankly at Capiam, as if wishing he had misheard.

Capiam sighed. He was not at all happy with a discussion that he had hoped to put off until he had completed a plan of action. People were less apt to panic if they were presented with a course of action. He had nearly completed his computations for the amount of vaccine needed, the number of dragonriders (and he had to assume they wanted to avoid a repetition of the plague as much as he) needed to distribute the vaccine, and the halls and holds where it would be administered. The confrontation had been precipitated by apprentice gossiping: speculations about why healers were still asking for blood donations for more serum when the reported cases of the "flu" were dropping and why the internment camp had not been struck.

"Next one?" Tirone's voice was incredulous.

"Oh, dear me, yes," Master Fortine replied from his corner, thinking his colleague needed support. "So far we have found four distinct references to this sort of viral influence. It seems to mutate. The serum which suppresses one kind does not always have any effect on the next."

"The details would bore Master Tirone, I fear," Capiam said. No sense in fomenting total alarm. Capiam had seized on the hope that, if they could immunize everyone in the Northern continent, catching all the carriers of *this* type, they would be in less danger from further manifestations, the symptoms for which would now be easily recognized and speedily dealt with.

"I am less bored by details than you might imagine," Tirone said. He strode forward, pulled out the chair at Capiam's desk, and seated himself, folding his arms across his chest in an aggressive fashion. He stared pointedly at Capiam. "Acquaint me with the details."

Capiam scratched at the back of his neck, a habit he had recently acquired and that he deplored in himself.

"You know that we looked back into the Records to find mention of the viral influence..."

"Yes. Stupid name."

"Descriptive, however. We found four separate references to such 'flus' as periodic scourges before the Crossing. Even before the First Crossing."

"Let us not get into politics."

Capiam opened his eyes in mild reproof. "I'm not. But I always thought you were of the Two-Crossings school of thought and the language in the texts supports that theory. Suffice to say," Capiam hurried on as Tirone twitched his eyebrows in growing irritation, "our ancestors also carried with them certain bacteria and viruses which were ineradicable."

"Indeed they were, but they are necessary to the proper function of our bodies and the internal economy of the animals brought on both Crossings," Master Fortine said in earnest support of his colleague.

"Yes, as Fortine says, we cannot escape some infections. We *must* prevent a second viral infection. It can recur. Here. Now. As doubtless it does periodically on the Southern Continent. We know to our sorrow that it only takes one carrier. We can't let that happen again, Tirone. We have neither the medicines nor the personnel to cope with a second epidemic."

"I know that as well as you do," Tirone said, his voice rough with irritation. "So? Do those precious Records of yours say what the Ancients did?" He gestured at the thick Records on Capiam's desk with a contempt based on fear.

"Mass vaccination!"

It took Tirone a moment to realize that Capian had given him a candid answer.

"Mass vaccination? The whole continent!" Tirone made a lavish sweep of one arm, glaring at Capiam. "But I've *been* vaccinated." His hand went to his left arm.

"That immunity lasts only about fourteen days with the sort of serum we can produce. So you see, our time is limited... and might even be running out in Igen and Keroon unless we can vaccinate everyone and anyone who might harbor the virus. That's the challenge. My Hall provides the serum and the personnel to vaccinate; yours keeps Hall, Hold, and Weyr from panic!"

"Panic? Yes, you're right about that!" Tirone jerked his thumb in the direction of Fort Hold where Lord Tolocamp still refused to leave his apartment. "You would have more to fear from the panic than the plague just now."

"Yes!" Capiam put a great deal into that quiet affirmative. Desdra had moved perceptibly closer to him. He wasn't sure if her intention was supportive or defensive, but he appreciated her proximity. "And we have to proceed with speed and diligence. If there should be a carrier in Igen, Keroon, Telgar, or Ruatha..."

The vulnerable angry look in Tirone's eyes reminded him of his own reaction when he had had to admit the inescapable conclusions drawn from the four references Fortine, and then Desdra, had reluctantly shown him.

"To prevent a second epidemic, we must vaccinate now, within the next few days." Capiam turned briskly to the maps he had been preparing. "Portions of Lemos, Bitra, Crom, Nabol, upper Telgar, High Reaches, and Tillek have not had contact with anyone since the cold season started. We can vaccinate them later, when the snow melts but before the spring rains, when those people begin to circulate more freely. So we have to concern ourselves with this portion of the continent."

Capiam brought his arm down the southern half. "There are certain advantages to the social structure on Pern, Tirone, particularly during a Pass. We can keep track of where everyone is. We also know approximately how many people survived the first wave of the flu and who has been vaccinated. So it comes down to the problem of distributing the vaccine at the appointed day. As dragonriders are vulnerable to the disease, I feel we can ask their cooperation in getting vaccine to the distribution points I've marked out across the continent."

Tirone gave a cynical snort. "You won't get any cooperation from M'tani at Telgar. L'bol at Igen is useless—Wimmia's running the Weyr and it's a mercy Fall is a consolidated effort. F'gal might help..."

Capiam shook his head impatiently. "I can get all the help I need from Moreta, S'ligar, and K'dren. But we must do it now, to halt any further incidence of the flu. It can be halted, killed, if it does not have new victims to propagate it."

"Like Thread?"

"That is an analogy, I suppose," Capiam admitted wearily. He had spent so much time arguing lately, with Fortine, Desdra, the other Masters, and himself. The more he presented the case, the more clearly did he feel the necessity for the push. "It takes only one Thread to ruin a field, or a continent. Only one carrier is needed to spread the plague."

"Or one idiot master seaman trying to stake a premature claim on the Southern Continent—"

"*What?*"

Tirone took from his tunic a water-stained sheaf, its parchment pages roughly evened.

"I was on my way to see you about this, Master Capiam. Your healer at Igen Sea Hold, Master Burdion, entrusted this to my journeyman. I wanted it for an accurate account of this period."

"Yes, yes, you badgered me on my sickbed." Capiam made to take the book from Tirone, who reproved him with a look.

"There was no floating animal, no chance encounter, Capiam. They *landed* in Southern. Burdion was quite ill, you know, and during his convalescence he read the log of the good ship *Windtoss* for lack of anything more stimulating. He's been in a sea hold long enough to know sailing annotations. And he said that Master Varny was an honest man. He logs the squall, right enough, and that did send them legitimately off course. *But* they ought not to have landed. Exploration of the Southern Continent was not to be undertaken until this Pass was over. It was to be a combined effort of Hall, Hold, and Weyr. They were three days in that anchorage!" Tirone punctuated his remarks by stabbing his finger at the journal in such a way that Capiam couldn't see the page properly. Then Tirone relinquished it to his grasp, and Desdra sidled up to look.

"Oh, dear, oh, dear, how very presumptuous of Master Varney," Master Fortine said. "But that means this is not a case of zoonosis, Capiam, but a direct infection."

"Only if there were humans in the Southern Continent," Capiam said hopefully.

"The log entries do not suggest there are!" Tirone sank that possibility.

"Indeed the Records concerning the Second Crossing are clear on that point."

"Are we sure," Desdra asked, "that they *were* in southern waters?"

"Oh, yes," Tirone said. "A seabred journeyman harper confirmed that the positions correspond to the Southern Continent! He said there wouldn't *be* any place shallow enough to anchor anywhere *short* of the landmass of the continent. Three days they were there!"

"The log says"—Desdra was reading—"that they had to jury-rig repairs to the sloop after it was damaged by a storm."

"That's what it *says*," Tirone agreed sardonically. "Undoubtedly they did make repairs, but Burdion added a note"—Tirone produced a scrap that he flourished before he read it—" 'I found fruit pits of unusual size in the unemptied galley bucket and rotten husks of some specimens which were unknown to me though I have been many Turns in this Hold.'" Tirone leaned toward Capiam, his eyes brilliant. "So, my friends, the *Windtoss* made a premature landing. And look where it has landed us!" Tirone threw his arms wide in another of his grand gestures.

Capiam sank back wearily in his chair, staring at the maps, flicking his careful lists with his fingers.

"The log may shed light on certain aspects of this, my good friend, but also warns us against that projected return to the Southern Continent."

"I heartily agree!"

"And it reinforces my conclusion that we must vaccinate to prevent the spread of the plague. And vaccinate the runners as well. I really hadn't counted on that complication."

"Look on it as a challenge?" said Desdra dryly, her hands kneading at the tense muscles of Capiam's shoulders.

"Not one which I think our unofficial Masterherdsman is capable of answering, I fear," said Capiam.

"Would Moreta know? She was runnerhold bred, her family had a fine breeding hold in Keroon..." Even the brash Masterharper paused, knowing of the tragedy there. "She did attend that mid-distance runner at Ruatha Gather. That was the first case to be noted here in the west, remember."

"No, I don't remember, Tirone," Capiam said irritably. Did he have to cure the sick animals of this continent, too? "You're the memory of our times."

"Surely if we have a human vaccine, we can produce by the same methods an animal one," Desdra said, soothingly. "And there's Lord Alessan, who certainly has enough donors. I did hear, did I not, that some of his runnerbeasts survived the plague?"

"Yes, yes, they did," Tirone said swiftly, glancing with an anxious frown at the despondent Masterhealer. "Come, my friend, you've solved so many of our recent problems. You cannot lose heart now." Tirone's bass voice oozed entreaty and persuasiveness.

"No, no, my dear Capiam, we *cannot* lose heart now," Master Fortine added from his corner.

Tirone rose, his manner suddenly brisk. "Look, Capiam, I'll drum for a convey. You can go to Fort Weyr, see what Moreta can tell you. Then on to that new man—what's his name, Bessel?—at Beastmasterhold. Meanwhile, since I take it that this vaccination program of yours is more urgent than ever. I'll sweeten hall and hold. I'll start with Tolocamp." Tirone jerked his thumb toward Fort Hold. "If he agrees, we'll have no trouble with the other Lords Holder, even that crevice snake Ratoshigan."

"Considering Tolocamp's mental state, however will you accomplish his cooperation?" Capiam asked, jarred from his depression by Tirone's obvious confidence.

"If you recall, my fellow Master, Lord Tolocamp has been deprived of our services for the past few days. As he has never encouraged any of his children or his holders to have ideas, he is going to need *ours*. He's had long enough to reconsider his intransigence," Tirone replied with a deceptively bland smile. "You take care of the vaccine; I'll organize the rest."

The Masterharper was careful to retrieve the log of the *Windtoss* from Capiam before he left with an energetic stride and a brisk slam of the door.

The elation that Alessan had experienced after his visit to Fort Weyr was compounded of renewed hope and the unexpected sympathy of Moreta. He would have liked to savor that incident but the most urgent problem, producing a usable vaccine for runnerbeasts, especially those he devoutly hoped that Dag had saved, took precedence over any personal consideration.

M'barak returned Alessan and Tuero to Ruatha Hold, landing in the forecourt. The speed with which Oklina emerged from the Hold suggested she had been anxiously awaiting her brother's return. She paused on the top steps, her face turned up to him. As he slid down the blue dragon's side, Alessan let out a joyful whoop and her expression turned to relief as she rushed to meet him. Exuberantly Alessan swooped her up in his arms, achingly aware of the difference between his sister's slight body and Moreta's. He gave Oklina a gentle kiss on her cheek.

There had been scant time for affection between brother and sister lately, and, during her illness, Alessan had come to know how much he valued Oklina. A kiss, he had good reason to know, was a kind gesture!

"Moreta said the serum idea is valid. We're going to try it! Now!" Alessan told her. "If it does work, then Ruatha is open again and my holders cannot deny me their labor. If it doesn't work, we're no worse off than we have been."

"It *has* to work!" Oklina cried fervently.

Alessan shouted for Follen. "We'll need his help, his implements, and that old brood mare. I know she caught the plague and I can't risk any of the team animals."

"Arith! Behave yourself. That's Lady Oklina!" M'barak called. The blue dragon had turned his head round toward brother and sister, and was now wiffling closer and closer to Oklina, his eyes whirling. By no means afraid of such attentions, Oklina didn't know what to do and clung to Alessan.

At his rider's reprimand, Arith made a tiny little noise, a disappointed snort, and turned his head away while M'barak apologized profusely.

"I really don't know what came over him. Arith is usually very well behaved. But it is late, he is tired, and we'd better get back to the Weyr." Arith snorted audibly and M'barak looked startled. "*I'd* best be back at the Weyr."

Thanking M'barak and Arith for their convey, Alessan guided Oklina out of the way, a bemused Tuero following.

"Blue dragons are not usually fascinated by the opposite sex," the harper remarked dryly to Alessan.

"Really?" Alessan's reply was polite for his mind was on the mechanics of turning runner blood into serum vaccine.

"There *is* a queen egg on the Fort Weyr Hatching Ground."

"And?" Alessan's courtesy turned crisp. He had a lot to do before he could see what Dag had salvaged of the Ruathan herds.

Tuero's grin broadened. "As I recall it, Ruatha has quite a few bloodties with dragonriders."

Alessan stared from Oklina to the dragon already airborne, and remembered K'lon's remark the day he had brought the vaccine to Ruatha Hold. "It couldn't be!"

At that point, Follen rushed out of the Hold, his expression hopeful, and Alessan devoted his full attention to putting vaccine theory to test.

Tuero brought the brood mare in from the field; she was quiet enough to be led by her forelock. Follen, Oklina, Deefer, and the trustworthy fosterlings bore the medical equipment to the beasthold. The momentum of exhilaration was briefly checked when they discovered that they didn't have large enough glass containers for the quantity of animal blood. Then Oklina remembered that Lady Oma had put away huge ornamental glass bottles long ago presented by Master Clargesh to Lords Holder as samples of apprentice industry and design. To spin such large bottles, Alessan, Tuero, and Deefer contrived a big centrifuge from a spare wagonwheel attached to spitcogs and a crank.

The runner mare stood quietly impassive since the bloodtaking caused no discomfort.

"Strange," Follen said as the first batch was completed and the straw-colored fluid drawn off. "It's the same color as human serum."

"It's only dragons who have green blood," Oklina said.

"We'll try the vaccine on the lame runner," Alessan said, wondering which blue rider was harassing his sister and why. All the time the wheel was turning, Alessan fidgeted. Since he'd no other option, he had been patient, but now that he could search out Dag, he was fretting to be gone. "If there's no ill effect on that creature, we can assume— we have to assume—that the serum works, since the same principle is efficacious for humans."

"It's too late to do more tonight anyhow," Follen said with a vast yawn when he had injected the serum in the lame beast.

"No one at the Harper Hall will think kindly of a message at this hour," Tuero agreed, knuckling his eyes.

"I think I'll just stay here tonight, in case there's a reaction." Alessan nodded toward the lame runner.

"And you'll be off first thing in the morning, won't you?"—Oklina leaned toward her brother, her dark soft eyes on his, her comment for him alone—"to find Dag and Squealer?"

He nodded and gave her shoulders an affectionate squeeze before he sent her off after the healer and the harper. Alessan watched the three until the glowbaskets they carried were out of sight in a dip of the roadway. Then he fixed himself a bed of straw in the stall next to the runner. Despite his good intention to remain alert enough to check on the beast, he slept soundly until first light. The injected runner was still lame but it exhibited no signs of a distress, no mark of sweat, and had eaten a good deal of the clean bedding with which it had been furnished.

Reassured, Alessan saddled the runner that Tuero had nicknamed Skinny—not a mount he would have chosen for anyone, but beggars couldn't be chosers at Ruatha those days. Alessan carefully packed the serums, needlethorns, and Follen's glass syringe into the saddlebag, cushioning them with clean straw, then mounted and urged Skinny onto the roadway.

The night before, he had had many doubts as they waited for the serum to be produced: doubts about many things, including Moreta's unexpected response to him. He thought of kindness and the kiss he had given his sister. Had Moreta only meant to be kind? Today, in the dawn of a bright fresh spring morning, he knew it had not been mere

kindness in Moreta. He and the Weyrwoman had been of one mind in
that brief instant. And the dragon queen had trilled in concord.

Skinny shied at some imaginary bogey in the greening bushes by the
track. Alessan swayed to the motion, checking the animal's sideway
plunge with a firm pressure of that leg, while he made sure that the
flaps on the saddlebags were secure. Alessan liked an active mover but
he couldn't risk the precious fluid or pause to school a fractious beast.
He must concentrate on riding and not be diverted by visions of the
impossible. Moreta was the Fort Weyrwoman. Although she might,
just might, enjoy a discreet relationship with him, might even allow a
pregnancy—and suddenly Alessan longed for a child as he had not
with Suriana—Alessan was still Lord of a severely depleted bloodline.
He had to have an acknowledged wife, and others to bear his children,
as many as he could beget.

Old Runel was dead, he thought with a flash of regret. Old Runel
and all the Ruathan begets as well as the bloodlines of runners back to
the Crossing. He'd never thought he would rue the loss of that man.

Skinny trotted, its hocks well under it and with a fine forward ex-
tension. Too bad the creature was gelded. Ruatha had once had far
better specimens to propagate. Alessan inhaled against the hope at the
end of this track. He tried to keep from wondering which animals Dag
had seen fit to take with him. If only Dag had included one breeding
pair of the Lord Leef's heavy carters... The records of animals destroyed that Norman had started to keep had been lost when the race-
flats temporary hospital had been abandoned. Alessan wished futilely
that he had made time to look in on the beasthold that frantic morning
before he had taken ill.

Alessan came to the fork in the track, each direction leading to
nursery fields. Dag would have taken the less accessible one, he decided,
but he paused long enough to see if there had been a message left at
the division. Not a rag, a bone, or an unnatural formation of the pebbles.
Nine days had passed since Dag left with Fergal. Fear burrowed from
the trap in his mind to which Alessan had banished it.

He dug his heels into Skinny, and the beast responded instantly,
skittering at a good rate up the track, high breathing as it caught the
excitement generated in its rider. Runners were considered stupid, had
few ways to communicate with riders, and yet occasionally one seemed
to know exactly what was going on in the human it bore. Alessan laid
a soothing hand on Skinny's arched neck and brought the animal to a
more sensible pace.

Then they were at the rise that led to the pasture and, for a heart-
breaking moment, Alessan could see nothing of man or beast in the
rolling fields. But the barrier had been man-made, with prickly hedge
and stone, high enough to contain docile beasts. He rose in his stirrups,
numb with the fear that Dag had brought the plague with him and died

with all the animals. Then he saw the thin column of smoke to his right, saw the flapping of a shirt drying on a branch. He heard a piercing whistle.

From the slope down to the stream, runners trooped obediently in answer to the summons. Alessan felt tears prick his eyes. He hauled Skinny smartly back down the road, turned, set his heels to the bony ribs, and Skinny charged the barrier, sailing nobly over it, clacking with surprise when they landed on the far side. Alessan hauled the delighted animal to a more sedate pace, remembering his mission. It was only then that he saw, among the beasts jogging up the slope, the wobbly-legged awkward infantile bodies, the waddling pace of the gravid. Alessan let out a whoop of jubilation and it reverberated from the hills. Had Dag taken *all* the pregnant mares with him? Alessan had bleakly had to assume that all the anticipated foals had died of the plague or been aborted, for all he found in the fields of the Hold proper had been gelded males and barren mares.

His whoop was answered from the rude shelter dug into the high side of the slope. The small figure standing at its entrance waved both arms. One small figure! Inadvertently Alessan checked Skinny and then urged it forward. One small black-haired figure, now with impudent arms cocked against ragged pants. Fergal!

"You took your time, Lord Alessan!" The boy's expression was as impertinent as his words were resentful and unforgiving.

"Dag?" Alessan's voice broke in consternation. He could not move from the saddle. Until that moment, he hadn't realized how much he had looked forward to seeing the old handler, how sorely he needed Dag's knowledgeable advice if Ruathan runners were ever to regain their former prestige.

Annoyingly, Fergal shrugged and then cocked his head up at Alessan.

"I thought you'd *forgotten* us!" He stepped to one side and gestured toward the shelter. "*He* broke his leg. I took care of all the runners, even the ones who birthed. Didn't I do a good job?"

Alessan would have swatted him for impudence had he been able to catch him but Fergal, grinning with positive malice at his little hoax, had slipped neatly out of range into the shelter of his charges.

"Alessan?" Dag's summons came from the shelter and Alessan put aside any thought of discipline to rush in to his old ally. "I saved all I could for you, Alessan. I saved all I could."

"You have also saved Ruatha!"

"I do apologize for intruding on the Hatching Ground, Moreta," Capiam said, peering cautiously around the entrance.

"Come in. Come in!" Moreta beckoned him eagerly to join her in her temporary accommodation in the first tier.

Capiam looked back over his shoulder a moment and then entered, keeping an anxious eye on Orlith among her eggs.

"She does seem quite serene, doesn't she?"

"Oh, she is!"

"M'barak, who conveyed Desdra and me here, said that she will even show off that splendid queen egg she clutched." With due respect for the hot volcanic sands, Capiam walked quickly to Moreta.

"Desdra's here? I've heard a great deal about her from M'barak and K'lon."

"She's chatting with Jallora so I could have a private word with you." Capiam cleared his throat in an uncharacteristic show of nervousness.

Moreta thought he was wary of Orlith and extended her hands to him. She supposed she must get used to the changes wrought in people by the plague. Capiam appeared only to have lost weight, for his eyes sparkled out of a craggy face that would become more attractive with age. His hair was thinning at the temples and she fancied that the gray had encroached farther into the black, but there was no diminution in the force of his personality, or in his grip as he clasped her hands.

"To what do I owe this unexpected pleasure?" she asked.

His eyes twinkled. "An unexpected . . . challenge is what I told Master Tirone."

Alerted by his geniality, Moreta searched his face. "What sort of a challenge?"

"I'll come to that in a moment, if I may. First, would you know if runnerbeasts would respond favorably to a serum vaccine against the plague they also suffer?"

Moreta stared at him a moment, surprised to be asked the same question twice in a short space of time, and surprised that the question had to be asked at all. She was angry that no one had taken steps to safeguard the runnerbeasts, which were such valuable assets of the Northern Continent. She had tried to appreciate that saving human life had been the priority, but surely someone must have been rational enough in one of the runnerholds to apply the principal to the beasts. She had been complimented and touched that Alessan had sought her advice yesterday evening and, despite her varied irritations, slightly amused that she, Weyrwoman of Fort, was now being approached by the Masterhealer.

"I answered that same question for Alessan last night."

"Oh!" Capiam blinked with surprise. "Oh, and how did you answer Lord Alessan?"

"Affirmatively."

"He contacted Master Balfor?"

"It was too late to drum up the Keroon Beasthold. Is Balfor the new Masterherdsman?"

"He is acting in that capacity. Someone must."

"Alessan ought to have informed you, or at least the Harper Hall . . ." Moreta frowned. Tuero should have done it if Alessan was too busy. Perhaps Alessan had not had enough time to produce a serum? No. She had the impression that he wouldn't have wasted any time.

"It is not quite noon," Capiam said tactfully, willing to give the harried Lord Holder the benefit on any doubt. "In theory, serum vaccine ought to produce similar immunization in the runners. Alessan needs all the luck and help he can get."

Moreta nodded in solemn agreement. "So why does the Healer Hall concern itself suddenly with animal vaccines?"

"Because, unfortunately, I have good reason to believe that the plague is transmitted to man by animals and may break out again—'zoonotic' and 'recrudescent' are the terms the Ancients used to describe those qualities."

"Oh!" Moreta struggled to assimilate the information. The ramifications were staggering. "You mean, we could easily have a second epidemic? Shards! Capiam, the continent couldn't survive a second epidemic!" She threw up her arms in an excess of dismay that had to be vented. "The Weyrs are only barely able to get the requisite number of wings in the air with every Fall, what with riders recovering from secondary infections and new injuries. If the plague went through us again, I doubt there'd be a full wing available!" In her agitation, she began to pace then she noticed his patient watching. She halted and gave him a closer scrutiny. "If the animal vaccine works, then you could stop the zoonosis? You would vaccinate both man and animal against it? And your challenge is . . ."—she had to smile at the way he had led her to the conclusion—"to the dragonriders for their assistance in distributing the vaccines?"

"Preferably on the same day to all distribution points." Capiam carefully unfolded a copy of his plan. He peered at her from under his brows, watching her reactions as he handed her the document. "Mass vaccination is the only way to stop the plague. It would require a tremendous effort. My halls have already started to accumulate human vaccine. To be candid, my Hall had not quite evaluated the runner susceptibility. Between Tirone's reports and Desdra's exhaustive investigations, we can find no other way than zoonosis for the plague to have spread so rapidly and so far. We now know that the only way to prevent a recurrence of this viral influence is to stop it within the next few days or endure a second wave."

Moreta shuddered with dread. She studied his plan.

"Of course," he added, tipping the edge of the parchment, "the scheme depends first on the feasibility of the runner vaccine and the cooperation of the Weyrs to circulate both."

"Have you approached any of the other Weyrs yet?"

"I needed an answer to my question on runner vaccine and you are the nearest authority." He grinned at her.

"Surely Lord Tolocamp—"

"I'm leaving Lord Tolocamp to Master Tirone." There was considerable acrimony in the healer's voice. "And such a question as this to someone who can give me a rational answer. Not only have I an answer, I have a source."

"That is also an assumption—"

"Which I will confirm as soon as you can also assure me that the Weyrs can assist us in delivering the vaccines. One of my journeymen is a wizard at figuring out what he calls time-and-motion processes. If we could rely on a minimum of six riders from each Weyr to cover their traditional regions, in a scheduled roster of stops to the various halls, holds, and Weyrs, that would be sufficient."

Moreta was doing some calculations of her own. "Not unless the riders—" She caught herself and gulped in astonishment. In Capiam's broadening grin she had an unexpected answer.

"I've been doing rather a lot of reading in the Archives, Moreta." Capiam sounded more pleased than apologetic for the shock he had given her.

"How did that bit of information come to be in the Healer Archives?" she demanded, so infuriated that Orlith came fully alert, claws hooking protectively about the queen egg.

"Why shouldn't it be?" Capiam asked with deceptive mildness. "After all, my Craft bred the trait into the dragons. Can they really go from one time to another?" he asked wistfully.

"Yes," she finally replied, as austerely as she could. "But it's not encouraged at all!" She thought of K'lon, knew very well how often the blue rider had been at the Healer Hall, and wondered about such convenient Records. On the other hand, Capiam's Craft had been credited with many incredible feats and displays of skill, secrets forgotten by disuse. She chided herself for doubting the integrity of Master Capiam, especially at such a critical hour when any strategy that might restore the continent to balance might be condoned. "Capiam, traveling in time produces paradoxes that can be very dangerous."

"That's why I suggested the progressive delivery so there is no overlapping." The eagerness in his manner was disarming.

"There might be some trouble convincing M'tani of Telgar."

"Yes, I'd heard of his disaffection. I also know that F'gal of Ista is very ill of a kidney chill and L'bol of severe depressions—which is why I specify the minimum number of riders the effort would require. I don't know how the continent would have survived without all the assistance the dragonriders have given hall and hold up to this point."

"You have enough vaccine for people?"

"We will have. Master Tirone is adroitly broaching the subject to hall and hold."

"A wise precaution."

Capiam heaved a sigh. "So, what must be ascertained now is whether or not Lord Alessan has successfully produced the animal vaccine."

Go to Ruatha with them, Orlith said. After a flicker of a pause, she added, *Holth agrees.*

Illogically, Moreta resisted that gratuitous permission—and wondered why. She had a perfectly natural wish to see the results of Alessan's experiment, not necessarily Alessan. Was she resisting the attraction she felt for him? She was not normally bothered by indecision.

You have always liked runnerbeasts. They deserve your help now. Holth–Orlith was speaking, Moreta decided from the doubly deep tone. *You will have to see Ruatha sometime again.* That, undeniably, was spoken only by Orlith.

Moreta sighed deeply and sadly. Orlith had touched the core of her resistance, for Moreta did not want to see Ruatha in the ruins K'lon had described.

"I think, Capiam," she said slowly, steeling her mind, "that I should accompany you."

Arith is more than willing. He likes the girl, Orlith said. She unsheathed her claws from the queen egg. From the Bowl, Arith bugled agreement.

"Which girl?" Moreta was surprised at the remark.

Orlith shrugged and went about making a depression in which she rolled her egg. So, trying not to appear resigned, Moreta collected her flying gear.

"Arith says he will take us to Ruatha Hold."

"You can leave her?" Capiam looked toward the queen.

"My going is her idea. She's not a broody dragon, like some who must have their rider in constant attendance. Leri and Holth are nearby. I shan't be gone very long, you know." She gave Capiam a dour glance and then smiled at his startled expression.

When Moreta and Capiam reached the Bowl, Jallora was talking earnestly with a dark-haired woman who was standing a few lengths from M'barak and Arith. Desdra was older than Moreta had expected from K'lon's comments, older than Moreta herself, but then Jallora had said that the woman was taking her mastery at the Fort Healer Hall. Desdra had a reserved air about her, not quite haughty but certainly a woman who kept herself to herself—a trait that did not, however, keep her from being keenly aware of the activity in the Bowl. Two wings from Fort would fly later across Bitra and Lemos. Sh'gall had gone forward to Benden to see K'dren. The Benden Weyrleader was tactful, as M'tani of Telgar was not, and Moreta counted on K'dren to smooth matters over in the day's consolidation. She would be everlastingly grateful when the Weyrs could return to traditional territories.

"Desdra, Moreta is coming with us to Ruatha," Capiam was saying. "It would seem that Lord Alessan has anticipated the matter of runner vaccine."

Desdra inclined her head courteously to the Weyrwoman, her large gray eyes calmly taking Moreta's measure.

"Don't let Desdra make you uncomfortable, Moreta," Capiam said. "She takes no one at face value; claims detachment is required of a healer."

"Jallora had told me of the superb reconstruction work you do on Threadscored dragon wing," Desdra replied in a low unhurried voice, her eyes flicking a glance to Moreta's hands as she put on her gloves.

"When there is time again, please return and examine Dilenth. The Istan Weyr Healer, Ind, taught me the technique. I've had opportunity to perfect it."

"I'd forgot about Fall today, Moreta," Capiam was saying uncertainly, as he looked about and saw the unmistakable preparations.

"I must be back for the *end* of Fall, certainly," Moreta replied, now perversely compelled to go to Ruatha. "As it happens, the wings have taken fewer injuries since the plague. It might just be that flying against other Weyrs has improved performances."

"Really? How interesting." Capiam's surprise was genuine.

Then M'barak courteously gestured for Moreta to mount Arith first. She did so, settling herself at the back and assisting Desdra. Although Desdra made no comment and appeared perfectly composed, Moreta decided that the healer had not often ridden adragonback.

Capiam was clearly delighted, twisting about to grin past Desdra at Moreta then checking discreetly that Desdra was comfortable. "Four riders are not excessive weight for your Arith, M'barak?" he asked as the blue rider swung into his forward position.

"Not my Arith," the boy replied stoutly, "or I'd've mentioned it."

As if to prove his ability, Arith leaped from the ground so enthusiastically that his passengers were abruptly pressed backward. Moreta instinctively locked her legs and grabbed the ridge behind her to balance Desdra, who was pushed back by Capiam's weight. Arith made a quick adjustment as M'barak rapped his neck. Conscious of his Weyrwoman's presence, M'barak made a ceremony of taking leave of the watchrider, accepting and returning salutes as Arith winged to a respectable altitude. M'barak looked back at Moreta with a warning nod of his head before he gave Arith directions.

"Black, blacker, blackest—"

Moreta's litany broke as they appeared in the sky again above Ruatha.

She caught her breath, closing her eyes against the sickening view of the violated field, the rutted racing flat, the great fire circles, and the appalling burial mounds. She knew that her grip on Desdra's waist had locked and she was aware, too, of warm hands that lay gently on hers in shared sympathy and dismay.

All too clearly, Moreta could recall her compliments to Alessan on Ruatha's Gather gaiety, a bitter memory now that she was faced with the grim reality of the Gather's aftermath. Arith glided across the racing flats, directly at the Hold. Moreta could see the starting poles forlornly tumbled about where the spectacular dead heat of the last race had been run. Moreta forced herself to look at the raw earth of the burial mounds and accept the fact of so many casualties from that carefree throng of visitors in their Gather finery. And to accept as well the cremation fires that had consumed dead animals, winners and losers both, of the ten races that had drawn them to Ruatha on that fatal occasion. For a callous moment she thought that Alessan could have found the time to clear the pathetic debris of travel wagons, trunks, and Gather stands from the roadway and the fields. She marked where campfires had blackened the stubble field from which she and the young Lord Holder had so blithely watched the racing. Where banners had brightly flown, the upper tiers of Ruatha Hold were shuttered, unneeded, reminders that Ruatha had withstood a siege more savage than any Threadfall.

Yet, even as her heart contracted at the disheveled look of the proud Hold, her eyes went to the fields and the runners grazing there—not the large, solid beasts that Alessan had bred on Lord Leef's instructions but the wiry, thin-boned runners of Squealer's ilk. The irony helped restore her composure. Her tears would not comfort Alessan now.

Arith was not going to land at the forecourt, for which mercy Moreta was extremely grateful. His line was taking them along the roadway to the beasthold where considerable activity was evident. Three runners were being disengaged from plows, saddles lay on the ground, and a small cart had been pulled from storage. People were rushing up the road, carrying baskets with careful haste. The basic vitality of Ruatha appeared resurgent.

"M'barak says that he has seen Alessan at the beasthold," Desdra said to Moreta, projecting her voice sufficiently to counter the glide breeze. Nothing in her expression indicated that she was aware of Moreta's painful first reaction to the plague-scarred Hold.

Those at the beasthold had become aware of the dragon's approach and, just as Arith landed neatly on the far side of the roadway, two men emerged. Both were tall and their faces in shadow but Moreta identified Alessan on the right. That he recognized her was apparent by his sudden start before he strode to meet his visitors as fast as a Lord's dignity would allow. And he walked like the Lord of Ruatha again, Moreta was relieved to see—confident and proud.

"Sorry to arrive at an awkward moment, Lord Alessan," Capiam called as he dismounted.

"Your arrival could never be awkward, your appearance is always welcome," Alessan replied, but his eyes held Moreta's for a long instant before he courteously handed Capiam to the ground. "Tuero and I"— he indicated the tall harper who had followed him—"were composing a message to you." Then Alessan abandoned his formal manner and grinned broadly up at Moreta. "Dag saved Squealer! We've foals, too. Three fine males!" He shouted the last sentence, giving vent to a joy he could no longer contain.

"Oh, how marvelous, Alessan!" Moreta swung her right leg over and behind her and dropped down Arith's side. Fortunately, for Arith was rather higher than she had thought, Alessan caught her about the waist and eased her to the ground. She turned in his arms, very much aware of his hold on her, his light-green eyes bright with elation and, she hoped, her unexpected visit. "And to think it's Squealer's breed that survived! And foals! Oh, how relieved you must be!"

"I'm only just back from the nursery meadows," he told her as he led her away from Arith, his hands moving along her arm, anxious to remain in contact with her and happy at a civil excuse to do so. "I didn't have enough vaccine with me. I never counted on foals. And Dag's got a broken leg so we have to send the cart. There'll be Fall here in six days! But Dag saved bloodstock for us. He saved enough and he's saved Ruatha!"

Moreta found herself grasping and shaking his hand repeatedly and wondering suddenly if anyone was noticing, but surely she could publicly congratulate him for such splendid good fortune. Then Capiam brought Desdra forward to introduce her, and Moreta saw that Desdra was measuring Alessan with the same penetrating gaze to which she had already been subjected. Moreta felt protective of Alessan and worried that the healer would divine her attraction to him.

"I deduce that you have produced a serum vaccine and used it."

"I have indeed, Capiam, for I couldn't risk the bloodstock in this infected area." Alessan's hand eloquently swept the Hold proper and its fields. "Journeyman Follen is in the process of making more." He nodded toward the beasthold. "The plague dealt us terrible losses both in men and animals." He motioned them all to follow him into the beasthold. "We prepared a serum as soon as I returned last evening, and I injected that beast." Alessan pointed to the lame one, its right front leg pointing despite the depth of the straw of its bed. "It seems none the worse for it. . . ."

"It won't be, I assure you," Capiam said warmly, adroitly steering them to an isolated area, away from others. "The theory is as sound for animals as it has proved for people. And"—he lowered his voice, peering first at Alessan and then at Tuero with a meaningful stare— "absolutely essential at this juncture." He shot Desdra a quick look at his inadvertent use of one of Tirone's favorite phrases. A twist of her lips showed that she had marked it. With a quick motion of his hands, Capiam circled the others closely around him, tucking his hands about Alessan's and Tuero's arms. He glanced about to be sure that everyone was busy, Follen with his group around the centrifuge and the holders about the animals being retacked. "Lord Alessan, the plague could break out again."

Moreta caught Alessan's free arm as he staggered back from Capiam. The Healer supported him on the other. Tuero's first reaction was to see how Alessan coped with the news. The harper's expression was unusually serious and compassionate.

"Animals as well as humans must be vaccinated this time round," Capiam continued. "All across the continent. I have worked out a plan of distribution, and Moreta will seek dragonrider assistance. What is needed is serum from recovered animals. You have them, sufficient at least to supply the needs of this Hold, Fort, Southern Boll, and that portion of Telgar which marches your boundaries. Lord Shadder, I know, will accommodate us in the east."

"But the herds in Keroon are vast . . ." Alessan was clearly stunned by the enormity of the project.

"No longer," Capiam said gently. "If this Dag of yours has saved bloodstock for you, you are richer than you think. May we have your help?"

Alessan looked at the Masterhealer, a curious expression playing in his light-green eyes and the oddest twist to his lips.

"Ruatha lost much—of its people, its herds, its honor, and its pride. Any help which Ruatha can now offer may perhaps remove the stain of our enduring"—Alessan indicated the burial mounds—"hospitality."

There was no bitterness in the young Lord Holder's voice but there was no doubt in anyone's mind that the aftermath of his first Gather had burned indelibly into his soul.

"What makes you think that *you* are responsible for that? Or any of this?" One flourish of Capiam's hand indicated the burial mounds, the next their meeting in the beasthold and the veterinary preparations being made to one side. "No blame adheres to you, Lord Alessan. Circumstance, unpredictable circumstance, drove the *Windtoss* from her course. Opportunism prompted its master to land in the Southern Continent, and greed kept him there for three days. What prompted the crew to transport that animal to the unprotected north will never be known for every witness to that reprehensible decision is now dead. But that circumstance was beyond your control. What *has* been in *your* control,

my Lord Alessan, is the courage with which you have conducted yourself, your care of the sick, your effort to sow crops, and the preservation
of Ruathan bloodstock. Most of all"—Capiam drew in a deep breath—
"most of all, that you are, in the midst of the severe trials you have
endured, willing to *help* others.

"When bad fortune occurs, the unresourceful, unimaginative man
looks about him to attach the blame to someone else; the resolute accepts
misfortune and endeavors to survive, mature, and improve because of
it.

"A fishing ship is blown off course in an unseasonal squall and that
minor event has influenced us all." Capiam's expression was rueful.
He glanced at Desdra, who was staring at him in a baffled manner. "If
you view justice as the foundation of your life, then it has been served—
for captain, crew, and cargo are dead. *We* live. And *we* have work to
do." Capiam gripped Alessan by the shoulder, emphasizing his words
by shaking him. "Lord Alessan, take no blame to yourself for any of
this. Take credit for your vision!"

Outside Arith suddenly bugled in welcome and was answered by a
deeper note.

"A bronze? Here?" Moreta hastily made her way to the entrance of
the beasthold. M'barak stood by Arith, who was gazing skyward. The
blue was not agitated even if Moreta feared that Sh'gall might have
followed. "M'barak! Who comes?" Why hadn't Orlith contacted her?

"Nabeth and B'lerion," M'barak said without concern, shielding his
eyes from the sun.

"B'lerion!" Moreta was relieved but, when a slender figure rushed
down the ramp from the Hold, she began to understand B'lerion's
presence.

Arith rose on his hindquarters, emitting what Moreta could only
interpret as a challenge.

"I don't know what's got into him, Moreta," M'barak cried, embarrassed. "He's gotten to be awfully protective of Lady Oklina."

"There is a queen egg on the Hatching Ground, M'barak," she said,
and added when it was obvious her explanation eluded the weyrling.
"Blue dragons are often very keen on Search. Arith would seem to be
precocious, though." She frowned, observing Oklina awaiting B'lerion.
"I don't think Fort Weyr has the right to deplete Ruathan resources..."

She swiveled around. Alessan was escorting Capiam, Desdra, and
Tuero to the centrifuge. The big wheel was slowing and the next batch
of serum could be examined. Turning her head, she saw that Nabeth
had landed and B'lerion was sliding gracelessly from the bronze back.
Oklina greeted him with restraint, pointing toward the beasthold. B'lerion caught her hand, and the girl fell in step with him willingly enough
but did not reclaim her hand. As the pair turned down the roadway,

Moreta could see B'lerion's left arm was in a sling. He could not fly Threadfall. Had he been glad to escape from his Weyr when the High Reaches wings rose? Did B'lerion feel—as she did when the wings rose without her—an irrational compulsion to be with them? Or did he feel the injury was little more than a valid excuse to visit Oklina?

Drawing back into the shadow, Moreta turned to join the group by the centrifuge, standing a little to one side—the better to watch Alessan— as the healers discussed the quantity of vaccine they would need, the minimum effective dose, and how they could discreetly discover how many runners were in-holded.

"Body weight is always the factor," Moreta said, slipping into the conversation.

"We must make the determination of dosage as easy for the uncertain and the inept as possible," Alessan said. "Some of the handlers in the back holds are going to be incompetent as well as skeptical. Where handlers are still alive, that is." He flushed as Capiam fixed him with a reproving eye.

"We have been relocating capable people and trying to ascertain where more might be needed. It is amazing what people can do when they have no other options available."

"Master Capiam, how crucial is it that the runners be vaccinated . . . at this juncture?" Desdra asked, her gray eyes intent on the Healer's face.

"With zoonosis the determining factor—and I thought we had agreed on that point—"

"We have, but we cannot also waste effort." Desdra indicated the ornamental glass, the layers of blood now at rest. "I am forced to admit to you now that we have barely enough needlethorn to vaccinate the *people*, much less the animals. It would be unwise to reuse needle-thorns," Desdra went on softly. "The danger of contagion—"

"I know. I know." Capiam pulled his hand across his forehead and down his cheek, rubbing at his jaw. He gave a weak laugh, tossing his hand in the air in a futile gesture before he eased himself to a bale of straw. "And we can only be sure of eradicating the threat of plague if we vaccinate both."

"It is just needlethorn which you lack?" Moreta asked, catching Capiam's despondent gaze. The Masterhealer's eyes began to widen and his stricken expression changed to incredulity as he realized what her question implied.

"And will lack, unfortunately, until autumn," Desdra was saying, turning away from the disappointment she had just inflicted on her master. She did not see the exchange that passed between Moreta and Capiam. "I have appealed to every hall and hold on the drum network to send us their inventory. As it is, we may be forced to exclude some people—"

"How? Who? When?" Capaim's terse questions to Moreta were hoarse whispers but so intense was his voice that it caused a hush and Desdra whirled to face him.

Shrugging off discretion with a nervous laugh, Moreta answered him. "*How* is walking down the roadway. *Who* is us, for I can count on your silence and *that* is as essential as needlethorn, and *when* has to be now, before I have time to reconsider this aberration." She grinned in reckless glee. Knowing it was a dramatic gesture, but unable to resist, she pointed to the entrance just as B'lerion and Oklina entered. "Are you badly injured, B'lerion?" she said, hailing the bronze rider cheerfully and, in a lower voice to Capiam, "He can't be that bad or he wouldn't have risked *between*."

"No, my shoulder was only dislocated," the bronze rider replied diffidently, "but I can't stand seeing the wings form without me. Pressen needed someone to bring Ruatha what we can spare from our stores, so I volunteered." B'lerion did not look at Oklina, who was standing breathlessly beside him, but bowed with tacit sympathy to Alessan. "I have wanted to express—" He broke off, sensing Alessan's distress.

"There is something you can do to help, now that you're handy," Moreta said, and B'lerion gave her a startled look. She drew him to one side and explained the situation and made her audacious request.

"I concede," he said, darting quick glances at Capiam and Alessan, "that the matter is urgent, even overwhlmingly so"—he spread the fingers of his uninjured hand in appeal—"but it is quite one thing, Moreta, to add a few more hours to a day, and a completely different matter to flit across months. You know very well that it's damn dangerous!" He kept his reply low while trying to argue sense into her. Though B'lerion might often behave with apparent disregard for proprieties, he was far from careless and irresponsible.

"B'lerion, I know where we need to go, in both Ista and Nerat. I know when needlethorn is ripe to be harvested. The *ging* tree is always in bloom. I have seen the rainforest resemble a green face with a thousand dark-rimmed eyes—"

"Highly poetic, Moreta, but not exactly the guide I'd need."

"But it is a *when*. And to get the proper coordinates we've only to check the autumnal position of the Red Star. Alessan would have the charts. It's rising farther and farther west. One only has to calculate the autumnal degree." She could see that that argument did much to reassure B'lerion.

"I had not really expected to spend my free afternoon harvesting needlethorn . . ." His protest was halfhearted as he came to a conclusion that Moreta hastily reinforced.

"We can spend as much time as we need there, B'lerion, and still harvest what is so desperately needed now. But we must go *now*. I have to be back at the Weyr for the end of Fall. Nabeth is equal to the feat."

"Of course he is. But *they'd* know"—he jerked his thumb at the waiting group—"that we had traveled forward in time, Moreta."

"Capiam and Desdra already know it's possible." She grinned at the expression on his face. "After all, the Healer Hall bred dragons."

"So they did." B'lerion recovered from his astonishment.

"We will also have to use the ability on the day the vaccine is distributed."

B'lerion blinked wildly, glancing about him, but his gaze fell more regularly on Oklina's figure and Moreta began to relax. "I could, actually, see the Weyrs condoning *that* application, Moreta."

"They do not need to know we have taken time today. Who knows you've been here?"

"Pressen and that lad out there."

"I'll send M'barak off on an errand. Surely we can expect silence from Oklina, so that gives us a working party of six. We must make the time, and take it, B'lerion. Weyr, hold, and hall cannot sustain a second epidemic."

"I have to concede that, Moreta." B'lerion looked out over the debris strewn in the roadway and fields. "The change here is staggering." He grasped her hands tightly, his grin giving her the assent she required. "I'll have Nabeth speak to Orlith. If she agrees, what difference would a few moments make among friends?"

"Tell Orlith it's for the runners. They deserve our help."

"You and your runners!"

When Moreta outlined her plan to Capiam, Desdra, and Alessan, she received startled demurrals from each one that they didn't have the time to join the expedition.

"Master Capiam, it *takes* no time from now, today, this hour, to do what I have in mind," she replied to their protests with vexed severity. "Alessan, you can surely arrange matters in your Hold for an hour's absence. It will take longer than that for the cart to collect Dag and the men to herd the mares and foals down. What will you do? Watch bottles spin? The risk I fear is a breach of discretion about the entire project. Capiam and Desdra already know about the dragons' ability, and they earnestly require the needlethorn. I know I can count on Ruathan honor to respect dragonrider privacy. B'lerion is fortuitously here, willing and able. Nabeth is well able to carry six of us and, in a day's hard harvesting, we will accomplish what is necessary to insure the plague does not spread across the continent again. No one else will be the wiser. And that is also essential!"

"Six?" Alessan asked into the thoughtful pause.

"It is your sister's company B'lerion seeks."

Desdra chuckled. Capiam grinned after he considered that development. Alessan reacted in surprise and then with dour amusement.

"You mentioned time paradox, Moreta," Capiam began.

"That would not apply to us in this venture, so long as none of us return to Ista on the day the *ging* trees flower."

"Highly unlikely," Capiam agreed with a humorous grimace.

"The ravines I have in mind can only be reached from a high cliff. I harvested there many Turns while I was still at Ista."

Alessan hesitated a moment longer, his eyes straying from Follen to the men waiting outside with saddled runners and the beast in the cart shafts.

"Another minor but extremely important detail, Alessan," Desdra said. "Your beasthold is well kept, but not exactly the proper environment if one is producing quantities of a serum which must be free of contamination." She indicated the droppings of the lame beast.

"A wise precaution," Alessan agreed, then smiled wryly as he added. "The removal should take not much more than an hour. What supplies should we bring with us?"

"Carry-nets," Moreta replied quickly. "The rainforests will provide everything else we're likely to need."

B'lerion came striding back, a grin wide on his face.

"Nabeth found it unusual to talk to two queens at once but you have permission to go and not be long about it. I sent M'barak off to High Reaches Hold for more of Master Clargesh's apprentice bottles. And there'll be more at every major hold in the west, I shouldn't wonder. Clargesh was so proud of them. That will keep *him* busy."

"Good, B'lerion, now find a jacket for Oklina to wear."

"She *is* rather special in an understated way, isn't she. Clever of Arith to notice. No wonder I've been attracted to her."

"Wait till the egg has hardened, my dear friend. Each one splits in its own way."

Capiam and Desdra were directing Follen and Tuero to reposition the vaccine manufactury. When Alessan returned from dispatching the men to collect Dag and the runnerherds, he suggested the vaccine apparatus be moved to the main Hall of the Hold since most of its patients could safely be moved to the upper storeys or their own cotholds. Moreta helped Alessan secure all the carry-nets hanging from the walls of the beasthold, lashing them into one large bundle. By the time B'lerion and Oklina returned from the Hold, the other four were impatient with the delay.

"Had to find the charts, my dear Moreta. I am not jumping without a more positive coordinate than 'a green face with a thousand dark-rimmed eyes.' We'll have to arrive at dawn to be perfectly certain, for the moons will both be visible then." He brandished his fist to signal success and readiness.

As they began to mount the stalwart Nabeth, Moreta turned to Alessan.

"Tuero's watching us. Has he any idea?"

Alessan moved his hands about her waist more than was strictly required to heave her toward B'lerion, who was already seated on Nabeth's neck.

"One can't keep a harper from having ideas, but he should be under the impression that we are going to see Master Balfor at the Beasthold about the animal vaccine. Moving everything up to the main Hall presently will occupy even his active mind."

Then all were aboard. B'lerion had insisted that Oklina ride before him, where he could secure her with his fighting straps. Moreta he positioned behind him to help direct Nabeth. Alessan rode behind Moreta, then Desdra and, finally, Capiam as the most experienced of the other passengers.

Orlith. I shan't be long but I must go, Moreta said.

So Nabeth has told me. Orlith sounded unconcerned.

"Moreta!" B'lerion's voice and a hard nudge of his right elbow interrupted her private communication. "I've got the moons and the Red Star visualized. Facing northwest, the Red Star is horizon, Belior half full ascending, and the quarter horn of Timor mid-heaven. You will please concentrate on how Ista looks with those *ging* trees in bloom. Think of them as *now* and in Ista, and the heat of autumn and the smell of those rotting rainforests."

Nabeth was excited but his launch had the smooth precision of the experienced dragon and did not even sway his passengers as he took off.

Moreta had become accustomed to two dragon presences in her mind; now a third one, a lighter one but by no means weaker, added itself. She conjured the image of Ista's southern palisades in their autumnal finery, the Red Star balefully glowering above the western sea, Belior half full and rising, and the quarter horn of the smaller Timor demurely above. She held that vision locked in her mind as she felt Nabeth take them *between*. She wanted to make use of her usual litany, but the blossom eyes of the *ging* tree and the heaven-held guides were sufficient comfort. Then, fearfulness mounting to an incredible pressure in heart and lungs, they were suddenly in the warm air, high over Ista's rocky coast, the creamy eyes of the *ging* tree blossoms seeking the early-morning sun just rising in the east. B'lerion let out a whoop and Oklina a tiny scream. This time it was Alessan who clung to Moreta for reassurance.

Nabeth immediately noticed the rocky ledge where Moreta had often landed Orlith to harvest needlethorn. It was high above the incoming tide that battered diligently at the rock palisade. Nabeth landed as competently as he had taken off, his wing strokes flattening the thick brush that clung to the very edge of the cliff.

"Needlethorn will be down that slope," Moreta called as they prepared to dismount.

B'lerion made an ostentatious descent from Nabeth, causing the dragon to turn his head with a startled exclamation.

"You could have broken your other arm, B'lerion," Moreta said, but she had to laugh because he'd succeeded. She explained to Oklina the proper and safer way of dismounting a tall dragon, and Nabeth obediently lifted his foreleg.

"Are we really in the future?" Capiam asked as Alessan handed out the cargo nets. He looked about him with an expression of awe.

"We'd better be," B'lerion said, glowering with mock ferocity at Moreta before taking another speculative glance at the three guides in the lightening sky.

"We are," she replied as calmly as she could, for she was becoming increasingly aware of a curious sense of disorientation within her—a sensation of weightlessness and a growing euphoria, neither of which she had ever experienced before. Action would dispel such contradictory agitations. She pointed down the slope. "We'll go this way and we'll know soon enough if we find needlethorn. I harvested here myself last year, with Ista's permission since they gather on more accessible slopes." And she led the way.

The ravine was ten or more dragon-lengths from the cliff edge, and Moreta was suddenly filled with apprehension. She hadn't cleared the bushes completely last autumn, but then the moons had been in a different conjunction and the Red Star was higher in the west. No one was more relieved than she to break onto the lip of the ravine and see needlebushes thick with brown spikes. Above them the rainforest closed over the sky. The ravine, winding away to the north and the south, had been caused by an ancient earthquake, and the shallow soil over solid rock could not support many of the lush rainforest plants though creepers draped its sides, keeping well clear of needlethorn bushes. Alessan commented on that.

"The needlethorn is omnivorous," she said. "The spines are poisonous through spring and summer. They'll suck the juice from anything that comes near them until the autumn when the thick stem of the plant has stored enough moisture and food, vegetable or animal. The vine grows during the winter and has to shed its old corona or leave too many unprotected gaps. I understand that the flesh is tasty."

Oklina shuddered, but Desdra went down on one knee by the specimen they were examining.

"During spring and summer the bush has an odor to attract snakes and insects. The hollow spines suck essential juices from the creatures the plant impales, and also rainwater. See, on that one there, the top is scarred. Some animal broke off the spines. That'll make it easier to harvest."

"You said the spines are poisonous." B'lerion was not too keen to start picking.

"In spring and summer, but right now the poison has dried up. See where new thorn buds are capping the scarred one? It's the new growth that forces the spines off. So all you do is—" With a sweep of her hand starting in the scar, she cleared a swath of needlethorns, holding the handful for all to see. "Very simple, but don't get too ambitious. Clear a small area first to give your hand room. You don't want to tick off the point and you want to avoid the fine hairs on the skin of the plant. They can cause an irritation and possibly an inflammation that would be rather difficult for us to explain."

"We can't transport them like that," Capiam said, looking at Moreta's handful.

"No. We have to wrap them in the fronds of the *ging* tree. Slice the edge, and sap from the frond provides its own glue. Very handy, and the fronds are thick and spongy enough to cushion and protect the needlethorn. It takes only a moment to strip a bush, so it might be more efficient if we paired off, one to pick and the other to pack."

"I'll pack for you, Moreta," Alessan suggested, and, taking his belt knife out of its sheath, went off to hack down the nearest *ging* frond.

"A grand idea," B'lerion said, his eyes dancing as he laid a possessive hand on Oklina's shoulder. "If you don't mind working with a one-handed man?"

"My dear journeywoman, pick or pack?" Capiam asked in high good humor as he bowed to Desdra. "Though we can switch off as the whim takes us."

"I daresay I've picked more often than you, good Master Capiam." She laughed as she led Capiam off down the ravine. "You'd best see how it's done."

"Take the tenderer fronds, Alessan," Moreta cautioned. "They've more sap and suppleness."

He had cut several, muttering about doing hatchet work with a table knife, when Moreta showed him how to break the frond off at the stem of the tree with a quick downward jerk. She laid the needlethorns on the petiole that was sufficiently concave to form a bed, and, deftly cutting away the excess leaf, she closed the needlethorns in a tough, tight little envelope, sealing the ends with the sap of the severed frond.

"No wonder you said we'd have everything in the rainforest. It's easy once you get the trick of it."

"That's all there is to it. Just a knack." She grinned up at him. "That package has roughly two hundred needlethorns. I tried to count as I picked but my concentration is abominable. Time distortion, I expect. Some of the bigger bushes will have thousands of spikes, each big enough for the largest runners on the continent."

Alessan caught her hand and she stopped her babbling, suddenly shy. They were alone, even though Desdra's amiable taunting of Capiam for his timorous dexterity and B'lerion's cheerful encouragement of Oklina were audible.

"You said that we could remain here as long as it took to complete the harvest," Alessan said quietly. He was kneeling beside her now. "And return with no more than an hour elapsed there....." His eyes searched her averted face, and his hands captured hers before she could reach for more needlethorns. "Can we not make a *little* time for ourselves?"

Oklina's delighted laugh rang out, followed by B'lerion's startled curse.

"Damn things bite!"

Moreta grinned at the outrage in the bronze rider's voice and her eyes met Alessan's, saw his amused reaction. She lifted her hands to Alessan's face, her fingers tracing the lines that tension and anxiety had etched on a young man's countenance. Merely touching him in light intimacy evoked a response in her body, and she swayed quite willingly into his arms as they kissed. The resurgence of her own sensuality dispelled the last vestige of restraint and she slid one arm about his neck, the other clasping his strong hard body against hers as they knelt together by the needlethorn bush they had been stripping.

"What more can you expect of a one-handed man?" B'lerion demanded in a loud complaint.

Moreta and Alessan broke apart, but the bronze rider was still out of sight, if audible. Alessan grinned for their discomfiture, expressing regret at the parting.

"It will be far too hot to work midday, Alessan, and I have no doubts that we can find some privacy then."

"Clever of you to bring mixed pairs, wasn't it?"

"One is always more sorry for the things one didn't do than the things one has done." Moreta spoke with mock severity, and Alessan quickly silenced her the most effective way.

"Personally, I don't like it when it's too hot," Alessan was saying, releasing her lips to give her eyes and cheeks and ears and throat equal attention. An injudicious movement brought his arm in contact with the needlethorn bush and he spun away, dragging Moreta with him. "They really do bite, don't they?" He rubbed his arm where a fine row of bloody beads rose on the skin.

"Oh, dear, they do." She reached for the cut *ging* and squeezed some of the sap onto the punctures. "There, that'll seal them too. Really,

Alessan"—and she gave him a quick kiss, fondling his ear—"we have to do what we came here for!" She tried to be stern, but he was still frowning from the indignation of having his ardor abruptly pricked.

"I'll settle a score for myself, too," he said, snatching handfuls of the needlethorns from the bush that had wounded him. "That'll teach you, my spiny friend! There! There! and There! You're stripped!"

Laughing at his outraged monologue, Moreta worked as fast as she could to pack the products of his vindictive harvest.

"You picked the first one. Now you pack for me!" Alessan said with a growl. But his hands impeded hers as she worked to close the last package. He kissed her at the base of her throat, then on her chin.

"Fastest packer on Pern," he said in a complimentary tone while his hands made investigations of their own.

"Now it's my turn to pick," Moreta said, nibbling at his ear and running her hands through his thick hair. "Someone must be able to give you a trim," she murmured solicitously. Alessan was beginning to look like his former shaggy self, and that annoyed her.

"I'll trim you if you don't get to work, Moreta."

"I work faster than you." She allowed herself to sound peevish as she snapped quick handfuls off the nearest bush, piling them for him to pack.

"Can't you two get along together?" B'lerion demanded, bursting suddenly from around a bend of the ravine.

"She'll learn!" "He'll learn!" they said in chorus, waving cheerfully. B'lerion looked at them for a long moment then stalked off.

"Work now, play later," Moreta said, continuing to strip the needlethorns down.

"It's as easy to combine work and play." Alessan drew a gentle finger from her ear to her shoulder.

They worked steadily, but each utilized every opportunity for a quick caress or a kiss exchanged as deft hands folded *ging* over a pile of needlethorns. They knelt by the bushes, knees or thighs touching. Moreta felt the light hairs of her arms rising toward his, she was becoming so sensitized to the delightful friction of his proximity. She had an idiotic desire to giggle and saw that Alessan, too, wore a rather foolish grin on his face most of the time. They were scarcely conscious of the others and almost forgot their existence until B'lerion and Oklina crashed to the top of the ravine.

"You have been busy," B'lerion said with grudging approval. "Haven't you noticed the heat?" He had stripped to the waist, and Oklina had tied her shirt up under her breasts, leaving her midriff bare. She carried four nets of packaged needlethorns. "I'm hungry, too, even if you aren't." He swung his shirt by the sleeves so that its burden was discernible. "Found some ripe fruit and chopped down one of those palms for the edible heart. You can't keep on at the pace you've been going"—he gestured to the filled nets—"without sustenance—and a bit of a rest in this humidity. Capiam! Desdra! Let's eat!"

Capiam and Desdra were arguing about the astringent properties of the *ging* sap when they sauntered up to join the others. Capiam, too, had stripped off his tunic, which was now draped over his shoulders. He was very thin, his ribs showing plainly.

"I know it's hot," Moreta began adroitly, "but none of us can return to Ruatha suffering from sunburn."

Capiam exhibited a leaf he was using as a fan. "Or heat prostration." He raised his eyebrows in satisfaction with the filled nets. "We left ours back a bit. I rather thought we should rest, as is the custom on this hot island, during the hottest part of the day."

Everyone agreed that that was a sensible idea.

"I found some melons and the red roots that Istans are so fond of," Desdra said, producing her contribution.

"There're clusters of softnuts on all the trees, Alessan. That is, if you can climb at all," Moreta said.

"I climb, you catch."

Alessan took off his shirt to keep it from being torn. Moreta used it as a receptacle for the softnuts. He was a dexterous climber and a swift picker. When finished, he sought his reward in a close embrace, his hands slipping up the back of her tunic, caressing her shoulders as she found, to her surprise, that his skin was as soft as Orlith's and the smell of him almost spicy in his maleness.

They recalled themselves to the task, not wishing to take too long for what was a simple enough operation. Moreta decided that her flush would be attributed to an incipient sunburn.

"Sun's rays at this latitude are too strong for winter-white skins," Desdra said, lounging on some *ging* fronds that she and Capiam cut just for that purpose. "And that heat's enough to drain anyone," she added, making use of Capiam's fan.

They relaxed during the meal. The red roots were succulent, the softnuts just ripe, and the melons so close to fermentation that the juice had a winey tang to it. The palm heart was crisply cool and crunchy, a nice texture to complement the others. Throughout the meal, B'lerion kept up a stream of quip and comment about his being one-handed in a venture that was destined to save the continent. Would he receive full marks for his participation or just half for the hand that had worked?

"Is he always like this?" Alessan asked quietly after B'lerion had told an extravagantly funny tale at the expense of Lord Diatis's reputation. "He's better than most harpers."

"He sings a good descant, but B'lerion's always seemed to be the epitome of a bronze rider."

"Why, then, is he not your Weyrmate?"

"Orlith chose Kadith."

"Do *you* not have any say in the matter?" Alessan was irritated for her sake. From remarks he had made during their morning's work, she knew that Alessan didn't like Sh'gall and wondered just how much their new relationship would strain Ruatha's dependence on Fort's Weyrleader. She was struggling to find an honest reply to a question she had evaded in her own heart, when Alessan contritely covered her hand, his expression pleading with her to forgive his rash remarks. "I'm sorry, Moreta. That is a Weyr matter."

"To answer you in part, B'lerion *is* always like that," she said. "Charming, amusing. But Sh'gall *leads* men well, and he has an instinct about Fall which his predecessor, old L'mal, considered uncanny."

"Well, well, B'lerion, I'd never heard that particular narrative." Capiam was still chuckling as he hoisted himself to his feet. "I suppose harpers must be discreet in circulating their tales." He extended his hand to Desdra. "Can you remember exactly where you saw those astringent plants, Desdra? I know we're here for needlethorn, but the Hall's supplies are dreadfully short."

"We'll look at the plants but, my dear Master Capiam, you are also going to rest through the heat of the day." Neither healer looked back as they disappeared up the ravine and around the first bend.

"Well, I suppose that one must allow an older man some rest," B'lerion said. "Come, Oklina, there's plenty of shade in our patch of needlethorn, and a smart breeze. We shall put our time to the use intended!"

Smiling affably, B'lerion made a running leap up the ravine, turning only to lend a long arm to Oklina. They disappeared from view, and the thick foliage settled to stillness in the thick noontime heat.

"If he expects me to believe that . . ." Alessan finished his sentence with a chuckle. Then, taking a deep breath, he pulled Moreta against him and kissed her deeply and sensually, his hand deftly stroking her to arousal. "Come on, Moreta, I'm not chancing another attack by those needlethorns." He led her from the ravine toward the cliff. "What I'd like to understand is why that blue dragon of M'barak's is sniffing around Oklina. I could understand Nabeth with B'lerion entranced by her, but Aritha . . . Would it have anything to do with that queen egg on the Hatching Ground as Tuero suggested?"

"It might, but Fort Weyr would not deplete your bloodline by Searching Oklina, Alessan."

"This will do. Let's just throw down some *ging* fronds," Alessan said, hauling on the nearest at hand. "I won't have you bruised, either. That would be almost as hard to explain as a sunburn or heat prostration." Moreta helped him arrange a bower, all her senses suddenly awake, wishing that Orlith, not Nabeth, were on the Istan ledge. "About Oklina, now, since I've been reliably informed"—Alessan paused to grin at her, his light eyes vividly sparkling with merriment—"that she already has dragonrider blood in her. . . ." Then he turned briefly serious. "If it could be understood that her children would return to Ruatha, I would not stand in Oklina's way if she had the chance to Impress a dragon." He dumped his last handful of frond on the ground with a decisive gesture and pulled Moreta into into his arms. "I'm not my father, you know."

"I wouldn't *be* in a rainforest with your father."

"Why not? He was a lusty man. And I intend to prove that I'm a suitable heir to his reputation!"

She was laughing as he laid her down on the sun-dappled frond bed. And her proved himself as lusty—and tender—as any woman could wish a man. For a shining moment at the height of their passion, Moreta forgot everything but Alessan.

The heat of the day did overcome them briefly, and they slumbered in each other's arms until tiny insects sought the moisture of their bodies and made them uncomfortable enough to wake.

"I'm eaten alive!" Alessan cried, pinning one of the biting insects to his forearm.

"Take some of that broad-leafed vine, the one climbing the tree by your side," Moreta said. "Bruise its leaves. It'll neutralize the sting."

"How d'you know so much?"

"I did Impress at Ista. I know its hazards."

They spent considerably more time neutralizing one another's insect bites than was necessary. When Alessan, trying to kiss her, got too much of the astringent liquid on his lips and his mouth began to pucker, they laughed and were still laughing about that when they returned to the ravine, slightly cooler now that the westering sun no longer shone directly above it.

When the tropical dusk had made work impossible, the six of them gathered on the ledge where Nabeth lounged somnolently and began to stack filled nets.

"Nabeth says"—B'lerion thudded the bronze dragon affectionately on the cheek—"that the only moving things he saw were fire-lizards fishing! He's got a good sense of humor, my bronze lad. I hope we've got enough for your purpose, Master Capiam, because I'm telling you, this single hand of mine"—he held it out to display the tracery of thorn scratches—"has done enough today!"

Capiam and Desdra gazed speculatively at the nets and then at each other. Desdra covered her mouth and turned away. Capiam looked distressed.

"Did anyone remember to count?" he asked, beseeching each one in turn.

"I'll tell you another thing," B'lerion said firmly, "I'm not going to count 'em now."

"I wouldn't suggest it!"

"However, I would gladly return to this secluded spot to pluck whatever number you find you lack."

Moreta tapped him on the shoulder. "Not here, B'lerion. If, by any possible chance, we did not pick enough today, go to Nerat. Not here."

"Oh, yes. That would prevent a time paradox. And the moons would be in roughly the same alignment on Nerat tip."

"Well, if that's settled, I expect we'd best return," Capiam said wearily.

"On the contrary, my dear Master Capiam, that would be a sure clue to our day's employment." B'lerion clucked his tongue. "We leave Ruatha energetic and in great spirit and arrive, an hour later, exhausted, reddened, hungry. Oklina, which one is the dinner net? Oh, here we are. Just settle yourselves. Use Nabeth as a backrest. There's more than enough of him to go round."

Oklina handed him a net of tied vines, which he hoisted so that all could see balls of hard-baked mud.

"Did a bit of fishing during my rest," B'lerion said, his broad grin daring anyone to challenge the truth of his statement, "and Oklina found the tubers. So we baked them. On the rocks in the ravine this noon it was hot enough to fry a dragon egg—begging your pardon, Moreta. A good meal would go down now without a struggle, wouldn't it? And while there's light enough, Alessan, if you and Moreta could find a few more of those ripe melons, why, we'd have a feast fit for a— Hatching!" B'lerion caught himself so quickly that only Moreta knew that he had quickly substituted one festive occasion for another less painful one.

She had distracted Alessan by pulling him after her to find the melons. They knew exactly where to find more, since they'd raided the patch several times in the afternoon to slake their thirst.

Hunger was part of the fatigue they all felt, and Moreta was glad to take her share from Oklina and thank the girl for such foresight.

"It was B'lerion's idea, you know," Oklina said. "He actually tickled the fish to catch them."

"Did he teach you how?" Alessan asked.

"No," Oklina replied with admirable composure. "Dag did. The same principal works in our rivers as Ista's."

Moreta could not resist chuckling at Alessan's expression as he sank beside her.

"On mature reflection, I think she deserves to be in a Weyr," Alessan said in a severe undertone. Then he realized that he was leaning against a bronze dragon and jerked forward apprehensively.

"Nabeth won't mind. He's an old friend of mine, too."

With a mutter of mock discontent, Alessan cracked the mud to produce a long slender tuber, then Moreta broke one open to prize out the fish, and they shared bits of the contents, keeping the second course warm.

"What a clever fellow you are," Capiam said, his mouth half full. He and Desdra had arranged themselves in the curve of Nabeth's tail. Desdra nodded agreement, too busy licking her fingers to speak.

"I have a few talents," B'lerion said with a becoming show of modesty. "Eating is one of my few bad habits. Fruit is all very well in the heat of the day but something warms soothes the belly before sleep . . ."

"Sleep!" Capiam and Moreta protested simultaneously.

B'lerion held up a restraining hand. "Sleep"—he pointed his finger sternly at Moreta—"for you have to mend dragons after Fall in another four hours. You can't do that effectively after the day you just put in." He flipped his hand toward the carry-nets lying in the shadows. "You, Alessan, will have to vaccinate and escort those priceless brood mares and foals of yours down from the meadows. I do not see you permitting anyone else to head that expedition. Desdra and Capiam, you will be returning to the pressures of expanding this vaccination program of yours to include runnerbeasts. So we shall finish our meal and then we shall sleep." He allowed the sibilance of the word to emphasize his meaning. "When Belior has risen, Nabeth will rouse us, won't you, my fine fellow?" B'lerion thumped his dragon's neck. "And we'll all be the better for the time spent *here*."

"B'lerion," Moreta protested vigorously, "I really should get back to Orlith."

"Orlith's fine, my dear girl. Fine! You're only going to be gone an hour in real time. And frankly, dear friend, you look dead right now!" B'lerion leaned over to ruffle her hair in a proprietary gesture that made Alessan tense beside her. Moreta quickly checked him with a hand on his thigh. "And anyway," B'lerion continued affably, "you've no choice, Moreta." And his grin widened with keen amusement. "You can't leave here except on Nabeth and he follows *my* orders."

"You're a managing soul," Capiam said without rancor.

"He's sensible," Desdra said, making a minor correction. "I was dreading the thought of being plunged back into all that must be done. Not to mention explaining these." She examined her scratched hands.

"If you keep everyone as busy as you usually do, Desdra," Capiam replied at his dryest, "no one will have time to notice."

"So just make yourself comfortable beside Nabeth. He won't mind being pillow as well as windscreen, but there's enough cover on the ground to keep you from scratching yourselves and the landward breeze will keep the midges off."

B'lerion then had Nabeth stretch out his neck so that he and Oklina could settle themselves. Capiam and Desdra arranged themselves in the tail curve so Moreta lay down against Nabeth's ribs and gestured for Alessan to join her.

"He won't roll over or anything?" Alessan whispered to Moreta as he lay down.

"Not while B'lerion's lying on his neck!"

So Alessan fitted himself against Moreta, drawing her arms around his waist and clasping them in his. She could feel his breath slow as he began to relax, and she pillowed her forehead against his strong shoulder blade.

The tropical night was warm and fragrant. Moreta tried to compose herself for sleep. She could hear Capiam's baritone murmur and then silence. Alessan slept and she wanted to but was haunted by the sense of disorientation she had left that morning. Then the spicy smell of dragon, still tainted by a hint of firestone, began to soothe her and she realized that—for the first time in twenty Turns—she had passed a day without Orlith. She did miss her. Orlith would have liked Alessan's exuberant loving. All that had been missing from that experience had been the dragon's share of her rider's gratification. Comforted, Moreta slept.

The moment Nabeth burst into the air above Ruatha, Moreta felt Orlith's distressed touch.

You are there! You are there! Where have you been?

Where could you have been? That deep-toned question was from an equally distraught Holth.

To Ista. As Nabeth told you.

We could not find you there! That came from both queens.

I am here. I have what we went for. All is well! I won't be long here now.

The time distortion that accounted for the strange feeling of separation and disorientation lingering even in her dreams at Ista had dissipated the moment Moreta felt Orlith's touch. She was not only rested but extraordinarily revived, to the point that the warm sphere of euphoria in her belly expanded to fill her entire body with strength. B'lerion had been sensible indeed to insist they take time for rest.

Seated behind Moreta, Alessan became suddenly tense, his hands tightening about her waist fiercely. She knew he was swearing though the wind of Nabeth's glide obscured the words. She looked down at sad Ruatha and knew that a dragonback perspective of the ruins could not fail to distress him. When she managed to twist to speak to him, his expression was full of urgent determination.

As soon as Nabeth came to a graceful landing across the roadway from the beasthold, he turned to Oklina. "Surely some of the convalescents must be strong enough to do maintenance, Oklina. Did you have a good look at the Hold proper? It's a shambles. Here, Moreta, I'll give you a hand." Alessa slid down Nabeth's side and extended his hands to her. It was, Moreta quickly realized, an excuse to hold her, and he kept one arm loosely about her shoulders as they backed far enough away from the dragon's bulk for Alessan to address the other riders. "I'll continue making the serum, Master Capiam, and wait for any further instructions. Oklina, have you seen what I mean? Then I'll help you down. My duty to you, Nabeth, and my eternal gratitude." Alessan bowed formally to the bronze dragon, who winked at him from eyes that whirled pleasantly green-blue.

"He says his duty was a pleasure," B'lerion replied, smiling as he handed Oklina down to his dragon's raised forearm. He waited until she was clear and then waved cheerily as Nabeth sprang aloft again.

They had made most of their farewells at Ista when Belior rose, round and greenly gold in the dark Istan sky. B'lerion would convey the two healers to their hall with the needlethorns. If more should be needed, B'lerion would harvest it discreetly at Nerat with Oklina and Desdra. Capiam had composed messages for the Masterherdsman and all the holds that bred or kept runners. Relays would go to drumless settlements.

The dust of Nabeth's departure was blowing away from them when Tuero came out of the beasthold, a look of surprise on his homely face.

"That didn't take you long," he said. "Alessan, we can't make up another batch unless M'barak finds more glass bottles. I don't know what's taking him so long."

The three travelers recoiled in a group, but before Tuero could comment on their reaction, Arith and M'barak hurtled across the fields to land almost exactly in the spot Nabeth had just occupied. Moreta clung to Alessan's hand for support.

"Who's he got with him?" Tuero demanded. As the blue dragon settled, it was obvious he bore three passengers as well as the carry-nets.

"Moreta!" M'barak called, gesturing to her urgently. "Hurry up. I need help with these silly bottles and I've people here who say they can handle runners. And we've got to hurry because I have to prepare for the Fall. F'neldril will skin me if I'm late!"

So Alessan, Tuero, Oklina, and Moreta rushed to unburden Arith of passengers and ornamental apprentice-blown glass bottles. Then Alessan gave Moreta a leg up to Arith's back and if his hands lingered on her ankle as she settled herself, no one remarked on the Lord Holder's behavior. As Moreta looked down at Alessan's upturned face, she wished she might give him more than a smile in farewell. Then he stepped back and one of the newcomers touched his arm. The woman was tall and thin, with dark hair as close-cropped as a weyrwoman's. She reminded Moreta of someone. Then they were airborne, and M'barak warned her that they'd go *between* as soon as Arith had air space.

Back at Fort Weyr, there was so much activity in the Bowl, readying the two wings, that no one noted their arrival though M'barak had craftily come in over the lake. Arith glided to deposit Moreta at the Hatching Ground cavern. After remembering to give the blue's ribs a grateful thump, Moreta ran toward Orlith across the sands, not totally surprised to see Leri's figure beside her.

You're here! You're here! Orlith was bugling in relief, her wings extended, sweeping sand over Leri's small figure.

"It's all right, Orlith. I'm here! Don't make so much commotion!" Moreta raced to her dragon, throwing her arms around Orlith's head and hugging her as tightly as she could, then scratching eye ridges and murmuring reassurances.

"By the first Egg," Leri was saying, leaning against Orlith's side, "am I glad to see you! What have you been doing? Holth couldn't find you either. Oh, do be quiet, Orlith! *Holth!*"

You have finally returned. There was more reproof in Holth's voice than Orlith would ever express.

"Couldn't you contact Nabeth?" Moreta asked Orlith, then Leri and Holth. Orlith's color was very poor and there was an ashen hue to Leri's complexion. She was full of remorse for having caused them a moment's anguish. "Why didn't you speak with Nabeth?"

I wanted you, Orlith said piteously.

"Could you spare me a word of explanation?" Leri asked in a caustic tone, her voice breaking effectively. Contrite, Moreta grasped Leri's shoulder. "The past hour has been dreadful. It took all my tact and patience to keep Orlith from blasting after you, wherever you were— which was where?"

"Didn't Nabeth explain? B'lerion said he had."

Leri waggled her hands irritably. "*He* only said that you had to go on an imperative journey that would take no more than an hour."

"And we were back at Ruatha within that hour." Moreta knew that had to be the truth and, indeed, now that she was back with Orlith, the past subjective twenty hours seemed the dream, not the reality. "Just an hour?"

"No, actually," Leri said firmly, "a little longer than an hour. You were talking with Capiam about something"—Leri underscored her ignorance of that interview by a significant pause—"before you, he, and that journeywoman of his went skiting off to Ruatha on M'barak. The next thing I hear is a request through Holth from Nabeth and B'lerion." She gave Moreta a stern look, an effect that was slightly spoiled by her changing from one foot to another during her reprimand.

"You look a bit uncomfortable on these hot sands, Leri. I think we'd better get off the Ground. I've rather a lot to tell you. No, Orlith, I won't leave your sight but what suits your eggs is hard on your rider." Moreta gave Leri a gentle shove toward her temporary living space and then fondled Orlith's muzzle.

Leri had already seated herself before Moreta had sufficiently reassured Orlith. The queen gently pushed her weyrmate off and began to reposition the queen egg.

"It all began," Moreta said to Leri as she settled herself, "when Master Capiam came to ask me the same question Alessan had"—Moreta caught herself before she could blurt out "two nights ago"—"about vaccinating the runners."

Leri gave a disgruntled snort. "I would have thought he had enough on his hands healing humans."

"He does, but the plague is an instance of zoonosis—animals infecting people *and* other animals."

Leri stared at Moreta, her jaw dropping in alarm. "Zoonosis? Even the term sounds repulsive!" She fiddled with the cushion behind her back. "So, now that I'm comfortable, give me all the details."

Moreta told Leri about Capiam's visit, his fears for the continent's health, how via zoonosis a second, more virulent wave of the viral infection could spread, and why mass vaccination was so essential. Capiam had left his chart behind, and Moreta produced it for Leri to examine.

"Capiam has it all planned so that a minimum of dragonriders would be needed—" She broke off, seeing the shock on Leri's face as the method of distribution became apparent to the older Weyrwoman.

"The riders would have to time it!" Leri stared at her, the nostrils of her straight, finely arched nose flaring with indignation. "You did say that Master Capiam brought this—this incredible plan *with* him?" When Moreta nodded, Leri's voice crackled with fury. "*How,* may I ask, *how* did Master Capiam know that dragons can move in time? I'll flay K'lon to his bones!" Leri all but bounced off the stone tier. From above, Holth bugled a protest.

"It wasn't K'lon," Moreta said as she clasped Leri's wildly gesticulating hands in hers. "Calm Holth down. She'll have Sh'gall on us!"

"If you told Capiam, Moreta—" Leri freed one hand to raise it aggressively.

"Don't be silly. He knew!" Remembering her own outrage at Capiam's knowledge, Moreta could well appreciate Leri's reaction. "He knew because, as he had to remind me, his Craft bred the ability into dragons."

Leri opened her mouth to protest that statement, then took a deep breath and nodded her head in belated acceptance. "You still have some explaining to do, Moreta. Where have you been the past hour where neither Orlith nor Holth could reach you?"

Moreta was not so certain, suddenly, of Leri's reaction to the truth of her whereabouts, especially now that it was obvious that Nabeth's explanation had been somewhat less than candid. And she'd given B'lerion far too good a reason to prevaricate.

"We went to Ista. We went forward in time to Ista to harvest needle-thorn. There's not much point in producing vaccine if there's no way to administer it."

Meekly Moreta endured Leri's piercing stare, the expression of disbe-lief, anger, anxiety, and finallly resignation that flashed through the woman's eyes.

"You just casually"—Leri flapped one hand in a careless motion—"jumped four or five months ahead?"

"Not *casually*—B'lerion checked the position of the Red Star and the two moons to be sure he was near the autumnal equinox. And we arrived back in Ruatha in an hour. Nabeth told you that much, didn't he?"

"That much!" Leri drummed her fingers on her short thighs, indi-cating a displeasure she evidently couldn't express in another way.

Moreta put out a tentative hand, a request for absolution, and Leri caught it, noticing for the first time the delicate tracery of needle scratches.

"Serves you right." With a snort of disgust she released the hand. Then, with a grudging smile, she added, "I'd have thought you'd've taken a lesson from K'lon's ineptitude. Sunburn. Scratches!"

"Nothing that redwort won't hide this afternoon." But Moreta tucked both hands under her thighs, the stone cool on the deeper slashes. "Nabeth didn't tell you he took us to Ista? I chose a spot that isn't easily reached through the rainforests. There're only two places on the northern continent where needlethorn grows, and I thought the ravine on Ista safer than Nerat. We were perfectly safe the entire time."

"We?" Leri eyed Moreta with renewed alarm.

"I could scarcely harvest the quantity of needlethorn required by myself." Then Moreta realized that, in her effort to reassure Leri, she had said altogether more than was strictly necessary.

"Who went?" Leri was quietly resigned to her indiscretions.

"B'lerion..."

"He would have to."

Moreta winced at Leri's dry sarcasm.

"Master Capiam and Desdra, the journeywoman. She knows about timing because she found the entries in the old Records."

"Could we ask Master Capiam to *burn* those old Records?" Leri asked hopefully.

"He's agreed to 'lose' them. Which is why *I* agreed to go."

"That makes four of you. So! Who else went? We've known each other far too long, my dear, for you to delude me!"

"Alessan and Oklina."

Leri sighed heavily, covering her eyes with one hand.

"Alessan has too much at stake and too much honor in him to prate about dragon capability. And judging by the way Arith has been snuffling around Oklina, she would make a candidate for Orlith's egg."

"You couldn't—you wouldn't take his sister from Alessan..." Leri was astounded.

"I wouldn't, but the queen might. Alessan said he'd be agreeable if any children she bears are allowed to go back to Ruatha."

"Well!" Leri's exclamation was complimentary. "You accomplished rather a lot in one hour, didn't you?"

"B'lerion insisted that we sleep six hours in Ista in *that* time, but we did have to leave an hour's leeway before appearing back at Ruatha!"

"So you skited back to Ruatha Hold bearing nets full of needlethorn and no explanations tendered?"

Moreta began to relax. Once Leri got over her shocks, she'd begin to see the humor of the whole adventure, that the sheer reckless momentum had worked to their advantage.

"B'lerion dropped off Alessan, Oklina, and me, and took off to the Healer Hall with Capiam and Desdra. The dust hadn't settled before M'barak arrived with more glass bottles and volunteers and...Besides, who will ask the Lord of Ruatha to explain an hour's absence or inquire of Master Capiam where he got needlethorn? He has it! That's all anyone needs to know!"

"A point to remember." Leri's humor had been restored enough for her to be witty.

"So," Moreta said, having achieved another minor miracle in soothing Leri, "tomorrow I have only to approach the other Weyrs to ask for aid in distributing the vaccine. I promised Capiam."

"My dear girl, you can skite out of here for an hour on a mysterious time-consuming errand, but what excuse could you possibly find to go Weyr-hopping?"

"The best. There's a queen egg in front of us. I can visit them on Search. Even Orlith would agree to the necessity for that! And if I remember correctly, the Weyrleaders promised at that historic Butte meeting of theirs that they would supply candidates for Orlith's clutch."

"Ah, but that was *then*," Leri pointed out sardonically. "This is now. You have surely been aware of M'tani's disaffection. He's unlikely to part with the dullest wit in his Cavern."

"I thought of that. Remember the lists the Weyrleaders gave S'peren? Or did you give them to Sh'gall?"

"Don't be ridiculous. They're safe in my weyr."

"We can figure out which of the bronze riders at Telgar are likely to time it. I can't imagine that Benden or High Reaches would renege on the offer of candidates—"

"Of course *they* wouldn't. T'grel would be the bronze rider you should see at Telgar. And you *could* apply to Dalova at Igen. She may tend to babble but she's basically rather a sensible person. You *have* thought this all out, haven't you?" Leri gave a little chuckle at Moreta's cunning. "My dear, you've the makings of a superior Weyrwoman. Just shuck that bronze rider and get someone you're happy with. And I do not mean that light-eyed Lord Holder, with his convenient stashes of Benden white. Though mind you, he's a handsome lad!"

Outside, the bronze voice of Kadith called the fighting wings to the Rim.

CHAPTER XV

Fort, Benden, Ista, Igen, Telgar, and High Reaches Weyrs, Present Pass, 3.21.43

"ONE DAY, M'BARAK, and not too distant at that," Moreta told the slim young weyrling the next morning, "we'll all have nothing to do but lounge in the sun."

"I don't mind conveying, Moreta. It's such good training for Arith." Then M'barak averted his eyes and she could see the color staining his neck and cheek. "F'neldril explained to me last night the responsibility of Search dragons and why Arith's been so discourteous."

"It isn't discourtesy, M'barak."

"Well, it's not proper dragon behavior and it doesn't *look* right for him to be doing such things to people like Lady Oklina."

"M'barak, she understands, too. And it is an instinct that we want very much to encourage in Arith. He's a fine sensitive blue, and you've been of great assistance to Weyr, hall, and hold! Now, today we must Search first at Benden. The Weyrleaders promised us candidates—"

"Ones who've been vaccinated—" M'barak added hastily.

Moreta gripped him by the arm, amused by his conditioned qualification. Then they mounted Arith and left Fort Weyr.

"You are always welcome at Benden," Levalla said when Moreta was ushered into the queen's weyr, "as long as you arrive without Orlith to plague Tuzuth." The Benden Weyrwoman cast a sly glance at K'dren. "I trust she is welded to the Hatching Ground."

"That's one of the reasons I'm here." Moreta was alone with K'dren and Levalla since she had been able to recommend to M'barak that he remain in the Bowl with Arith. Both Weyrleaders looked tired and she wished that she did not have to tax their resources further, but there was no way one Weyr could manage to distribute the vaccine.

"Orlith's a reason for coming here?" K'dren grinned. "Ah, yes, of course. Candidates for your Hatching. Never fear that I will go back on that pledge. There are some promising fosterlings in our caverns. *All* have now been vaccinated—"

"That's the other reason I'm here." Moreta had to blurt out her real mission at the first opportunity he gave her.

K'dren and Levalla heard her out in weary silence, K'dren scratching at his sideburns, Levalla sliding a worry-wood piece through her fingers, its surface smooth from long use.

"What we don't need is another epidemic. I quite see that," Levalla said when Moreta had finished outlining the plan. "We didn't lose that many runnerherds here in the east but I'm sure Lord Shadder would be glad of the vaccine. Imagine Alessan being able to produce it with all he's been through!"

"I don't like asking riders to time it, Levalla."

"Nonsense, K'dren, we'll only ask those who do it. Only last Turn, Oribeth had to discipline V'mul, and he's only a brown rider. Bone lazy, the pair of them. You know how brown riders can be, Moreta. And you know perfectly well, K'dren, that M'gent makes time whenever it suits him."

"Then we'll put him in charge of the Benden riders assisting the Healer Hall," K'dren said with a snap of his fingers. "Just the sort of challenge to keep him out of mischief. He was annoyed, you know"— and he winked at Moreta—"that I recovered from the plague so quickly. He enjoyed Leading to Fall. He'll make Weyrleader soon enough, won't he, mate?" He cast such a ludicrously suspicious look at his beautiful Levalla that it was obvious he had no anxieties on that score.

Levalla laughed. "As if I had time for any dallying these days. You're looking exceedingly well, Moreta. Any injuries in your Weyr from yesterday's Fall?"

"A few Threadscores and another dislocated shoulder. I'd say that this consolidation puts each wing on its mettle."

"My thoughts, too," K'dren said, "but I shall be eternally grateful when we can resume our traditional regions. It isn't Sh'gall, I'll have you know—he's a bloody fine leader; it's that sour excrescence from Telgar—"

"K'dren..." Levalla spoke in firm remonstrance.

"Moreta's discreet, but that man..." K'dren balled his fists, setting his jaw as his eyes flashed with antipathy for the Telgar Leader. "He won't assist in either of your requests, you know, Moreta!"

"*He* might not." Moreta took out the lists. K'dren exclaimed in surprise at seeing them.

"So they will serve a purpose after all. Let me have a glance." He flipped the sheets till he came to the angular backhanded scrawl of M'tani's. "T'grel would be the man to contact at Telgar. Even if he weren't a responsible rider, he'd do it in reprisal for some of M'tani's tricks. And you must have riders from each Weyr, ones who know how to find the hole-in-the-hill cots that aren't well marked. Well, you *can* be sure of Benden support. I wondered why our healer was bloodletting again!" He rubbed his arm with a rueful smile.

"And Capiam's sure about this vaccination of his?" Levalla asked. Her fingers betrayed her anxiety by the speed with which she flipped her worry-wood.

"He likens it to Thread. If it can't get a grip, it can't last."

"About your Hatching, now. We do have a very keen young man from a Lemos highlands minehold whom we found on Search two Turns ago," Levalla said, reverting to Moreta's ostensible errand. "I don't know why he didn't take, but we'll have him back if he doesn't find a mate on your Ground. Dannell's his name, and he's eager to keep up with his mining craft if he can."

"Are you Searching more among the crafts than the holds these days?"

"With the end of Pass in sight, it's best to have men who can occupy their spare time profitably for the Weyr."

"We receive the tithe whether there's Pass or not," Moreta said with a frown.

K'dren looked up from his perusal of the names. "To be sure, but once a Pass is over, the Lords may not be quite so generous." K'dren's expression indicated that his Lords had better sustain the quality of their tithes. "I've underlined the riders who I suspect do time." His grin was raffish. "It's not something anyone admits to but T'grel must *have* to use it to cope with M'tani. Don't bother with L'bol at Igen. He's useless. Go directly to Dalova, Allaneth's rider. She lost a lot of bloodkin at Igen Sea Hold. She'd know who among her riders time it. And Igen has all those little cotholds stashed in the desert and on the riverbanks. Surely you've got a few good friends left at Ista. You were there ten Turns. Have you heard that F'gal's bad with kidney chill?"

"Yes, I'd planned to speak to Wimmia out of courtesy. Or D'say, Kritith's rider."

"You have a son by him, don't you?" Levalla said with a tolerant smile. "Such ties seem to help at the most unexpected times, don't they?"

"D'say is a steady man and the boy Impressed a brown from Torenth's last clutch," Moreta said with quiet pride. She rose. She would have liked to stay longer with the Benden Leaders but she had a long day ahead of her.

"We'll give Dannell time to pack up and send him on to you at Fort tomorrow, with M'gent. You can use the opportunity to go over any details with him. Shall I have a discreet word with my Lords?"

"Master Tirone is supposed to be sweetening them but your endorsement would be a boon."

As K'dren escorted Moreta to the stairs, Levalla waved an idolent farewell, still worrying the wood in her left hand.

The encouragement that Moreta received from the Benden Weyrleaders did much to sustain her during her next three visits. At Ista, F'gal and Wimmia were in her weyr, bronze Timenth on the ledge, the tacit signal for privacy. So Moreta directed M'barak to land Arith at D'say's weyr, where Kritith greeted Moreta with shining blue spinning eyes, rearing to his hindquarters and extending his wings. He peered out to the ledge, patently disappointed that Moreta had arrived on a blue instead of with her queen. Then D'say emerged from his sleeping quarters. To her chagrin she had obviously awakened him from a much-needed sleep. He was one of the few who had not succumbed to the first wave of illness, and he had ridden Fall continuously, nursed other sick riders, and tried to bolster F'gal's leadership during the latter's kidney ailment.

As she argued with D'say on the necessity of once again cooperating with the Healer Hall, she wished that he had had the plague; then he would not be so slow to comply. D'say resisted her presentation in such a glum silence that she was becoming depressed when their son M'ray suddenly charged up the steps.

"I beg your pardon, D'say, but my Quoarth told me that Moreta is here." The boy—in his height he was more manly than boyish—paused just long enough in the threshold to receive permission to enter. Then he rushed to Moreta, embracing her with a charming enthusiasm. He peered anxiously into her face with eyes the color of her own, set in a head with the same deep sockets and arching brows. Yet he was far more D'say's child in build and coloring. "I knew you were ill. It's very good to see you well."

"Orlith has clutched. I've had little to do except repair scored riders and dragons."

M'ray opened his arms, looking from sire to dam, hopeful of answers to his outspoken questions.

"Moreta needs help, which I don't think she'll get from F'gal in his state of health." D'say replied noncommittally. He refilled Moreta's cup with klah, tacitly giving her permission to tell their son.

She did, and the boy's eyes widened with apprehension and a growing eagerness that answered the challenge.

"Wimmia would agree, D'say—you know she would. We only have to present the urgency to her. She's not a passive person, like F'gal. He's—he's changed a lot recently." As M'ray blurted out his opinion, he eyed D'say to see if the bronze rider would try to refute him. D'say shrugged. "Anyway, *I'd* like to help and my wingleader, T'lonneg, is hold-bred. If there's anyone who'd know the rainforest holds, it's him. He caught the plague, too, and lost family. He should *know* about this, D'say, really he should. This isn't the sort of request you can deny, is it? No more than we can stop rising to Fall." M'ray faced his sire, shoulders back, jaw forward, a pose she remembered striking when she had acted on her own initiative in treating a runner in her family's hold. "I rose with Ista's wings at every Fall. Haven't got so much as char in my face."

"Keep it that way," D'say remarked in a flat voice that masked the pride he had for his lad. "T'lonneg says they fly well, M'ray and Quoarth."

"What we'd expect," Moreta said fondly, smiling all the more warmly at the lad. It was a pity that she hadn't been able to give him more time but she'd had to go on to Fort Weyr, and D'say had remained at Ista. "K'dren thought that six or seven riders would be needed from each Weyr."

D'say rose to stand beside his son; there wasn't a hair's difference in height between them. Moreta had never been motherly toward her children; as a queen rider, she'd had to foster them immediately. She could be proud of M'ray, though, of his eager enthusiasm. Though he was committed to the Weyr, it suddenly occurred to her that she had other children and her bloodline could be sustained in Keroon.

"We will recruit riders who are adequate to the task and will discharge this duty to the Hall," D'say assured her. "I'll speak to Wimmia as soon as she's free. She'll review the fosterlings for your queen's clutch, though I must remind you that we had heavy losses among the weyr and hold folk. Everyone wanted to see that peculiar beast when it passed through here on its way to the Gather."

"I grieved to know you had such heavy losses." Moreta looked up at the fine lad, grateful he had been spared. "When you've arranged the matter, send a messenger to Master Capiam. He has all the details worked out."

"I'll see you at the Hatching?" M'ray winked impudently at her.

"Of course!" Moreta laughed, and he embraced her again, a little more certain of where his arms should go and not quite so fierce with his strong arms.

Both riders walked her to the weyr entrance.

"You're off to Igen now?" D'say asked. "See Dalova. She'll agree." D'say's smile showed some of the charm that had once attracted her. The bronze rider had always been slow to make up his mind, but his loyalty never faltered after he had. "Don't try to talk to M'tani at Telgar. Ask for T'grel. He's sensible."

Then the bronze and brown rider locked fingers to give Moreta a lift to Arith's back, warning M'barak in a jocular fashion that he'd better be careful with that conveyance. M'barak replied solemnly that it was his sworn obligation.

Then they were above Igen Weyr, the brilliance of the sun glancing off the distant lake painful to eyes *between* blinded; but the heat, the dry intense desert heat, was welcome to chilled bodies as Arith bugled his request to the watchrider.

Dalova was at her weyr ledge to greet Moreta, her tanned face wreathed in delighted smiles for her visitor.

"You come in Search?" she cried, embracing Moreta and drawing her into the cool of her quarters. Dalova had a demonstrative and affectionate nature, though the strains of the recent past were apparent in her nervous gestures and grimaces, the way she constantly shifted her position by her queen, often tapping her fingers on Allaneth's forearm as she listened to Moreta's explanation of her double Search.

"There's no question of my refusing help, Moreta. Silga, Empie, and Namurra won't refuse either. Six, you say Capiam'll need? I'd wager any amount"—she laughed, a high nervous laugh—"that P'leen times it. You *do* get to know, you know. As I'm sure you do." She grimaced, causing the sun-lines around her sad brown eyes to crease. "If only L'bol were not so terribly depressed. He feels that if he hadn't let our riders convey that dreadful beast about—" She broke off and threw her arms out as if she could scatter all the unpleasantness and misery. Absently she patted her dragon's face, and Allaneth regarded her fondly. "I can help you distribute the vaccines but I cannot, in conscience, give you any candidates. We have so few young people to present to hatchlings, much less a queen. Besides, Allaneth should rise soon; I'm counting on it." A flash of desperation crossed Dalova's mobile face.

"There's nothing like a good mating flight to buoy the spirits of the entire Weyr," Moreta said, thinking ahead to Orlith's next flight with increasing anticipation.

"Oh, my, not you, too?" Dalova asked with a shaky little laugh. Tears formed in her expressive brown eyes, and now her queen licked her hand.

Without hesitation, Moreta took Dalova in her arms and the woman wept, in the quiet forlorn way of someone who has cried often without relief.

"So many, Moreta, so many. So suddenly. The shock of it when Ch'mon and Helith went. Then . . ." She could not continue for sobbing. "And L'bol is sunk in apathy. P'leen has risen with the Igen wings. That's not out of order, but when we're no longer consolidated, if he cannot *lead* . . . So I'm counting on Allaneth's rising, and me! Once there's been a good mating flight, everyone's spirits will improve. And once the fear of this hideous plague is over, everyone will be restored."

Dalova raised her head from Moreta's shoulder, drying her eyes. "You know how firestone makes me sneeze, and I nearly burst myself to keep from doing it because a sneeze frightens people so! Ridiculous, but it is the truth." Dalova sniffled, found her kerchief, and blew her nose lustily. "I must say, I do feel better because *you* know what it's like. Now, let me have a look at our Weyr maps. Yes, I see what Master Capiam means and he's worked so much of the detail out, it'll be no trouble. I'll organize Igen. Have you been to Telgar yet? Well, ask for T'grel. Then you'll go to High Reaches? Is Falga improving? Will Tamianth really fly again? Oh, that is good news. Look, much as I'd love you to stay, you'd better go or I'll drip tears all over you again. I try *not* to for L'bol's sake because Timenth tattles on me and that depresses L'bol even more. You can't imagine what a relief it is to weep all over you. Look, I'll send Empie when we've decided, and I might not ask more than the queens or P'leen. I can trust them but L'bol never approves of timing it, for *any* reason, and now is not the moment to upset him on minor matters." Dalova had been ushering Moreta to the weyr entrance, holding tightly to her arm as they walked. She smiled warmly up at M'barak, stroked Arith's nose, and gave Moreta a leg up.

At Telgar the brown watchdragon bugled threateningly to Arith, ordering the blue to land on the Rim instead of proceeding down to the Bowl.

"My orders, Weyrwoman," C'ver said with no apology. "M'tani wants no strangers in the Weyr."

"Since when are dragonriders strangers to each other?" Moreta demanded, offended by the order and insolence with which it was delivered. Arith trilled with concern over their reception and he could sense Moreta's fury. "I've come in Search—"

"And left your queen alone?" C'ver was openly contemptuous.

"The eggs harden. I call M'tani to honor his promise to S'peren to send us candidates for Impression. I have vaccine with me if it is needed for the weyrfolk I seek."

"We have all of *that* we need for those who deserve it."

"If I were on Orlith, C'ver—"

"Even if you were on your queen, Moreta of Fort, you wouldn't be welcome here! Take your Search into your own Holds. If there're any holders left, of course!"

"If those are your sentiments, C'ver—"

"They are."

"Then have a care, C'ver, when this Pass is over. Have a care!"

C'ver laughed and his brown reared to his hind legs, trumpeting derisively. Arith trembled from muzzle to tail tip.

"Get out of here, M'barak." Moreta spoke through clenched teeth. Telgar could burn in fever and she'd never answer them. They could be down to the last sack of firestone and she'd not send them a sliver. The Weyr could be full of Thread and she—"Take us to the High Reaches."

A Rim landing indeed! The cold of *between* did not dampen Moreta's fury, but Arith stopped trembling only when the High Reaches watch-dragon caroled a welcome.

"Ask Arith to request permission to land in the Bowl near Tamianth's quarters. Say we come in Search."

"I already did, Moreta," M'barak said, his eyes still shadowed by Telgar's rejection. "We are twice and twice times twice welcome at the High Reaches. Arith says Tamianth is warbling."

As Arith glided past the Seven Spindles and the waving watchrider, they could indeed hear Tamianth's intricate vocalization. B'lerion's Nabeth answered then charged out of his weyr to its ledge. S'ligar's Gianarth emerged as if catapulted, flapping his wings and uttering high crackling trills as Arith made his landing.

M'barak turned to grin at Moreta, his shattered confidence restored by the spontaneous greetings and goodwill. Then Moreta saw B'lerion standing in the wide aperture to the weyrling quarters that accommodated the wounded Tamianth. He waved his right arm vigorously and then trotted out to meet her.

"Just a quick word alone," he said, folding his good arm around her shoulders with careless ease. "I took Desdra and Oklina to the Nerat plantations late last night. We've all the needlethorn we could possibly require. I've not mentioned either of your Searches to Falga and S'ligar and there have been no awkward questions from any other source." He raised his voice, chatting casually. "Tamianth's wing is dripping ichor, and she's got a tub for diving; S'ligar's improving, the sun is shining, the Weyr is righted, and Pressan and I were just giving Falga a little walk. Pressen thinks very highly of you, my dear Moreta. Cr'not may *tell* me that Diona did it, but we know Diona, don't we? Pressen attended the dragon injuries from yesterday's Fall. Spends his free time badgering Falga about dragon cures, which keeps her from feeling useless. Ah, here we are, Falga, your waterbearer!"

The first thing Moreta noticed was the enormous water butt conveniently placed at Tamianth's left, full to its brim. Then she saw the neat stack of buckets.

B'lerion chuckled. "My idea. Everyone who wants to visit Falga goes by way of the lake and brings in a full bucket. Every hour a weyrling returns the empties to the lake. If you count the current buckets, you'll realize that Falga's been having entirely too much company. Or Tamianth's thirst has finally been slaked."

Falga was propped against cushions on a wide couch that had been

made of several weyrling beds tied together. Moreta was delighted to
see the good color in Falga's face and returned her embrace, almost
embarrassed by the woman's profuse thanks for saving her queen's life.
Then, out of deference to Falga's fervent request, Moreta checked the
progress of Tamianth's wing with Pressen while Tamianth hummed
softly, watching Moreta with softly glowing eyes.

Holth says Orlith sleeps. It was Tamianth who spoke.

Startled, Moreta glanced at Falga, who was equally surprised but
smiled warmly at her.

"You've come on Search," Falga began. "Surely it's early, and even
a shade unwise to assemble candidates." Falga indicated that Moreta
should sit on one end of the couch, B'lerion on the other.

Moreta heistated, glancing at Pressen, but he was busy in the far
end of the large room.

"I've two reasons for coming."

"But there's only one queen egg." Then Falga slumped back against
her pillows, resigned. "What else has gone wrong then?"

"No, I think you could say that something has come right," Moreta
said in a positive manner, "but Master Capiam needs our cooperation."
Quickly Moreta once more explained, irritated by the sincere way in
which B'lerion expressed astonishment. "Parts of Nabol, Crom, and
the High Reaches are totally isolated. Master Capiam feels that they
could wait so your involvement won't be as large—"

"Moreta, after saving Tamianth you can have anything in this
Weyr...except S'ligar and Gianarth. Fortunately"—Falga's delightful
laugh pealed out—"he's feeling his age. B'lerion, I know you time it
as a matter of everyday convenience. This is the sort of thing you're
good at organizing. Besides, I doubt if there's a cot you don't know in
any western hold."

"Falga!" B'lerion affected indignation and hurt, laying his right hand
on his heart. "May I see this plan of Master Capiam's?"

The bronze rider was a very shrewd dissembler for he examined the
plan as if that were his first viewing. Moreta wished that B'lerion were
not so comprehensively charming.

"Moreta," Falga said, eyeing her thoughtfully, "if Tamianth says
Holth says Orlith's asleep, High Reaches has not been your first stop."

"No, I kept the best for the last."

"Could that be why Tamianth tells me Holth now informs her that
Raylinth and his rider have arrived, in great agitation, at Fort?" When
Moreta nodded grimly, she added, "M'tani would have none of it?"

"The watchrider made Arith land on the Rim."

B'lerion cursed with real fervor, all langor gone.

"If I'd been on Orlith, that squatty mildewed brown of C'ver's
would—"

"Consider the source," Falga said earnestly. "A mere brown rider! Really, Moreta, save your wrath for something worth the energy to spit at. I don't know what has got into M'tani over the last Turn. Maybe he's battle-weary from fighting Thread for so many years. He's gone sour totally, and it's affecting his whole Weyr. That would be disastrous enough in ordinary times, but this plague has only shown up his deficiencies. Do we have to force a change there? We'll take up that matter later. Meanwhile, High Reaches will take up distribution on the eastern side of Telgar's region. Bessera can time it, and has, which accounts for that smug look so often on her face. B'lerion, which of the bronzes?"

"Sharth, Melath, Odioth," B'lerion closed a finger into his palm with each name. "Nabeth, as you suspected, Ponteth and Bidorth. That makes seven, and if my memory serves me, N'mool, Bidorth's rider, comes from Telgar Upper Plains. Of course, T'grel's not the only rider who's dissatisfied with M'tani's leadership. I told you, didn't I, Falga, that once those Telgar riders had had a taste of *real* leadership, there'd be trouble." He smiled winningly at Moreta. "I actually do defer to Sh'gall's abilities. He may be a dull stick in other matters—oh, no, you can't fool your old friend B'lerion—but he *is* a bloody fine Leader! Don't waggle your finger at me, Falga."

"Do stop your chatter, B'lerion. Holth has told Tamianth that Moreta had better get back to her Weyr. And we'll send you over a few weyrlings from our cavern. You can take your pick. If we discover any more likely lads and girls while we're delivering Master Capiam's brew, we'll bring them in."

"I'll just give Moreta a leg up," B'lerion called back over his shoulder as he hurried out with her.

"It's a good thing you've only the one arm, B'lerion," Falga called after them goodhumoredly.

"I was going back by way of Ruatha," Moreta said anxiously.

"I thought you might be. You don't have to. They're doing splendidly. Capiam's sent more people in to help. Desdra's overseeing. She says Tirone and his harpers are doing a magnificent job with the Lords Holder and Crafthallmasters."

"He must be. I haven't seen K'lon in days."

"Good fellow, K'lon; and I don't say that about just any blue rider."

Then they were beside Arith and, one-armed or not, B'lerion nearly lifted her over the blue dragon.

Orlith was awake on Moreta's return to Fort Weyr because Sh'gall had roused her while looking for Moreta. He was pacing up and down in front of the tier and whirled belligerently at her when she entered.

"M'tani sent a green weyrling," he cried, fuming, "hardly more than a babe, to give our watchrider the most insulting message I have ever received. He has repudiated any agreement made at the Butte, a meeting at which I was *not* present." Sh'gall shook his fist first at Moreta and then in the vague direction of the Butte. "And at which arbitrary decisions were made, which I cannot condone, though I've been forced to comply with them! M'tani has repudiated any arrangement, agreement, accord, understanding, undertaking. He is not to be bothered— bothered, he says—not to be bothered by problems of any other Weyr. If we are so poor that we have to beg and Search from other Weyrs, then we do not deserve to have a clutch at all." Sh'gall ended up swinging his arms about like a drum apprentice.

Moreta had never seen him so furious. She listened to what he had to say but offered no response, hoping he would vent his rage and leave. Having repeated himself at length on his displeasure with her shameless venture for the Weyr that had resulted in such an insufferable message from M'tani, he ranted on through his usual grievances, about his illness, about the puny size of the clutch. Finally Moreta could bear no more.

"There *is* a queen egg, Sh'gall. There have to be enough candidates to give the little queen some choice. I applied to Telgar Weyr as I did to Benden, Igen, Ista, and the High Reaches. No one else thought my appearance or my request importunate. Now leave the Ground. You've upset Orlith sufficiently for one day."

Orlith was visibly upset as Moreta ran across the hot sands to her, but not, Moreta knew very well, by Sh'gall. By Telgar Weyr. She paced in front of her eggs, her eyes wheeling from red to yellow and orange as she recited to her rider a list of the damages she would inflict on bronze Hogarth in such detail that Moreta was torn between laughter and horror. A mating dragon could be savage with the drive of that purpose, but a clutching dragon was usually passive.

Moreta scratched Orlith's eye ridges and head knob to soothe her, urging the dragon to have a care for her eggs and come lie down again and let the hot sands lull her.

She has some very good ideas, came the unmistakable voice of Holth. *Leri says that Raylinth's rider understands all that is necessary. She says that in the interests of tranquility, you are to stay in the Ground, eat and sleep well.*

Do you miss anything, Holth–Leri?

No. If Orlith does not finish Hogarth appropriately, I will do so.

Leri says—and the voice was now only Orlith's, her tone sullen— *that we must not stop Holth. Why not? If you had ridden me, you would not have been insulted.*

"Actually, I'd rather have C'ver's skin for a floor rug," Moreta said in a considered tone. "He's hairy enough."

The notion of flaying a rider was originally Leri's, but thinking about the process restored Moreta and indirectly placated Orlith. Perhaps she should go for Sh'gall's hide, too, except that she was fond of Kadith and wouldn't cause him anxiety.

Kamiana comes, Orlith said, her tone calmer, her eyes more green than yellow.

Moreta looked up and saw the Weyrwoman beckoning urgently for Moreta to join her on the tier.

"Leri told me to wait until you'd both had a chance to cool down!" Kamiana said, rolling her eyes and grinning sympathetically at Moreta. "Sh'gall will drone on when he's offended, won't he? You'd think the plague had been invented to annoy him alone. And that M'tani? We're all tired of Thread but we still do what is expected. He may find himself flying by his lonesome, and I know his Weyr's at half strength. Can *we* not replace him? Or must we wait until Telgar's Dalgeth rises to replace him as Leader? However, we're flying for Capiam tomorrow, Lidora, Haura, and myself. I wish you could persuade Leri not to, but she does know the hole-in-the-hill places better anyone else in the Weyr. She's talked S'peren into taking a few runs and K'lon, though he's only a blue." Kamiana frowned dubiously over that choice. "I think P'nine would have been wiser but he got scored."

"K'lon's already stumbled onto timing; besides, he's done a lot of conveying lately, you know."

"I didn't know"—Kamiana rolled her eyes expressively again—"just how much was going on around here, Moreta, and your queen on the Hatching Ground, pushing sand about to warm her eggs!"

3.22.43

In the main Hall of Ruatha Hold, which had so recently been a hospital, forty cartwheels had been rigged as centrifuges. A hundred or more ornamental bottles had also served their purpose and were now stacked against the stair wall where once the banquet table of Ruathan Lords had graced the raised end of the long Hall. The frenzied activity of the past three days had, in the late hours of this night, abated to weary preparations for the morning's final effort. It was no comfort to the fatigued that similar activity had wearied anxious men and women in Keroon Beasthall and Benden Hold.

In the corner nearest the kitchen entrance, a trestle table had been serving as dining table at appropriate hours and a worktable at all other times. The remnants of an evening meal were at the end nearest the wall, where maps and lists had been tacked to the hangings. On its long benches sat the eight people whom Alessan called his Loyal Crew, relaxing with a cup of wine from Alessan's skin of Benden white.

"I wasn't so taken with that Master Balfor, Lord Alessan," Dag was saying, his eyes on the wine in his cup.

"He's not confirmed in the honor," Alessan said. He was too weary to take part in an argument and well aware that Fergal was listening with avid ears to store bits and pieces of irrelevant information in his cunning young mind.

"I'd worry who else might have the rank, for Master Balfor certainly hasn't the experience."

"He has done all that Master Capaim asked," Tuero said with an eye on Desdra, who apparently was not listening.

"Ah, it's sad to realize how many good men and women have died." Dag lifted his cup in a silent toast. "And sadder to think of the fine bloodlines just wiped out. When I think of the races Squealer will walk away with and no competition to stretch him in a challenge."

Alessan poured a bit more wine in his cup, Fergal's eyes on the business. He'd been offered a portion but disdained it with an insolence that Alessan excused only because the lad had worked so diligently at any task assigned him. But then, the work had been to save runners, and the boy had obviously inherited his grandfather's total commitment to the breed.

"You say Runel died?" Dag continued, finding it hard to comprehend how few of his old cronies remained. "Did all his bloodline go?"

"The oldest son and his family are safe in the hold."

"Ah, well, he's the right one for it. I'll just have a look at that brown mare. She could foal tonight. Come along, Fergal." Dag swung his splinted leg off the bench and took up the crutches Tuero had contrived for him. For just a moment, Fergal looked rebellious.

"I'll come with you if I may," Rill said, rising and unobtrusively assisting Dag. "A birth is a happy moment!"

Fergal was on his feet in an instant, extremely possessive of Dag and unwilling to share the man's attention with anyone, not even with Nerilka, for whom he had taken a curious liking.

Tuero watched the curious trio until they had left the hall. "I know I've seen that woman before."

"I have, too," Desdra said, "or maybe her kinfolk. Faces have got blurred. Overdose!" She was leaning back against the wall behind her, hands limp in her lap, a few wisps of dark hair escaping from the tight braids. "When this is over tomorrow, I'm going to sleep and sleep and sleep. Anyone, anyone whosoever attempts to rouse me, shall be . . . shall be . . . I'm too tired to think of something suitably vile."

"The wine was excellent, Lord Alessan," Follen said, rising. He pulled at Deefer's sleeve. "We've just three more batches to decant tonight. There could be breakages, so we must have spares. It won't take long now."

Deefer yawned mightily then belatedly covered his mouth, apologetically glancing around. But a yawn was not in the same category as a sneeze or a cough.

"When you think that I thought," Tuero began with a long sigh as he regarded the interior of his empty cup, "that a Ruathan Gather would be less tedious than a Crom wedding, you may wonder what I was doing for wits that day."

Alessan looked up, his light-green eyes sparkling. "Does that mean, my friend, you have considered my offer of a post here at Ruatha?"

Tuero gave a little chuckle. "My good Lord Holder Alessan, there comes a time in a harper's life when he decides that the variety and change of temporary assignments begin to pall and he wishes a comfortable living where his capabilities are appreciated, where he can be sure of witty conversations over the dinner table—to save his fingers from the harping—where his energies are not abused—"

"I wouldn't post to Ruatha in that event," Desdra remarked caustically, but she smiled.

"You weren't asked," Alessan replied, mischief in his eyes.

"It's no joy to serve a cautious man." Tuero flung an arm about Alessan's shoulders. "There is one condition, however, which"—the harper held up a long forefinger, pausing before his stipulation—"must be met."

"By the first Egg," Alessan protested, "you've already got me to agree to a first-storey apartment on the inside, second tithe of our Crafthalls—"

"When you've got them staffed again—"

"Your choice of a runnerbeast, top marks as journeyman, and leave, if you wish, to take your mastery when the Pass is over. What more can you ask of an impoverished Lord Holder?"

"All I ask is what is fitting for a man of my accomplishments." Tuero humbly put one hand on his heart.

"So what is this final condition?"

"That you supply me with Benden white." He spoiled the gravity of his pronouncement by hiccuping and gestured urgently for Alessan to fill his cup. He sipped wine to stop the spasms. "Well?"

"Good Journeyman Harper Tuero, if I can procure Benden white, you may have your just share of it." He raised his cup solemnly and Tuero touched his to it. "Agreed?"

Tuero hiccuped. "Agreed!" He tried to swallow the next hiccup.

Desdra looked at Alessan then leaned forward and prodded the wineskin under his elbow. She made a noise of amused reproof.

"There's not much left in it," Alessan assured her.

"That's just as well. Tomorrow your heads must be as clear as can be," she said. "Come, Oklina, you're half asleep as it is."

Regarding her through the lovely euphoria produced by several cups of his superlative Benden white, Alessan wondered if Desdra was being solicitous of his sister or merely needed support up the stairs. The progress of the two women was steady but uncertain, and their indirect course not entirely due to the cartwheels, apparatus, and equipment that lay strewn about the spacious whitewashed Hall. That was another thing he must do, Alessan decided suddenly—repaint the Hall. The austere white was too much a reminder of too many painful scenes.

"I say, Alessan," Tuero said as he tugged at the Lord Holder's sleeve, "where do you get all that white Benden?"

Alessan grinned. "I have to have a few secrets." His head was wobbling and if he wasn't careful, it would fall sideways onto the table.

"Secrets? Even from your harper?" Tuero tried to sound indignant.

"If you find out, I'll tell you if you're right."

Tuero brightened. "That's fair enough. If a harper can't find out—and this harper is very good at finding things out—if a harper can't find out, he doesn't have the right to know. Is that right, Alessan?"

But Alessan's head reposed on the table; a snore issued from his half-open mouth. Tuero stared at him for a moment in mixed pity and rebuke, then pushed at the wineskin under his elbow and sighed in disgust. There wasn't more than a dribble in it.

Footsteps sounded behind Tuero. He turned.

"Has he finished it?" Rill asked.

"Yes, it's empty, and he's the only one who knows where the supply is!"

Rill smiled. "The foal is a male, a fine strong one. I thought Lord Alessan would like to know. Dag and Fergal are watching to be sure it stands and suckles." She looked down at the sleeping Lord Holder, an expression of ineffable tenderness lending her a look of quiet beauty.

Tuero blinked to be sure it was the wine that had enhanced the tall woman. She had good bones in her face, he decided after making an effort at concentration. With a bit of thought to her clothing, brighter colors, with hair longer than that unattractive crop, she'd be attractive. Unexpectedly her expression altered, and so did the illusion of beauty— once again she bore the resemblance that perplexed Tuero and Desdra.

"I know I know you." Tuero said.

"I'm not the sort of person a journeyman harper knows," she replied. "Get to your feet, Harper. I can't allow him to sleep in this uncomfortable position and he needs a proper rest."

"Not so sure I can stand."

"Try it." Her terse reply was issued with an authority that Tuero found himself obeying though he was shaky on his legs.

Rill was only half a head shorter than Alessan so she looped one limp arm over her shoulder, urging Tuero take the other. Between them they managed to get Alessan upright, though he remained only half-conscious of their efforts. Tuero had to cling with his free hand to the bannister but fortunately, Alessan's rooms were the first apartment past the head of the stairs. They got him through to the bedroom where Rill arranged his limp body comfortably before she covered him. Tuero was mildly jealous that Alessan could arouse such tenderness.

"I wish... I wish..." he began but lost the words to express that longing.

"The doss-bed is still in the next room, Harper."

"Will you cover me up, too?" Tuero asked wistfully.

Rill smiled and merely pointed to the pallet on the floor and shook out the blanket folded on it. With a sigh of weary gratitude, Tuero lay down on his side.

"You're good to a drunken sot of a harper," he murmured as he felt the blanket spread over him. "One day I'll rememmmm..."

The morning began as any other in the Weyr. Though bothered by a lingering cough, Nesso had otherwise recovered from her illness. She brought Moreta breakfast and so many complaints about Gorta's management of the Lower Caverns during her illness that Moreta cut short the tirade by saying she had to check Leri's harness.

"I can't imagine why the queen riders would fly with Telgar after what M'tani did yesterday."

Moreta was grateful that the Fall would mask the queens' real activities and grateful, too, that Nesso had obviously not discerned that the rising to Fall was merely an excuse, that Telgar had nothing to do with the queens' flight that day.

"It's the last time," Moreta said, hastily draining her cup. "We had our duty to hold and hall!"

Orlith was carefully turning eggs on the hot sands, testing their shells with a gentle tongue. She was more solicitous of the queen egg and turned it nearly every hour; the lesser ones were rearranged only three or four times a day. Moreta would see Leri safely off on her mission and then take Orlith to the feeding ground. They would have to insist that drovers restock the Weyr, once the threat of plague was over. Just then there wasn't much choice among what beasts were left. She'd speak to Peterpar. Maybe wild wherries could be found nearby fattening on the spring growth in the lower range. Once the day was over, there'd be a lot of details she'd best attend and get affairs back to a normal pace. And then a real Search for candidates would be initiated.

Leri was dressed in her flying gear but grumpy.

"Maybe you'd better not fly your run if your joints are bothering you so much. Did you take enough fellis juice in your wine?"

"Hah! I knew there'd come a day when you'd beg me to take fellis juice!"

"I'm not begging you—"

"Well, you don't need to remind me either. Just didn't sleep well last night. Kept going over the details of what goes where and with whom. M'tani couldn't have picked a better time to be obnoxious." Leri was blackly sarcastic. "You're going to have to cope with Sh'gall today, you know, and all that injured dignity. Good thing we planned for you to stay in the Hatching Ground; otherwise he'd get suspicious."

"He's asleep."

"He should be! Gorta tells me he put away two wineskins on his own. Now, if you'll just pass that strap?—There!"

Holth nuzzled Moreta with unexpected affection as she bent her head to accept the neck strap, and Moreta gave her eye ridge a scrape.

"You'll take good care of Leri today, won't you, Holth?"

Of course!

"Of all the nerve. Talking behind a rider's back!" Leri pretended indignation, but she smiled warmly at Moreta before she tugged at the harness to be sure that the clips were secure. "There!" She thumped Holth on the neck. "We'd best be off. I'm taking the upper ranges. When I collect the animal vaccine from Ruatha, shall I leave in any messages?"

"You'll wish them well, of course. And see what Holth thinks of Oklina."

"Naturally!"

Moreta accompanied Leri to the ledge and, as Holth crouched low, helped her mount. Leri fastened her riding straps, settled her small frame against Holth's ridge, and waved a negligent farewell. Moreta stepped back against the wall while Holth leaped off, her wing strokes strong and sure. She flew toward the feeding ground and then, in an instant, was gone *between*. Moreta worried at Holth's habit of flipping *between* so soon after takeoff, but the dragon was old. After they had treated everyone, Moreta was going to present the strongest possible arguments to Leri about continuing flight at all. The wise old Weyr-woman could be exceedingly useful down at Ista where the climate would be much kinder to both dragon and rider.

Other dragons were at the feeding ground, Moreta noticed, after reaching her decision about Leri's future. The sparse numbers of the Weyr herd stampeded to the lake and some ambled into the water. A pursuing green had a fine time splashing after a wherry, and sprays of water made rainbow dazzles in the midmorning sun. The green's triumphant bugle was somewhat muffled by the wet mass in her mouth. Instead of flying up to her ledge to savor her meal, the green veered low and deposited the wherry at the feet of the blue dragon on the far side of the lake. Tigrath had preyed for Dilenth, A'dan and F'duril standing by. Unless Moreta's eyes deceived her, the third man watching the exchange was Peterpar, the Weyr herdsman.

When she joined the trio, Peterpar was finalizing the details of a

wherry hunt to be held that afternoon if the weather kept fair.
"They've nooks they squeeze into up in the ravines, Moreta," Peterpar explained. "If it stays sunny"—he twisted round to view the cloudless horizon—"and it looks to, they'll be out, browsing. A'dan here says he's willing."

"I was thinking of asking S'gor to join us," A'dan said. "Malth could use an excuse to spread her wings, and the chase would do S'gor a power of good!"

"He oughtn't to stay immured like that," F'duril agreed, glancing up toward S'gor's weyr in the western arc of the Bowl. "We'll do it," he added with a wink and a nod at Moreta. "A'dan here could get a snake to walk when he sets his mind to it." Grinning, he hooked arms with his friend.

"Nonetheless, Moreta, we'll hunt the hills out right quick," Peterpar said with a shake of his head. He frowned as he pushed together some stones with the toe of his boot. "How soon d'you expect the holders'll be willing to send up a drove?"

"Could we not just ask for permission to hunt until there's no more fear of spreading plague?" A'dan asked. Neither he nor F'duril had been infected since both had stayed close to F'duril's injured blue Dilenth during the worst of the contagion.

"That would spare holders the necessity of a drove when they're shorthanded and behind on spring work," Moreta agreed, adding that detail to the others she was accumulating.

"Round up the strays for people in Keroon and Telgar," Peterpar said, nodding sagaciously. "I did hear that animals were let run when folk took sick with no one to care for them." Then he pointed skyward. "Where're the queen riders going? Is that S'peren with them?"

"On Search," Moreta said casually.

"Queens don't go on Search," Peterpar said presumptuously.

"They do when a Weyrwoman has been treated as uncivilly as Telgar treated me," Moreta declared with sufficient severity to quell Peterpar's curiosity. "Orlith does need to be fed. Do please get a few juicy bucks for her in your hunt."

Smiling, she left the men. Trust Peterpar to take an interest in everything. He hadn't mentioned Holth and Leri so perhaps Holth's shallow-angle approach to *between* had been justified. K'lon must have left earlier, but he was in and out of the Weyr so frequently on convey that his departure would not cause comment. It amused Moreta that she could turn M'tani's disaffection to advantage, so he was made useful instead of being merely obstreperous. Now if Sh'gall would just sleep all day. . . .

She felt inordinately good that morning, aware of the smell of the spring in the air, the warmth of the sun, the laughter of the children

playing near the Cavern. Once the dragons had finished feeding, they
would return to the lakeside, their favorite spot for games. The atmosphere in the Bowl was returning to a normal buzz of pleasant activity,
no longer silent with anxiety. However, an air of anticipation, of suppressed excitement, hung over the infirmary when she visited looking
for Jallora, who was vaccinating one of the riders scored the day before.

"Good morning, Moreta," Jallora said. "A well-timed arrival. Now
I can give you the second vaccination which Capiam has ordered for
the Weyrs. Dragonriders travel so much," she said with a mild apologetic smile. Nothing in her expression indicated that the procedure
was anything but routine. She administered Moreta's dose with the
deftness of long practice.

"Can I give you a hand?"

"I wouldn't object. I've got the Lower Cavern to do. I vaccinated
the queen riders before they left on their errand."

Did Moreta imagine a twinkle in Jallora's eyes? At least she could
keep busy helping the journeywoman, and so she passed the morning
well occupied. When she saw Peterpar with A'dan and S'gor, she went
to tell Orlith that there'd be more choice if she could contain her appetite
until later in the afternoon.

Wild wherries are tough, Orlith remarked a trifle petulantly, *but
generally tasty,* she added, sensing Moreta's concern and nuzzling her
rider. *Kadith sleeps. Holth says that the errand proceeds well.*

Moreta was very grateful that Kadith still slept. Inevitably Sh'gall
would discover that Fort Weyr riders had taken part in Capiam's vaccine
distribution—preferably after he had recovered from the wine and when
he had calmed down over M'tani's insult. Moreta could have been
mistaken, but she had a fleeting thought that Sh'gall was obscurely
pleased by M'tani's attitude toward her.

Suddenly Orlith reared up, her eyes flashing reddish orange with
such alarm that Moreta whirled to the Hatching Ground entrance, alert
to danger.

*He will not let the bronzes go. Sutanith is worried. He is dangerous.
Dalgeth, the senior queen, restrains all.* Orlith sounded perplexed as
well as defensive.

"Sutanith is speaking to you?" Moreta was amazed. Sutanith was
Miridan's queen and she was a very junior weyrwoman at Telgar.
Moreta didn't know her well at all for Fort did not often combine with
Telgar Weyr even when traditional territories were observed.

The Leader has gone between *to the Fall, so Sutanith warns you of
the trouble—that the bronzes cannot help.*

"M'tani found out that T'grel was going to distribute the vaccine?"

Sutanith has gone. Orlith relaxed her posture.

"And Dalgeth restrains? *How* did M'tani find out? I thought Leri and T'grel had worked out every detail. And Keroon *must* have the vaccine." Moreta began to pace, scrubbing at her short hair as if she could tease out a plan. "If Keroon doesn't get the vaccine, the whole plan could fail!" She dashed across the sands to the tier and found Capiam's notes. Keroon and Telgar had to be covered and there were many halls and holds. Who else among her riders knew Telgar and Keroon well enough to—

Oribeth comes. This time Orlith jumped in front of her eggs, spreading her wings, arching her neck in instinctive protection of her clutch from the proximity of a strange queen.

"Don't be silly, Orlith. Levalla's here to see me!"

Astonished that the Benden pair should appear in Fort Weyr, Moreta rushed out to meet Levalla. They had landed in the center of the Bowl, well away from both Hatching Ground and Cavern. As Moreta rushed out to meet her visitors, Levalla sighted the sun's position in relation to the Star Stones before sliding down her queen's shoulder to await Moreta.

"I timed that very well indeed. I didn't want you to worry unnecessarily."

"You timed it here? Orlith just relayed Sutanith's cryptic message. Do you *know* about it?" Moreta had to bellow over the noise made by the Weyr's dragons, which were bugling in bewilderment at Orlith's alarm and Oribeth's presence. Moreta sent powerful reassurances to her queen, who stopped bugling.

"Do calm everyone down. I didn't mean to put the Weyr in a panic. My apologies to Orlith and the watchrider and all that, but I had to see you instantly. I did rather well, you know, timing it across the continent on top of everything else." Levalla had stripped off one glove and now fingered the worry-wood. "And yes, we know all about it in the east. About midmorning, our time, M'gent thought something was amiss when Lord Shadder said no one from Telgar Weyr had collected any vaccine from him or Master Balfor—so we were slightly forewarned. Sutanith got her warning through to Oribeth, Wimmia, and Allaneth so I give Miridan full marks for courage. But then, K'dren says she's mating with T'grel, and *he's* determined against M'tani now. So we took a little time"—Levalla smiled eloquently at Moreta—"and we have assigned two brown riders who know Telgar Plains and the River holds. D'say has agreed to send one of his group on the runs along the Telgar coast to the delta. Dalova says she can expand her responsibility to include the mountains, skipping back pre-Fall because that's where it would chose to Fall today. But we don't have anyone who knows the Keroon Plains well enough." She paused then from her swift recital of emergency measures and gave Moreta a long stare. "You do. Could you fly it on that young blue?"

Holth comes. I come, said Orlith and Holth in different tones on the same breath.

"Oho, and here comes trouble without a shirt." Levalla looked up at the weyr steps and pulled Moreta to one side, to be shielded by Oribeth's bulk. "Does Sh'gall know, or was it Orlith's fussing that roused him?"

"He doesn't know." Moreta wasn't sure if she understood what was happening or half of what Levalla had so tersely explained. Then Holth arrived, no more that two wingspans above the Bowl.

"Shells, but she's flying near the mark!" Levalla instinctively drew back. "Sh'gall thinks you were only on Search yesterday, is that right?" When Moreta nodded, she went on. "All right then. I'll delay him. You do Keroon on anything that will fly you. Those runnerholds *must* get the vaccine. Master Balfor has it all ready, in order, and with handlers to help out at the appropriate holds. Find a dragon to ride. Oribeth and I have done all we have time for in one day!"

Then Levalla shoved the worry-wood back into her belt and strode off to meet Sh'gall, who was bellowing at such rude awakening and strange queens threatening the peace of his Weyr.

Holth had continued her glide to land right at the Hatching Ground entrance, glaring at Oribeth, who was beginning to react to the air of hostility. Moreta rushed to intercept Leri before Sh'gall saw her.

"What has been going on? Orlith called Holth in sheer panic about Sutanith and Oribeth—"

Moreta made wild gestures up at the steps, indicating Sh'gall. Holth crouched down on the ground so that Moreta didn't need to shout up at Leri, and the old queen hissed soothingly in Orlith's direction.

"M'tani had Dalgeth restraining T'grel and the other bronzes. No vaccine has been conveyed in Dalgeth or Keroon. Sutanith got a warning out to some of the queens but M'gent of Benden had already suspected something was wrong because no riders from Telgar had collected any vaccine. Levalla has made arrangements for Telgar Plains and River, D'say has taken charge of the coast to the delta, and Dalova is taking the mountains—"

"Which leaves the Keroon Plains and you! Get your riding things. The day's half done in the east. I'll tell Kamiana to take over the rest of my run. S'peren can do the western coast from the Delta. I had the oddest feeling that something was going to go wrong. I did all the hidey holes in the top range first. The others are easy to find. Go, girl! I'll stay with Orlith. In truth"—Leri had difficulty swinging her leg to dismount—"my bones are very weary today and I'll be quite content to sit sipping my fellis juice and wine by Orlith's side."

"Peterpar's gone to hunt wild wherries for her. Make her eat."

"I'll save a few fat ones for Holth when you two get back. She'll need to eat by then." Leri called cheerfully after Moreta as she ran to grab her riding gear. She started toward Orlith to give her a parting hug, but Leri cautioned her. "You've no time to waste and a lot to make. I'll give her all the affection she needs."

You must go to Keroon, Orlith said, still keeping one eye on the Benden queen in the center of Fort Weyr Bowl. *Holth will take you. I must guard my eggs.*

"Oribeth doesn't *want* your eggs," Moreta cried, scrambling up Holth's side.

I have told her that, Holth said.

Moreta quickly lengthened the riding straps to accommodate her longer body, secured them, then told Holth she was ready. Holth turned, charged a few lengths toward the lake, not quite in line with Oribeth, and then launched herself in the air. Moreta caught a glimpse of Levalla standing on the steps in earnest conversation with Sh'gall, who didn't even look up as Holth took to the air. With relief, Moreta realized that the bronze rider had not noticed the switch of riders.

"Please take me to Keroon Beasthold, Holth," Moreta said, visualizing the distinctive pattern of the fields that she knew as well from the ground as from the air. She didn't have time to think of her verse— she had to think of how much time she had to make. The Keroon region blazed in her mind, a map she had seen daily as a child in the big room of her family's hold. She knew it even better than she knew the northern holds, for she had trotted around it on runnerback as a child; she knew the north only from the back of a queen dragon.

The beasthold itself, set in its complex of paddocks, was a sturdy group of stone buildings and quadrangles of low, slate-roofed stables. It was there that the feline had been brought for identification and from those fields that runners had carried the disease. Few enough beasts occupied the fields, but more than she had expected. Perhaps in her family's hold the strays had been rounded up and all her father's careful breeding had not been wiped out. Holth glided in to land near the building where a group of men obviously awaited them, a line of nets arrayed on the ground.

Moreta recognized Balfor, an unsmiling man who generally confined his remarks to monosyllables. Or perhaps he had always diplomatically deferred to the affable and verbose Herdmaster Sufur. Balfor was certainly vocal now as he hurried to Moreta and Holth, beckoning his men to bring the first of the nets.

"We have them all in order for you, Weyrwoman," he said, "if you know the holds from east to west. We've taken pains to be sure there is enough vaccine for every beast and human registered with the drum census. Go speedily, for the afternoon is half gone."

Balfor exaggerated, too, for the sun was just past zenith.

"Then I shall make the most of it. Don't go wandering off. I'll be back directly."

Moreta angled Holth in takeoff so they both had a good look at the angle of the sun. Then she checked the first label: Keroon River Hold, situated where the river rushed through a gorge in its first wild charge from the higher plateaus. Holth jumped for the sky and went *between* as Moreta kept the gorge hard in her mind. She was met by the healer of Keroon River Hold and her delivery received with thanks. They had begun to worry since the vaccine had been promised for early morning. Moreta did not dally.

Next they went slightly northeast to the High Plateau Hold where the runners were cleverly penned in a canyon, awaiting the vaccine. The holder wanted reassurance about "this stuff" since they'd only had drum messages and no contact with anyone "below" since the quarantine was sent, and he wanted a fuller account of all that had been going on below. She answered him tersely but told him that once the vaccination had been administered, he could go below and hear the whole story. Her next stop was westward, along the great plateau fault at Curved Hill Hold where there had been a great in-gathering of runners—and that was the last of the first run she did.

She did four more holds, and each time she landed at the Beasthold for more vaccine, the sun had dipped by another hour's arc, though she and Holth had been on the move hours longer than the sun told. And each jump Holth made seemed just that much shallower. Twice Moreta asked the dragon if she wanted to take time to rest. Each time Holth replied firmly that she was able to continue.

The angle of the sun dominated the coordinates Moreta envisioned for Holth in her valiant leaps: It had become a blazing beacon, turning slowly orange as it dipped farther down in the west. Moreta began to think of the sun as her enemy, fighting the time it took for Holth to recognize each new destination, to glide in to the hold or cot, hand over the bottles of vaccine and the packets of needlethorn, to explain, patiently over and over, exactly the dosage for animal and that for human, repeating instructions already sent by drum and messenger. Yet Moreta had to admit that, despite Master Tirone's best efforts, there was still panic in the more isolated holds that had not been touched by the plague and dreaded it more for its unexperienced terrors than its known qualities. Only the fact that she came adragonback allayed some suspicions. Dragons had always meant safety, even to the most secluded settlers. She had to use valuable time reassuring Holth and still make it back to the Beasthold for the next load of vaccine and the next run.

All during the last round, she kept the sun at a midafternoon position, feeling the strain of timing it in her bones, in Holth's heaviness. But when she asked Holth if they should stop, the dragon replied that she wished Keroon had a few mountains instead of all these dreadful plains.

Then they had delivered the last of the vaccine and the net across Holth's withers was empty at last. They were at a small western hold, stark amid the vast rolling plain, the runners held in an uneasy assembly around the great waterhole that supplied them. The holder was torn between administering the vaccine as long as he had light and offering hospitality to the dragon and rider.

"Go, you have much to do," she told the man. "This is our last stop."

Thanking her profusely, the man began to hand out the contents of the net to his handlers. He kept bowing to her and Holth, walking backward to his herd, all the while expressing his gratitude for their arrival.

She watched him go, numbly aware that Holth's body was shaking under her legs. She stroked the old queen's neck.

"Orlith is all right?" She had asked the question frequently, too.

I am too tired to think that far.

Moreta looked at the midafternoon sun over Keroon plain and wondered with a terrible lethargy exactly what time it was.

"One last jump, that's all we have to take, Holth."

Wearily the old queen gathered herself to spring. Moreta gratefully began her litany.

"Black, blacker, blackest—"

They went *between*.

"Shouldn't Moreta be back by now, Leri?" The blue rider had been prowling uneasily in the tiers, occasionally barking his shins.

Leri blinked, looking away from K'lon. His restlessness deepened her anxiety despite the soothing effect of the fellis-laced wine she had been sipping all afternoon. It had eased the pain in her joints caused by the morning's concentrated flying but did not allay her worry. She jerked her shoulders irritably, arching her back, and peered down at Orlith who lay drowsing beside her clutch of eggs.

"Take a hint from Orlith. She's relaxed enough. And I won't disrupt their concentration with an unnecessary question at what could be an awkward moment," she replied testily. "They'll be very tired. They'll have had to fight time and make every minute into twenty to get the vaccine distributed." Leri balled one hand into a fist and pounded her thigh. "I'm going to rend M'tani." She flexed her fingers as if to encircle M'tani's neck. "Holth'll rake that bronze of his into shreds."

K'lon regarded her with startled awe. "But I thought Sh'gall—"

Leri gave a snort of contempt. "L'mal would not have needed to 'discuss' the matter with K'dren and S'ligar. He'd have been at Telgar, demanding satisfaction."

"He would? What?"

"No Weyrleader can disregard a continental emergency. Capiam has not revoked his priority. Well, M'tani will wish he *had* cooperated. And"—Leri's smile was malicious—"Dalgeth will answer to the other queens."

"Really?"

"Hmm. Yes. Really!" Leri drummed her fingers on the stem of her wine cup. "As soon as Moreta comes back, you'll see."

K'lon peered out of the Hatching Ground. "The sun's nearly down now. It must be dark in Keroon..."

Afterward, K'lon realized that both the rider and the dragon knew in the same instant. But Orlith's reaction was vocal and spectacular. Her scream, tearing at his taut nerves, brought him round to witness the initial throes of her bereavement. Orlith had been lying at the rear of the Ground, her eggs scattered on the sand before her. Now she reared up on her hind legs, her awkwardly coiled tail all that prevented her from crashing backward as she arched her head back, howling her despair. The sounds she emitted were ghastly ululations in wierd dissonances, like throat-cut shrieks. Then, in an incredible feat, Orlith launched herself from that fully extended posture, over her eggs, missing them by a mere handspan. She sprawled, muzzle buried in the sand as all color faded from her golden hide. Then she began to writhe, thrashing her head and tail, oblivious to the fact that she had caught her right wing under her, flailing the air with the left.

Holth is no more, Rogeth told K'lon.

"Holth dead? And Moreta?" K'lon could barely comprehend that statement and frantically tried to deny the corollary even as he watched its effect on the stricken queen.

Leri!

"Oh, no!"

K'lon whirled. Leri lay against the cushions, gasping, her mouth working, her eyes protruding. One hand was pressed to her chest, the other clawed at her throat. K'lon leaped toward her.

She cannot breathe.

"Are you choking?" K'lon asked, horror mounting as he scanned her contorted face. "Are you trying to die?" K'lon was so appalled at the thought of Leri expiring before his eyes that he grabbed at her shoulders and shook her violently. The action forced breath back into her lungs. With a thin wail more piteous than Orlith's shattering cries, Leri went limp in his arms, her body wracked with sobs.

Hold her. Rogeth's voice was curiously augmented.

"Why?" K'lon cried, suddenly aware that in his selfish panic, he had thwarted Leri. If Holth was dead, she had the right to die, too. His heart swelled with a crippling ache of compassion, anguish and remorse.

"How?" he demanded, unable to comprehend what terrible circumstance could have robbed Orlith of Moreta and Leri of Holth.

They were too tired. They ought not to have continued so long. They went between... to nothing, the composite voice replied in the sad conclusion perceived by all the dragons in the Weyr.

"Oh, what have I done?" Tears streamed down K'lon's face as he rocked the frail body of the old Weyrwoman in his arms. "Oh, Leri, I'm so sorry. Forgive me. I'm so sorry. Rogeth! Help me! What have I done?"

What was necessary, the augmented Rogeth spoke in a tone ineffably sad. _Orlith needs her to stay._

Now the air was filled with the lamentations of the Weyr's dragons as they joined Orlith's dreadful keen. Sound battered the Hatching Ground, echoing wildly in the great stony cavern. As K'lon rocked Leri, the dragons were respectfully gathering at the entrances to the Ground. They lowered their great heads, their eyes dulled to gray as they shared the grief of a dragon who was unable to follow her rider in death, held to the Ground by the clutch of hardening eggs.

People had edged past the guardian dragons now, pausing briefly in deference to Orlith. Then K'lon recognized S'peren and F'neldril, closely followed by the other queen riders and Jallora. Kamiana turned with a peremptory gesture to the weyrfolk to remain at the entrance. But Jallora hurried to the steps, sliding to the blue rider. The healer murmured tenderly to Leri, stroking her hair, before she took the weeping woman from K'lon's arms.

"She wanted to die," K'lon stammered, lifting his empty hands in mute apology to Kamiana. "She nearly did."

"We know." Kamiana's face was wretched.

"Pour some wine, Kamiana," Jallora said, rocking Leri as K'lon had. He was obscurely relieved that he had, at least, done that right. "Use plenty of fellis juice. From that brown vial. Pour a cup for K'lon, too."

"We could all use some," Lidora muttered as she helped Kamiana.

But when Jallora held the cup to Leri's lips, the Weyrwoman pressed them tightly closed over her sobs and turned her head away.

"Drink, Leri." Jallora's tone was deep with compassion.

"You must, Leri," Kamiana insisted, her voice breaking. "You're all Orlith has."

The rebuke in Leri's pained eyes was more than K'lon could stand and he buried his head in his hands, shaking with reaction. F'neldril laid a gentle arm across his shoulders to support him.

"Dear Leri, L'mal would expect it of you. I implore you. Drink the wine. It _will_ help." S'peren's voice was hoarse.

"Oh, brave Leri, courageous Leri," Jallora murmured in approval and K'lon looked up as the old Weyrwoman accepted the wine.

Lidora pressed a cup into his hand. It must be half fellis juice, he thought as he recklessly downed the draught. Not that it would do any good. Not all the wine in Pern could assuage the pain and remorse in his heart. He willed the potion to numb his senses but he couldn't stop weeping. Even F'neldril's seamed face was tear-stained as he stroked S'peren's shoulder in comfort.

"Let's get her up to her weyr," Jallora said, motioning for S'peren and F'neldril to assist her.

"No!" Leri's response was vehement. Orlith screamed in echoing protest.

No, said the voices and K'lon caught S'peren's arm.

"I'll stay." Leri pointed toward Orlith. "I'll stay here."

"Will *she*?" Jallora asked the other queen riders, meaning the dragon.

"Orlith will stay," Kamiana said in a barely audible voice while Leri slowly nodded affirmation. "She will stay until the eggs are ready to hatch."

"Then we'll both go," Leri added softly.

Her words would forever remain in his mind, K'lon knew, as indelible as the rest of the terrible scene. S'peren and F'neldril stood beside him, drooping in grief, their faces suddenly aged. Haura and Lidora clung to each other weeping, while Kamiana stood to one side, her figure taut. Beyond them, the arched entrances to the Hatching Ground framed the press of dragons, all gray in sorrow, and the silent cluster of weyrfolk bewildered by the grievous loss. Just then there was a stir and three riders slowly moved onto the Ground, Sh'gall escorted by S'ligar and K'dren. Sh'gall continued forward alone, his body bowed with grief. He fell to his knees, covering his face with his hands, unseen by the inconsolable Orlith who writhed in the soul-rending agony of separation from her beloved rider, Moreta.

AFTERMATH

Present Pass, 4.23.43

THE OCCASION OF a Hatching ought to be a joyous one, Master Capiam thought without a single buoyant fiber in his body as he watched the dragons glide to the knots of passengers awaiting conveyance to Fort Weyr.

He had not attended to what Tirone had been saying to him. Then the Masterharper's parting phrase penetrated his gloomy reflections.

"I will be singing my new ballad, composed in celebration of Moreta!"

"Celebration?" Capiam roared. Desdra caught his arm and prevented him from being trampled on by Rogeth. "Celebration indeed? Has Tirone gone mad?"

"Oh, Capiam!" Desdra's soft exclamation was unusually gentle for that caustic lady, newly made a Masterhealer. Capiam glanced quickly about to see why. Then he saw K'lon's grief-stricken face as the rider dismounted.

"Leri and Orlith went before dawn," K'lon said, his voice breaking. "No one could—would have stopped them. But we had to watch, to be with them. That's all we could do!" K'lon's tear-filled eyes begged for solace.

Desdra folded her arms around him, and Capiam stroked his back, offering the blue rider a kerchief that he needed himself in that instant. Desdra didn't weep but her face was flushed, her jaw muscles tight, and her nose very red.

"They only stayed because of the eggs, to be sure of the day. But we had to see them go." K'lon sobbed.

Wondering if he should administer a restorative, Capiam caught Desdra's eye, but she gave a little shake of her head.

"They were so brave. So gallant! It was dreadful, knowing they would go. Dreadful knowing that one day we would wake up and they would be gone! Just like Moreta and Holth!"

"They could have gone that day..." Capiam began, knowing that wasn't the thing to say, struggling to find something to ease K'lon's grief.

"Orlith could not have gone till the eggs were hard," Desdra said. "Leri stayed with her. They had a purpose and now it is accomplished. Today must also be a glad day, for dragons will hatch. Surely that is a good day for going. A day that had begun in unmeasured grief will end in great joy. A new beginning for twenty-five—no, fifty—lives, for the young people who Impress today begin a new life!"

Capiam stared in wonder at Desdra. He could never have expressed it so well. Desdra might not speak often but she chose the right words when she did talk.

"Yes, yes," K'lon was saying, dabbing at his eyes, "I must concentrate on that. I must think of the beginnings of this day. Not of the endings!" He straightened his shoulders resolutely and remounted the doleful Rogeth.

Dragons did not weep as humans did, but Capiam thought he might prefer tears to the gray tinge that came to their eyes and hides. Rogeth bore the color of mourning. They mounted and K'lon conveyed them to Fort Weyr. Old tears froze briefly on Capaim's cheeks, to be renewed as he saw the dragon-crowned Rim of Fort Weyr. He'd no time to count but surely even Telgar's disaffected Weyr must be represented to produce such an assembly. K'lon angled Rogeth to land as close to the Hatching Ground as possible, seemingly a dangerous task for dragons were leaping and landing all over the Bowl.

Everyone will have to make an effort today, Capiam thought and tears streamed down his face again. Desdra was stroking his hands and he knew she was aware of his intense feelings. He knew she wasn't untouched by the tragedies; but grief can be exhibited in many ways, and her quiet summary to K'lon had given Capiam some comfort, too.

They dismounted quickly from Rogeth, smiling up at K'lon, who had mastered his tears if not his mournful expression. Then the blue dragon leaped skyward again.

Capiam noticed that the usual tables and benches had been set outside the Lower Cavern for the Impression feasting. He hoped to get drunk enough at it not to hear Master Tirone's ballad. Capiam could smell the roast meats but they did not rouse his appetite as they usually did. It was a lovely day. It would have been a magnificent dawn, he thought, and rubbed his face harshly, to stop the ready tears. If the Masterhealer of Pern could not maintain his composure, what a poor example he would set. The day was a beginning not an ending!

As Desdra pulled him toward the Hatching Ground, he inadvertently looked to his right, to where Moreta had lived the last days of her life. He blew his nose fiercely and looked directly ahead of him, now pulling Desdra to a place as far from that tier as was possible within the confines of the Ground.

The eggs took his attention. They lay, neatly spaced, the queen egg separate on a neat mound of sand, lovingly piled to cushion and display it. He blew his nose again and stumbled on the first step of the tier.

There seemed to be a good deal of nose blowing, and kerchiefs of all colors were being flourished. There was no end to the sounds people made in clearing their nasal passages. Obscurely Capiam felt cheered that so many people were affected by the aura.

Could the dragons massed on the Rim have prevented Orlith and Leri going? Capiam chided himself for such wistful futile thoughts. No, the halves that were missing could never be replaced. Orlith yearned for Moreta, and Leri for Holth. As K'lon had done, Capiam must accept the inevitable.

Then he felt the vibration though his boot soles and looked down. It took him only a moment to realize that Hatching was imminent. The dragons had begun their hum. Not just the dragons taking their place at the top of the Ground, but those outside, until the solid rock of Fort Weyr was resonating. The note managed, in some inexplicable manner, to be melancholy as well as expectant. It was low, the crescendo to Hatching, but it produced an impetus. The audience rushed in.

Capiam looked around him again, to identify faces no longer obscured by kerchiefs. On the upper tier, to his left, he saw Lord Shadder and his lady, Levalla, K'dren and M'gent beyond, sitting next to Master Balfor, who had declined the honor of becoming Masterherdsman. Some said he felt keenly responsible that Moreta had died helping his Hold.

Desdra's hand tugged at his and he followed her gaze to see Alessan entering the Hatching Ground with Lady Nerilka. They were a striking pair, Alessan a half head taller than his consort, but, even at this distance, Capiam could see that Alessan was pale. He walked steadily, if slowly, his arm linked through Nerilka's. Tuero was on his right side, Dag and little Fergal a respectful pace, for once, behind their Lords Holder. Capiam had been surprised by Alessan's choice of wife, but Desdra said that Rill would support Alessan and he needed that.

Master Tirone arrived, with Lord Tolocamp and his ridiculous little wife. Capiam wasn't certain if the emergence of Lord Tolocamp from his self-imposed isolation was a tribute to the occasion or would be a trial, but he had made the effort today. As Nerilka had noted to Capiam, the man had never known he had a daughter missing. When told that

Nerilka had become Alessan's wife, Tolocamp had remarked about Ruatha swallowing up his women, and that if Nerilka preferred Ruathan hospitality to his, that was the end of her in his eyes.

Lord Ratoshigan arrived, alone as always, mincing across the hot sands to the fast-filling tiers. The dragon hum was swelling now, more confident, less mournful. Other Lords Holder and Mastercraftsmen scurried to the tiers. S'ligar supported Falga, who still walked lame though she rode every Fall; B'lerion walked by himself, quickly, and took a place without glancing about. Amid the journeymen, small holders, apprentices, folk from all the Weyrs, Capiam saw few wearing a Telgar badge—but many displaying Keroon.

The hum became excited as the dragons, gripped by a sense of occasion, sang their welcome. One of the eggs began to rock, and a hush of expectancy fell over the visitors while the dragon's song became ecstatic.

Sh'gall escorted the candidates in their white robes, the four girls leading. Sh'gall fussily motioned for the boys to walk on while he deferentially led the girls to the queen egg. Capiam rapidly counted the boys: thirty-two. Not as much choice as usual but then...

Capiam thought Oklina looked stunning. He remembered her as so shy and diffident in the bustling, lusty family that had once cramped Ruatha Hold as to be unremarkable. She had certainly bloomed. Then he noticed B'lerion watching her intently. He, too, had changed dramatically since Moreta died. *There*, the phrase had come out, hurtful though it was. Tears stung his eyes again. Desdra's hand renewed its clasp on his. Did she always know when sorrow overcame him?

People stirred and pointed as the first egg continued to rock and cracks became visible. The humming reached a new pitch of excitement, and Capiam felt his breath quickening. Another egg became agitated...and a third. One didn't know where to look first. The hum became more than vibration: It became a sound enveloping everyone in the Hatching Ground, almost visible about the eggs. They responded by frantic rolling and pitching.

The first one broke, and a moist dragon head appeared, crooning piteously as the dragonet shook itself free of the shell. It was a bronze! A sigh of relief rose from every throat. For a bronze to hatch first was a good sign! Pern needed every one it could discover. The little beast staggered directly toward a tallish boy with a shock of light-brown hair. That was also a good sign, that the dragonet knew whom he wanted. The boy didn't quite believe his good fortune and looked in appeal to his immediate neighbors. One of them pushed him toward the dragonet. The boy no longer resisted and ran, to kneel in the sand beside the little bronze and stroke his head.

Capiam had tears in eyes again, but they were joyful ones. The miracle of Impression had occurred and spread its anodyne, dispersing sorrow. While he was blotting his face, a second dragonet, a blue, found his rider. The hum of the mature dragons was joined by the crooning trill of hatchings and the excited exclamations from the newly chosen riders.

Suddenly a fresh flurry signaled activity about the queen egg, which rocked, Capiam thought, more imperatively than the others. In fact, three good wobbles and the egg cracked neatly in half, the fragments falling away from the little queen who seemed to spring from the shards. Another excellent omen! Two of the girls wavered in their stance but in Capiam's mind there was never any question of which girl the little queen chose.

Capiam turned to embrace Desdra in celebration. Clinging together, they watched Oklina lift shining eyes, her gaze instinctively finding B'lerion in the mass of faces confronting her.

"Her name is Hannath!"

DRAGONDEX

IN ORDER OF FOUNDING
THE MAJOR HOLDS AS BOUND TO WEYRS

Fort Weyr

    symbol:
    color: brown

Weyrleader: Sh'gall; dragon bronze Kadith
Weyrwoman: Moreta; dragon queen Orlith
Wingleader: S'peren; dragon bronze Clioth

    Fort Hold (oldest hold), Lord Holder Tolocamp
    Ruatha Hold (next oldest), Lord Holder Alessan
    Southern Boll Hold, Lord Holder Ratoshigan

Benden Weyr

    symbol: **II**
    color: red

Weyrleader: K'dren; dragon bronze Kuzuth
Weyrwoman: Levalla; dragon queen Oribeth
Wingleader: M'gent; dragon bronze Ith

High Reaches Weyr

    symbol:
    color: blue

Weyrleader: S'ligar; dragon bronze Gianarth
Weyrwoman: Falga; dragon queen Tamianth
Wingleader: B'lerion; dragon bronze Nabeth

    Tillek Hold, Lord Holder Diatis

Igen Weyr

    symbol:
    color: yellow

Weyrleader: L'bol; dragon bronze Timenth
Weyrwoman: Dalova; dragon queen Perforth

Ista Weyr

    symbol:
    color: orange

Weyrleader: F'gal; dragon bronze Sanalth
Weyrwoman: Wimmia; dragon queen Torenth
Wingleader: T'lonneg; dragon bronze Jalerth
Wingleader: D'say; dragon bronze Kritith

    Ista Hold, Lord Holder Fitatric
    Nerat Hold, Lord Holder Gram

Telgar Weyr

    symbol:
    color: white

Weyrleader: M'tani; dragon bronze Hogarth
Weyrwoman: Miridan; dragon queen Sutanith
Wingleader: T'grel; dragon bronze Raylinth

PERNESE OATHS

By the Egg

By the First Egg

By the Egg of Faranth

Great Faranth

Scorch it

Shards

By the shards of my
dragon's Egg

Shells

By the Shell

Through Fall, Fog, and
Fire

SOME TERMS OF INTEREST

agenothree: a common chemical on Pern, HNO_3. Agenothree fuels the flamethrowers used by groundcrews to burn Thread, and traditionally carried by riders of the queens' wings.

Belior: Pern's larger moon

between: an area of nothingness and sensory deprivation between here and there

Dawn Sisters: a trio of stars visible from Pern; also called Day Sisters

Day Sisters: a trio of stars visible from Pern; also called Dawn Sisters

deadglow: a numbskull, stupid. Derived from "glow."

Dragon: the winged, fire-breathing creature that protects Pern from Thread. Dragons were originally developed by the early colonists of Pern, before they lost the ability to manipulate DNA. A dragon is hatched from an egg, and becomes empathically and telepathically bound to its rider for the duration of its life.
  Green: Female (20–24 meters). The smallest and most numerous of the dragons. Light, highly maneuverable and agile, the greens are the sprinters of dragonkind. They breathe short bursts of flame. Greens are rendered sterile through a sex-linked disability triggered by chronic use of firestone.
  Blue: Male (24–30 meters). The workhorse of the dragons. Medium-sized, the blues are as tough as the greens but not as maneuverable. They have more stamina under pressure and are capable of sustaining flame longer.

274

Brown: Male (30–40 meters). Larger than greens and blues, some well-grown browns are as big as smaller bronzes and could actually mate with the queens if they so dared. The browns are the real wheel-horses of the dragons, reasonably agile and strong enough to go a whole Fall without faltering. They are more intelligent than blues or greens, with greater powers of concentration. Browns and their riders sometimes act as Weyrlingmasters, training the young dragons and riders.

Bronze: Male (35–45 meters). The leaders of the dragons. All bronzes compete to mate with the gold queens; the rider whose dragon succeeds becomes Weyrleader. Bronzes are generally trained for leadership and assume Wingleader and Wingsecond positions along with browns. Bronzes and their riders often act as Weyrlingmasters, training the young dragons and riders.

Gold: Queen, full female (40–45 meters). The bearer of the young, the queen is traditionally mated by whichever bronze can catch her. Although browns can mate with queens—and sometimes do, in the case of junior queens—this is unusual and not encouraged. The queen is fertile and bears eggs which she oversees until they hatch. Clutch sizes range from ten to forty; generally, the larger clutches occur during a Pass. The senior queen, usually the dragon of the oldest queen rider, is the most prestigious dragon and is responsible for all the dragons in the Weyr and for the propagation of her species.

fellis: a flowering tree

fellis juice: a juice made from the fruit of the fellis tree; a soporific

firestone: a rock bearing phosphorous that, when eaten by a dragon, is digested to produce phosphine gas, which ignites on contact with air

glow: a light-source that can be carried in a hand-basket

harper: Harpers are the teachers and entertainers of Pern. They educate the young in hall, hold, Weyr, and cot; they guide the elders in the practice of their traditional duties. The Masterharper of Pern is responsible for the training of harpers, the appointment of trained harpers to Weyr, hold, hall, and cot, and the discipline of harpers. The Masterharper acts as judge, arbitrator, and mediator in disputes between Lords Holder and between Weyr and hold or hall, but any harper can be called in to mediate if necessary.

Headwoman: Selected by the Weyrwoman to run the Lower Caverns, the Headwoman supervises the general domestic machinery of the

Weyr and the individual weyrs of the riders. Among her duties are the care of the young; the supervision of food collection, storage, and preparation; weyr maintenance; and nursing, under the aegis of the Weyr healer(s).

High Reaches: mountains on the northern continent of Pern (see map)

hold: A hold is where the "normal" folk of Pern live. Holds were initially caverns in rocky cliffs where Thread could gain no foothold; they began as places of refuge. They grew to become centers of government, and the Lord Holder became the man to whom everyone looked for guidance, both during and after the Pass of the Red Star.

Impression: the joining of minds of a dragon and his or her rider-to-be. At the moment of hatching, the dragon, not the rider, chooses his partner and telepathically communicates this choice to the chosen rider.

Interval: the period of time between Passes; generally two hundred Turns

klah: a hot, stimulating drink made from tree bark and tasting faintly of cinnamon

Long Interval: a period of time, generally twice the length of an Interval, during which no Thread falls and Dragonmen decrease in number. The last Long Interval is thought to herald the end of Threads.

looks to: is Impressed by

month: four sevendays

numbweed: a medicinal cream that, when smeared on a wound, kills all sensation; used as an anesthetic

Oldtimer: a member of one of the five Weyrs that Lessa brought forward four hundred Turns in time. Used as a derogative term to refer to one who has moved to Southern Weyr.

Pass: a period of time during which the Red Star is close enough to drop Thread on Pern. A Pass generally lasts fifty Turns and occurs approximately every two hundred Turns. A Pass commences when the Red Star can be seen at dawn through the eye rock of the Star Stones.

Pern: third of the star Rukbat's five planets. It has two natural satellites.

Red Star: Pern's stepsister planet. The Red Star has an erratic orbit.

Rukbat: a yellow star in the Sagittarian Sector, Rukbat has five planets and two asteroid belts.

runnerbeast: also called "runner." An equine adapted to Pernese conditions from fetuses brought with the colonists. Quite a few distinct variations were bred: heavy-duty cart and plow animals; comfortable, placid riding beasts; lean racing types.

sevenday: the equivalent of a week on Pern

Star Stones: Stonehenge-type stones set on the rim of every Weyr. When the Red Star can be seen at Dawn through the eye rock, a Pass is imminent.

Thread: mycorrhizoid spores from the Red Star, which descend on Pern and burrow into it, devouring all organic material they encounter.

Timor: Pern's smaller moon

Tunnel-snakes: Tunnel-snakes are a minor danger and an annoyance on Pern. Of the myriad types of Tunnel-snakes, two are the most insidious: the type that lives in tunnels, and the type that makes tunnels by burrowing in the sand on beaches. The latter has a great appetite for fire-lizard eggs.

Turn: a Pernese year

watchdragon: the dragon whose rider has pulled watch duty on the Weyr roster. A watch is generally four hours long. Essentially Weyrs are military camps. Sentries are part of that ethos. During a Pass, they watch for any chance erratic Fall of Thread, for anyone entering or leaving the Weyr.

watchwher: the ungainly, malodorous product of an attempt to breed larger, more useful animals from the genetic material of the fire-lizard, an indigenous Pernese life form. Watchwhers are nocturnal, exceedingly vicious when aroused, and highly protective of those they recognize as friends. A watchwher is conditioned to know the people of its hold, hall, or cot, and to give warning of intruders of any sort; used as a watchdog, it is generally chained to the front entrance of the hold, hall, or cot. Watchwhers can communicate with dragons, but as they tend to be very trivial and rather stupid, dragons are not fond of touching their minds.

Weyr: a home of dragons and their riders

weyr: a dragon's den

Weyrleader: generally the rider of the bronze dragon who has mated
    with the senior queen dragon of the Weyr during her mating
    flight. The Weyrleader is in charge of the fighting wings of the
    Weyr, responsible for their conduct during Falls, and for the
    training and discipline of all riders. During an Interval, he is
    responsible for the continuance of all Thread-fighting tactics, for
    keeping alive the fighting abilities of dragons and riders. His rank
    symbol is a dragon.

weyrling: an inexperienced dragonrider under the tutelage of the
    Weyrlingmaster. His rank symbol is an inverted stripe.

Weyrlingmaster: usually an aging rider with good skills and the
    ability to discipline and inspire the young. Responsible for the
    training of young riders and their dragons.

Weyrsinger: the harper for the dragonriders, usually himself a
    dragonrider

Weyrwoman: The rider of a dragon queen and coleader, with the
    Weyrleader, of the Weyr. She is responsible for the conduct of
    the queens' wing during Fall, under the Weyrleader's orders; for
    the care of dragons, riders, and all Weyrfolk; and for the peace
    and tranquillity of the Weyr during a Pass and during Intervals.
    She appoints all subordinates, insures that all tithes are delivered
    or collected, and mediates all disputes except honor contests
    among riders. She is responsible for the training, fostering, and
    disposition of the Weyr's children and nonrider personnel,
    overseeing with the Weyrleader the training of weyrlings under
    the Weyrlingmaster. As any dragon will obey a queen, even
    against the wishes of his or her rider, the Weyrwomen are in fact
    the most powerful people on Pern. Weyrwomen have autonomy in
    their own Weyr, but will act in concert with other Weyrwomen
    when necessary for the good of the Weyrs. Her rank symbol is a
    dragon.
        Each Weyr has from two to five queens, the larger numbers
    occurring during a Pass. In the event of the death or voluntary
    retirement of a Weyrwoman, the position will be assumed by the
    oldest of the other queenriders in the Weyr. Although candidates
    for Impression generally come from nearby holds and halls, the
    Search for a queen candidate may extend throughout the
    continent.

weyrwoman: a female dragonrider. Her rank symbol is a gold star.

wherries: a type of fowl roughly resembling the domestic turkey of Earth, but about the size of an ostrich

Wingleader: the dragonrider in command of a Weyr's fighting wing, subordinate to the Weyrleader. His rank symbol is double bars.

Wingsecond: the dragonrider second in command to the Wingleader. His rank symbol is a single bar.

withies: water plants resembling the reeds of Earth

THE PEOPLE OF PERN

A'dan: rider, at Fort Weyr; dragon green T'grath

Alessan: Lord Holder of Ruatha Hold

A'murry: rider, at Igen Weyr; dragon green Granth

Baid: cropholder, at Ruatha Hold

Balfor: Master, at Keroon Beasthold

Barly: (deceased) Healer, at High Reaches Weyr

Berchar: Masterhealer, at Fort Weyr

Bessel: a man at Beastmasterhold

Bessera: weyrwoman, at High Reaches Weyr; dragon queen Odioth

B'greal: weyrling, at Fort Weyr

B'lerion: wingleader, at High Reaches Weyr; dragon bronze Nabeth

Boranda: Healer, at Healer Hold

Bregard: Healer, at Peyton Hold

Burdion: Healer, at Igen Sea Hold

Campen: heir to Tolocamp, Lord Holder of Fort Hold

Capiam: Masterhealer, at Fort Hold

Ch'mon: rider, at Igen Weyr; dragon bronze Helith

Clargesh: Mastercraftsman, glass, at Tillek Hold

Cr'not: Weyrlingmaster, at High Reaches Weyr; dragon bronze Caith

Curmir: Harper, at Fort Weyr

C'ver: rider, at Telgar Weyr; dragon brown Hogarth

Dag: runner handler, at Ruatha Hold

Dalova: Weyrwoman, at Igen Weyr; dragon queen Perforth

Dangel: brother to Alessan, Lord Holder of Ruatha Hold

Dannell: candidate for Impression from Lemos Minehall, at Benden Weyr

Declan: candidate, at Fort Weyr

Deefer: warden, at Ruatha Hold

Desdra: Journeywoman healer, at Fort Hold

Diatis: Lord Holder of Tillek Hold

Diona: weyrwoman, at High Reaches Weyr; dragon queen Kilanath

D'ltan: weyrling, at Fort Weyr

D'say: wingleader, at Ista Weyr; dragon bronze Kritith

Empie: weyrwoman, at Igen Weyr; dragon queen Dulchenth

Emun: Journeyman harper, at Ruatha Hold

Falga: Weyrwoman, at High Reaches Weyr; dragon queen Tamianth

Farelly: harper, at Ruatha Hold

F'duril: rider, at Fort Weyr; dragon blue Dilenth

Felldool: Healer, at Hold Brum

Fergal: grandson to Dag, runner handler at Ruatha Hold

F'gal: Weyrleader, at Ista Weyr; dragon bronze Sanalth

Fitatric: Lord Holder of Ista Hold

F'neldril: Weyrlingmaster, at Fort Weyr; dragon brown Mnanth

Follen: Journeyman healer, at Ruatha Hold

Fortine: Master of Archives, at Fort Hold

Gale: Healer, at Big Bay Hold

Gallardy: Healer, at Healer Hall

Galnish: Healer, at Hold Gar

Genjon: Master, glassblower at Tillek Hold

Gorby: Healer, at Keroon Runnerhold

Gorta: Apprentice to Headwoman, at Fort Weyr

Gram: Lord Holder of Nerat Hold

Haura: weyrwoman, at Fort Weyr; dragon queen Werth

Helly: race rider, at Ruatha Hold

H'grave: rider, at Benden Weyr; dragon green Hallath

Ind: Healer, at Ista Weyr

Jallora: Journeywoman healer, at Fort Weyr

J'tan: rider, at High Reaches Weyr; dragon bronze Sharth

Kamiana: weyrwoman, at Fort Weyr; dragon queen Pelianth

K'dall: rider, at Telgar Weyr; dragon blue Teelarth

K'dren: Weyrleader, at Benden Weyr; dragon bronze Kuzuth

Kilamon: Journeyman harper, at Ruatha Hold

K'lon: rider, at Fort Weyr; dragon blue Rogeth

Kulan: smallholder, at Ruatha Hold

Kylos: Healer, at Sea Cliff Seahold

L'bol: Weyrleader, at Igen Weyr; dragon bronze Timenth

Leef, Lord: father of Alessan, Lord Holder of Ruatha Hold

Leri: inactive Weyrwoman, at Fort Weyr; dragon queen Holth

Levalla: Weyrwoman, at Benden Weyr; dragon queen Oribeth

Lidora: weyrwoman, at Fort Weyr; dragon queen Ilith

L'mal: (deceased) previous Weyrleader, at Fort Weyr; dragon bronze
    Clinnith

Loreana: Healer, at Bay Head Seahold

L'rayl: rider, at Fort Weyr; dragon brown Sorth

L'vin: rider, at Benden Weyr; dragon bronze Jith

Makfar: brother to Alessan, Lord Holder of Ruatha Hold

Marl: handler of herdbeasts and runnerbeasts, at Ruatha Hold

Masdek: Journeyman harper, at Fort Hold

Maylone: candidate, at Fort Weyr

M'barak: weyrling, at Fort Weyr; dragon blue Arith

Mellor: Weyrwoman, at Telgar Weyr; dragon queen Dalgeth

Mendir: Healer, at Ground Hold

M'gent: wingleader, at Benden Weyr; dragon bronze Ith

Mibbut: Healer, at Keroon Beasthold

Miridan: weyrwoman, at Telgar Weyr; dragon queen Sutanith

Moreta: Weyrwoman, at Fort Weyr; dragon queen Orlith

Mostar: son of Tolocamp, Lord Holder of Fort Hold

M'ray: rider, at Ista Weyr; dragon brown Quoarth; son of Moreta by
    D'say

M'tani: Weyrleader, at Telgar Weyr: dragon bronze Hogarth

Namurra: weyrwoman, at Igen Weyr; dragon queen Jillith

Nattal: old Headwoman, at High Reaches Weyr

Nerilka (Rill): daughter of Tolocamp, Lord Holder of Fort Hold

Nesso: Headwoman, at Fort Weyr

N'men: rider, at Fort Weyr; dragon blue Jelth

N'mool: rider, at High Reaches Weyr; dragon bronze Bidorth

Norman: race manager, at Ruatha Hold

N'tar: rider, at High Reaches Weyr; dragon bronze Melath

Oklina: sister to Alessan, Lord Holder of Ruatha Hold

Oma, Lady: mother of Alessan, Lord Holder of Ruatha Hold

Pendra: Lady Holder of Fort Hold

Peterpar: herdsman, at Fort Weyr

P'leen: rider, at Igen Weyr; dragon bronze Aaith

P'nine: rider, at Fort Weyr; dragon bronze Ixth

Pollan: Healer, at Big Bay Hold

Pressen: Healer, at High Reaches Weyr

Quitrin: Healer, at Southern Boll Hold

Rapal: Healer, at Campbell's Field

Ratoshigan: Lord Holder of Southern Boll Hold

Rill: see Nerilka

R'len: rider, at High Reaches Weyr; dragon bronze Ponteth

R'limeak: rider, at Fort Weyr; dragon blue Gionth

Runel: old herdsman, at Ruatha Hold

Scand: Masterhealer, at Ruatha Hold

Semment: Healer, at Great Reach Hold

S'gor: rider, at Fort Weyr; dragon green Malth

Shadder: Lord Holder of Benden Hold

Sh'gall: Weyrleader, at Fort Weyr; dragon bronze Kadith

Silga: weyrwoman, at Igen Weyr; dragon queen Brixth

Sim: drudge, at Fort Hold

S'kedel: rider, at Fort Weyr; dragon brown Adath

S'ligar: Weyrleader, at High Reaches; dragon bronze Gianarth

Sneel: Healer, at Greenfields Hold

Soover: smallholder, at Souther Boll Hold

S'peren: wingleader, at Fort Weyr; dragon bronze Clioth

Sufur: Masterherdsman, at Keroon Beasthold

Suriana: deceased wife of Alessan, Lord Holder of Ruatha Hold

Talpan: Healer of Animals, at Keroon Beasthold

Tellani: woman at Fort Weyr

T'grel: wingleader, at Telgar Weyr; dragon bronze Raylinth

Theng: guardleader, at Fort Hold

Tirone: Masterharper, at Fort Hold

T'lonneg: wingleader, at Ista Weyr; dragon bronze Jalerth

T'nure: rider, at Fort Weyr; dragon green Tapeth

Tolocamp: Lord Holder of Fort Hold

Tonia: Healer, at Igen Seahold

T'ragel: weyrling, at Fort Weyr; dragon blue Keranth

T'ral: rider, at Fort Weyr; dragon brown Maneth

Trume: Masterherdsman, at High Reaches Hold

Tuero: Journeyman harper, at Ruatha Hold

Turvine: cropholder, at Ruatha Hold

Turving: smallholder, at Ruatha Hold

Vander: smallholder, at Ruatha Hold

Varney: Master of the *Windtoss*

V'mal: rider, at High Reaches Weyr; dragon brown Koth

V'mul: rider, at Benden Weyr; dragon brown Tellath

Wimmia: Weyrwoman, at Ista Weyr; dragon queen Torenth

W'ter: rider, at Benden Weyr; dragon bronze Taventh

W'ven: rider, at Fort Weyr; dragon green Balgeth

PASSES AND INTERVALS

Planetfall plus 8 years

First Fall		
	58	First Pass
	258	Second Pass
	508	Third Pass
	758	Fourth Pass
		First Long Interval
	1208	Fifth Pass
	1458	Sixth Pass
	1505	Moreta's Ride (The Plague)
	1758	Seventh Pass
	2008	Eighth Pass
		Second Long Interval
	2405	Lessa's Impression
	2408	Ninth Pass

ABOUT THE AUTHOR

Born on April 1, Anne McCaffrey has tried to live up to such an auspicious natal day. Her first novel was created in Latin class and might have brought her instant fame, as well as an A, had she attempted to write in the language. Much chastened, she turned to the stage and became a character actress, appearing in the first successful summer music circus at Lambertsville, New Jersey. She studied voice for nine years and, during that time, became intensely interested in the stage direction of opera and operetta, ending this phase of her life with the stage direction of the American premiere of Carl Orff's *Ludus De Nato Infante Mirificus*, in which she also played a witch.

By the time the three children of her marriage were comfortably at school most of the day, she had already achieved enough success with short stories to devote full time to writing.

Between appearances at conventions around the world, Ms. Mc-Caffrey lives at Dragonhold, in the hills of Wicklow County, Ireland, with two cats, two dogs, and assorted horses. Of herself, Ms. McCaffrey says, "I have green eyes, silver hair, and freckles; the rest changes without notice."